Praise for
My Soul to Keep

"*My Soul to Keep*, the third and best Dylan Foster thriller, again demonstrates Melanie Wells's wit, intelligence, and knack for telling a swiftly paced, complex story. Through a wonderful network of plots and subplots—and the ruminations of the ever-complicated Dr. Foster—the novel reveals the helplessness and fierce love at the heart of parenting, as well as the way that each of us is responsible for children, our own and others. Wells takes kids seriously—their fears, their vulnerabilities, their spiritual wisdom and resiliency. Written with passion, a good dose of humor and, dare I say it, soul, this novel reminds us that we all, with grace and good fortune, bumble our way toward salvation."

—K. L. Cook, author of *Last Call* and *The Girl from Charnelle*

"*My Soul to Keep* is a rich and meaningful story. Like water rising to a boil, its suspense sneaks up on you—before you know, you're in the thick of a frightening drama. This is a story painful to witness but a pleasure to read. Superbly crafted."

—Robert Liparulo, author of *Deadfall, Germ,* and
Comes a Horseman

"*My Soul to Keep* is a great example of gritty reality colliding with spiritual questions. Melanie Wells proves to be one of the most consistent writers around, threading mystery and supernatural intrigue around memorable characters. I'm a huge fan."

—Eric Wilson, author of *A Shred of Truth* and the
novelization of *Facing the Giants*

"*My Soul to Keep* is a marvelous book. Lyrical and moving, the story and characters will stay with you long after you turn the last page. I can't wait for Melanie Wells's next novel."

—Harry Hunsicker, Shamus Award-nominated
author of *Crosshairs*

"In *My Soul to Keep*, Melanie Wells delivers tightly-woven mystery and profound drama with nail-biting intensity and a light touch. The struggles and triumphs of the wry and delightfully-flawed Dylan Foster allow us a glimpse of God's mercy at our worst and His best. *My Soul to Keep* is Melanie Wells's best book yet and one not to be missed. I can't wait for the next one."

—KATHRYN MACKEL, author of *Vanished*

"One moment, *My Soul to Keep* will have you laughing out loud, and the next you'll be under the covers with a flashlight, questioning unseen things, and hoping the ride never ends. Melanie Wells has one of the freshest, most uniquely readable voices in fiction. A few pages will have you hooked."

—CRESTON MAPES, author of *Nobody*

My
SOUL
to KEEP

PREVIOUS NOVELS BY MELANIE WELLS

When the Day of Evil Comes
The Soul Hunter

My SOUL TO KEEP

A NOVEL OF SUSPENSE

MELANIE WELLS

MULTNOMAH
BOOKS

MY SOUL TO KEEP
PUBLISHED BY MULTNOMAH BOOKS
12265 Oracle Boulevard, Suite 200
Colorado Springs, Colorado 80921
A division of Random House Inc.

ISBN 978-1-59052-428-2

Library of Congress Cataloging-in-Publication Data
Wells, Melanie.
   My soul to keep : a novel of suspense / Melanie Wells. — 1st ed.
      p. cm.
   ISBN 978-1-59052-428-2
   1. Psychology teachers—Fiction. 2. Kidnapping—Fiction. 3. Children—Psychic ability—Fiction. 4. Texas—Fiction. 5. Psychological fiction. I. Title.
   PS3623.E476M9 2008
   813'.6—dc22

                                                      2007037278

Printed in the United States of America
2008—First Edition

10 9 8 7 6 5 4 3 2 1

For Dot and Ron, who inspired me

He leaves the creature to stand up on its own legs—to carry out from the will alone duties which have lost all relish.... He wants them to learn to walk and must therefore take away His hand; and if only the will to walk is really there He is pleased even with their stumbles.

—Screwtape to Wormwood in
The Screwtape Letters by C. S. Lewis

1

WHEN DID I GIVE up on certainty?

At what hour on what day did I realize that you never get to know the answers? Especially not the juicy ones?

It was a misguided affectation, I realize, my little preoccupation with verity. One that served no more purpose than a set of wisdom teeth or a manual typewriter—fitting, perhaps, in some other millennium, but out of place if not archaic in a postmodern world of news cycles, reality shows, and million-dollar half-minute Super Bowl ads. I never saw it as dangerous, though. Of course, that was back when I was young and dumb and blissfully wafting through my days as though nothing sinister was sharing the air with me.

But the air is indeed crowded. And the other inhabitants rarely announce their presence, much less their intentions. Which sends the rest of us spinning around in unexpected directions, bumping into invisible barricades and teetering off into unseen ravines.

Eventually, of course, if you have any spunk at all, you right yourself and find your bearings. But just when you think you've spotted the lodestar, you discover that what you thought was true north is neither. That truth in the universe is the most elusive of the elements. And that if you're dumb enough to go looking for it, you're liable to get smacked in the face by one of the legions of liars you're trying to outwit.

My own personal liar—the one assigned to me by some force out there in the ether—is named Peter Terry. He's a nasty, ratfink bottom-dweller—a mind-stalking, soul-dissing prevaricator of the first degree. He lies, cheats, and steals, amusing himself by shoplifting, pickpocketing, breaking and entering, or outright armed robbery.

I thought I'd seen the worst of him. But with beings like Peter Terry,

I've learned, low expectations cannot possibly be low enough. And where Peter Terry is concerned, I have lowered my expectations all the way down to the black pit of hell.

This time it began on a sunny Saturday in May. Graduation day. My favorite day of the academic year.

I teach psychology at Southern Methodist University. Like most professors, I experience a powerful surge of enthusiasm every August when classes begin. In those first moments standing at the blackboard, chalk smudges on my fingers, my students' faces aglow with curiosity, I swell with the intellectual and spiritual stimulation of my craft. I love a fresh roomful of unsuspecting minds, the smell of new school supplies, the squeak of the freshly waxed floors of Dallas Hall, the sound of the crowd at football games (a small crowd since 1987, unfortunately).

Of course, that sentimental nonsense lasts about forty-eight hours. And then, like the rest of my colleagues, I spend the following nine months wishing the little darlings would quit bothering me and go home. The students are equally sick of us by May, however, which is one of the reasons graduation is a uniformly glorious occasion on campuses around the world. It's one of the few Hallmark holidays about which everyone involved is truly unconflicted.

On this warm summer Saturday (the solstice comes early in Texas, whether we want it to or not), I found myself hooded and tasseled, wrangling a roomful of rowdy degree candidates. Technically, they would not be graduates for another hour or so—which ensured my last, tenuous thread of authority over them. Our caps and gowns gave us all an impressive, if misleading, air of credibility, at least until you glanced down at the wild variety of (mostly tasteless) footwear on display.

I was shouting instructions, trying to herd them all into a reasonably straight, alphabetically ordered line, when my cell phone rang. Amid hoots from my charges—I'd confiscated cell phones from several conspirators who were plotting to interrupt the festivities with coordinated Pink Floyd ringtones—I hiked up my gown and fished in the pocket of my cutoffs, which, paired with my stilettos, made me look like a streetwalker on a *Dukes of Hazzard* episode. I smiled sweetly and flipped open my phone.

"We're here, Miss Dylan!" the caller shouted.

It was my little friend Christine Zocci, due to arrive from Chicago today to celebrate her sixth birthday with me.

"Did you know this airport is called Love? *Love, love, love,*" she sang.

"Where did you learn that song?"

"Everyone knows love, love, love," she said, clearly disgusted with me. "It's the Bees."

"I think that's Beatles, Punkin."

"I don't like beetles. I like bees."

"*Beatles* is the name of the band that sang the song. Not a bug."

"I like bees," she insisted.

And that was the end of that.

"Are you guys getting your bags now?"

"The pilot has our suitcases."

"I don't think so, Punkin. The pilot flies the plane. He doesn't carry the bags."

"His name is Captain George. He's nice."

As though that explained it.

"How do you know his name is George? Did he tell you?"

She sighed. "I had a bee in a jar once, but it stang me and died."

"How about if I talk to your mommy?"

I heard a series of clunks as the phone changed hands, and then her mother came on the line.

"Hi, Liz. Where are you guys?"

"All I know is, we landed at Love Field. We're..." She paused. "I don't see any signs. I'm not sure where we are."

"Baggage claim is on the bottom floor. Take the escalator down."

"The pilot has our bags."

"Um, okay, Liz. Have you guys been doing a lot of craft projects lately involving glue? Because glue fumes can cause serious brain damage. You should be aware."

"Oh, there he is." I heard her shout to someone named George. I pictured an American Airlines pilot carrying Christine's lavender Barbie suitcase. And then, of course, I realized what was going on.

Liz and Andy Zocci are the primary shareholders in a Midwestern regional airline called Eagle Wing Air, founded by Andy's father. They have more money than the Mormon church.

"You guys brought your own plane, didn't you?"

"It was just easier," Liz said, sounding embarrassed.

"Oh sure, well, I always think it's easier to take my own plane. Because, you know, the other ones are so…crowded. All those peeeople!"

"Dylan…"

"And the snacks are just not acceptable. Crummy little packets of pretzels passing for food. And don't even get me started on those filthy blankets. I hate those things."

"Dylan, this is very original humor. I'm laughing hysterically. Really, I am."

"You can see other people's hairs on them. It's disgusting."

"Are you done? Or is there more?"

"Hmm…that's about it. Do you want directions to my house, or should I meet you at your hotel?"

"I think we'll go unpack and then meet you at your place. Christine has been talking about this for weeks. I don't think I can hold her back much longer."

"I've got another couple of hours here in the salt mines," I said. "Can she make it that long?"

"We'll unpack and get some lunch. It might take me a while to find something Christine will eat. You know how she is."

"Is she still on crunchy food?"

"It comes and goes. For now it's crunchy food mainly. And orange, if at all possible. Carrots, Cheetos, things like that. Yellow's okay too. We eat a lot of vegetables and corn chips."

"Your kid is weird."

"I try not—Christine, gum and hair don't mix—try not to think about it."

"Did Andy and the boys come?"

"They're out of the country."

"Well, la-di-da," I sing-songed. "They're not even in kindergarten, and they're already world travelers?"

"It's an Angel Wing mission."

"Oh."

"To your friend Tony DeStefano's orphanage in Guatemala."

"Well, that's different."

"Thank you. I thought so. Want to retract your la-di-da?"

"Da-di-la."

Angel Wing Air is the Zoccis' charity airline. They fly small planes into remote areas around the world to supply and transport medical personnel and missionaries. Tony DeStefano was a friend from my seminary days. He'd also been a sort of spiritual touchstone in recent years, an ally in that whole Peter Terry, life-disintegration fiasco. He and Jenny had recently returned to the mission field.

"I made a cake," I offered, more to change the subject than to announce the menu. "A regular, spongy, noncrunchy cake."

"What kind?"

"Strawberry. Isn't that what you said?"

"Yep. She makes exceptions for strawberry anything. What time do you want us? We've got a car."

"La-di-da again. You didn't bring a limo too, did you? Like, in the cargo hold?"

"We're renting a regular, run-of-the-mill car, just like the little people."

"Where are you staying?"

"The Crescent. Do you want me to call you? Or just show up?"

"I'll call with directions when I'm done here. Hey, you didn't tell Christine about her present, did you?" I said. "I want her to be surprised."

"Not a word."

"Great." I checked my watch. "I think I can be out of here by two o'clock, assuming no one blows anything up or passes out or anything."

The students in my immediate vicinity began making explosion noises and pretending to faint.

"I gotta go, Liz. I'm losing control here."

Someone shouted, "She never had control!" into the phone as I hung up.

I spent the next two hours sweltering under my regalia—surely one of the more enduring medieval torture devices—enjoying one of the slim gratifications of another year of largely thankless effort. As much as I gripe about my work, there's no fighting off the joy when my students high-five me as they walk off the stage toward the rest of their lives, clutching four years of hard-won education in a maroon leather folder, their families cheering from the seats. It's one of the few times of the year when I feel proud of my incredibly low-paying, bottom-of-the-academic-ladder job.

The rest of the time I feel poor, mainly.

After the ceremony, I walked a hot half mile to faculty parking, swept off my mortarboard, and drove my crummy pickup home to my tiny house. I parked in the driveway under the sycamore tree that always needs pruning and cut the motor, which shrugged reluctantly to a stop. I hauled my stuff to the porch and unlocked my front door. The air conditioner hummed a pleasant little greeting, which is always good news on a hot Dallas afternoon. I threw my keys on the kitchen table, placed my once-a-year heels in the back of my bedroom closet, tossed my graduation gown into the dry-cleaner hamper, Frisbeed my mortarboard onto the dryer for sponging and Febreze, and walked over to the rabbit hutches in the corner of my bedroom.

"Bunnies, I'm home," I cooed, peering into the cages. Two small rabbits hopped over to greet me—a little red one, whose auburn coat matched my hair color exactly, and a tiny gray lop-ear. Melissa and Eeyore. I reached down and scratched them behind their ears.

I've never really been a pet person. All those bodily fluids and floaty little hairs are prohibitive for a person of my obsessive inclinations. Even the smell of a pet store is a problem—I order all pet supplies online to avoid that trauma entirely. But both bunnies had been orphaned the previous winter when their owners were caught in one of Peter Terry's snares.

So I had taken them in—Melissa first and then, later, Eeyore.

It turns out that nonverbal roommates are better than no roommates at all. And as an added bonus, rabbits are relatively tidy little creatures. These two were actually housebroken. But since almost no one has need of two bunnies, especially two bunnies of the opposite gender (though Melissa had recently surrendered her femininity at the vet), Eeyore was to be my birthday gift to Christine.

I couldn't wait to give him to her. I'd gotten him a big, purple bow—Christine's favorite color—and had his name painted on a set of (mail-order) ceramic bowls. I could now send his hutch home with the Zoccis as well, since cargo room was clearly not a problem.

I showered quickly and went to the kitchen to set out some refreshments. I was squeezing lemons for lemonade when the doorbell rang. I glanced out the kitchen window and wiped my hands on a cup towel. My friend Maria Chavez had arrived with her little boy.

Maria is an OB-GYN at the local public hospital and one of my All Time Favorite People. She also happens to be a fellow Peter Terry target. She is my only local friend, the first recruit in my campaign to improve my abysmal social life—an effort I commenced last year along with a rigorous Thigh Recovery Program. (I like to believe in the possibility of Total Overhaul.)

I opened the door and greeted her with a best-friend hug, then knelt down and said hello to my groovy little friend, Nicholas.

"Hey, doodlebug." I gave him a quick hug, squeezing the air out of him as he tried to say my name.

"Hi, M(squeeze)iss (squeeze) Dy(squeeze)lan," he coughed out.

We did The Squeeze every time I saw him. It was our little thing. He giggled. "Do it again!"

I did it again. He coughed out my name in spurts.

Nicholas had wild, curly brown hair just like his father, who at that moment was sitting in a hot cinderblock cell down in Huntsville, serving ten flat for aggravated sexual assault. That crazy mop of hair framed bright blue eyes and a face so flushed and pink with innocent vim, you couldn't possibly imagine he'd been conceived through violence.

"What do you have behind your back?" I said to Nicholas. "Did you bring your G.I. Joe?"

He shook his head and giggled.

"Is it your turtle?"

Another giggle.

"Is it a skyscraper? I heard one was missing from downtown. Or maybe a buffalo? I've always wanted my own buffalo. Let's saddle him up and go for a ride."

"A buffalo is too big," he said, giggling. He swung his hand around and pointed a plastic gun at me. "BANG!"

I pretended to die, clutching my heart and crumpling to the ground.

"Don't shoot people, Nicholas," Maria said. "It's bad manners."

"But that's what it's for," he whined.

I picked myself up. "He's got a point, Maria."

"Enrique gave it to him," she said. "He's recruiting him, I think. It came with holsters and a badge and a little red siren for his bicycle. It runs on batteries."

"The holsters sound cool. I could use a set of those myself."

"I may never forgive him."

"How is he?"

"Enrique? Charming. Handsome. Overworked." Her brown eyes twinkled mischievously. "Slightly unavailable."

"Ooh, I love that in a man," I said.

"Very sexy," she agreed. She gave me her girlfriend-confrontation look. "I still think you should call David."

"It's a procedural violation to call a man six months after he breaks up with you."

"You're stubborn."

"Check the handbook."

"And it's only been four and a half months."

"I think he's made it perfectly clear, Maria, that he doesn't want to be with me."

"I keep hoping."

"You're an optimist. I hate that about you, you know that? I truly do. You really should get it seen about."

Liz and Christine arrived then in a regular, run-of-the-mill, rented Suburban. I made the introductions, and we all trailed inside. Christine went nuts over Eeyore, as I knew she would. We sent the kids to the backyard with the rabbits while we blew up balloons and lit candles, then we brought them all in and gathered at the kitchen table for cake and presents.

We'd all gotten gifts for Nicholas too. And though Christine was officially the birthday girl, she let Nicholas wear her Barbie birthday princess tiara while she sported the cowboy hat I'd bought for him. Eeyore wore his spiffy satin bow and sat in Christine's lap eating crumbs from her strawberry birthday cake.

I was setting up my homemade version of pin the tail on the donkey when Christine announced she wanted to take Eeyore to the park. I decided to bring the game along, just in case the kids got bored. I threw the blindfolds, tails, and donkey—which I had drawn myself in a misguided fit of Martha Stewart ambition and which, I'm proud to say, actually looked sort of like a donkey—into a shopping bag, tossing in my staple gun at the last minute.

I live in a Dallas neighborhood called Oak Lawn, which is funky and artsy and pleasantly rickety. It has groovy old houses, giant, mis-shapen trees, cracked sidewalks, and quirky people. My next-door neighbor has a bubble machine on his balcony. That's how cool my neighborhood is. The parks, however, are full of weeds, doggie poo, and sticker-burrs.

Two streets over is Highland Park, a much nicer, nonfunky, not-at-all-rickety neighborhood that has fabulous parks with manicured azalea bushes and banked flowers and lacy white gazebos. Sort of like a Thomas Kinkade painting.

Highland Park, for me, is like the Bermuda Triangle. My luck is ter-rible there.

It's a low-crime area with huge houses, fancy cars, and its own police force. Which means it's crawling with bored cops trolling around all day in a shiny fleet of Suburbans.

They care if you go thirty-five in a thirty.

Interlopers like me driving loud, crummy vehicles with lousy mufflers and cracked windshields, stand out like goats in the piano parlor. Since I am a fast driver and a slow learner, I'd received, at last count, three—count 'em, three—speeding tickets in Highland Park. And that was in one year.

Given the nature of our mission, however, I caved to the sticker-burr issue and let Liz drive us over to Highland Park, banking on her luck to overcome mine.

Apparently, lots of other birthday groups had the same idea. The place was crawling with kids—balloons tied to their wrists, cake smeared on their faces. Their defeated moms trailed behind them yelling out halfhearted prohibitions. Off to one side, someone had set up a petting zoo with a tiny Brahman calf, two saddled, bored ponies, a little herd of baby goats, and a few baby rabbits hopping around in a pen. Melissa and Eeyore sniffed sympathetically through the pickets at their imprisoned relatives.

Maria, Liz, and I found a bench and watched the kids as they made friends and played on the swings. The breeze blew softly as sunlight dappled in through the leaves of the live oak trees. A soccer game buzzed like a hive in the center of the green lawn. A gardener clipped hedges with manual choppers and swept up the leaves with a real rake, not one of those obnoxious, nuclear-decibel leaf blowers.

An ice-cream cart came by, and we all bought Popsicles. I got one of those orange push-up things that taste like sherbet but are probably made out of xanthan gum and high-fructose corn syrup. I tried not to think about it. It's important to not blow such lovely moments obsessing about food additives. I've spent a modest fortune on therapy to learn that little trick.

It was a beautiful day. A perfect, grade-A, blue-sky day, in fact. I licked my xanthan pop and searched my memory for the last time I'd been this happy.

While Liz and Maria talked, I got up and began stapling my donkey to a tree. He looked a bit like a special-needs donkey, now that I got a good look at him. A special-needs donkey in need of orthodontia and maybe orthopedic shoes. Several children left the swings and came over to check out the afflicted animal. Nicholas pointed his gun at the donkey, no doubt intending to put it out of its misery.

"BANG!" he said and then ran off, sprinting away and scooting behind a tree. He stuck his head back around and pointed his plastic gun, took another shot at the donkey, then ran all the way to the other end of the park and ducked behind the tennis courts.

"Have you mentioned to him that the headwear might be a problem?" I said to Maria. "I mean, the gun is kind of manly. But the tiara…" I tsked. "It ruins the look."

Maria shrugged. "Maybe with the holsters…"

The tennis courts were fenced, with black wind netting covering the chain-link way up past eye level.

"Where's Nicholas?" Christine asked.

I pointed. "I think he's hiding behind the tennis courts. Go see if you can find him."

"Could you tell him to come back over here, sweetie?" Maria asked. "I don't want him that close to the street."

Christine ran to the fence, then stopped short and cocked her head.

Liz shouted over to her. "What is it, Christine?"

Christine pointed at the area behind the tennis courts. "Mommy, that man is mean."

"I'll go." Liz stood up to fetch the kids.

Christine screamed, and we saw a hand—a large hand, a man's hand—grab her by the arm and yank her behind the netting, her cowboy hat flying out behind her and spinning onto the ground.

We all covered the ground in seconds. By the time we got there, Christine stood behind the fence, her panicked face red and wet with tears, her birthday tiara in the dust at her feet.

Nicholas was gone.

2

I RACED TO THE other end of the tennis courts, Maria screaming and running at my heels. With the staple gun still clutched in my hand, I rounded the row of shrubs that led to the street. As we got there, a blue minivan pulled into the street and took off. I'd learned how to shoot a gun the year before. Instinctively, I stopped, assumed the stance, and raised the staple gun, shooting industrial staples at the back of the van. They landed all around me in the street, pinging harmlessly on the asphalt.

Maria kept running, following the van as it turned onto a side street and sped away. When I caught up to her, the van was gone and she was standing in the middle of the street, her mouth open, her hands at her sides. Her eyes darted around frantically. She kept opening and closing her fists, like she was trying to pump blood into her hands.

I stopped beside Maria, my chest heaving. "I got two letters and a number off the plate. *AK* and a *9*."

Maria turned and began pounding her fists on one of the cars parked in the street, yanking on the door handle. The alarm began wailing loudly, splitting the still silence of the quiet, tree-lined neighborhood.

"Where are the keys?" Maria shouted.

"Maria, this isn't our car. Try to calm down."

"Where's Liz? We have to go after them. He's got my baby!"

"Maria, they're gone. We can't catch them. Look at the street." I pointed. The lane was empty, the van long gone. "We have to call the police."

She stared at me.

"Did you see the license plate?" I shouted over the car alarm.

Her face was blank.

I raised my voice. "Maria?"

Her eyes were vacant. Empty. I put my hand on her shoulder. "Maria, look at me." Still no response.

The street around me began to blur. I felt myself get dizzy, the panic choking the air out of me. I struggled to hold on to consciousness, blinking the darkness away and taking a few deep breaths.

Maria was looking at me as though we'd just met. Like she didn't even know who I was.

"Maria, did you see the plate? Did you get the number?"

"He's got Nicholas. We have to—"

"Did you see the plate?" I had her by the shoulders now, yelling at her. "Do you remember the license-plate number?"

Maria wrenched free from my grip, yanked on the car door again, and pounded the window. Then she sank to her knees and began to cry. Frantic, gulping cries, sucking in mouthfuls of hot asphalt-scented air.

I screamed for help—a shout in the general direction of the house next to us—and knelt down to hold her. By now people were coming out of their houses and staring at us. We were still in the middle of the street. I tried to stand Maria up. A car had come up behind us and was waiting for us to move. The man behind the wheel tapped the horn.

I turned around and glared at him. He averted his eyes, ducking behind a baseball cap.

I stood Maria up and led her back toward the park, letting the car pass beside me. The car alarm stopped abruptly. A crowd of women from the park had reached us by then, holding their children in white-knuckle grips. Several of them were talking on cell phones, looking around for street signs and house numbers to get their bearings.

We made it back to the park in a clump, all of us clinging together and moving in unison—frightened zebras after a lion has attacked the herd. Police cars began to arrive from both the Highland Park and Dallas police departments—lights flashing on the tops of their cruisers. Someone pointed in our direction, and a Highland Park cop walked over to us.

"Are you the mother?" he said to me.

I pointed at Maria. "This is Maria Chavez. Dr. Chavez. Her boy Nicholas is…he's the one that…" I didn't want to say it.

Maria had collected herself. She looked at him and began to recite. "My son's name is Nicholas René Chavez. He's five years old. He weighs thirty-nine pounds, and he's forty-one inches tall. His hair is blondish-brown and curly, and his eyes are blue. He was wearing denim shorts, white sneakers, and a Dallas Cowboys jersey with the number twelve on it. He had a"—she choked back a cry—"a little toy gun." She put her hand to her mouth and began to shake, tears streaming down her cheeks. "It was a blue van. That man in the blue van took my son."

I hugged Maria. The cop kept talking.

"You saw someone get in a van with your son?"

I told him the story, pointing at the bench, the tennis courts, and the street as I filled in the details. "We saw a man's hand reach out and grab Christine." I gestured toward Christine, who was draped over Liz's shoulder in a heap, hugging her mother tightly.

"But you didn't see anyone actually get in the van with the kid?"

I shook my head. "No."

"Where's the boy's father?" the cop asked.

"Um, that's sort of a long story." I glanced around at the gathering crowd, wanting to spare Maria's privacy. She saved me the trouble.

"He's in prison in Huntsville. It wasn't his father."

"One of your husband's friends, maybe?" the cop asked. "Criminal associate—"

I interrupted. "He's not her husband. And, um…that's really not a possibility, Officer."

He raised his eyebrows at Maria.

"He's never met Nicholas," Maria said.

He looked back at me and let it go.

"Did you get a plate?"

"*AK* something, *9* something something."

"Texas plate?"

I nodded.

"Happen to notice whether it was a vanity plate? Or one of those fund-raiser plates—State of the Arts, Humane Society?"

"No. I think it was just a plain Texas plate."

"What kind of van?"

"I think it was a Chrysler."

"Are you sure?"

"Maria? Did you see?"

She shook her head. "No. It was blue. It had a sticker on the back."

"What sort of sticker?" the cop asked.

"Ducks Unlimited," she said.

"On the bumper?"

"The back window."

"Right or left side?"

"Upper right. And one of those."

She pointed at a sticker on another car. It was the logo of one of the local Christian schools.

"That's the Dickersons' van," someone said.

The cop turned around. "Ma'am?"

A woman stepped out of the huddle around us and said, "Richard and Anne-Marie Dickerson. Their little girl is on my daughter's soccer team. They carpool with us."

"Were they here today?" he asked.

"Anne-Marie was, and Lauren. I never saw Richard. I think he travels."

"Do you have an address for them?" the cop asked.

The woman gave the address, and the cop gestured to his partner to call it in.

"Is there any way you can contact Enrique Martinez?" I asked. "He's a detective with the DPD."

"What division?"

"Robbery."

"Kidnappings go to robbery. They'll get the call anyway."

"Aren't we in Highland Park?"

"Something like this, it'll go to DPD. You know him?"

"He dates Maria." I glanced over at her. "And he's a DPD chaplain. I think it would be good to have him here."

He raised his eyebrows but didn't comment. "I'll try to raise him for you, if you want."

I nodded my thanks.

Martinez came, along with a crowd of uniformed cops, detectives, and a van full of crime-scene investigators. I hugged him and led him over to Maria, who leaned into him and held on for a minute, then squared her shoulders and stepped away. Maria handled herself well, answering questions with astonishing poise under the circumstances, though the strain was obvious. Martinez, pacing around and asking questions, seemed more agitated than she did.

Christine couldn't stop crying. The bad man was real mean, she kept saying.

"How did you know he was mean?" Liz asked.

"He was all black, and I could just tell."

"You mean he was a black man? His skin was black?" I asked. She hadn't mentioned this to the cop who questioned her.

"Noooo, *he* was black," Christine insisted. "Not his skin."

"Punkin, I'm not sure what you mean," Liz was saying. "Were the man's clothes black?"

"Noooo, *he* was black," she said again. "And really mean." She stuck her thumb in her mouth. "Where's Eeyore and Melissa?"

We'd all forgotten about the bunnies. When we got back to our stuff, the petting-zoo guy had given them some water and rabbit pellets and put them in the pen with the other rabbits. We thanked him and loaded them up. We were all due at DPD headquarters to give statements. They wanted us to come in while our memories were still fresh. I needed to take the rabbits home first, so we agreed that I'd meet Liz and Christine at the station. Maria would ride with Martinez.

An alert had been issued for a missing child, with Nicholas's name and description and a description of the van. It flashed on a sign over the highway as I drove downtown from my house. Flashing yellow, over and over again.

Kidnapped child. Kidnapped child. Kidnapped child. Male. Five years old. Abducted.

3

I'D BEEN DOWNTOWN TO DPD headquarters a few times last winter, but I got lost anyway. When I finally walked into the lobby, it was almost empty. A bright expanse of sparkling-clean, waxed floors reflected the sunlight streaming in through floor-to-ceiling windows. A few disheveled, distracted people stood near a row of benches that were scooted against the wall near the metal detectors. I gave my name to the officer at reception and waited at the desk, away from the benches.

Martinez appeared in a few minutes. I could feel the stares of the small crowd as he hugged me, walked me around the metal detectors, and escorted me to the elevators. We were silent as the elevator took us up to the fifth floor. We stepped out past a sign that read Crimes Against Persons (CAPERS).

I saw Maria sitting at a desk. "They can't find the van," she said. "They went to those people's house. But no one was home."

"Was it that family's van? What's their name—Dixon?"

"Dickerson," Maria said. "They're trying to find them. It's a really good sign, don't you think? That it was a family? Maybe it's just a mistake. Maybe they just grabbed the wrong kid. Maybe they thought he was someone else. Someone who was supposed to ride with them or something."

I looked at Martinez. He met my eyes, and we silently agreed not to say anything. Let her think that if it would keep her calm.

"It's a good lead," Martinez said. "You want something solid like this in the first forty-eight hours."

"I saw the alert," I said. "On the highway signs."

"Did you know most of those kids get found?" Maria asked.

"They told me. Eighty percent last year. That's pretty good odds, don't you think?"

"Did you see anyone?" Martinez asked me. "Anything at all?"

"The only thing I can come up with was one guy who looked funny to me. He was standing with all the parents at the soccer game, but I never saw him with a kid. All the other parents seemed to have kids running on and off the field, and they were yelling for their kids by name. He was watching the game, but not the same way."

"What sort of way?" Maria asked. "What do you mean?"

A stocky, necktied man with thick black hair and wire-rims interrupted us. He greeted Martinez and then turned to me. "I'm Detective Ybarra. Are you Dr. Foster?"

I nodded, and he said, "Could you follow me, please?"

I trotted obediently behind him down a short hallway and past a tidy kitchenette. I caught the acrid scent of coffee left too long on the warmer.

"Offer you a cup?" the detective asked.

I glanced at the stained carafe. "No thanks."

He opened the door to a small room furnished with a white Formica table and two chairs. "Mind if we record this?"

"Not at all."

"Have a seat."

He took down my name and contact info, my profession—all my vital signs except temperature and blood pressure—and asked me some general questions about the afternoon and about how I knew Maria and Nicholas. She'd told the police by then about how Nicholas was conceived. I filled in a few blanks about my brush with his father the previous winter. Gordon Pryne was his name. Career criminal, serial violent offender. Nasty slick of a man.

"He's back in Huntsville. At least, I assume he's still there."

He paused. "We're still confirming that."

I wondered if he knew something I didn't.

"Listen," I said. "I was just telling Maria—the one thing I do remember is this parent. At least, I assumed he was a parent. He was standing with the crowd, but thinking back on it, I don't think he really fit in."

"Why would you say that?" He began to scribble notes.

"Well, he was pretty tall, for one thing. Like, almost NBA tall. So he stood out that way. But the other thing is, he didn't seem connected to any of the kids. He wasn't rooting for anyone."

"Could he have been there with another parent? Was he talking to any of the adults?"

"Not really. But he was watching the game very closely."

"A coach, maybe. Or a scout."

"Do scouts come to little-kid soccer games?"

"No, you're right. Probably not. But a coach, maybe."

"I think a coach would be more engaged than he was."

"Engaged how?"

"He seemed disconnected from them. He was watching them like they were objects, not people. Objectifying the kids, I think. He had a look on his face that was…" I searched for the word. "Predatory," I said at last.

"You got a good look at him, then?"

"I got a decent look, but I'm not sure I can tell you much about him. I wasn't really paying attention."

"Sounds to me like you were."

"I was paying attention to the dynamic—the interaction between the people. But not really to the people themselves."

He looked at me skeptically. "Is that a shrink thing?"

I shrugged. "Occupational hazard."

"So you can't describe him?"

"Tall, like maybe six-six or so? And white or maybe Latin. Not black, definitely. I think he had on a white shirt and shorts. Khaki, maybe. But honestly, that's a wild guess. I may have imposed that in hindsight."

"Hair color?"

"Don't remember."

"Get a look at his face?"

"No."

"Facial hair or anything?"

"Not that I noticed. Did you guys interview anyone like that? You talked to all the parents, right?"

"We're talking to everyone who was in the park when we arrived. If he left before that, I can't say." He hunched thick shoulders over the table and scribbled on his notepad for a minute, making lists and drawing arrows between columns. He was left-handed, his writing square and precise, his manners genteel. He wore a gold wedding ring that had clearly gone the distance.

He looked up and caught me staring.

"Would you be able to identify him?" he asked.

"From a photo? Or in person?"

"Either one."

"Probably not from a photo. I don't remember a face. Maybe if I saw him in person, dressed the same way? I don't know. I'm sorry. I guess my memory isn't very reliable."

"Nobody's is, really," he said. "That's only on TV. Eyewitness testimony is always the least reliable evidence in any case."

"I didn't know that."

"Yep."

A knock at the door, and Martinez came in.

Ybarra told him what I'd said.

"How's your girlfriend?" Ybarra asked.

"Tougher than I would be."

"Did you guys talk to Christine Zocci?" I said. "She got a good look at the guy."

"We talked to her," Martinez said. "She wasn't too helpful. Just said he was mean and black."

"Dr. Foster just said he was white," Ybarra said.

"I said white or Hispanic. But we may not be talking about the same guy. I saw the guy on the field. I didn't see the guy behind the tennis courts. Christine was the only one who saw him."

Ybarra checked his notes. "The kid told me he was white." He turned to me. "Didn't you say you saw the arm when he grabbed her?"

I nodded. I'd forgotten. "It wasn't black."

"She also told us he had a snake," Martinez said. "Did she mention that to you?"

"A live snake? How is that possible?" I said.

"She couldn't elaborate. I don't know if she saw a real snake or maybe he had one on his T-shirt," Martinez said.

"Or maybe a tattoo," Ybarra said.

"She could have meant he was mean as a snake," I said.

Ybarra looked at me blankly.

"Christine"—I hesitated—"has a way of seeing things from... I don't know how to say this without sounding like a lunatic," I said, realizing even as I said it that I sounded exactly like a lunatic. I slowed down and thought about how to word it. "She has a way of seeing things from another point of view."

"What point of view would that be, Dr. Foster?" Ybarra asked.

"A spiritual one."

Martinez watched him, waiting for his reaction.

Ybarra was looking at me like I'd just coughed up a live frog.

I stammered on. "It could be what she meant when she said he was black. That he had a mean, dark soul."

"What, you mean she sees things? Like, literally? As in 'I see dead people'?" Ybarra said.

"No, not like that," I said. "She just has a vivid imagination and a good feel for spiritual things. It's like a radar."

Ybarra rolled his eyes, irritated.

Martinez poked him and winked at me. "Seriously. I've seen it before. My grandmother was that way. She could tell things before they happened." He shrugged. "The kid could have a gift."

I figured this would be an inappropriate time to mention that I'm cursed with the same gift. A gift I would give back in an instant if I could locate the customer-service department and acquire the necessary forms.

Ybarra rolled his eyes again. "I'll make a note."

"It's just a possibility," I said. "I'll see if I can clear it up—"

Ybarra interrupted me. "I'd prefer you didn't talk to her about any details like that."

"Why not?" I felt strangely hurt.

"Kids' testimonies are fungible enough without anyone poking around in there trying to suggest things."

"I wasn't going to suggest anything. I was just—"

"All the same, Dylan," Martinez said. "It's better if you stay out of it." He turned to Ybarra. *"Fungible?"*

"My eight-dollar word for the day. Look it up."

Ybarra turned to me. "We'll add the snake to the description as a possibility, just in case it wasn't a 'radar' thing."

I forced a smile and thanked him. "Who does your kid interviews? Do you guys have a child psychologist or something?"

Martinez nodded. "She's in with them now."

"Could you write her name down for me?" I asked. "I'd like to talk to her."

"I thought we just agreed you were going to stay out of our investigation," Martinez said.

"Sorry." I held my hands up in defense. I'd try to pry it out of him later.

I answered a few more questions but had nothing more to contribute. Ybarra eventually thanked me and cut me loose.

Martinez decided to stay with Maria. She had no family in the area and obviously needed the company. I hugged her good-bye and promised I'd check on her later. I waited around for Liz and Christine to finish with their interviews. I walked a path between the coffee makers and the bathrooms, resisting an overwhelming urge to clean both. When they finally emerged, Christine was tearful, sucking her thumb and whining for her new bunny.

Since Eeyore wasn't welcome at their hotel, we stopped there to pick up clothes and toothbrushes, and then we all went back to my house.

Christine, usually a buoyant, joyful child, was grouchy and weepy. She cried throughout the evening, fussing over the littlest things. Wanting the stereo on, then off. Wanting to be outside, then in, always on the wrong side of the door. Complaining about her supper. Making picky requests and then refusing to eat anything at all. All she wanted was to hold Eeyore and Melissa. We finally settled her on a pallet on the bedroom floor, the three of them nestled into a pile of pillows and old quilts, and at last she fell asleep.

Liz and I talked into the night, trying to come to terms with what had happened.

As much as you know otherwise, this sort of catastrophic event seems unreal, impossible. Almost imaginary, as though it happens only to fake people in some distant netherworld. You see them on news programs, their faces flushed and wet with tears, their sanity leaking out a drop at a time, and you want to believe it's not possible for such a thing to happen to you.

It's a necessary form of denial. If we didn't think about it that way, most of us could never leave our houses.

But now we were the ones in the drama. Live action, real time, real life. It wasn't virtual. It was actual. And it was too terrible to take in.

It wasn't that I couldn't allow myself to think about it. I was just missing the circuitry to comprehend it. I couldn't get my brain to imagine where Nicholas might be or who might have him. It was as though the passageway, the avenue, was just blocked.

It wasn't until the middle of the night—3:30 a.m., to be precise—that the passageway gaped open, an empty hole of the blackest blackness, smelling of rotting eggs and death. Peter Terry stood right there in the doorway, bald and emaciated, his pasty white skin looking pickled and lifeless. He wore khaki shorts and a white polo shirt—a nice little dig, and just like him to pay attention to such details.

He walked over to the bed, pulled an ashen hand out of his pocket, and tossed something heavy onto the mattress.

"For you, Dylan," he said with a snide smile. "And we begin again."

He turned and walked away from me, showing me the bloodstain on the back of his shirt—evidence of an ancient badge of dishonor. A gash running blade to blade, where wings had long ago been ripped away.

I looked down to see a snake writhing on the quilt—and then woke with a lurch to a dark, cozy room, Liz breathing quietly behind me.

I lay there and shivered, though the night was hot and thick with humidity.

Christine had woken up on the floor. I got out of bed and tiptoed over to her, whispering for her to follow me. We scooted into the kitchen and shut the door behind us. I poured her a glass of milk and cracked open a fresh package of Oreos.

I sat on the table, my bare feet in the chair next to hers. "Christine." I handed her a cookie. "Is there anything you haven't told me?"

She dipped it into her milk three times and took a slow bite.

I waited until she washed it down with a swallow of milk. "Was his skin black?"

She took another bite and chewed with her eyes down, looking into her glass.

"Or was it his soul? Did you mean maybe his soul was black?"

I heard her mumble something.

"What did you say, sweetie?"

She took another sip of milk. "His heart."

"His heart was black."

"Uh-huh."

I handed her another cookie and watched her dip it into the milk. Three times, each bite.

"Why didn't he take you?" I said. "I mean, he grabbed you. But then he left you there behind the fence, all safe and sound. Why would he do that?"

"It was scary," she said.

"I'm sure it was."

"He was mean."

"I know he was."

I waited for her to answer my question.

She started to cry.

I got up and got her a Kleenex, kneeling down beside her chair so my eyes would be level with hers. "Christine?"

She took the Kleenex and wadded it up in her hand, wiping her nose on the sleeve of her pink jammies.

"He didn't want me," she said at last.

"What? Did he say that?"

She nodded.

"He said that out loud, in words? That he didn't want you?"

She nodded.

"Why did he grab you, then?"

"It was a mistake. He said he made a bad mistake and it burned his hand."

"When he grabbed you, he burned his hand?"

She looked down at her glass and nodded. "And then he said something to Jesus."

"To Jesus?" It took me a moment to realize what she meant. "You mean, he yelled Jesus's name when he burned his hand?"

"Uh-huh."

"Did he say anything else?"

"Not to Jesus."

"To you. I meant to you."

"He said he didn't want me. He wanted Nicholas."

"He mentioned Nicholas by name?"

She nodded.

"What else did he say to you? Did he tell you why he wanted Nicholas?"

She looked down at her glass again.

"Christine, I know you're holding something back. You need to tell me so we can find Nicholas. It's okay, honey, whatever it is."

I saw a tear plunk into her glass of milk.

"What did he say? What did he tell you?"

"He said he came to get Nicholas."

"Did he say why? Or where he was taking him?"

She looked up at me, brown eyes fringed with miles of lashes, too serious and wise for a newly minted six-year-old.

"He said it was to keep him safe."

4

To keep him safe. Right. From what? His own mother?

I knew Christine was telling the truth. But that didn't make the story true for one split second.

I didn't think Peter Terry was actually the one who snatched Nicholas, you understand. He'd never do the dirty work himself. But it was clear to me now that he was behind it somehow. I don't know why I hadn't realized it. This was just like him.

I tucked Christine back in with the bunnies and left a message on Ybarra's voice mail about Christine's exchange with the kidnapper and the burn on his hand. Then I made myself some tea and sat in the kitchen alone, listening to the clock buzz as the seconds slipped away.

I first met Peter Terry—the pasty-pale phantom with an ugly gash in his back, blade to blade—a couple of years ago. It was a hot August afternoon at a cold spring-fed pool in Austin. He walked right up and introduced himself to me in broad daylight, setting off a storm of gale-force chaos that ripped the roof off my life in no time flat, just like a Texas tornado in the summertime.

That day I'd received a groovy silver necklace, my mother's wedding ring (which had been buried with her two years before), and a full-on · blast of terror, uncertainty, and dread. In the ensuing months, I'd seen my career almost scrubbed off its foundations and my house infested with flies and various other vermin. I'd also managed to get myself dragged into the wakes of a couple of tragic, ambiguous suicides and the bloody murder of a young girl—a talented but lost college student—by a hapless loser in Wolverine work boots.

After all that, you'd think I'd be onto Peter Terry. And yet somehow I'd let myself be caught by surprise again—flatfooted and off my guard.

As nasty as I knew him to be, I never expected him to start kidnapping kids. Much less a sweet, funny little boy with nothing to protect him but a few knock-kneed women, two rabbits, and a staple gun.

After a few hours of fitful sleep, we all got up the next morning unsure about how to proceed. How do you act when someone you love—a helpless little boy—is out there somewhere in the hands of a kidnapper?

Sitting still for any length of time was an impossibility, so we went over to Maria's and did what anyone would do, I suppose. We paced. We worried. We cried. We speculated obsessively. We prayed.

Then we paced and worried and cried and speculated some more.

The speculating quickly became counterproductive, so we put a stop to that. The worrying we couldn't do anything about. That would have been like holding back a freight train with a rubber band.

The praying we kept up. Maria was particularly good at it. She must have crossed herself a thousand times, eyes cast upward, murmuring in Spanish.

I always forget God is multilingual. Half the time, I forget He's there at all. You'd think I'd learn, but spiritually, I have ADHD and am still in the third reading group.

He has to smack His ruler on my desk a lot to get my attention.

We spent the day calling around to let Maria's relatives and friends know what was going on. We fielded phone calls. We answered her door for her and received casseroles and fended off nosy neighbors. We made flyers and stapled them to every telephone pole and bulletin board we could find. We got Maria pulled together enough to go on the Sunday night news shows to ask politely for her son back. That was a particularly galling activity.

The whole thing was surreal. We all floated through it like we were swimming through JELL-O. And after another sleepless night, we got up and did the whole thing again.

We could feel the futility every time we stapled another flyer to another telephone pole. What were the chances that someone would see it and think, *Why, my goodness! That's the little boy my uncle brought to*

*the picnic last night, the one that was screaming and crying for his mother
and had duct tape around his wrists?* I mean, really. But we did it anyway. Because it was all we could think of to do.

I even called the milk-carton people. But those kids have been missing a while, it turns out. That's the rule. So, of course, we didn't want
Nicholas ever to qualify for milk-carton space.

Christine was a champ. She stapled flyers with the rest of us. It was
her idea to add the ribbons. She wanted purple, but when Liz explained
that yellow is the color for wishing someone you love would come
home, she agreed that yellow was the only choice. So I took her to the
craft store, and we bought a couple of miles of yellow ribbon and started
stapling bows with the flyers to the telephone poles.

A cop came by one time and told me it was against a Dallas city
ordinance to display flyers on telephone poles. I shoved a flyer in his face
and said, "You want to tell that to this kid's mother? Give me your
phone number, and I'll have her give you a call." He handed the flyer
back to me and walked away without a word.

On rare occasions, my natural hostility can be an asset.

Monday evening found us all sitting on my front porch, sipping
tepid lemonade and trying to fan away our exhaustion.

Maria looked at her watch. "That's it. Forty-eight hours. If they
don't find him in the first forty-eight hours, the chances go down by
half."

"That's got to be an estimate," I said. "I mean, they have to have
some time markers to evaluate things, right? But it can't mean forty-
eight hours exactly. It's probably, like, in the first few days."

She put her head in her hands, then pushed back her thick dark
hair and looked at me. "I feel like someone stuck my tongue in a light
socket. Every nerve I have is just gone. Charred to a crisp." She took a
sip of her drink and leaned her head back in the rocking chair. "I can't
cry anymore. I don't think I have a single tear left." She closed her eyes
and rocked slowly. The sun had gone behind the trees, and a breeze had
come.

"He's alive. Somewhere out there. I can feel it. I would know it if he…" Her voice trailed off. None of us could think about it, much less say it.

Christine was sitting cross-legged on the porch boards, cutting strips of yellow ribbon and tying them into lopsided bows. The warm air moved a strip of ribbon across the porch in a long curl.

"Does Nicholas like Kool-Aid?" she said without looking up.

"Yes, he does," Maria said. "He loves Kool-Aid."

"What color does he like?" Christine asked.

"Red," Maria said. "He likes red."

"He's thirsty," Christine said. "He wants red."

Liz looked up. "Christine, that's not—"

Maria sat up and looked at Christine. "What did you say?"

"He's all thirsty and he wants some Kool-Aid. Can I have some too?"

"Sure, Punkin," I said. "What kind? I've got red and purple."

"Nicholas wants the red kind."

Liz flashed her daughter a mother-of-three-in-the-grocery-store look. "Christine, you could not possibly know if Nicholas is thirsty. You're upsetting Maria. Now tell her you're sorry," she said sternly. "And if you want the red kind, it's *may I have the red kind, please?*"

Christine looked up at her mother and furrowed her brow. "But it's real hot."

"I know it's hot. You can have all the Kool-Aid you want," Liz said. "Just don't—."

"No… Nicholas. He's real hot. He wants some Kool-Aid. The red kind."

"We don't know where Nicholas is, Christine," I said. "We don't know if it's hot there or not."

"It's not nice to say something like that when Miss Maria is so worried," Liz said. "Christine, say you're sorry."

"But—"

"Say you're sorry," Liz said.

Christine rubbed her eyes and dropped her head. "I'm sorry," she mumbled.

I reached over and pulled her into my lap, leaning my head back on the porch column, my legs stretched out in front of me on the porch, ankles crossed. She put her head on my shoulder.

"Do you think it's hot where Nicholas is?" I asked.

"Really super-duper hot," Christine said.

"That's pretty hot." I pushed the hair out of her eyes, off her forehead, which was damp with sweat. "You think he's okay?"

"Uh-huh," she said. "I think he's okay."

Maria was sitting on the edge of her chair. "Christine, how do you know Nicholas is hot and thirsty?"

"Because he wants some Kool-Aid."

I had a thought. "Punkin, did Earl tell you Nicholas is thirsty?"

Maria looked puzzled. "Who's Earl?"

"Christine's guardian angel," I said. "She named him Earl, and she believes he talks to her sometimes."

Christine began to cry. "He *does* talk to me! I didn't make him up. His name *is* Earl, and he's real."

"Oh, sweetie, I didn't mean—"

"And Earl told you Nicholas is thirsty?" Maria said.

I winced at the hope in Maria's eyes.

But Christine just shook her head petulantly. "Not Earl."

"Christine," Maria said again, "how do you know Nicholas is thirsty?"

"Because of the Kool-Aid," Christine whined.

"Do you know who has him?" Maria asked.

"The man was real mean, and he had a snake on him," Christine said.

Maria kept pressing. "You told us that already. Is there anything else? Do you know anything about where the mean man took him? Or why he might be thirsty? Did he say where he was taking him? Is that how you know he's thirsty?"

Christine shook her head again.

"Maria, I'm sorry." Liz stood and began winding Christine's ribbon onto its spool. "We should go. It's been a long couple of days. I think we'll stay at the hotel tonight and see if we can get a good night's sleep. Dylan, do you mind keeping Eeyore for another night or two?"

I felt a stab of alarm. "You guys don't want to stay with me?"

The thought of being alone with so much tragedy clogging the air in my house wasn't the slightest bit appealing. I could feel a fetid cloud of depression sinking on me at the very thought.

"I think we'll put on our bathing suits and go for a nice swim, and then we'll see if we can order a pizza or maybe some crunchy carrots from room service," Liz said. "Or we could stop at 7-Eleven on the way there and get you some Fritos and an orange Popsicle. Would you like that, Punkin?"

"I want to stay with Miss Dylan."

"We can't, honey. We need to go stay at the hotel tonight."

Christine started to cry again and shoved her thumb in her mouth. I looked over her head at Liz. "Are you sure?" I mouthed silently.

She rolled her eyes.

"Please?" I mouthed.

She sighed. "Okay, Christine. One more night. But no more stories about Nicholas."

"It's not a story," Christine mumbled. She climbed off my lap and went inside the house, letting the screen door slam behind her just as Martinez pulled up in front of my house.

He parked his squad car in the driveway and headed up to the porch. He had a slow, ambling sort of walk that made him look wise and pensive and worldly all at once. Maria got up to greet him and stepped into his arms. He held her for a long minute—long enough that Liz and I began to feel awkward and intrusive.

He wiped the tears from her face with his thumbs, said something to her in Spanish, and kissed her on the forehead. When he finally let go, Maria was crying again.

The look on his face offered little hope. "We took the van apart."

"And?" I said.

"We found a couple of long, brown, curly hairs."

Maria started to say something, but he held his hand up to stop her. "They're not his. We're trying to match the daughter's hair."

"Have they interviewed that family?" Liz asked. "The Dickersons?"

"Repeatedly." He sat on the porch swing and pulled Maria over next to him. "They've been fully cooperative. No lawyers. No resistance. Nothing. They let us crawl over every inch of their cars. We've been through their entire house. They all gave hair samples. Everything. They're clean."

"Are you sure?" I asked.

"I'm positive. I've watched every minute of the interviews. They're not hiding anything."

"Then how do you explain the van?" Maria's eyes began to tear up again. You could just see the hope leaking out of her.

"Coincidence," Martinez said. "They must have pulled away at about the same time Nicholas was abducted." He hugged her. "*Mija*, Nicholas was never in that van."

Maria drew away from him and crossed her arms. She walked to the other end of the porch, staring into the street.

"What now?" Liz asked.

"We start interviewing the witnesses again. See if anyone remembers anything."

"Like what?" Maria said. "It happened so fast."

"Like another car," Martinez said. "He got away from that park somehow."

"With a kicking, squirming kid who didn't want to go with him." I nodded in agreement. "He must have had a car. How else could he have—"

Maria whirled around. "Dylan, we saw another car."

"What car? When?" I said.

"When we were in the street. A car honked at us."

"All I saw was the van."

She gestured at Martinez. "I can't believe I forgot. It wasn't a van. It was…" She paced around in a circle, then stopped and looked at me. "What was it, Dylan? What kind of car was it?"

I shook my head. "Maria, I don't know what you're talking about. I don't remember another car."

"Yes, you do! It was after you caught up to me and I was losing it in the street. Remember—a car came up behind us and honked for us to get out of the way? What was it? Don't you remember?"

I thought for a minute. "I really don't. I'm sorry."

"Are you sure you saw another car, Maria?" Martinez asked. "Sometimes people inject details in hindsight."

I stood and headed inside for my bag and keys. "Let's go over there. Right now. Maybe it'll jog my memory."

5

LIZ STAYED WITH CHRISTINE while the rest of us headed back to the park. We hadn't been there since Nicholas disappeared. It had an eerie, abandoned feel to it. The swings were still. A deflated soccer ball sat beside a backstop. The fountain had been turned off. The pond emitted a putrid, brackish stench. Even the katydids were silent—strange for a summer evening.

At first, Maria couldn't get out of the car. We backed away and let her take her time. She eventually took a few breaths and stepped out like she was stepping off a boat into a deep body of water. She walked slowly, her arms crossed tightly, one hand at her mouth, biting her thumbnail, the other twirling the St. Christopher medal she wore around her neck.

We started at the park bench. The special-needs donkey was still stapled to the tree, looking more forlorn than ever. I pulled it down and followed Martinez to the trash bin. The trash had been confiscated by the DPD two days before. A piece of yellow crime-scene tape formed a cross over the bin opening. Martinez broke it, and I shoved the donkey inside.

We retraced our steps, walking past the benches, the swings, the water fountains, the tramped-down grass where the petting zoo had been. We circled the tennis courts and stopped. Beside the tennis courts, a bronze statue of children playing had been made into a shrine of sorts. Flowers and notes and teddy bears were piled up at the children's feet, looking almost like an impediment to their gleeful play. Maria reached down and picked up a few of the notes. She read them silently, then tucked one into her pocket and crossed herself.

As she stood there, a couple pushing a stroller walked up the street behind us. Their big yellow dog tugged at its leash, pulling them all forward. They put their heads down, graciously declining to stare. Maria waited until they had passed and began to cry. She crossed herself again, kissed her St. Christopher, and turned to walk into the street. We followed her around the block to the center of the street, one block over. Maria and I stopped there and looked around.

"Let's try something," I said. "Maria, kneel down like you were the other day."

She knelt and looked up at me.

I nodded. "Okay now, Maria, look the other way, in the direction the van was moving." I knelt down beside her and held her shoulders like I had before. I stared into the distance, summoning my memory, picking through the fog for the visual. In my mind I could hear the honk, but I couldn't see the car.

"The horn was a medium horn," I said finally. "Not a little beepy one. Not a loud foghorn one. Just medium." I looked up at Martinez. "Could have been a sedan."

Martinez was watching me intently. "Okay, that's good. Anything else? Can you see the hood? Is there an emblem or anything?"

I let go of Maria and walked around, looking up and down at the cars parked in front of houses. The streets in this part of Highland Park are narrow. When two cars are parked on opposite sides of the street, there's room for only one car in the middle. I walked over and stood between two cars, closed my eyes, and then turned my head over my shoulder, putting myself in the exact position I'd been in the moment I'd seen the car.

"White," I said. "I think it was white."

"Are you sure?" Martinez asked.

"Nope. But it's the best I can do."

"I think that's right," Maria said. "I think it was white. I remember now."

Martinez looked at her without saying anything. Maria wanted to believe it so badly.

"It seems like the hood had some gray patches," I said.

Martinez pulled a notebook from his back pocket and began scribbling. "Sanded down, maybe? Like someone was repairing the finish?"

I nodded. "Could be. That's what I'm seeing in my mind. A ratty sedan with white, patchy paint."

"Driver?" Martinez asked.

"White guy."

"Age?"

"Maybe forties? Not old. And definitely not a kid."

"Anyone else in the car with him?" Martinez looked up from his writing.

"Nope."

"Headrests?"

I raised my eyebrows. "Good question. That would narrow the model year down a bit, wouldn't it? I don't think there were any headrests. Could have been a bench seat."

"An old car, then," Martinez said. "Engine noise?"

"I heard it come up behind us, so it must have been a little loud. Not a nice, new, whirry sound. Old and clunky is closer, I think. Kind of like my truck, come to think of it."

"But a car, not a truck," Maria said. "It was definitely a car."

"Don't you think someone would have noticed a car like that in this neighborhood?" I asked. "Especially on a Saturday when none of the work crews are around."

"What does that have to do with anything?" Maria asked.

"No one living in this neighborhood would drive a car like that," Martinez said. "Construction workers, yard men—you'd see them on weekdays. Everywhere. But not on a weekend. A car like that would stand out."

"Like a chicken in a duck pond," I said.

"We'll recanvass with the description," Martinez said. "Someone should have seen it. Anything else about the driver? You said he honked?"

"Yeah, and I turned around and glared at him." I pointed at Martinez as I remembered. "He had a hat on. He ducked behind it when I turned around."

"What kind?"

"Baseball cap."

"Anything on it? Emblem or anything?"

"No idea."

"What color?"

"Dark, maybe black."

"Like the guy in the park."

"Maybe. That's a long shot, though, Enrique. I can't say for sure."

"Everything's a long shot," Martinez said. "It's a lead. Let's go."

We checked in with Liz and Christine, then headed down to the station to look at photos of cars. I studied books of sedans and narrowed it down to a white, early- to midsixties Ford or Chevy. Red or brown interior.

Martinez put it on the wire, and we called it a night.

He dropped me back at my house, then left to take Maria home. I stood on the porch for a minute before I went inside, looking into my house from the outside. I could see straight into my living room. The light was yellow and warm, streaming through the bamboo shades I'd bought for thirty dollars apiece at Home Depot. It looked homey in there, inviting. Liz and Christine were sitting on the floor, playing with the bunnies.

I rarely allow myself to think about how alone I am in the world. It's an indulgence I cannot afford. But standing there, looking at that little bit of family in my living room, I blew every cent of serenity I'd saved up. I had never felt so alone in my life.

My mother had died several years ago, not long after she and my dad split up. My father and brother and I were all that was left of our shoddy little family, and we were fractured and fragmented, separated from one another by unforgiving miles and profound disinterest.

My brother, who lived in Seattle, had recently gone through a bruising divorce. He'd wound up stuck in a town that gets three hundred days of rain a year, living alone in a house he can't afford with two cats he can't stand.

My dad had taken up with his ding-a-ling scrub nurse, Kellee with two *e*'s, about fifteen seconds after he and my mother divorced. The two of them had married and were about to produce their first, and I hoped only, offspring—a little girl I wanted to love but with whom I felt no connection whatever. They'd already named her Kellee Shawn—Sean is my father's middle name—and were busy planning to transform her into a tiny extension of themselves.

I was prepared to jump through the requisite big-sister hoops—though I had managed to schedule myself a speaking gig at an academic conference the weekend of the Big Baby Shower. I intended to purchase flowers for Kellee when the baby was born, buy savings bonds, send the kid a tiny SMU cheerleader outfit. Rah, rah, rah. But the hard truth is, my heart wasn't in it. Every time I imagined that sweet, untarnished face, I felt a wave of resentment knock into me like a hot, dusty wind. When I looked at my father looking at Kellee and imagined Kellee's little replica lying there on her Oilily blankie, wearing her pressed Lilly Pulitzer prints, I felt subordinated. Tossed aside. Replaced.

Now, I admit that these are childish sentiments. They are especially childish given the fact that I recently passed into the latter half of my thirties. I'm not the baby of the family whining because I've lost my mommy's rapt attention. My mother wasn't the rapt-attention type. The sad truth is, I'm the baby of the family whining because I never had my father's attention at all.

Neither will little Kellee Shawn, of course. She's just a prop on the stage of Kellee's paper-doll fantasy life. She's got the heart-surgeon husband, the cruise wear, the implants, the French tips, the "natural blond" highlights. And now she's working on the tow-headed, bow-haired daughter to match. She'll have Kellee Shawn in French tips in no time.

And as for my dad, he'd just about finished assembling his little picture-perfect family kit. Which we had never been. My brother and I were childhood reprobates, running around barefoot with dirty ankles and ripped jeans and T-shirts with inappropriate messages on them, shoplifting cigarettes from the local convenience store. And my mother was earthy and cerebral and interesting and refused to wear pantyhose or color her auburn hair when it began to gray.

When my dad was young and idealistic, a hippie medical student headed for the Peace Corps, our scruffy little family had fit the bill. But once he grew the horns of ambition, we'd become a sour disappointment to him. I've never forgiven him for that.

I periodically summon weak resolve to stop flattening tires on this particular pothole in my otherwise orderly life. I bulldoze in a load of gravel and tar, dump it in the hole, tamp down the asphalt, and smile with satisfaction at my newfound mental health. But then Father's Day comes around. Or I hear a John Lennon song on the radio. And suddenly I feel like Cynthia's kid Julian—heir to nothing when the legacy is rightfully mine. And I sink back into self-pity, and I fantasize about retribution.

Not my finest quality, admittedly. It's easily one of my Top Ten Terrible Traits.

As I stood there in the warm evening, looking inside the windows of my house, I marveled at my astonishing lack of progress on this issue and resolved once again to patch the hole, wondering how much gravel there was available in the world. Then I walked inside and locked the door behind me, settling myself on the floor with the rest of the group. We played pin the tail on the bunny using Scotch tape and the donkey tails I'd made for the birthday party and chased the bunnies around the room. We liked the game better than the rabbits did, of course. It was a silly, witless distraction that could probably get us into trouble with the PETA crowd. But it served its purpose and popped the bubble on the tension. In the end, the bunnies seemed none the worse for the wear and were rewarded for their trouble with an extra helping of purple carrots from Whole Foods.

I'd just about shaken off my funk when my doorbell rang. I checked my watch. Who would knock on my door at ten thirty? I looked through the peephole, gasped, and felt the asphalt rumble and crack as a brand-new hole gaped open under my feet.

6

DAVID SHYKOVSKY IS QUITE possibly the most perfect male I've ever met. He says "thank you ma'am" and "please" and rises from his chair when a woman enters the room. He has the shoulders of a linebacker and the waist of a dancer, knows his downward dog from his warrior pose, and can quote every word of every Lyle Lovett song ever written. He makes a mean chocolate pie with cooked pudding, not instant. He can rebuild a transmission and choose the right wine to go with the fish he just grilled. Take him to a party, and he can hold an animated, engaging conversation with a sack of shelled corn.

And he never leaves crumbs in the butter.

His one failing, other than the fact that he owns a funeral home in Hillsboro, is that he put up with me for almost a year and a half. Which, of course, is why I eventually lost respect for him.

I met David shortly after Peter Terry ran a bowling ball through my life and scattered every scrap of my carefully ordered world into the gutter with a slap and a clatter. I was the worst version of myself during our time together—catastrophically anxious, chronically forgetful, and relentlessly self-involved. I was even more cranky, compulsive, and impulsive than usual. And obsessive, of course. That goes without saying. The smell of Pine-Sol alone would have been enough to run off the average boyfriend candidate. David, however, remained sweet, thoughtful, and thoroughly magnanimous throughout.

Then, to his credit, he broke up with me.

Since I'm not completely mentally challenged, I realized in short order what an idiot I'd been. I promptly threw myself at his mercy and begged him to take me back. He declined a golden opportunity to gloat, told me he cared about me but cared about his own sanity more, and wished me well. Then he wiped my tears, walked me to my truck, checked my oil for me, and kissed me good-bye.

I'd been pouting ever since.

And now here he was, standing on my front porch at ten thirty on a Monday night, handsome and clean and patiently waiting for me to let him in. And I was demonstrating all the backbone and resolve of a wad of chewed Juicy Fruit.

I turned and whispered to Liz. "It's David. What do I do?"

"Open the door."

"No."

"Dylan, open the door."

"I can't."

He knocked again. "Dylan? I can hear you in there. It's me."

"Dylan!" Liz said.

"What?"

"The man is standing on your porch. Open the door."

"How do I look? Do I need lip gloss?"

"Dylan, let the man in."

I checked my fly and straightened my shoulders, then undid the latch and swung the door open a few inches.

"Wow," was all I could think of to say. Not a particularly brilliant choice in hindsight, but at least I was able to vocalize.

He gave me a little wave. "Surprise."

"What are you doing here?"

"Can I come in?"

I took a step back into the foyer and opened the door.

David walked inside and gave me a kiss on the cheek. He was wearing the cologne I'd bought him in Italy—an earthy, tobaccoish scent that used to drive me off a cliff every time I smelled it on him.

"Liz, you remember David, right?"

"Of course I do. David, it's good to see you again." Liz picked herself up and stood to greet David, who gave her a gentlemanly air kiss on the cheek and a warm, genuine hug. Then he bent down to say hello to Christine, who jumped into his arms and clung to him like a baby monkey.

"Where have you been?" she asked plaintively.

"Just real busy, sweetie."

"I turned six, and I got a bunny," Christine said. "Why didn't you come to my birthday party?"

He looked at me.

I smirked back at him.

I wasn't about to bail him out. It's not the dumpee's responsibility to smooth things over with mutual friends. Everyone knows that.

"I saw a funny purple pen with a big hairy ball on the top the other day, and it made me think of you," David said. "If I'd known you were coming to town, I would have bought it for you."

Christine conned him into sitting on the floor with her to play pin the tail on the bunny, which David did because he's a fabulous human being who is impervious to self-doubt or fits of ego. How many men do you know who would sit cross-legged on the floor with a six-year-old and try to tape a paper tail to a bunny's rear end?

I studied him. He was wearing old chinos that were faded and worn and butter soft and looked devastating hanging on his lean frame. A T-shirt that said "I'm big in Japan" hugged his shoulders and matched his blue eyes. He had new flip-flops, which he'd kicked off to sit on the floor with Christine. His skin was browned from the sun, his hair glinting in the light.

I was in real trouble here.

I watched the three of them play and talk, unable to join in, of course, because I was too busy obsessing. What was he doing here? Had he been out with anyone else? How did I look? I glanced down at my chipped toenail polish. When was my last pedicure—Christmas? Was that a tattoo peeking out from under his shirt sleeve? His hair looked lighter. Had he been to the beach or something? Who went with him?

What if he wanted me back? Should I play hard to get or sign up now without the recommended twenty-four-hour waiting period?

He started telling Christine knock-knock jokes, sending her into spasms of laughter and inspiring her to make up her own.

"Knock, knock," Christine said.

"Who's there?" David said.

"Orange."

"Orange who?"

"Orange you gonna kiss Miss Dylan on the lips?"

She squealed and giggled as I cowered in the rapidly widening asphalt chasm in my living room floor.

"Time for bed," Liz said suddenly.

"Mommy, no!"

"It's way past bedtime, Punkin. Let's go."

She dragged Christine out of the room, returning a few minutes later. She hugged David, then stepped back and looked him over. "You look terrific. I'm glad you came by. We all needed some bad knock-knock jokes."

He feigned disappointment. "I was shooting for terrible."

"I'm turning in," she said. "See you in the morning, Dylan."

They said their good-byes. We heard Liz shut the bedroom door.

He turned and looked at me. "Hi."

" 'Hi'?" I crossed my arms and shifted my weight to one foot. "That seems insufficient, don't you think?"

"How about, 'Hello'?"

"You've had all this time, and you came up with 'hi' and 'hello'?"

He grinned. "I worked on it, though. Did you notice how polished my delivery was? I practiced in front of a mirror."

"You drove an hour in the dark to say hello?"

"Didn't you see *Jerry Maguire*?"

"Tom Cruise?" I laughed. "Pick someone else. He's a nut."

"Yes, but he can deliver a line."

"Try it again."

He backed up a couple of feet, mustered a look of tearful sincerity, and put a hand across his chest as though in pledge. "Hello."

I squinted at him. "Nope. No buzz, David. Sorry."

"You complete me?"

I raised an eyebrow. "Our status would make that seem disingenuous."

"How about, 'You had me at hello'?"

"That's her line."

He threw up his hands. "Got any Shiner?"

"Sure."

We walked to the kitchen. David made himself at home on a bar stool. I opened a can of pistachios—my class-A company snack—and put out an extra bowl for the shells. David started in on the pistachios as I popped the top on his beer. My beer mugs had been in the freezer since January, unused. It was strange to need them again.

"I saw you on the news," he said.

"I was on the news? When?"

"Sunday night."

"I was on TV?"

"The interview with Maria. You were standing behind her." He set his beer down and looked at me. "You were there, weren't you? When it happened?"

I nodded.

"I'm sorry, Dylan. I don't even know what to say."

"There's nothing to say."

"How is she?"

"Better than you'd expect, I guess. She's keeping it together."

"It must have been terrible."

"It's still terrible." I rubbed my eyes, then ran my fingers through my hair. "I feel like I could sleep for a week, but I have these appalling dreams. I can't get away from them. I have these awful visions of what might be happening to him."

"This is Gordon Pryne's kid, right? The man who raped Maria?"

"Yeah. Nicholas. He looks so much like his dad, but he's such a sweet little boy, David. So trusting. He's kind of small for his age and really shy. You have to draw him out. He has this pet turtle named Bob that he walks on a leash." I fought off tears, reaching for a paper towel to dry my eyes, then looked at David and shook my head. "What are you doing here? Why show up after all this time?"

He cleared his throat. "When I saw you—on the news, on TV, standing there behind Maria… You didn't know the camera was on you. And I hadn't seen you in such a long time." He pushed his beer away. "Your hair's longer."

"That happens."

I waited for him to finish his story.

"You looked so sad, Dylan. I just didn't…" He stared at his beer.

"Didn't what?"

"I just didn't think…"

"Didn't think what, David?"

He pursed his lips and looked at me. I could tell he was trying to decide whether to tell me what was on his mind.

"Come on…"

"You'll say I'm being patronizing."

"David, just spit it out."

He took a breath and interlaced his fingers around his beer mug. "I didn't want you to go through this alone."

"I'm not alone," I said defensively.

"I realize you're not literally alone—"

"I have friends."

"I know you do. I didn't mean that. I just meant—"

"What, exactly?"

"I care about you, Dylan. I wanted to help. I'm trying to be nice here."

"Nice? It's not nice to show up on my doorstep like this. It's been six months."

"Four and a half."

"Okay, practically five. Why did you have to show up at my house? And why now, of all times? I'm holding myself together with Scotch tape and paper clips."

"I wanted to see you. That's all. I thought I could offer some—"

"Comfort? I don't find your presence comforting, David. I find your presence upsetting. Couldn't you have been nice in a voice mail? Or an e-mail?"

"Can you cut me a break here?"

"A break? You broke up with *me*."

"Yes, but reluctantly."

"You insulted me."

"I did not."

"You said I was too much trouble."

"I never said that."

"You did."

"I said I couldn't handle all the trouble you had in your life. I said I wanted to be more important to you than the latest catastrophe."

"Well, here's a little news flash for you, David. You're not more important to me. This catastrophe is officially and appropriately more important to me than you are. It's more important than I am. That's the natural order of things. Catastrophes are, well, catastrophic, David."

"I realize that. That's not what I meant."

"Life doesn't just go on without skipping a beat, you know. Some things demand immediate attention."

"I didn't mean that. I just—"

"What did you mean then, David? I don't ask for these things to happen." I took a breath and walked the length of the kitchen, trying to calm myself down. "Look, I'm not even really involved. I'm just some target in a gigantic video game. Running around hiding in manholes, trying not to get vaporized. You think I like all these bombs going off in my life?"

He pushed his beer away. "No. I don't. If I implied that to you ever, I'm sorry."

Neither of us said anything. David got up to leave. I stopped him and pulled him back to the bar stool. I sat him down and stared at him for a second while I forced myself into the penitence I knew he deserved, then hiked myself up on the bar and sat facing him, my bare feet on the worn knees of his chinos.

"I owe you so many apologies, I don't know where to begin." I reached for both his hands. "I'm sorry. I am." I shook my head and squeezed his hands, loving the feel of his fingers wrapping around mine. "But geez. After all this time…" I looked down and blinked away a tear. "Why do I always manage to feel attacked when there's no enemy in the room?"

He shrugged. "Who says there's no enemy in the room?"

I looked around, half expecting to see Peter Terry standing in the doorway, overcome suddenly with that eerie feeling you get when someone's watching you.

"You're shooting at the wrong guy, sugar pea," David was saying. "Next time, maybe you should find out if you're dealing with friend or foe before you unload your clip into him."

"So which is it? Friend or foe?"

"Friend."

"Friend. I don't know if I can be friends with you, David."

"I don't know if I can be anything else, Dylan."

I hopped down and went to the fridge and poured myself a glass of wine. I set the bottle down on the bar, took a sip, and closed my eyes, letting the taste settle in on my tongue.

"Sauvignon blanc," he said, tilting the bottle so he could read the label. "New Zealand?"

I nodded. "It's the best." I took another sip and held out my glass. "Want a sip?"

"I'll stick with my Shiner."

I set my glass down, and our eyes locked in a long clinch. "You broke my heart," I said finally.

"I'm sorry. I didn't want to hurt you."

"Sure you did."

He shrugged. "Okay, maybe a little."

"Don't do that anymore, okay?"

"Hurt you?"

"Yeah. I can't take it. I haven't got any fight left in me."

"All evidence to the contrary." He looked at me, then down at his hands. "I can't get back together, Dylan."

MY SOUL TO KEEP

I felt a tear slide down my cheek. I reached up and swiped it away quickly, before he looked up. It is a rule in the universe that a girl should never break down and sob hysterically in front of an ex-boyfriend. I intended to adhere to the handbook on this one. I had my self-respect to consider.

"I don't want to get back together either," I lied. "But you are the one person in the world who isn't qualified to comfort me right now, David. You DQed yourself the last time you walked out that door."

"DQed?"

"Disqualified. Technical foul. Penalty for piling on."

"For what? I play a fair game."

"You broke my heart."

"You mentioned that," he said.

I thought I caught at least a glimpse of remorse in his eyes. I looked at him expectantly. "Where's my apology?"

"I'm, sorry, Dylan. I really didn't think you cared that much."

"Well, I did."

"I couldn't tell."

"I know," I said. "You deserve better. I'm sorry."

"You're right. I do."

He stood and picked up his keys. I followed him to the door, resisting a sudden, overwhelming impulse to drop to my knees, grab his legs, and beg him to stay. If I'd thought it had a gnat's chance of working, I might have done it. I'd have regretted it, of course. Begging is not an optimal relationship tool. But still, it was tempting.

He stopped at the front door and hugged me. I closed my eyes and breathed in the smell of his shirt.

"Nice touch," I said when we stepped back.

"What?"

"The cologne."

"I wear it all the time."

"That's not why you wore it tonight."

He blushed. "Dirty trick, huh?"

"A little bit, yeah."

"Take care of yourself, will you, Dylan? And will you please let me know what I can do?"

"Oh, sure. Absolutely. You'll be the first one I call."

"Liar."

"I'm trying to be nice."

"Don't." He kissed me on the forehead. "I like the real you better."

I shut the door and watched through the peephole as he walked down the walkway, got into his car, and made a phone call. I felt a spike of jealousy as he smiled and laughed through a brief conversation. Then he started the car, turned on the headlights, and drove off into the night.

I sat in the kitchen and cried into my wineglass for a while, trying to convince myself I wasn't an unredeemable loser who'd just managed to run off a perfectly good boyfriend. But since I *was* an unredeemable loser who'd just managed to run off a perfectly good boyfriend, my task was a little tough. I eventually admitted the obvious, blew my nose, put my dishes in the dishwasher, and scrubbed the sink with my new bottle of lemon-scented Soft Scrub with Bleach, just to cheer myself up, buffing the porcelain to a high shine with a clean cup towel. I reached into the fridge for a bottle of water and began contemplating a bubble bath.

I had just flipped off the kitchen light and put my hand on the bedroom doorknob when I heard the first scream come from behind the door.

7

~

I FLIPPED THE KITCHEN light back on, flung the door open, and let a stream of light into the otherwise dark bedroom. The bunnies were racing around in circles, whimpering and squealing, their little rabbit toenails scratching against the wood floor.

Liz was kneeling on the floor beside Christine's pallet. She looked up at me with wild eyes. "She's not breathing." She began slapping Christine on the cheeks and shouting her name, screaming hysterically and begging her to wake up.

I grabbed the phone and dialed 911. After a quick conversation I was back in the bedroom, peering into Christine's lifeless face. Her skin was pallid, her lips blue.

I shoved Liz aside and started CPR. My last refresher course had been when I was a lifeguard my last summer in college, several presidential administrations ago. But the instructor's advice turned out to be true; it was indeed like falling off a bike. I cleared Christine's trachea and started compressions, yelling at Liz to breathe into Christine's mouth on my count.

The rabbits scooted in and snuggled next to Christine, puffing themselves up into warm, fluffy balls, their eyes half-closed, their ears laid back as though they were sleeping. There was no sound in the house other than our barked communications and the puffs of air as Liz breathed into Christine's lungs at regular intervals. We plugged along in rhythm until the ambulance arrived a few minutes later.

The paramedics made quick work of getting oxygen into her. Christine pinked up right away. Her brown eyes flew open, and she started blinking frantically, her chest convulsing as she tried to cough the tube out of her mouth. She began to fight, struggling to push the paramedics away. One of them grabbed her arms and pinned her down. She started kicking then, her little feet punching their legs and stomachs until she nailed one of them in the groin. They finally gave her an injection to calm her down. Her body went limp, but her eyes remained wide, darting around the room, big wet tears running down her cheeks and pooling in her ears.

Liz wasn't much easier to manage. She kept trying to claw her way past them to get to Christine. One of them finally shouted at me to get her out of there, which I did. Liz and I stood in the kitchen and hugged while they finished their work and got Christine onto a gurney.

Liz rode in the back of the ambulance. She was holding Christine's hand and whispering into her ear when they closed the doors and sped off, lights flashing red against the gray-painted bricks of my little house.

I hopped into my truck and followed them, dialing David as I drove. He didn't pick up.

I cursed violently, threw my phone down, and sobbed the entire way to the hospital.

On the way there, weaving through late-night bar traffic, it finally occurred to me to pray, though I can't say I followed the prescribed routine. I mentally stamped my feet and demanded that God heal Christine immediately—without that whole TV-preacher, slain-in-the-Spirit routine—and return Nicholas to his mother right this minute. In mint condition. I reminded the Almighty of my reasonably good behavior in recent months. I promised a lifetime of devotion to the entire Trinity, even though we all knew I couldn't deliver. And then I screamed obscenities at Peter Terry, ordering God in the next breath to flatten him without mercy and to doom him to suffer cruelly for all eternity.

God has a tendency to not follow my orders, a niggling little policy of His I find quite maddening. After all this time, He still refuses to budge.

By the time I parked my truck in the lot at Children's Medical Center and threaded my way through the ER, Christine and I had both calmed down. She was alert and placid, lying there in her hospital bed, blinking in the fluorescent light and clutching a white blanket.

Liz was still hysterical, however. I pulled aside an ER doc and asked her to prescribe some Xanax for Liz. Two hours later we were all in a room on the seventh floor, limp and exhausted.

They'd removed Christine's breathing tube in the ER, though she was still tethered to an IV and a breathing monitor. She had so many drugs in her system at that point that she slept like a stone through that long, brutal night as nurses walked in and out of the room, flipping on lights and checking her monitors.

After they'd settled Christine into her room, I went downstairs to the cafeteria. I don't usually drink coffee, but there was no tea in sight. Coffee would have to do. I ordered some for Liz and me, and I brought a little cardboard tray back up with two steaming cups, complete with sugar packets and that crummy fake cream in the little plastic thimble cups with the peel-off foil tops.

I handed Liz a steaming cup and offered her a plastic straw to stir her coffee with.

Her eyes were swollen and red, her nose stuffy.

"My head's killing me," she said.

"Want some aspirin?" I asked. She nodded. I got up and felt around in my bag for Sudafed and aspirin. I found a box of Kleenex in Christine's bathroom.

Liz took a sip of hot coffee, wincing as she tried to force the pills down her throat. She plucked a Kleenex out of the box, swallowed again, and closed her eyes. "You saved her life."

"The paramedics saved her life."

She dabbed her eyes. "I didn't know what to do."

I looked down at my coffee and didn't say anything.

"I took CPR," she said. "But I couldn't think. I panicked."

I scooted my chair away from an unwelcome blast of air conditioning and blew on my coffee. "You're not beating yourself up, I hope."

"No. I can't go there. I just… I'm grateful. That's all. Thank you."

I held up my foam cup. "To survival."

"To survival."

The coffee wasn't too bad. I guess they splurge for the parents of sick kids. We sat silently for a moment, listening to the beeps and bangs of a busy hospital in the nighttime and gazing at Christine, who was breathing peacefully, her thumb in her mouth. She slept deeply, her cheeks still sticky with tears.

"How did you know?" I asked.

"Hmm?" Liz asked. I'd jolted her out of a daze.

"How did you know she'd stopped breathing?"

"The rabbits."

"Come again?"

"The rabbits woke me up."

"Eeyore and Melissa?"

She nodded.

"You're kidding me."

"I am absolutely not kidding you. I heard this thump, and then they both started squealing and scratching the floor. I tried to shush them, thinking they'd wake Christine. But they wouldn't shut up. I got out of bed to find them and put them in their hutches. I didn't turn on the light because I didn't want to wake her. She's had so little sleep the past few days."

I realized I was listening with my mouth open. It was a mouth-open kind of story.

"I kept trying to catch them, but they were too quick. I could feel them hopping up onto her chest. I kept grabbing for them, but they'd hop down onto the floor for a second and then bounce right back up there. It finally dawned on me that she wasn't waking up."

"It's like one of those hero-dog stories."

"Except they're rabbits. Who ever heard of that?"

"We should call *People* magazine."

She took a sip, leaned her head back to swallow, and let out a long exhale.

"I finally thought to lean down and listen for her breath. It was still pitch black in there." The air conditioner rattled loudly behind us. "There was no breath."

"What do you think happened?"

"Maybe she choked on something? I can't imagine what. She didn't cough anything up."

"What did the ER doc say?"

"Asthma."

"I didn't know Christine had asthma," I said.

"She doesn't."

"Then how—"

"They don't know what happened. It's a guess—a bad one, I think. Christine has been healthy as a goat her entire life."

"I think asthma can start at any time, though."

Liz sipped her coffee and didn't say anything.

"Liz? What are you thinking?"

"Nothing."

"What?"

"Nothing."

"Tell me."

Liz looked at me. "I'm thinking bad things happen when we're with you."

I caught my breath and blinked back a sudden flood of tears.

"I'm sorry, Dylan. I know it's not intentional or anything. But there's this cloud or curse or something…"

There was no point denying it. "I know. I'm sorry, Liz. I'm so very sorry."

She touched my arm. "I don't think it has anything to do with you personally. Bad things happen all the time. But something is terribly wrong. And somehow, right now at least, you seem to be in the middle of it."

I put my head in my hands, briefly contemplating breaking into the nurses' station and foraging for narcotics.

"Dylan." She reached for my arm. "Look at me."

Liz met my gaze with kind, brown eyes.

"Christine is a special kid," she said. "An important kid. I've always known that. You've always known it."

I nodded.

"I think there are…forces out there fighting over her."

"I do too."

"So. The wrong side almost won tonight. That's all."

"Maybe Earl tipped off the rabbits."

"That wouldn't surprise me a bit." She set her coffee down. "They're fighting over you too, I think."

"Not over me. Around me, maybe."

She shrugged. "What difference does it make?"

We didn't talk any more that night. There was nothing more to say. We were both numb with exhaustion.

My cell phone rang at two that morning, jarring me out of shallow sleep. I groaned and reached for it, my bones stiff from dozing upright in a chair. It was David. I hesitated, then took the call on the fourth ring.

"You called me," he said.

"You didn't pick up."

"I'm calling you back."

"You didn't pick up."

"I'm sorry, Dylan. I didn't hear the phone."

I shoved the whine out of my voice and tried not to sound petty. "It's okay. It doesn't matter." I got up and went out into the hall.

"It does. I asked you to call and you did. I blew it."

"Okay. I take it back. It does matter."

"Give me another shot. Want to call me again and I'll pick up this time? On the first ring, even. Real eager."

I started to cry, hating myself for it. I am generally not a crier, but I couldn't control myself.

I could hear the alarm in his voice. "Dylan, where are you? Are you at home?"

I started to sob into the phone.

"Tell me what's happening."

I slid to the floor and crouched in the hallway beside the door, my head in my hand, my shoulders shaking. The nurses' shoes squeaked past me on the linoleum. Each little scuff, each tap rattled its way up my spine and jangled and pounded its way into my skull. I shut my eyes and tried to tune out the smells and sounds of broken children.

David didn't say a word. He just let me cry. He's good that way. He always knows what not to say.

When I could finally talk, I said, "I'm at Children's. Can you come?"

"Room number?"

"Room 709."

"Ten minutes."

Exactly ten minutes later, he walked out of the elevator. I was in the waiting room, curled up into a ball, clutching a wad of spent tissues, staring dumbly at a copy of *Dallas Child* magazine. The cover article was about birthday parties. I flipped the magazine over and threw it facedown on the sticky coffee table.

David sat down beside me on the hard, vinyl couch and took me into his arms. I felt a shock surge through my body as he touched me. It had been so long since I'd received comfort from anyone. I latched on to him and dissolved, my face smashed against his chest, dumping wet salty tears all over his "I'm big in Japan" T-shirt.

I finally collected myself and pulled back, blowing my nose for the hundredth time that night.

"Thanks for coming," I said.

"Of course."

"I almost didn't call."

"I'm glad you did."

"Me too."

"What happened?"

I told him the story, watching his face fall as he listened.

"Is she okay?"

"Christine? I think so."

"What caused it?"

"They're saying maybe asthma."

"Can I see her?"

I almost said yes, but then I noticed his smell.

"When did you start smoking?"

"Um, never?"

"You smell like smoke."

"I have not been smoking."

"I don't think you should go in there. The smoke might trigger another attack." I squinted at him. "What, did some dead emphysema victim roll into the shop tonight?"

"I've been at Poor David's…"

I raised my eyebrows.

"…listening to a band."

"By yourself?"

I shouldn't have said it. I knew as soon as it was out of the gate that I should have held it back. But it just charged out like a stallion at the bell.

My impulses never listen to me. Another of my Top Ten Terrible Traits.

I felt my chin quiver as I waited for an answer.

"Dylan, I'm not going to tell you who I was with tonight."

"Why not?"

"Because it's none of your business."

"Make it my business."

He shook his head. "You're really a piece of work—you know that?"

I sniffed and squared my shoulders. "I saw you make a phone call before you left my house."

He rolled his eyes and groaned.

"You seemed really happy. Did you have a date tonight?"

David pursed his lips and dropped his eyes, staring at his folded hands for a moment. Then he kissed me on the cheek, stood up, and looked at me with genuine sadness in his face. "Tell Christine I came to see her," he said softly.

I watched dumbly as he turned and walked away. He pushed the button for the elevator, his feet shifting uncomfortably as he waited, head down, shoulders tense. When the elevator came, he stepped inside and found a spot in the small crowd of hospital staff.

His back was still turned toward me as the stainless-steel doors closed behind him.

8

~

I COULD FEEL THE sun coming through the slats in the blinds. My hair was tickling my face, fanned forward by the blizzard of air conditioning blasting out of the vent behind me. My bones ached. I winced and rotated my shoulders to unstick them. The light shone in stripes on the smudged wallpaper—up and down, like the bars of a jail cell.

I looked around, remembered where I was, and grimaced as I tried to move, stretching my legs out in front of my chair. I'd dreamed I was sleeping on a bus. And not a nice Greyhound, either. One of those creaky yellow school buses with the stiff vinyl seats. With no heat. In winter.

But it was just a horrible, not-quite-reclining hospital chair—the kind that smells of old clothes and old germs and Lysol. I longed for some Clorox disinfecting wipes and a hot shower with antibacterial soap.

Liz was gone. Christine was curled up in her hospital bed, sleeping soundly, her thumb in her mouth and her feet tangled up in her blankets. I glanced at the clock. Six thirty.

I stood and slipped my feet into my flip-flops. The icebox chill in the room had purpled my toes. I wondered idly where I could score a pair of tube socks. I straightened Christine's covers, tucking her feet under her blanket and making a mental note to myself to bring her a quilt from home if she had to stay another night.

I checked my phone for messages. Normally I approach phone messages with a dread more appropriate for, say, facing a firing squad without a cigarette. But for once, I was crushed that there were none. I winced as I remembered the exchange I'd had with David a few hours before.

I wanted to claim stress-induced psychosis, but I knew it wouldn't fly. That unfortunate woman standing in front of David demanding that he justify his private behavior had been the real me—the worst me, to be sure, but the real one nonetheless. I keep thinking the other me, my better self, will wrestle the crummy one to the ground, hogtie her, and (quite literally) beat the hell out of her. But my better self, unfortunately, is a wimp and a sluggard. She's far too lazy to be bothered and probably afraid of me to boot, familiar as she must be with my legendarily poor attitude and foul disposition. Coward.

I wrapped myself in a thin cotton hospital blanket, sat back down in my chair, and began contemplating my future. The view from here was grim. I pictured myself living alone in some creaky house in a formerly middle-class neighborhood, one of those weird old women who smells vaguely of Avon products and talcum powder, wandering around in a sleeveless housecoat and ratty pink slippers. The scene was vivid and depressing: the lunchroom-lady arms, the wiry apricot hair flat on one side, an inch of gray at the roots. A weedy yard full of skinny cats and pet raccoons. I shut my eyes and tried not to sink completely into full-on despair.

"Dylan?"

I looked up. Maria stood there in pink hospital scrubs, name tag clipped to her shirt, stethoscope draped around her neck. She'd aged ten years since Saturday. She gripped a pen and hugged a clipboard to her chest like she needed something to hold.

"Tell me you're not working today," I said.

She shot me a look. "I can't sit home and do nothing. I'll lose my mind. What's left of it."

She walked over to Christine's bed and picked up the chart.

"Did Liz call you?" I asked.

"Martinez told me."

"How did he know?"

She shrugged. "I didn't ask." She looked at Christine. "How's she been?"

"She slept through the night."

Maria put her clipboard down and flipped open Christine's chart. "Asthma?" She looked up at me.

"Liz said she doesn't have asthma."

She paged through the chart. "Lindsay. He's good."

"Who's that?"

"The pediatrician who admitted her. Lucky break he was on call last night. If there were a better answer, he would have found it." She scanned the pages. "He hasn't ordered any more tests. Albuterol and Singulair…"

"What are those?"

"Asthma drugs." She slapped the chart shut and hooked it back on to the foot of the bed. She picked up her clipboard, crossed her arms again, and shivered. "Something's just wrong."

"What do you think she has?"

"I'm not talking about Christine." She looked around the room. "It's the whole thing. Everything's off center."

I cringed and felt goose bumps come up on my arms as the chill in the room intensified. "Liz said the same thing last night."

She grimaced. "It's like we fell into a wormhole or something. Like it all fell apart at once."

I thought maybe if I stayed real still and held my breath, Maria wouldn't notice my constant proximity to the wormhole and dump me as a friend.

"It's like we stepped into some other universe. Someplace I don't want to be."

I nodded. I didn't want to be here either. "Any word from Enrique today?"

She shook her head. "They're canvassing, asking about the other car, the white one. That's the last I heard." She stretched her neck side to side, her forehead creased with strain. "Two FBI agents showed up at my house last night and started plugging things into my phone lines."

"The FBI? DPD is off the case?"

"No, not off. The FBI comes in to help after a certain point, I guess. They have a whole separate unit for child kidnappings. They showed up with computers, phones, big black suitcases full of things with wires and plugs."

Something sparked vaguely in my mind. "That's right. Didn't that start with—"

Maria nodded ruefully. "The Lindbergh case. Fat lot of good it did. They found that kid too late."

There was nothing to say to that. We both just let it hang there.

"How are you?" I asked finally.

She sat down and massaged her temples. "Don't ask me. I can't talk about it. If I even think about it, I'll fall apart."

Her pager buzzed. She glanced at the message. "I gotta go."

"ER?"

"Delivery. She's ready to push." She sighed. "Life is so insistent."

"I can't believe you're delivering babies today."

"I told them I'd take it four hours at a time. We'll see how I do after the first half-shift. I'm off at eleven. I'll check in with you then." She stood and adjusted her stethoscope. "Babies give me hope."

She left and I sat there alone, staring at Christine, watching her breathe.

A nurse came in bearing a partitioned meal tray and a foam cup. She set the tray down on the bed table and scooted it over to me.

"Brought you some breakfast, honey."

She pulled the lid off the foam cup and handed me some coffee, which I accepted gratefully. Then she lifted the cover off the tray and revealed two slices of limp toast, a dried-up sausage that looked like old dog poo, and the crowning blow, a slimy pile of runny, far-too-yellow scrambled eggs.

I loathe eggs—a lifelong aversion to which I am irrevocably committed. The smell alone almost doubled me over.

I looked up at her and smiled weakly, checking the ID hanging on a lanyard around her neck. "Thank you, Wanda. You're very thoughtful."

"You gotta eat. Keep your strength up." She fussed over Christine's monitors for a minute, then checked her vitals.

"Have you seen her mother?" I asked.

"Thought you were the mother." The nurse glanced down at Christine's face. "She favors you. You an aunt or something?"

"Just a friend."

"I came on at seven. I'll check at the nurses' station, see if they know."

She left, and I slapped the cover back onto the breakfast tray. I held the tray at arm's length, walked it across the room to the closet, closed the door tightly, and dropped a towel in front of the crack to seal it off completely.

I foraged around Christine's night table, found a pen and a pad of paper, and began scribbling notes. I needed to figure out a way to talk to the DPD shrink who had interviewed Christine. I scratched out a list of questions. I made another list for the ER doctor. I wanted to talk to him, if possible, though I figured he couldn't tell me anything without a family member present.

Where was Liz anyway? I checked the clock. Almost eight. She'd been gone over an hour.

Christine stirred. I walked over to the bed and put my face down by hers, waiting for her to open her eyes.

Her brown lashes fluttered and parted. She smiled when she saw me. "I knew you were here."

"Of course I am. I'm right here, Punkin." I brushed the hair out of her eyes. "How you doing, sweetie?"

"My throat hurts."

"I think it's from the tube they had in you. It might hurt for a little while."

She moved her eyes around the room.

"Where's Mommy?"

"She had to leave for a minute. She's coming right back."

Her gaze settled on the closet door. "Will you move that towel away?"

I turned to look at the towel, still shoved against the crack to block the egg smell.

"The one on the floor?"

"Uh-huh."

"Sure, sweetie." I walked over to the closet and picked the towel up, folding it neatly and laying it on the floor beside the closet.

"Better?"

She smiled. "Can I have some ice cream?"

"You bet."

She stuck her thumb in her mouth. "Strawberry," she mumbled.

"Coming right up."

I stepped out into the hall and signaled Wanda, who came in and checked on Christine while I hustled down the hall, and returned a moment later with some strawberry ice cream.

I pulled the cardboard off the top of the cup and handed it to Christine, who pushed her spoon into it weakly and shoveled a small bite into her mouth.

She smiled dreamily. "Yummy for my tummy."

I watched her eat, adoring this kid who was breaking my heart with her sweet, quirky personality. Next time I crossed paths with Peter Terry, I was going to skin him alive for coming anywhere near my little borrowed family.

Christine was perking up, her face gaining color with each bite of Blue Bell. Then her brow furrowed. "Where's Nicholas?"

I could feel my shoulders tighten. "Nicholas is gone, Punkin. Remember?"

She looked at me quizically. "I saw him in the closet."

"I think that might have been a dream, sweetie. Remember? He's with the man from the park."

She frowned and took another bite.

I sat next to her on the bed. "Did you have some bad dreams?"

"Uh-huh."

"Did you dream about Nicholas?"

"Uh-huh."

I pulled her to me and hugged her. "It's okay now. They were just dreams. Dreams can't hurt you."

Most of the time, anyway.

"I like Nicholas," she said. "He's funny."

"Did you know bunny rabbits hate ice cream?" I said brightly. "All they like is crunchy food."

"I used to like crunchy food. Now I like ice cream. Does Eeyore miss me?"

"Of course. He can't wait for you to come home."

She finished her ice cream and then drank a full cup of water, slurping it greedily.

"Thirsty, huh?" I said.

She nodded and handed me the cup, which I refilled and handed to her.

She drank the whole thing, handed it back to me, then snuggled into her pillow and quickly fell asleep.

I tiptoed over and checked the closet, just to satisfy my paranoia. It was empty, of course, except for the stinky cafeteria tray, which I took out to the hall and left on the floor outside the room.

I'd dialed Liz's number a dozen times that morning. Now I sat in my Lysol-scented chair and pushed Redial over and over again. It went straight to voice mail every time. I checked the two waiting rooms at either end of Christine's floor. Both were full, but there was no sign of Liz. By the time she finally appeared, I'd edged past worried and was closing in on frantic. She'd been gone at least two hours.

"Where have you been?" I demanded in a whisper, my anxiety quickly transposing into anger, as it so often does. Another Top Ten Terrible Trait. I scolded myself mentally and tried to calm down.

"Dispatch," she whispered back.

"What's dispatch?"

"The hospital has a radio dispatch station for helicopter landings and ambulance communication. I was trying to reach Andy."

It hadn't dawned on me once in this entire time that she hadn't mentioned talking to him. "Doesn't he have a phone?"

"He has a satellite phone with him, but it hasn't been picking up. If the phone's not working, they can only be reached by radio."

She pulled me out into the hall. I could tell by the look on her face that something was wrong.

"I'm not even sure they got there," she said quietly.

"When did they leave?"

"Saturday afternoon."

"That's three days ago. How long does it take to get to Guatemala?"

"Chicago to Guatemala City with a stop for fuel—somewhere around six hours in the Gulfstream. They'd switch to a twin engine in Guatemala City and fly into the jungle. That's another couple of hours."

"So what does that mean?"

"It means nobody knows where they are."

9

I STARED AT LIZ, the dumb, open-mouthed feeling numbing me once again. I was completely unable to process what I was hearing. "Did they land?" I asked, finally. "Surely someone knows whether or not they landed. Did you call the airport?"

"There is no airport. Just a landing strip. A short landing strip. Out in the middle of nowhere."

"What could have happened to them?"

"How should I know?"

"Well, what are they doing all the way down there anyway? Who takes preschoolers into the jungle?" I asked, exasperated.

She crossed her arms and glared at me. "Why, I believe we do, Dylan. Crazy us—we want our kids to grow up with a sense of gratitude for what they have and a burden for service to others who are less fortunate."

"Oh." I could feel my face turning red. "Well, that's a good reason."

"Thank you. I thought so."

"Did you try to reach Tony?"

"Of course, I tried to reach Tony. There's no phone, Dylan."

"What about the radio? What's wrong with the radio?"

"The radio must be out. I couldn't raise anyone. I talked to a ham operator in the area who said that a plane landed on Saturday, but he didn't have the tail number."

"What's that—like a license plate?"

She nodded.

"So there's no way of knowing if it was their plane."

"It probably was. There aren't too many planes landing in the area."

"Could you e-mail Tony and find out if he knows where they are?"

"Dylan, there is no e-mail. Okay? There's weather in the area. The infrastructure is terrible. Everything goes out when it storms." At this point she was so exasperated with me, she was talking to me like I was a special-needs donkey. She slowed down and drew out her words. "They…cannot…be…reached."

"Is anyone looking for them?"

"They'll dispatch a rescue crew as soon as the weather clears. Until then, there's nothing to be done."

"What if they landed? What then? How long does it take to get to the orphanage?"

"Depends on the roads. It's three hours by Jeep in good weather. A local guide was going to meet them. They were going to camp for the night and drive in the next day."

I stared at her. "So you're telling me your husband and two little boys are missing in Guatemala."

"Yes."

"Why are you so calm?"

She threw up her hands. "Who said I'm calm?" She pointed at the door. "My little girl's in a hospital bed with tubes coming out of her. A little boy got kidnapped by a man that grabbed my kid too and then changed his mind. I think calm is out of the question, don't you?"

I took a step back. I'd never seen Liz angry before.

"Exactly what good is it going to do for me to fall apart now?" She began to pace in front of Christine's door.

"None. None at all."

"I can't help them. I can't reach them by phone or radio. If I wanted to go down there and look for them myself, it wouldn't do the slightest bit of good. I couldn't even get there, and even if I did, what use would I be? There's nothing to do but wait." She leaned against the wall and closed her eyes, the anger dissipating into fatigue, her face draining of color. "I'm sorry. I don't know why I'm yelling at you. I'm on my last nerve."

"I can take it." I smiled and shrugged. "It's one of my few strengths."

Her face softened as the tension eased.

"Look, this happens all the time on Angel Wing missions. They always come back. Always."

Always seemed like good odds, but the way our luck was running, I wasn't betting.

I left Liz in the hospital room and went to pick up cheeseburgers and fries at Jack's—one each for Liz and me, and for Christine a junior burger with meat and bun only and a strawberry milk shake. I didn't know if she'd eat the burger, but I thought the milk shake was probably a lock. By the time I walked into the room, Maria was sitting there with Liz, having just come off a three-baby half-shift. Christine was awake and energetic, sitting up in bed and listening to her own heart with Maria's stethoscope.

We divvied up the food and ate ravenously.

"When are they discharging her?" Maria asked.

"They haven't said." Liz dipped a french fry in ketchup and handed it to her daughter. Christine took it, licked the ketchup off, and dropped it on her plate beside another half-dozen that had been licked clean and discarded.

"I'll check on it after lunch. She should be out of here this afternoon at the latest. I guess you guys will be heading out after that?" Maria asked.

"George is on standby. We could load up and be out of here by..." Liz checked her watch, "...five or six, I guess. How does that sound, Punkin?"

I choked on my pickle.

"You okay, Dylan?" Liz asked.

I nodded. "Fine. Wrong pipe." I took a swig of Dr Pepper and tried to remain calm.

Once again, I felt strangely appalled that she and Christine might leave. Like it would jinx Nicholas's chances or something. The three of us had been through so much together.

"We can get Eeyore all settled in at home and then fix grilled cheese for supper. With the crunchy chips you like and some carrots?"

We turned to Christine, who was about to cry, her chin puckering, her eyes puddling with thick, drippy tears.

"I want to stay with Miss Dylan."

Liz rolled her eyes. "Christine, it's time for us to get out of Miss Dylan's hair and go back home to Chicago."

"We're not in her hair. Are we, Miss Dylan?"

I fluffed my hair, running my fingers through the thick tangle of auburn strands. "Nobody in there but me."

"We need to go see Dr. Friedman and see what she has to say about your breathing. You love Dr. Friedman." Liz turned to Maria and me. "Dr. Friedman always has Tootsie Pops." Then back to Christine, "Aren't you ready to take Eeyore home and show him your room?"

Christine crossed her arms and launched into a full-blown pout. Her lip curled into a defiant frown as tears ran down her face.

I, of course, was absurdly flattered, though I managed to maintain a convincingly neutral mask so as not to betray my staggering self-absorption.

"Christine," Liz said, "I'm not going to have any fits out of you. Not today. Now straighten up and finish your burger."

"I wanted cheese on it."

Christine wiped her tears, crossed her arms again, and refused to take another bite.

Liz ignored her and turned to Maria. "Will I be able to get copies of her records? I want her to get seen at home as quickly as possible."

"Of course. I'll make sure they have them ready for you."

"Did you tell Maria about the…communication issue you were dealing with this morning?" I asked.

Liz cocked her head toward Christine. "Haven't had a chance."

Maria raised her eyebrows. Liz looked at me, the hint obvious in her eyes.

"Want to take a walk?" I asked Christine.

She nodded. I walked out in the hall and signaled Wanda, who came in, unhooked Christine from the monitors, and got her all arranged, hanging her IV drip on a pole with wheels, which I slid alongside us as we walked. She named the pole Archie, chatting with it amicably as though they were fast friends. Christine wore a little yellow hospital gown with daisies on it and her Barbie sneakers that lit up when she walked. She looked sweet enough to eat, even after her little fit of temper.

We held hands and walked down the corridor, pausing often so Christine could introduce herself and Archie to everyone she encountered. Me, she forgot about completely. So much for her unflagging devotion to Miss Dylan.

When we got back to the room, I could hear my cell phone ringing through the thick door. I swung the door open and handed Christine off to her mother so I could take the call. It was Martinez. I stepped out into the hall and picked up.

"Where are you?" he said.

"At Children's."

"How is she?"

"She seems fine. They'll release her any time now, I think."

"Maria said she was going to check in with you guys."

"She's in there with Liz and Christine now. Do you want to talk to her?"

"No. I called to tell you something."

"What?"

"They found a body."

I fought off a violent urge to vomit, my face flushing and my skin suddenly clammy and cold.

"Is it Nicholas?"

"I don't know. Some kayaker spotted something in the reeds out at White Rock Lake. All I know is small frame, curly brown hair. They're on their way out now. I just wanted to make sure you were with Maria. Just in case."

"Does she know?"

"I just found out myself. I don't want to tell her unless it's Nicholas."

"Why put her through it?" I agreed.

"Can you stick with her for a while? I'm on my way out to the scene."

"Sure. Enrique?"

"What?"

"Do you think it's him?"

Silence. Then, "I'll know in a few minutes."

He hung up.

I slid once more to the floor in the hall, my back to the wall, hugging my knees. I couldn't go back in that room knowing that Maria's kid might be floating dead in a lake on the other side of town. I could feel myself sinking in a swirl of nausea mixed with rage mixed with panicky, frantic dread. I was losing my grip. My mind took off, spinning around like a lawnmower blade, ripping up everything it could find to run over and destroy. Shredding any remaining hope of calm, of common sense, of intentional optimism. My heart pounded, the blood pulsing loudly in my ears.

I mentally slapped myself around and tried to focus on my exchange with Liz. What good would it do to lose control of myself now?

I found a pulse in my neck and counted the heartbeats, focusing on slowing them down. Breathing slowly. In and out. In and out.

I stared at my phone, willing it to ring, then began walking down the hall and back, counting my steps. Twenty-three to the end of the hall. Turn. Twenty-three steps back.

From inside the room, I heard a loud, long beep, then voices.

The door flew open, and Maria stuck her head out the door and yelled at the nurses' station.

"She's crashing!"

As Maria shouted instructions to the staff, I pushed past her and ran back into the room. I knelt by the bed. Christine's eyes were open, but her lips were beginning to turn blue. I peered frantically into her face, as though I could keep her there by locking her eyes onto mine.

She looked at me knowingly and smiled, her mouth barely turning at the corners. Then she closed her eyes and was gone.

10

~

THE THING WITH Peter Terry is, his booty isn't cash or Social Security numbers or flat-screen TVs. What he's after is your mind. And your soul if he can get it. But in this game, your soul is just the bonus round. His eye is on your serenity. Your peace. Your sense of safety in the world. If he can lift those precious little items off you and toss them onto his pile, he's pulled off a score unlike anything you've ever read about over a morning cup of coffee or seen at a ten-dollar movie.

Naturally, intensive care is Peter Terry territory. You sit there, staring at your loved one, in the company of strangers who are also staring at their loved ones. And you're surrounded by the architecture of suffering—monitors, pumps, bags, needles, tubes. And you can feel the skin being ripped off your illusions. Flesh covers veins, and veins web through organs and muscles and bones. And they're all stuck together with the fragile, electric sinews of sensation, of movement. It's the perfect disguise, this farce of wholeness.

And the parts, they all break so easily. When you're sitting there, staring at your loved one, the one with the broken parts, you can't believe any of it ever works at all.

And then, as you pace between beeps and alarms and rhythmic whooshes of air, you hear the whispering and the murmuring. And you peek around curtains, where rosaries are fingered with confident intention, where heads are bowed, where hearts are turned upward because it's the only possible option. And the atmosphere of hope in the place is overpowering.

Then you realize hope is all there is. There's nothing else to live on. The rest is just parts and a jump-start.

I'd been adopted into the Zocci family on Maria's authority, since intensive care is a "family only" floor. So I sat there with Liz, gripping her hand as we sat by Christine's bed. Christine slept soundly after her near-death experience—or her death experience, to be more accurate. Technically, she *had* died, if only for a few seconds. Her breathing had stopped, her heart had arrested, and she was gone. But Maria tubed and bagged her, and Christine was back in no time, kicking and fighting and trying to pull the tube out again.

Liz got on the phone with the Cleveland Clinic and spoke with the nation's leading expert on childhood asthma. The doc implied that Christine's case was routine and suggested Liz get a good night's sleep. She hung up on him.

A quick call to Christine's pediatrician in Chicago relieved her mind. Dr. Friedman recommended they stay put, get Christine stabilized, have some tests run. No reason to risk putting her on a plane—with the altitude and limited medical resources—when she was already in one of the best children's hospitals in the country.

Don't panic, the doctor had said. Christine's tough. And asthma is treatable. They'd get to the bottom of it in no time and everything would be fine.

Looking at Christine's pinched little face in ICU made that hard to believe.

Martinez showed up an hour into it, having been unable to reach me by phone. No cell phones in ICU. He pulled me out into the hall.

"It's not him."

I dissolved into tears, clutching Martinez and sobbing all over his tie. He hugged me politely and waited for me to stop.

I pulled back eventually and choked out, "Who was it?"

"No ID yet. It's a woman. Shot in the face. Half the body was in the mud. Guy couldn't tell if it was man, woman, or kid. Just saw brown hair in the grass and called it in."

I closed my eyes and breathed a silent prayer of thanks, though I hurt for the nameless dead woman.

"Are you going to tell Maria?" I asked.

"I don't want her reading it in the paper. I'll find her and let her know."

As he went inside, I walked out to the waiting room and stared through the dirty window into the summer haze. I wondered where the dead woman had lived. What terrible trail of events had led her to a surly end in a muddy gully at White Rock Lake? Was she loved, or was she alone in the world? Was she married? Did she have a lover? Children? Had anyone noticed she was gone?

Whoever and wherever those people were, their pain was just beginning, though we'd won at least a brief reprieve.

My eye wandered over the neglected neighborhoods near the hospital—the buckling houses. The choked, lonely yards. The skinny dogs, chained and barking at aimless neighbors who were ambling along with nowhere to go and nothing to do. What sad-luck lottery had landed them here? Or had led me to stand on this mottled square of tile and stare at them from a window at Children's Medical Center on a bright Tuesday afternoon?

I could almost hear Peter Terry laughing. How do they know where the vulnerable ones are, these spiritual warlords? Are there pins on a map somewhere? Darts on a board? Do they do it because they get a kick out of it—imprisoning and starving their millions? Or is it part of some grand strategy? When does it count as genocide?

I turned and walked back to the room. Liz said that Martinez had taken Maria home for the day. No news was bad news, of course. We could all feel the clock ticking. The FBI was still camped at her house, tracing phone calls and monitoring e-mails on the chance of a ransom request, though Maria had no money to speak of and no connections to any. She'd submitted gladly to their presence, thawing tamales and tortillas for them from her freezer. Her parents had arrived that morning from El Paso. Maria had skipped the second half of her shift and gone home to check on them and collapse for a while.

I needed a break myself, so I got a list of items Liz needed, kissed her good-bye, and promised I'd be back in a few hours.

Walking to my truck in the warm May afternoon, I felt a strange and unwelcome sense of relief. It seemed ages since I'd been outside or noticed the feeling of the sun on my face. It was only the second time in days I'd been alone for more than a few minutes. I tried to wave away the guilt clouding what little pleasure I might have taken from the beauty of the day. But it hung on like a bad smell—guilt for my momentary relief from the cold, noxious air of the hospital, for my freedom to walk out of there, and for failing somehow to bar the gate to the wormhole.

I headed for SMU. I needed comfort, something familiar and normal and everyday. I love the SMU campus—mainly because the trees are big and all the buildings match. It's modeled after the University of Virginia, which was designed by Thomas Jefferson, a very orderly person and thus, to my mind, a pretty good sort (apart from that whole Sally Hemings thing, of course).

College students are seasonal creatures, moving in mass-migration patterns every three months or so. SMU's flock had taken off for their summer mating grounds shortly after graduation. So I pulled on to a largely deserted campus, my truck almost leading the way on its own in my perpetual search for a convenient, shaded parking place. I parked with a lurch in a near-empty lot and grabbed my swim bag.

I changed in the locker room and walked past a few student stragglers who were sunbathing in the pool's rickety lounge chairs. I spread my towel out on the starting block and sat there for a minute, watching the other lap swimmers slap the water in rhythm and trying to remember what it felt like to not be gripped with fear all the time. Not so long ago, I'd been one of them, swimming along with normal, general-issue worries knocking around in my head—the ever-present pressures of work and of money and the languid loneliness of living perpetually in a boyfriend-free zone. It had all seemed so heavy at the time. Now I felt trite and small for ever thinking any of it important.

I'd lost that innocence the day I met Peter Terry. It was a summer day, not unlike this one, when the gate swung open without a sound and Peter Terry walked into my life, sucker-punching me blithely as he strolled on by.

I sealed my goggles over my eyes, slipped into the pool, and pushed off the wall, feeling the awkwardness of my time out of the water. I summoned rusty self-discipline, the physical persistence—stroke, stroke, breathe—and the mental patience, waiting for my body to settle into the familiar movements, to shake off the stiff uncertainty that comes when I've spent too much time on land. The water felt good. A few hundred meters and I had my rhythm again, the water slipping over my skin, washing away some of the strain of these days.

I let my thoughts wander back to the day at the park.

Nicholas, with his tiara and plastic gun. The man watching the soccer game. In my mind, I could see him pace, staring at the game, turning and pacing again. Stopping to look over the crowd.

I flipped and pushed off the wall, holding a tight streamline and trying to keep the man's image in my head. Peering into his face, looking for something, anything. His eyes had been strangely intense, almost aggressive. His features were gone from my memory, though— only his expression remained. It was greedy. Hungry.

Another wall, another turn, another streamline. Stroke, stroke, breathe.

I could see the park clearly. The petting zoo. A little girl in yellow overalls, crying when her parents put her on the pony for a photograph. A gardener—the only black face in the park—dogged and solitary, clipping hedges and raking leaves and twigs into a pile. I hadn't seen anyone use a rake in a long time. Always those horrible leaf blowers.

Mentally, I scanned the crowd at the soccer game. A little herd of ponytailed girls, all five-and-unders, in their stiff shin guards and kneesocks and teeny team jerseys, running up and down the field in bunches, blindly following the ball around. Dads with excessive enthusiasm jumping and shouting and waving their arms. Moms with expensive hair and pastel outfits, talking idly to one another, ignoring the game. Me with my Supercuts hairdo and cutoffs, licking my xanthan pop and allowing myself to get swept up in the joyful simplicity of the day.

I glided into the wall and stopped, holding on to it with one hand. I shook my head to get the water out of my ears and heard a voice.

"Come over here, sweetie. That nice man doesn't want to play. He's busy working."

I followed the sound and watched as a mother reached for her little boy's hand, nudging him away from the lifeguard stand. It occurred to me they should have lifeguards for parks, with all those predators walking around. My eyes climbed the ladder and studied the lifeguard. Tanned and young. Cut from granite, those muscles of his. I thought of David, with his summer tan and the glint in his hair, his back to me as the elevator doors closed behind him.

I fought an overwhelming urge to cry, my goggles fogging up from a quick, unexpected flood of tears.

I washed out my goggles and wrestled my mind away from the stifling, persistent grip of self-pity. There was no time to go there. I finished my swim, hopping out of the pool an hour later physically renewed but mentally frustrated. I'd gotten exactly nowhere perusing my memories of the park.

I headed for the locker room, still obsessing over what I might be missing. I got myself reasonably well put together, my hair fluffed and clean for the first time since my hours under the sweaty mortarboard. Graduation seemed like months ago, though it had been only a few days.

I threw my stuff in my truck, swung by my office to pick up a few things, and headed home, glad to see my house in the daylight. The porch light was still on. I flipped it off when I walked in the front door and went to check on the rabbits, throwing my mail on the kitchen table as I walked by. Eeyore and Melissa were bored and lonely, I could tell. I let them out into the backyard and gave them each a few apple slices.

My answering machine light was blinking, as usual, that insistent red light screaming out a strident warning: "Do not approach. You are entering the Obligation Zone. Do not approach."

I punched the button and zipped through messages from the usual suspects. My father. My department chair. Twice. My father again. He never tells me what he wants. He just baits me into calling him back.

There was nothing from David. Answering machines are secretly programmed to accept only messages from people you don't want to hear from. Satan and his minions at work again.

I hit the Erase button and smiled at the satisfaction of demands unanswered.

I grabbed a pen and notebook, sat down at my kitchen table, and started to write. Too many details were stacking up in my head. I couldn't keep track of them all. Nicholas, the man watching the soccer game, the arm that grabbed for Christine, and the hand that burned when he touched her. The man telling Christine he didn't want her, only Nicholas. The man who knew Nicholas's name. The white car. The baseball cap. The snake that only Christine saw. The blue van that turned out to be nothing.

After half an hour of scribbling, moving the ideas around on paper like blocks in a Rubik's Cube, I still couldn't make sense of any of it. But it was a start. At least I'd dumped it out on the page.

The house smelled musty, so I opened a few windows to let the air in, then propped the back door open with a brick, locking the screen door with the little hook lock. I packed a bag for Liz. Fresh clothes, makeup, toiletries, jammies for her and Christine both, warm socks, a worn quilt, and Christine's scrap of a stuffed animal—a disintegrating teddy bear she aptly called No-Nose. I zipped it all into a bag, then fixed myself a glass of iced tea. I reached into the pantry for a package of lemon cookies dusted with powdered sugar, then sat down and opened my mail.

I leafed through a few bills and a catalog filled with stiff, conservative clothing I wouldn't be caught dead in. (It has long been a matter of twisted pride that I haven't worn plaid since elementary school—and even then, not by choice.) I picked up a letter from my employer. My heart always skips a few beats when I see the little SMU emblem on the corner of an envelope. A letter from your employer is almost never good news.

I ripped open the letter and groaned. My three-year academic review had been scheduled for August. That was only three months away. I'd known it was coming, of course. The letter was a benign formality. But somehow seeing it in print made it seem more menacing. I picked up the phone and dialed my boss.

Helene Levine rarely bothered with pleasantries. "Where have you been? I've called you twice."

"Why, I'm just fine, Helene. Thank you so much for asking. How are you?"

"Oh, hello and all that. Why do we have to go through a silly routine? Answer my question."

Helene is a rare breed of academic—brilliant mind, impeccable credentials, yet not at all boring. She possesses a searing sense of humor and an astonishing acuity for sizing people up. As an added bonus, she has an atypical knack for cutting through the truckloads of bull hockey that pile up thick on college campuses. She's impatient, imposing, and impossible to get along with. Everyone's afraid of her. I adore her.

"I've been tied up," I said.

"Tied up? You want me to tell that to the student who's trying to get an incomplete off his record before he goes home for the summer? Why don't you call his parents and tell them you're tied up?"

"It's after graduation, Helene. I'm off duty."

"Well, I realize that. You can still pick up your phone when I call, can't you? It does ring, right? Or is your phone off duty too?"

"What is wrong with you? You're in a worse mood than usual."

"You're no peach yourself," she shot back.

I waited.

"I can't tell you," she said at last.

"Why?"

"It's confidential."

"It's not about me, is it?"

"No. Well, not exactly about you."

"Not *exactly* about me? What is it about, exactly?"

She didn't say anything.

"Helene?" I tapped the phone loudly. "I can hear you breathing."

"What?"

"Come on. Cough it up."

She sighed. "A student came in today and complained about John Mulvaney. She says he's harassing her."

A former colleague of mine, John had been arrested the previous January and hauled downtown to Lew Sterrett Justice Center.

The whole thing had been a big, muddy mess, and I'd been in it up to my Thigh Recovery Program. The man was a nut-ball. A sicko, screw-loose fruitcake. Even so, I'd succeeded, I'm happy to say, in blocking him from my mind completely. I'd checked him off my worry list the minute the doors banged shut behind him. As far as I knew, he was still in there, contemplating his navel lint and awaiting trial.

"I thought John Mulvaney was locked up," I said. "Did he make bail or something?"

"He's still in jail. Apparently geography isn't much of a deterrent."

"Say something that makes some sense to someone other than you, please. Did the student go see him in the poky or something?"

"He has a blog."

"A blog? They let them have computers in there?"

"That's what I wanted to know. I spoke with the district attorney's office. I quote: 'No inmate in the Texas prison system has direct access to the Internet.'"

"Then how…"

"Lots of inmates have blogs, it seems. They send letters to people on the outside, who post the letters on the Internet for them," she said. "Death-row inmates' blogs tend to get the most attention."

"And people read them?"

"Apparently they attract a fair amount of traffic."

"That's sick."

"Someone on the outside is managing the blog for him."

"Who?"

"The blog says it's you."

I felt the room get cold. "You know that's not true."

"I know, I know. That's why I didn't want to mention it. Why can't you let anything go?"

"Notice how I'm letting that jab go," I said pointedly. "What are you going to do about the blog?"

"There's nothing I can do. The DA says it's a First Amendment issue."

"Even though he's using my name and directing the content at a particular person? That's not illegal?"

"This is America, not the Middle East. John Mulvaney has the same right to free speech as any other citizen."

"It just seems wrong that he can do that."

"Take it up with your congressman."

"Or woman."

"Or woman. Whatever."

"What did you tell the student?"

"I told her the DA recommended she get a new e-mail address."

"What did she say?"

"Nothing. She just sat in my office and cried."

"I don't blame her."

"I gave her your e-mail address."

"Great."

"Since you refuse to answer your phone."

I sighed. "You're going to be sorry you were mean to me when I tell you what's been going on."

I told Helene about Nicholas and about Christine's asthma attacks.

"You've got the worst luck," she said.

"Thanks for pointing that out. Because, you know, I hadn't really noticed."

"I'm just saying…"

"I'll try to get by the office and deal with the incomplete."

"When?"

"Soon."

"I'll call the parents and hold them off a little longer."

"Thanks, Helene. You're a sport."

"No, I'm not."

"Okay, you're not."

After we'd said our good-byes and hung up, I realized I'd forgotten to ask her about my review. I couldn't imagine concentrating on journal articles and teaching evaluations with Peter Terry staring over my shoulder, breathing his foul, cold breath onto my neck. I'd have to try to get the review rescheduled somehow. Or close the gate to the wormhole.

I stared at the phone and pondered Helene's news. John Mulvaney, of all people. A first-class loser and third-rate human—popping up now, of all times. How much worse could things get?

A lot worse, probably. I should know better than to tempt the universe by tossing out a stupid question like that.

I was determined, however, not to expend one ounce of energy worrying about John Mulvaney. He was surrounded by lots of armed, uniformed men who were paid (salary plus benefits) by the state of Texas to make sure he stayed locked up tight. That was going to have to do for now.

I spent a few minutes resetting my house, cleaning the kitchen and making the bed, folding up the blankets from Christine's pallet. We'd left in such a hurry, there was still medical packaging on the floor where the medics had been working on her—disarray I would never have tolerated under normal circumstances. It was a graphic sign of the severity of my distress that I'd forgotten about the mess entirely.

I opened the screen door for the rabbits. They hopped back in, and I settled them again in their hutches, with apologies for making them spend so much time alone. They twitched their noses at me and sniffed as though they understood.

11

~

WHEN I GOT BACK to the hospital, Christine had already graduated from ICU and was back in her room. She was awake and pink-cheeked, drawing with a purple pen that had a big, fuzzy ball on top.

She looked up at me. "Mr. David is nice."

I looked helplessly at Liz.

"You just missed him," she said.

I walked over and tucked a strand of brown hair behind Christine's ear. "Yes, he is. He's very nice."

"He said to tell you hi," Liz said.

I smirked at her. "Lucky me."

"Why don't you and Mr. David get married?" Christine said.

I waited for Liz to intervene, but she just crossed her arms and pursed her lips, holding back a smile.

"I don't think Mr. David wants to marry me."

"But you're so pretty!"

"It's more complicated than that, Punkin."

Christine thought for a second, her brow furrowing. "Is it your personality?"

Liz burst into laughter.

"Well, yes, it is, I think," I said.

"Oh." Her face fell. She thought for a moment, then brightened. "Maybe you should bake him some cookies."

"I'll try that, hon. Thanks for the suggestion." I sat down in my fake-leather chair and caught my first whiff of the sour disinfectant smell.

"I've got a great snickerdoodle recipe," Liz said to me.

"Mommy makes the yummiest snickerdoodles. They have cimmony on them."

"Cinnamon, Punkin."

"Cimanon."

"It's worth a shot." I stood and looked out the window. "The truth is, I'm better single than I am paired up. It suits my natural inclination toward self-absorption."

"What's self-distortion?" Christine asked.

I smiled. "Self-absorption."

"They're sort of the same thing," Liz said to me.

"It's when you think you're more important than you really are," I said.

"Like Paris Hilton?"

I laughed. It felt good to laugh. "How do you know about Paris Hilton?"

"I saw her in the grocery store."

"Magazines at the checkout stand," Liz said. "Try explaining Paris Hilton to a six-year-old sometime."

I unzipped the bag I'd brought. Christine squealed at the sight of No-Nose and immediately settled him in beside her on the bed. Liz excused herself and hauled the bag into the bathroom with her. After a few minutes, we heard the shower running.

"What are you writing, Punkin?" I asked.

"I'm practicing my letters. *S*'s are hard."

I walked over to the bed and looked at the paper. "Hmm. You make them backwards sometimes, huh?"

She shrugged. "I can't ever remember which way they go."

"Want to know a trick?"

She nodded.

"Well, if you think of the *s* as a snake, its head is at the top, and it's always pointed at the next letter. Like it wants to eat it up." I drew one for her, putting a little face on the top end of the letter, its mouth open and waiting. "See?"

"Hey! That's easy-peasy."

I sneezed and grabbed a Kleenex. "Easy-peasy-I-have-to-sneezy!"

She practiced a few, then frowned. "What if there's no letter for the snake to eat?"

"Snakes are always looking for something to eat."

"How do you spell *snake*?"

I spelled it for her and watched her carefully draw the letters. She picked up a red crayon and began drawing a snake.

"Can you draw the snake you saw on the man in the park?"

"I don't know how to draw that one."

"Why not?"

"I like to make the long ones." She drew a long, squiggly loop and put a face on it.

"That one wasn't long?"

"Um, I don't really know." She colored in the outline she had drawn.

"Why don't you know, sweetie?"

"All I could see was its face."

"Then how did you know it was a snake?"

"It looked real snaky."

"Where was it? On his arm? Like a tattoo?"

"On his head," she said matter-of-factly.

"His head? Coiled around on top?"

"No. Just stuck there."

I tried to get a picture. Did the man have a snake tattooed on his forehead? Surely someone like that would call enough attention to himself to have been noticed by someone.

Liz emerged, a little cloud of steam puffing from the bathroom as she stepped into the air conditioning. She wore the clothes I had brought, and her hair hung wet to her shoulders.

"I guess I forgot the blow-dryer," I said.

"I don't care," she said. "It's such a relief to be clean. Christine, you ready for a shower?"

Christine nodded, and Liz called the nurse to help her untangle tubes and unplug the breathing monitor. The nurse took Christine into the bathroom to bathe her while Liz and I sat together and looked out the window at the setting sun.

"Did the doctor come?" I asked.

"Finally. At three o'clock this afternoon."

"What did he say?"

"Nothing. Just ordered a bunch of tests."

"What's she having done?"

"I can't even remember. It's a long list."

"Does Christine know?"

"I haven't told her yet."

Liz picked up No-Nose and smelled him, closing her eyes. I saw a tear push past her lashes and fall silently to her cheek.

"You okay, Liz?"

She shook her head, opened her eyes, and hugged No-Nose. "I'm fine. I'm as fine as I can be under the circumstances."

"Any word from Guatemala?"

"Not directly."

"What do you mean?"

"Christine woke up this morning talking about Andy and the boys. She said they were eating tortillas and bananas and playing soccer." She smiled. "Earl told her."

"Earl's reliable." I grinned.

"He is that. The weather's probably cleared. I'm sure I'll hear something shortly."

"Let's hope for good news."

"I can't stand to think otherwise."

"Hey, did Christine say anything else to you about the snake she saw?"

"No, just that the man had a snake."

"She told me just now it was on his head."

"What's that supposed to mean?"

"I was hoping you'd know."

"I can't get a picture of that at all."

"All I can conjure up is something coiled on his head—maybe a turban or something."

"I think she knows what a turban is."

"How would she know that?"

"She saw *Aladdin*."

"Oh. I guess Disney is responsible for kids' cultural education these days."

"Such as it is."

"Maybe it was figurative," I said.

"Christine keeps saying the man was mean."

"Could be more than that," I said. "Maybe evil spirits have some sort of snake manifestation."

"On their heads? That's ridiculous."

"More ridiculous than believing in them in the first place?"

She shrugged. "Maybe it's what they have instead of a halo. Peter Terry would know. Maybe we should ask him."

I shuddered. "No thanks. I've got more trouble than I can handle already without bringing him into the conversation."

I told her about John Mulvaney and the blog he was using to harass a student.

"And he's saying you're involved?"

I waved my hand, swatting away the concern. "It's the kind of thing that can be easily disproved. I haven't had any contact with the man since he was arrested."

"But he's in jail, right?"

"Yep. Downtown at Lew Sterrett. Awaiting trial."

"Still?"

"Wheels of justice."

"Do you think John Mulvaney could be involved in Nicholas's disappearance?"

The thought hadn't occurred to me. "I can't imagine how."

"It just seems odd that his name would crop up now. Didn't he have some weird obsession with you?"

I felt a hint of nausea rise into the back of my throat. "He'd been taking pictures of me for…a year or so, I guess. He had them all over his apartment."

Liz looked at me expectantly.

"I can't see how it would be connected," I said.

She raised her eyebrows.

I pursed my lips and considered her point. "I'll call Martinez," I said finally. At this stage of the game, I was willing to follow any meager little trail of crumbs I could find.

I decided to leave the hospital to make the call. I wasn't too interested in being overheard talking about a sicko who was harassing someone in my name and who might possibly be involved in kidnapping a sweet little friend of mine. Not that any of it was my fault, you understand. But still, it's not like asking someone to pick up a gallon of milk on the way home.

I walked out the sliding doors and dialed. Standing there, the warm air settling in on me, I leaned my head back against the wall and closed my eyes. After hours in the dank air conditioning, my skin felt clammy and prickly. I felt as though I would never warm up. All this darkness and cold malevolence. It seemed to be everywhere—all around me.

Martinez picked up immediately. I told him about John Mulvaney and his sick little blog.

"Liz thought it might somehow relate to Nicholas's disappearance."

"How?"

"I don't know. But it does seem weird, don't you think? That this nut-job surfaces right after Nicholas disappeared?"

"How do you know he surfaced after Nicholas was kidnapped?"

I paused. "I guess I don't. That was an assumption."

"When did he contact the girl?"

"I don't know. I just know it was recently." I was starting to feel awkward and self-conscious. Why hadn't I thought any of this through? Clearly I was wasting the man's time.

"What's her name?"

"Um, I don't know. My boss said the girl was going to contact me."
The whole thing was starting to seem like a stupid notion.

"Blog address?"

"Don't know."

"Didn't ask many questions, did you?"

"Guess not."

"Call her back and get more information."

"Okay. Any leads on the white car?"

"*Nada.*"

He was about to hang up when I stopped him. "Hey, do you know
if anyone else saw the man in the park?"

"Which man in the park?"

"The tall one watching the soccer game. The one I said looked
predatory."

"I don't know off the top of my head. I'd have to check the witness
statements."

"Would you mind?"

"Sure. I'll call Ybarra."

"Would you ask him again if I could talk to the child psychologist?
The one who interviewed Christine?"

"He won't let you."

"Why won't he let me?"

"Dylan, we've been over this. You're a witness. He won't want to
muddy the stories."

"But I'm also a psychologist. I need to ask him some questions."

"Dylan, I hate to break it to you, but Casey Ybarra does not want
your help with his investigation."

"I know, but—"

"I'll ask him, but the answer is going to be no."

"Would *you* give me the name, then?"

He laughed. "Whose side do you think I'm on, anyway?"

"Nicholas's," I said sharply.

The line fell silent.

"Enrique?"

I could hear him breathing.

"Enrique, I'm sorry. That wasn't fair."

"I'll call you back." He hung up.

I mentally berated myself for being belligerent (another Top Ten Terrible Trait) and then dialed Helene.

"I need the student's name."

"Which one? The incomplete?"

"No. The one Mulvaney's harassing."

"Allegedly."

"Allegedly. Whatever."

"Do you have a pen?"

"Shoot."

"Molly Larken. L-a-r-k-e-n." Helene gave me her contact information but suggested I wait a day or two to see if she'd contact me first.

"Do you know when the harassment started?"

"I didn't ask," she said. "Why?"

"I'm wondering if it could have anything to do with the kidnapping. It just seems a little strange that both things would somehow connect to me. Do you have the blog address?"

I heard her shuffling around her desk. "I wrote it down…"

She read the address to me.

"Have you looked at it?"

"Why would I want to look at it?"

"You're going to have to eventually. You're at your desk, right?" I asked. "Type in the address, will you?"

I waited as she tapped on her keyboard.

She sighed. "You have the worst luck."

"Is it pictures or narrative or what?"

"You need to see it for yourself. I'm turning it off."

"How bad is it? Regular bad or unusually bad?"

"How could we not have known he was such a mess?" She sighed again. "You have the worst luck."

"You keep saying that."

"It's true."

"I can't help it."

"It keeps getting worse."

"Thanks for pointing that out, Helene."

"Maybe you need a sabbatical."

"It's summer, for crying out loud. I have two months off."

"I'm just saying…"

"Hey, speaking of needing a sabbatical—I forgot to ask you about my review. That was why I called in the first place."

"You're not ready, are you?"

"I'll be ready," I said, scribbling notes to myself. "When is it again?"

"Fall semester. Officially, August, but I can stall for you until October or November."

"What should I be working on?"

"Just make sure your work is up to par."

"My work's up to par." I waited for her to say something. "Isn't it?"

"Your student evaluations are wonderful. Your classroom work is superior. Your record…is pretty clean."

"*Pretty* clean?"

"The Zocci thing."

"That turned out to be nothing."

"A kid died."

"I didn't mean literally *nothing*. I'm just pointing out that it didn't have anything to do with me."

"It's still in your file."

Erik Zocci, Christine's uncle, had been a patient of mine in the student clinic a couple of years ago. He'd died under mysterious circumstances. That whole mess, which eventually led me to a friendship with the Zocci family, started the day I met Peter Terry. The creep dragged me into the fray with false accusations of professional impropriety. I'd been absolved, but still, it's not exactly the sort of thing you want in your personnel file.

"I haven't been watching your publication history," Helene was saying.

"I've got another journal article coming out in August. That makes eleven. I submitted a book outline six months ago. I'm still waiting to hear."

"Who's got it?"

"Harcourt."

"I'd call Harold. He did a book with them a few years ago. He might be able to get you out of the slush pile. Isn't he mentoring you?"

"Yep. I lucked out. He's the only one in the department with any people skills at all."

"Other than me."

"Obviously. That goes without saying."

"Stop kissing up. Call Harold. He'll help you through it."

I was still writing furiously. "I don't know if I have the energy for all this right now, Helene."

"Oh, stop whining. You have all summer to get ready. Things will have settled down by then."

"You're certainly optimistic."

"I'm optimistic by nature. Have been all my life. But you," she said, cackling, "have a way of surprising me."

12

I GOT UP EARLY the next day and went for a swim, then called Liz in the room and told her I had some errands to run. I blew off Helene's advice and called Molly Larken on her cell phone. She didn't sound too happy to hear from me but said she'd talk to me. We agreed to meet at Starbucks at one that afternoon.

I showered and changed, then moved my truck to faculty parking behind my building, pulling into a nice wide slot under a large, leafy live oak tree. Two for two. I threw my shoulder against the door of my pickup and forced it open against its will, wincing at the familiar donkey honk of the hinges. Time for another can of WD-40.

As I stepped onto the asphalt, I was struck once again by what a great place SMU is to work. Beautiful campus, supportive faculty, reasonably intelligent (if somewhat apathetic) student body. And—wonder of wonders, miracle of miracles—generous and proximate faculty parking. I felt a little alarmed at the possibility of bombing my review. I knew I'd never find another job like this one, especially with my legendarily rotten luck. Now that I understood the way the universe worked, I couldn't believe I'd landed here in the first place. I'd probably just squeaked past the gate while Peter Terry was off at the beach or something.

I walked quickly to Hyer Hall, my mind trailing off again toward Nicholas and the park and the rest of it. Preoccupied, I stalked up the steps to my office. I was determined, by sheer will if nothing else, to squint through the blinding glare of seemingly unrelated details—which all seemed to converge at a point unknown, some fractal disaster zone just out of sight. I unlocked my office and threw my bag down on my old leather chair, punched the button on my computer, and watched it warm up while I checked my phone messages.

There were several calls from disgruntled students. A couple of them wanted grade changes. Fat chance. Delete, delete. One call was from a student who had missed the final, claiming his sister had been in a car accident. I checked my records. The kid hadn't missed a class all year. I'd give him a makeup test and threaten him with his life if he took this magnanimous and unprecedented gesture for granted. The last call was from the boy who needed to get the incomplete off his record. I called him back and relieved his anxiety by letting him know I'd send in the grade today, then bumped him from a C+ to a B- as a guilt offering for my lack of availability. I didn't tell him that, of course. But it would be a nice surprise when his grades showed up. I finished returning calls, then got online and found John Mulvaney's blog.

The Internet is the modern version of an ancient cultural tradition. Instead of ripping open an overcoat and flashing at one or two strangers at a time, narcissists, exhibitionists, and the pathologically self-involved can now reveal their private parts (literal and figurative) online—and have access not just to one stranger at a time but to countless infantile voyeurs who wander into their cyberspace. I'd always found the odd, counterfeit intimacy of the online universe profoundly unsettling. Why anyone would want to spew their secrets into the cosmos for strangers to pick through and smell—a virtual garage sale of emotions and sentiments and opinions—was beyond me.

But there it was. Not only did John Mulvaney have his own blog, but the counter at the bottom of the home page proclaimed proudly that 2,574 "unique" visitors had actually taken a look. Make me 2,575.

I clicked the icon and stepped into John Mulvaney's strange online world.

My cell phone buzzed, yanking me back into my office. I looked around at my bookshelves, remembering suddenly where I was. I checked my watch. I didn't want to be late for Molly Larken. Then I flipped open my phone.

"I checked with Casey," Martinez said without saying hello.

"Casey?"

"Ybarra. No one else saw the guy at the soccer game."

"No one? Not one single person?"

"Just you." I heard him kick the door to his office closed.

I thought for a minute.

"Why would that be?" he asked me.

"No idea."

"You must have some idea, or you wouldn't have asked."

I didn't say anything.

"Dylan?"

"I'm not sure he was really there."

"What do you mean? You made him up?"

"No. I just mean—"

My phone buzzed as another call came in. "Hold on." I checked the number. My father. No way was I talking to him right now. "I mean that he may not be a regular human person."

"What's the alternative?" he asked.

"Remember the Peter Terry thing?"

"Yeah. The spooky white guy who haunted Gordon Pryne."

"The same thing happened the first time I saw him. I had a conversation with him in broad daylight. When I asked someone about it later, she said she hadn't seen anyone but me."

"You think the guy in the park was Peter Terry?"

"Definitely not."

"Then who?"

"Maybe a friend of his."

"You believe that?"

"I'm not sure. But why would it be that no one else saw him? Not one person out of...how many?"

He turned pages, then said, "One hundred eighteen. Not including kids."

"A hundred and eighteen people and I'm the only one who saw this guy."

"Maybe no one else was looking."

"I wasn't looking either. He only stood out to me because he was so predatory."

"So you're saying he was…"

"I don't know."

"A demon. Or something on the order of one. That's what you're saying."

"It's a possibility."

"That's—"

"Weird, I know."

We both fell silent. I was relieved when he changed the subject.

"Casey wouldn't give me the name of the shrink."

"Well?"

He sighed. "I shouldn't be doing this."

"Do it anyway."

"Carmichael. Joan Carmichael."

"I know her."

"What a surprise."

"We interned together at Parkland. Do you have her number?"

"I'm not giving it to you."

"I'm calling her anyway."

"I wouldn't."

"Why not?"

"We have procedures, Dylan. We're investigating a kidnapping."

"Not *a* kidnapping. Nicholas's kidnapping."

"I realize that."

"So I'm calling Joan Carmichael."

"Suit yourself."

"He's out there somewhere, Enrique. He's still alive. I know it."

"Let's hope so."

He hung up on me again. I picked up my bag and headed out the door for my meeting with Molly Larken.

13

I CALLED JOAN CARMICHAEL on my way to Starbucks and left her a girl-friendy-collegial type of voice mail. Sort of a "Hey, your name came up recently and I wanted to check in" type of thing. I was trading on good-will and professional courtesy, and cashing in on all that false intimacy we'd banked through our mutual suffering on the locked adult psych unit at Parkland during our internship year. I didn't tell her why I was calling, exactly. I figured it was seventy–thirty she'd return my call.

I parked my rattly truck in the immaculate, tree-shaded lot of immaculate, tree-shaded Highland Park Village shopping center, smack in front of the Chanel store between a sparkling navy blue Porsche 911 and a sparkling white Mercedes convertible. I shoved my shoulder against the door of my pickup, winced once again at the groan it emit-ted as it opened, and caught it just as it slammed into the side of the Porsche. I checked the Porsche—no ding, thank God, and no alarm—then feigned nonchalance and glanced around to see if anyone had noticed. I found myself in the stare of a Chanel saleswoman, who was looking at me through the store window as though I'd just dumped a truckload of manure in front of the store. I gave her a big "hi, there" smile, passed up a perfect hair-flip moment as I walked past her, and swung open the Starbucks door.

It was freezing inside, as usual. I'd spent many hypothermic hours in this Starbucks grading papers. My feet would be blue in a few min-utes. I scanned the store but didn't see anyone who had that anxious "are you the one I'm meeting?" look about her. I was early, for once, so I ordered some iced tea and took a seat just inside the door. A few min-utes later, Molly Larken walked in. Ten minutes late. I knew her imme-diately, though I was positive we'd never met.

She was maybe five-four, wearing frayed Levi's and a pink baby tee that said "I'm Bluffing" on it in big black letters. Her Converse sneakers were faded and worn. A peace-sign keychain jingled from the slouchy leather bag slung over her shoulder. Her auburn hair was pulled back in a ponytail, revealing beady earrings and a yin-yang drop on a leather choker. She wore no makeup. Her big, greenish eyes were set off by a creamy complexion. She sported a respectable tan for a redhead.

I stood as she walked in. "Molly."

She turned to look at me.

I stuck out my hand. "Dylan Foster. Thanks for meeting me."

Her eyes moved up and down my body, starting at my Converse sneakers, pausing at my slouchy leather bag, and settling on my auburn ponytail. "Wow. You look just like me. You could be my mother."

I cringed. "Ouch."

"I didn't mean—"

"Big sister. Cousin, I could work with. Aunt, even. But mother? Did you have to go there?"

"Sorry."

I smiled and waved away her apology. "Kidding. Don't worry about it."

"But you are too young to be my mother, right? Like, way."

"Thirty-five and lucky to have made it this far."

"Way too young. My mom's, like, fifty."

"What a relief."

She studied me. "Not a match, exactly. More like a conjugation."

Big-girl words too.

"Can I order you something?" I asked. "I'm having iced tea."

"That's okay. I'll get it."

She turned and walked to the counter. Odd for a student to pass up an offer for free coffee. They usually assume they're being treated, even though most of my students could buy and sell me a dozen times over.

She bought an iced coffee, followed me outside, and sat down opposite me, tucking the change into her pocket. She pulled the wrapper off the straw and began to twirl it into a knot.

"So, you teach at SMU?"

I nodded. "Guilty."

"What do you teach?"

"Psychology." I waited for the next question, intrigued that she had taken the lead.

She untied the wrapper and started in on it again without looking up. Clearly it was my turn.

"What about you? You're at SMU, right? Studying what? Business?"

"Art."

"Unusual. At SMU, anyway."

She glanced up. "Yeah, everybody's in the B school. It's a good department, though. There's cash behind it. Have you been to the museum?"

I nodded. "Lots of big Spanish art. Do you paint?"

"Some. I do sculpture, mostly." She twisted the paper into a half bow and curled it up on the ends. I looked down at her hands, which were calloused and rough looking, the cuticles torn and dry, the nails unpolished. She caught me staring. "Makes it tough to keep a manicure," she said.

"You don't seem like the manicure type."

The corners of her mouth turned up for the first time. "Neither do you."

"Guilty." I held out my hands for her review. They weren't as bad as hers, but I could have used a visit to Madge the Palmolive-manicure lady. "Tell me about your art. Figurative or abstract?"

"They make us do both, but I like abstract."

"What medium?"

"Mainly bronzes. That's what I like to do, anyway. We do a lot of clay—for pragmatic reasons. It's hard to get studio time for bronzes or any kind of metals. One of my professors has a studio, though. I do most of my bronze work there."

"Would I know his work?"

"He doesn't show much. His studio is in the garage behind his house. He helps me with my stuff more than he works on his own."

"Sounds like a good arrangement."

She shrugged. "I don't have to sleep with him or anything." She caught the look on my face. "It happens. Students get exploited like that all the time. Especially the poor ones like me."

"But not you."

"I let him know the first day he'd have to stay on his side of the workbench. I pay him for studio time. I don't owe him anything else."

She was self-possessed, much more so than I had been at her age.

"So why SMU?"

"My parents. They're mad for the place."

"They must be to pay the tuition."

She shrugged nonchalantly. "I have a full ride. It came down to SMU or one of the art conservatories if I decided to go away. But I didn't want to be stuck with artists all the time. They're too weird."

"You're on an art scholarship, then?"

"Academic. President's Scholar."

Oh. That was a whole different level of smart.

"I went all the way through school on scholarships," I said.

She laughed. "And look how you turned out."

"This," I said dramatically, "is your destiny." I gestured toward the window at my crummy truck.

"That's yours? I noticed it when I came in. It's so cool!"

"Well, I like to think so, but I'm usually the only one."

Her eyes were on the truck, but from the side I could see her expression lapsing, her eyes changing focus. She looked back at me.

"So." She took a sip of coffee. "John Mulvaney."

"Right. John Mulvaney. I hear he's been harassing you."

"E-harassing, I guess. Is that a word?"

"What's he been doing?"

"Mainly talking about me on his blog. E-mailing me all the posts."

"By name?"

"By name, by address, by description, by phone number, by e-mail. Pretty much advertising all over the Web who I am and where I live and how to contact me, just in case any of the sickos who read his blog want to know."

"Why would he do that?" I asked.

"He says I'm his muse." She rolled her eyes. "It makes me want to puke."

"What does that mean?"

She looked at me with a level, hardened gaze. "You tell me. You're the one who posts the content. He calls you his 'liaison to the free world.' A little grandiose, I thought."

"I don't have anything to do with the blog, Molly."

Her expression softened. "You don't, do you? I could tell as soon as I saw you. And not because you look like me." She cocked her head. "You just don't look like the type. You know what I mean? Those women who visit prisons and write letters to convicts and then marry them and never even spend one single night with them?" She took another sip of coffee and unwound the straw wrapper again. "Weirdos."

"That's the clinical term, I believe."

"So. Dr. Mulvaney."

"Weirdo du jour."

She folded the paper in half lengthwise and started to twirl it into a spiral. "I can't get much information from SMU. They told me he had to take an unexpected leave of absence. For personal reasons."

"Well, that's sort of true."

"I mean, it's not like he went home to nurse a sick relative. There's a difference."

"You found out what happened, though, right? It was all over the news."

"I looked it up in the *Morning News* archives."

"Well, I can't speak for SMU. I do know the department head, and she's terrific. I guess it was a judgment call."

"Whatever. The whole thing is freaky."

"I'm sorry."

"How well do you know Dr. Mulvaney?"

"Not well, I'm happy to report. Only professionally. I knew him well enough to know something was a little out of whack. I had no idea he was as disturbed as he turned out to be."

She looked away. "Yeah, well, you can't always tell about people."

"Did he ever, you know…"

"Come on to me? You're kidding, right? I don't even know the man. I only know what he looks like from the blog." She grimaced. "What a drip."

"I wonder how he knows your address?"

"Don't professors have access to students' addresses?"

"We have e-mail addresses because students log in to our online classes." My eyes mentally scanned my desk. "And come to think of it, we all have a campus directory. I guess he got it out of that."

"I'm not in the directory."

"Why not?"

"You can decline to be listed." She looked up at me. "For privacy's sake."

She shuddered.

"I wish I could help you," I said. "I can't think what—"

"I thought about visiting him in jail and asking him to stop."

"I don't think that would be a good idea. At all."

"It's weird that we look so much alike. Do you think that's why he's doing this? Did you make him mad or something?"

"Well, yeah, I did make him mad." A slight understatement, but she was better off not knowing the whole story. "I don't think that's why he's picking on you. I think he's picking on you because he's sick, and men who are sick like he is tend to stick to one physical type."

She sipped her coffee and stared at the parking lot as a motorcycle buzzed by. "Didn't someone marry, like, Ted Bundy?"

"I think so, yeah. After he was convicted."

"But before he was executed, I take it."

"I don't think they got much of a honeymoon."

"Yeah, and like Eva Braun?" she said, her face animating. "Didn't she marry Hitler and then kill herself, like, ten minutes later?"

"Wouldn't you have shot yourself too?"

"I thought it was poison."

"I think that was the Goebbels. They poisoned their children with cyanide. All six of them. Can you imagine?"

"Weirdos."

I laughed. I liked Molly Larken. I mentally put John Mulvaney on my skin-him-alive-next-time-I-see-him list. "So what are you going to do?"

"Move. Disappear. I've already changed my phone number and e-mail address."

"I'm sorry. It's not fair that you have to do that."

"Hey, it's a free country."

"As long as you're in jail."

"Makes you proud to be an American, doesn't it?"

She stood up and tossed her empty cup into the garbage, then tucked the twisted piece of paper into her pocket.

She dug around in her bag, pulled out a business card, and turned it over to write something on the back. She handed me the card and shook my hand.

"It was nice to meet you, Dr. Foster. You're pretty cool for a professor. Maybe I'll take one of your classes."

I groaned. "Don't take my class. You'll just be bored. But I would like to see your art sometime."

"I'm not working on anything now, but I've got some stuff in storage you might like." She pointed at the card. "My new e-mail's on the back. You already have my phone number."

"Right."

She turned to walk away.

"Good luck," I said. "Keep in touch."

She looked back and waved. Then she was gone.

I bought myself another iced tea and sat down to make phone calls. I called my father who, lucky for me, was in surgery. I talked to his office manager, Janet, who chided me for being so hard to reach.

Janet has a knack for scolding me and yet still managing to sound perky and nurturing. My father would have been sued out of the medical profession years ago, I'm convinced, if it weren't for her. The patients love Janet. My father they tolerate because he's so good. He's got a perfect surgeon's personality—works too hard, has no hobbies, no social life, unbelievably rigid personal habits. You can count on a guy like that to show up on time and concentrate on what he's doing. You'll never catch him making careless mistakes or bantering with the anesthesiologist.

I checked my voice mail at the office and was relieved to hear that Harold had returned my call. I called him back and caught him in his office.

"Helene tells me you're in a bit of a snit about your review."

"I don't know if I'd say *snit*. *Pickle,* maybe. *Frenzy,* surely. *Snit* sounds so…snippy."

"Snit, snip. It's all the same to me."

"It's more like a panic, truthfully. I mean, I know it's months away, and I'm pretty confident going into it…"

" 'Pretty confident' don't feed the bulldog, Dr. Foster. Let's aim a little higher, shall we?"

"Well, that's why I called," I said sarcastically.

"*Now* you sound snippy."

"Snippy, snitty, what difference does it make? My career's flapping in the wind, and you're commenting on my temperament?"

"Your temperament could use some improvement. And the wind—why, the wind will soon die down, and when you look around, you will see how far it has carried you. Why don't we get together Thursday? I'll take you to lunch."

"When and where?"

"You're one of those sushi people, aren't you? Maybe that new place over on—"

"Inwood? I love that place. Twelve thirty?"

"Perfect."

"What should I bring?"

"Just a pen and paper, your brilliant mind, and a reasonably good attitude."

"It's a stretch, that third one."

"It's what we all love about you, my dear. See you then."

I dialed Liz. "Any developments?"

"We're about to take Christine in for her first round of tests."

"What kind of tests?"

"Some chest x-ray thing. I don't know."

"They didn't explain it to you?"

"They did, but I heard from Tony DeStefano in the middle of it and had to step out. Andy and the boys are fine."

I felt the breath leave my lungs. "What happened?"

"It was what I thought. They landed safely but couldn't get through because of the weather."

"They're okay, though, right?"

"They're fine. They're playing soccer and eating tamales."

"Earl strikes again. Did you talk to them?"

"Andy and the boys were sleeping when he called. Tony said to tell you his wife was making spaghetti. He said you'd be jealous."

"Jenny's spaghetti is sublime. I think it's his mom's recipe. Like, from Italy—one generation removed. I practically pass out every time I have it, it's so good."

"They're in good hands, then."

"Very good hands. How's Christine?"

"Scared."

"Will it be invasive? There's no, like, dye or anything?"

"I don't think so. Besides, she already has the IV. They should be able to use that, right? She's just so little…"

"What time does she go?"

"They're on their way up."

I looked at my watch. I could beat the traffic if I left now. "Be there in ten."

I threw out the rest of my iced tea and stood to go just as the Chanel chick stepped out onto the sidewalk. She was a magazine ad—perfect makeup, heavy but tasteful jewelry, Chanel head to toe. Just the right shade of coral painted onto her sneer. She even had the pose down.

One foot delicately pointed forward, ankles crossed, as she reached into her quilted bag for her cigarette case.

The one flaw in her otherwise exquisitely crafted image was that she had this huge, cartoonish helmet of stiff, fake-blond, beauty-pageant hair. I was positive that if I stood downwind, I'd be smothered in Chanel No. 5 and Final Net fumes.

She looked me up and down with barely concealed disgust. As her eyes followed me to the truck, I felt my hostility rise up, take over my brain, and tackle what few weak instincts of proper social conduct I possess. It's an old reflex, one I'm not proud of, certainly. But honestly, I couldn't help myself.

I yanked open the door to my truck and slid onto the hot vinyl seat. As the engine coughed to life, I slammed the door, backed out of my space, and cranked down my window.

I waved gaily to her. "Love the hair!" I shouted. "Hope you win!"

As her jaw dropped and her face flushed to a lovely shade of magenta, I drove away sporting my first genuine smile in days.

Sometimes you have to create your own victories.

14

It's ten minutes from Starbucks to Children's Medical Center. But if you have bad traffic luck, which of course I do, the drive stretches quickly into an obstacle course of orange-and-white-striped barricades and stalled vehicles. You end up waiting in long, snaky lines of steaming SUVs with their hoods up and with steaming drivers inside them talking on cell phones.

The congestion today was even worse than usual—worse than I'd ever seen it, in fact. The epic traffic was surely part of some well-deserved reprimand from Jesus, but I didn't mind, honestly. Even in Dallas traffic in high afternoon sun with Stone Age air conditioning. Forty-five minutes after I three-point-landed my beauty-pageant joke, I pulled into the parking garage at Children's, sweating like a barn animal but still crowing with guilty satisfaction.

I had just missed Liz and Christine, so I had to track them down in radiology. Children's Medical Center is part of the Parkland system—a sprawling hive of buildings with byzantine signage and a maze of multicolored stripes painted on hallway floors. The stripes are supposed to serve as directional indicators but instead meld into a Daedalean mess that eventually leads you all the way to nowhere.

Three nurses' stations, two missed turns, and one wrong elevator later, I was standing in the radiology hallway, just outside the reception window, trying to con the guard-dog nurse into letting me in. His name was Patrick, and he was wearing pink scrubs and black eyeliner.

"Name of patient?"

"Christine Zocci."

"Social?"

I decided to try to charm him. "Yes."

He narrowed one eye at me.

"I mean, I guess she's pretty social. Why?"

A level of disdain I did not realize was humanly possible clouded his already dark expression. Someone should introduce him to the Chanel beauty contestant. They could share makeup.

He glared. "Security number. Social Security number."

I stubbornly maintained eye contact. He did have lovely green eyes—Irish eyes, set off by freckled skin and a shock of black hair, which had been waxed into a sharp center peak. He didn't need the liner at all, really.

"Oh. Well, I don't know her Social. I mean, I'm just the aunt."

"Aunt?"

"Yes. You know—like related to her parents? She's my…" I couldn't think. Cousin?

"Niece."

"Right. That's it. My niece." I have become quite an accomplished liar in recent years—an unexpected benefit of the Peter Terry debacle. I'm not proud of it, mind you, but it does come in handy occasionally. I was off my game today, though. No rhythm. Rhythm is everything in lying.

He pursed his lips and looked me up and down, then picked up the phone, punched a button, and waited a second, all the while keeping a sharp eye on me. I straightened my shoulders, copied Chanel's beauty-pageant stance, and shot him a big Miss Texas smile.

He turned his back to me and murmured something into the phone, then replaced the receiver and raised one eyebrow at me.

"They're expecting a friend, not an aunt."

"That's me. I'm the friend."

"A male friend."

I felt a surge of alarm. Was David on his way? I still hadn't gotten a pedicure!

"Did they give you a name?"

"I believe his name is Dylan Foster."

"That's me! I'm Dylan Foster."

He crossed his arms. "*Doctor* Dylan Foster."

"I *am* Doctor Dylan Foster."

The other eyebrow went up. "Really, now?"

"Yes, really now."

"Do you have your hospital ID with you, *Doctor* Foster?" He emphasized the *doctor* with palpable disdain.

"Um, no. I mean…I don't work at this hospital."

A raised eyebrow.

"It's just that, well, I'm not that kind of doctor."

"A veterinarian, perhaps? Or maybe you just play one on TV?"

I resisted the urge to sock him in the stomach. "Psychologist. I'm the family's psychologist."

"I thought you said you were the child's aunt."

"Well…that too. I'm the aunt, the psychologist, and the friend. I multitask."

"So…the man part?"

I wanted to point out that he was the one with the gender confusion, not me, but it seemed unwise.

"Maybe it was just an assumption the nurse made?" I suggested. "I mean, it happens to me all the time."

He looked me over. "Really now?"

"On paper. It happens on paper. Gender-neutral name."

He sighed and held out his hand. "ID?"

I handed him my driver's license and a copy of my American Psychological Association membership card, hoping he wouldn't notice that both were expired.

He sniffed and handed them back to me, walked wordlessly away from his desk, and opened the door between the hallway and the sacrosanct area into which unauthorized personnel like me were not allowed to pass.

On the other side of the door was a waiting room occupied by a few sick children and their exhausted parents. I scanned the room but didn't see Christine or Liz. Patrick strode past the wilted families and tapped on the glass between the waiting room and the nurses' station.

The frosted pane slipped open an inch, and my escort whispered for a moment to the person behind the window.

The window slid shut, and someone opened the door into the radiology unit. I waved a thank-you to Patrick, but he'd already turned on his heel and left, a vague sense of contempt wafting out behind him.

I followed the radiology tech (purple scrubs, orange hair, black roots, no eyeliner) into the holy of holies—a warren of curtained booths where patients changed into gowns and waited to be called for their procedures. I could hear Christine wailing as soon as I stepped into the hallway. I followed the sound and pushed back the curtain.

Liz was holding her and rocking in a fruitless attempt to settle her down. Christine was having none of it. She kept trying to push her way off Liz's lap, fighting with all the kick she'd shown the paramedics that first night at my house. Poor guy was probably still limping.

"I don't know why she's acting like this," Liz said over the din. "It's just an x-ray."

"Hi, Punkin," I said brightly.

Christine paused, wiped her eyes, and looked up at me, then buried her head in Liz's hair and glued herself to her mother. Liz looked helplessly at me over Christine's shoulder. She had circles under her eyes and a look of gray fatigue on her face.

"Want a break?" I asked.

Liz nodded gratefully. "I'll run to the restroom." She spoke into Christine's ear. "I'll be right back, Punkin. You keep Miss Dylan company."

Liz peeled Christine off herself and handed her over. Christine latched on to me, and I hugged her as she sniffed and cried.

After a few minutes of this, the curtain flew open, startling us both. Christine stopped for a moment, then took a breath and prepared to step up her screaming—expecting, surely, to meet the person who would usher her to her doom. I braced for a chewing out from someone fed up with the din.

Instead, a sixtyish man with close-cropped gray hair, a phenomenal tan, and a bright, affable smile leaned into the booth and tapped

Christine on the shoulder. He wore a faded hospital gown, his muscular, browned legs poking out the bottom and set off by a gleaming pair of white athletic socks. The man shot me a quick wave like he knew me and sat on the bench beside Christine. "Are you afraid?" he said to her.

She sniffed hard, laid her head on my shoulder, and nodded.

"You know what?" the man said.

She shook her head no and wiped her eyes on my hair.

"It doesn't hurt one bit."

She lifted her head. "It doesn't?"

"Nope. Not one teeny bit."

"Are they going to give me a shot?"

He leaned over and looked her in the eyes. "There's not one single shot involved. I promise."

She looked at him doubtfully, but he gave her another big smile. "All they do is, they take you into this room, and it's pretty cold in there. That's the part I don't like." He turned to me. "But you can just ask them for a blanket, and they'll give it to you, and then she won't be cold anymore." He looked gravely at Christine. "That's why I keep my socks on."

Christine's brow furrowed, and she wiggled her bare toes. I could see her making a mental note to ask for a blanket.

"They stand you on this little black square in front of this big white square, and they stick this big metal tray into the white square, and then they go behind a little wall and tell you to hold your breath."

"For a long time?"

"No. Just for a second or two. It's easy. Like this." He filled up his lungs and held the air in, a big, happy smile on his face, then blew into her face. She giggled.

"And then…" He leaned in, his eyes twinkling as though he were telling her a fairy tale. "Then they come out from behind the little wall and slide another tray into the big white square, and then you get to do it again. It's the easiest thing in the world."

"Easy-peasy," I said to Christine.

"Easy-peasy-I-have-to-sneezy," the man said.

"That's what Miss Dylan likes to say!"

"Really?" He winked at me. "That's one of my favorite things to say. Let's say it together."

They said, "Easy-peasy-I-have-to-sneezy," together, and Christine squealed with glee. I was positively slack-jawed at her transformation.

"And if you want," the man added enthusiastically, "I'll wait right next door until you finish, and then you can come out and tell me how easy-peasy-I-have-to-sneezy it was."

"You will?" she said.

"Of course!" He got up and waved good-bye to Christine. Then he looked at me, a bright twinkle in his eye, stepped inside his booth, and shut the curtain behind him.

Liz came back a few minutes later and raised her eyebrows in surprise. "Feeling better, Punkin?"

Christine nodded and laid her head on my shoulder again.

"We had a visit from another patient," I said. "He cheered her up."

The tech came then and called Christine's name. A brief look of panic crossed her face.

I pulled away from her and looked her in the eye. "Remember, Punkin? Easy-peasy."

Christine sighed heavily, climbed off my lap, and looked up at the tech. "Can I have a blanket?"

The woman had a kind smile. "Sure, sweetie. You bet."

Liz mouthed a silent thank-you to me as she took Christine's hand and led her down the hall.

I followed them to the x-ray room but wasn't allowed in, so I contented myself with pacing maniacally outside the door until they emerged about fifteen minutes later.

Christine came flying out the door, dragging her blanket. She charged past me and raced down the hallway looking for her new friend. Liz emerged behind her, and we walked together slowly down the long hallway.

"How'd it go?" I said.

"It was just a simple chest x-ray. I don't know why she was so scared. She's had x-rays before."

"What's it for?"

"Just to check out her lungs, make sure there's no obstruction or anything. They said the chances of that were practically zero, but they have to rule it out anyway."

"Did they tell you anything?"

"They're not allowed to, I don't think. Not until the doctor checks the films. But you know how you can usually tell by the tech's mannerisms? I got the impression everything was fine."

"That's good news."

"Sure, but it doesn't get us anywhere. She has some kind of breathing test next. I can't imagine the meltdown that's going to trigger. I really don't have the energy."

"Lucky break, that guy showing up, huh?"

Liz threw her head back and moaned. "Thank God for the mercy of strangers." We stopped at a vending machine. "Want anything?" She dug in her purse for change.

"Nope."

She turned back toward the nurses' station. "I'm going to see if I can find some change. I'll catch up with you."

Christine had found the man's booth and was sitting on the bench chatting amiably with him, telling him all about her x-rays and what a good job she'd done holding her breath and about how next time she'd know to take some socks, but her feet didn't get that cold because she'd asked for a blanket right away, just like he said.

I shook his hand and thanked him for his help.

"She's had a rough few days," I said. "You were a godsend."

Christine gasped. "Did God send you?"

The man's eyes twinkled. "Of course He did. God doesn't like for little girls to be afraid."

"Mommy said I have to do another one next." She looked up at me, a shadow of fear crossing her face. "What is it?"

"It's just a little breathing test. I think you get to blow up a balloon or something. It'll be great."

Christine looked over to the man. "Have you ever done that one?"

"Well, I haven't done that exact one. But I have it from a reliable source that it's not hard at all. You just blow into a machine as hard as you want."

"That sounds fun, doesn't it, Christine?"

Christine cast a worried gaze at the man.

"I wouldn't worry about it one bit if I were you," he said. "Not one bit."

Christine sighed but seemed resolved to take his advice.

"Bye, Punkin," the man said. "Remember, don't be afraid." He shot me a knowing grin and stepped back into his booth.

We waited a few minutes for Liz, who came bearing a bag of Cheetos and two cold Dr Peppers. Christine dove into the Cheetos. I popped the top on a Dr Pepper and took a long, fizzy sip. We sat for a moment and gathered ourselves. Then Liz picked up her handbag and the worn hospital blanket, which Christine refused to leave behind, and we got ready to take Christine back to her hospital room.

We'd left the holy of holies and made it almost past Patrick the eye-lined guard dog when I realized Christine's new friend had never mentioned his name. I wanted to find out his room number and buy him a new car or something, I was so grateful for the relief he'd given my little friend.

"Wait a second," I said. "I'll be right back."

I hurried back to Christine's empty booth and found the man sitting on the bench, his hands folded in his lap, ankles crossed, white socks gleaming, a contented smile on his face.

"I'm sorry to bother you again," I said. "I just realized we never caught your name." I reintroduced myself and thanked him again for his help.

"Very pleased to meet you, Dylan Foster." As he stood and held out his hand, I could see an ankh on a chain around his neck.

"Joe Riley." He beamed at me. "At your service."

15

By the time I stepped out of the hospital that evening, the parking lot was emptying out for the day, and the air smelled fresh and wet. Huge, puffy clouds were stacking high in a burnt western sky. I hadn't seen a forecast in days, but May is when the thunderstorms come. Violent storms, with thunderclaps so sudden and explosive, they're liable to sneak up on you without warning and knock you right out of your bed at night.

The summer sun had turned the clouds a bright, orangy scarlet. I stood, mesmerized, and watched the entire sunset, stunned by the grand magnitude of the view, feeling small and comfortably insignificant, my worries melting away in the warm yellow glow. How could any of it be important with all that going on up there?

I turned and walked to my truck, my thoughts turning to the journey home and the night ahead. I'd be glad for the rain. My yard was crunchy, my flowers wilted and bent.

It had been another endless day. I mentally cataloged the events that had crowded between sunup and sundown. One hysterical meltdown (not mine, for once), one unexpected stranger, one chest x-ray, and one pulmonary function test (also not mine). And as a last, final indignity, a long, agonizing conversation with Liz about my dismal prospects for reclaiming my boyfriend. By the time I left the hospital, I felt like I'd gone ten rounds with one of George Foreman's infomercials.

As the darkness settled in, I walked to my truck and mentally ran through the conversation with Liz. She'd been appropriately appalled when I confessed to her my recent (multiple) episodes of spectacular self-indulgence. I'd cried telling her about it all, and she—quite generously I thought, considering the circumstances—had hugged me, expressed profuse sympathy, and handed me Kleenexes. She'd actually seemed relieved to be the one doing the comforting for a change. After listening to my stories, however, she'd suggested that I just might have done it this time and run David off for good.

While I sulked, Christine had been busy whining for pizza. She'd then conked out halfway through her first slice, having successfully blown up the balloon every single time.

"This child does not have asthma," the tech had said flatly, ignoring the hospital's disclosure rules entirely. Liz and I had looked at each other, relieved to hear it but weary of what was turning out to be an endless rabbit trail of ambiguity.

We weren't counting on his diagnosis, of course. We'd wait to hear from the doctor. But we both knew it. Deep down to our bones, we knew it.

My house was dark when I got home. I parked my truck under the sycamore tree and slumped to the front door, fumbling for my keys in the dark. I'd tried to get Liz to switch with me—to take a night for herself while I did hospital duty—but she couldn't. Or wouldn't. They were both the same thing, as far as she was concerned. She couldn't leave her kid in the hospital and go home for a good night's sleep. It was an impossibility.

Though I'd have been happy to sub for her, I had to admit I was looking forward to an evening alone.

I threw my keys on the table and let the rabbits out of their hutches to wander around. I propped open the back door, sliced up an apple and some rhubarb for them—a new favorite of Melissa's—and set out to shed my day. To my profound relief, the mail held nothing extraordinary, and my answering machine was blissfully empty. I had no one to call, nothing to do, nowhere to be. I barely knew what to do with myself.

Supper was a ham sandwich on wheat and a handful of Fritos. I consider Fritos to be a health food, since they are the only snack food I've found that contains none of that nasty ethylmethylpethyl at all. All they are is corn, oil, and salt. Nice, pure, crunchy food.

I missed Christine. Christine and her weird crunchy food habits. After I'd put the dishes in the dishwasher and wiped down the counter-top with my new favorite cleaning product, Cinch (brought to us by God and the makers of Spic and Span), I fired up my laptop and sat at my kitchen table researching childhood lung conditions. Asthma was everywhere—all over the Web and all over the world, apparently trig-gered by everything from roach poo to anime cartoons to too much fun at Six Flags. The symptoms sort of fit, but not quite. And as the tech said, Christine had passed the breathing test with flying colors. She had no diminished lung capacity. The child did not have asthma.

My next search was for inmate blogs. I found several without much effort, with titles like "Meet Pete" and "Save Steve"—all self-aggrandizing, self-pitying manifestos. All of the sites positioned the prisoners as hap-less victims caught in the tortuous web of an overzealous justice system. There were long chat threads calling for the repeal of the death penalty, endless rants dissecting court cases—all in a naked effort to convince their readers that they were innocents, unjustly accused.

Any time the crime was mentioned, the language became imper-sonal, and the writer switched to the passive voice: "the alleged victim was supposedly made to kneel" or "he was struck with a bat or some other object while drunk." It angered me, the bald attempt to shift the blame from perpetrator to victim. And ultimately, of course, it was self-defeating. It just made them look more guilty.

I typed in John Mulvaney's blog address (DoctorBehindBars.com) and watched as the computer thought it over and took me there. Doc-tor Behind Bars, indeed. John had always insisted on the title, nudging people to call him Dr. Mulvaney in even the most casual of circum-stances. That single word—*Doctor*—had been his one claim to citizen-ship, his only ticket to any social standing at all, even in the drab, stiff, consolation-prize society of academia. He'd clung to that sad shred of identity with a closed fist and clenched teeth, convinced it was all he had.

I perused the entire site, steeling myself as I read every word, stud-ied every photo. Whoever was doing the blog had posted a photo of John as a toddler—pudgy, pouty, his clothes askew, his expression vague and disconnected. A pair of genderless hands—a parent or relative, per-haps—held him awkwardly in a lap and offered him a lollipop. As though his childhood was populated by candy and hands, but no real connection at all. Shadows on the wall behind him suggested a woman had taken the picture with the sun behind her so that her shadow pro-jected into the frame, shading part of John's face. John squinted uncom-fortably into the sun.

Other photos were of the SMU campus, overblowing John's aca-demic career, which was in fact undistinguished, though perfectly cred-ible. The absence of graduation photos—by the time you get your PhD, you've graduated half a dozen times—suggested to me that there had been no one to take them. John was so narcissistic he'd certainly have included cap-and-gown photos of himself if he'd had any. The only other photo of John was one I knew well—of him and his junior-high girlfriend, Brigid, whom I had met last January and who had revered him as "Dr. Mulvaney," her one missed chance out of trailer-trash pur-gatory. The caption under the photo read, "The professor's first and only love." The image was of two awkward misfits, their mismatched clothing and crooked, stiff smiles betraying the enormity of the social gap between them and their peers.

There were no photos of Molly Larken and, thankfully, none of me. No photos—but plenty of text. John's was the only inmate blog I'd found that singled out individuals on his page. Probably the others, fur-ther along in the legal process, had more sense than that. Or better lawyers. Naming names made him look predatory and disturbed.

He'd mentioned me, Molly Larken, and Gordon Pryne, who had been the cops' original suspect and who John was now claiming had committed the crime and framed him for it. Molly he claimed as his muse. Me he credited with maintaining his Web site. Profuse gratitude dripped in overwritten prose for both Molly and me.

I skimmed the site again. The rest of the copy was woodenly writ-ten and contained common but ignorant grammatical errors like the missing apostrophe in "professors," "might of" instead of "might have," "irregardless" rather than "regardless," "regime" rather than "regimen."

The copy had clearly been written by two different people.

One was surely John Mulvaney. My guess was that he'd written the drippy but grammatically correct part himself. The man had a PhD, after all. He had all the poise and social grace of a bucket of mop water, but he could at least complete a sentence.

I was just starting my research on serpents and the subconscious mind when Joan Carmichael returned my call and saved me the trouble.

"Dylan," she said, sounding friendly but not warm. "It's good to hear from you. I hope you're well?"

"Yeah, I'm doing great. Thanks for asking. I really appreciate your calling me back." I'd decided to shoot straight with her. I figured it would only handicap me to go in the back door, especially with the recent deterioration in my lying skills. She'd spot the deception a mile away.

"Listen, Joan, the reason I'm calling is—I know you may not be able to talk to me about this—but I'm calling about the Nicholas Chavez case."

Silence.

"Joan?"

"I'm here." She paused. "You know I can't disclose—"

"Yeah, I know you can't be specific. But it's just that the little girl you interviewed, Christine Zocci, is a friend of mine."

"You know her?"

"Pretty well. And I was there when the boy disappeared. They'd all been at my house that afternoon."

"Do you have a release from the family?"

Why hadn't I thought of that? I mentally bludgeoned myself and said, "No, but I can certainly get one and fax it over to you tomorrow."

"That would be good. I'd feel better about talking to you."

"Sure, I understand. But since I've got you on the phone, do you think we could do the hypothetical thing? Just so I can get a few things knocked off my worry list?"

"Sure. Shoot."

"Well, I was wondering if she mentioned a snake to you. Anything at all about the kidnapper having a snake with him?"

"That's not a hypothetical question."

"Oh, right. We just said that, didn't we? Okay, can you discuss, in general, the connection between snakes and the child psyche? I mean, I doubt any human person would be walking around carrying a snake with him while he's out kidnapping children. It seems that perhaps a child who witnessed an abduction or some other traumatic event might insinuate that image into the scene somehow. I wonder if you think that's possible?"

"Children do imagine such things in stressful or traumatic situations. My guess is that a child in the situation you describe could very well have done that. Perhaps she saw something that suggested a snake—a tattoo maybe, or an image on a T-shirt—and was unable to process the information in the heat of the moment, so to speak. She might then animate the snake in her mind, imagining it was real."

Bingo.

"And what would such imagery suggest to you, Joan? I mean, child psychology is not my field. Adults, I know, associate snakes with subversion, with power, with subterfuge. And there's the whole phallic Freudian thing, which I always thought was pretty misogynistic."

"It's a primal image in dreams for both children and adults," Joan said, "suggesting the associations you mentioned. Jungian archetypes, of course, are more sophisticated than Freud's. In the case of snakes, rather than being simply a phallic symbol or a simple power image, Jung suggests they're symbolic of the conflict between conscious attitudes and unconscious instincts."

"You mean, like the fight between good and evil?"

"I guess that's a possibility. But an internal struggle. It's a common phobia as well, one that develops in very early childhood, whether or not the individual has had any direct contact with snakes. This in itself suggests a universality of meaning."

"The subterfuge thing is important, don't you think?" I said.

"Stolen power. If a child witnessed the kidnapping of another child, after all, what better, more graphic image of stolen power could you possibly construct?"

"I agree."

"Do you get any sense at all that the snake was real?"

"That's not a hypothetical question."

"But it could be an image. An image of some kind."

"Yes."

"What about the color black? What if the child suggested the perpetrator was black, when it's known he was white?"

"Hypothetically?"

"Yes. Hypothetically, of course."

"Some children have an innate sense about people. They don't see auras, per se—none of that drippy hippie stuff—but they might see a person as dark or troubled and associate that with a color. It shows up in their art, for instance. They'll choose colors to represent feelings. Blue for sad, black for angry or sad, red for mean."

"This child has an astonishing spiritual acuity. She sees angels."

"Literally?"

"Yes. Literally."

"Any other signs of psychosis?"

"I don't think that's a sign of psychosis."

"You don't think she really—"

"Yeah, I do. I know it's strange."

"Very."

"It's like a radar. A spiritual radar."

"So the spiritual images—"

"Make sense. For this kid in particular, yes."

"You mean, in general. Hypothetically."

"Right. Hypothetically. I'm also wondering, what sort of effect do you think an event like that might have on a child?"

"The witness or the victim of the kidnapping?"

"Both."

"Trauma. Plain and simple. More for the victim than the witness, obviously. But you could expect PTSD symptoms for both children, varying in severity and duration according to the level of trauma and the sensitivity of the child."

"Could that involve somatization? Sudden onset of asthmalike symptoms, for example?"

"Absolutely."

I thanked her for her time. She'd gone way out on a professional limb by talking with me, even under the thin veil of a hypothetical conversation. We arranged to get together for lunch in a few weeks and hung up.

I'd just fired up an Internet search on snakes in Jungian literature when the rabbits came scuttling into the room. I looked up, startled at the speed they moved past me. Eeyore and Melissa are not exactly assertive pets. Or ambitious. They generally move one hop at a time unless a purple carrot is involved. Now, though, they bolted through the kitchen and scooted into the bedroom. I looked around the corner in time to see them both dive under the bed, then stood up to see what all the fuss was about.

I didn't see anything unusual in the house, so I stepped outside and flipped on the light, illuminating the yard with the yellow glow from my GE Bug Lite bulb. (Moths swarmed the light immediately, of course.)

Summer sounds greeted me—sprinklers in my neighbor's yard, katydids in the willow tree next door, and the occasional cicada or cricket. But otherwise the yard was quiet. I went inside and got a flashlight. The grass crunched under my feet as I walked the fence line, rattling bushes and shining my light around corners.

I got all the way around to the back steps before a sharp clap of thunder startled me just about out of my skin. I looked up as the rain began, thinking I needed to check my truck windows. And then I heard under the back porch a sound that stopped me dead in my tracks—a sound any corn-fed Texan knows by heart.

The unmistakable buzz of a rattlesnake.

Since I am not a complete idiot, I did not stop right then and personally search for the snake. I bolted back into the house, slammed the door, and locked it behind me, as though somehow that would make a difference. Like snakes have fingers or something.

I spent a few frantic minutes in the Yellow Pages, hands shaking, looking for a snake-removal service—which, by the way, does not exist in the Greater Dallas phone book. And then I came across the business card of an exterminator I'd used the last time Peter Terry showed up and let a bunch of unwelcome creatures into my house.

I don't know why it didn't occur to me until that moment that Peter Terry had sent the snake. He loves to use vermin to torment me. It's like a calling card. It had been flies the first time, then rats. Since he doesn't play fair, he'd just about gotten the better of me both times. I'd had to reclaim my territory one kill at a time. Now that I was onto him, I had no intention of letting that happen again.

"Come on," I said out loud. "Snakes and evil?"

I slapped the phone book shut. "You can do better than that."

16

~

NOW, I REALIZE THAT any normal person would be scared at this point. With a snake rattling under my house and a demon floating around my kitchen, panic was in order, surely. Or at least a good, hearty scare. But to tell you the truth, I was just sick of the whole thing. Peter Terry had become a nuisance. A stalker. Like a one-date mistake who refuses to take the hint. The kind who won't stop calling and then eventually starts screaming into your answering machine when you won't pick up the phone. And then disappears for a while before he shows up at your office and lets the air out of your tires.

He was insufferable. Intolerable. Inexcusable. Incorrigible. And as far as I was concerned, he had to go.

Getting rid of beings like Peter Terry is no simple matter, unfortunately. I'd seen enough movies about medieval monks and chalices and crucifixes to know that. And it's not as though I hadn't tried. I'd stood my ground, run like a madwoman, stamped both feet, cursed the ground he walked on, and prayed repeatedly to the Good Lord Jesus Himself for deliverance. I'd done everything I could think of, in fact, short of grabbing a dagger and letting an exorcist paint sacramental oil on my door frames. It was going on two years now, in fact, and I wasn't having any luck at all.

I had to wonder, once again, if it was me. Maybe I was the problem. Was I an easy target? Had my foul temper, poor mental health, solitary lifestyle, and lousy spiritual condition set me up for all this?

It was a reasonable conclusion, certainly. The truth is, if Christianity were a merit-based society, I would have gotten kicked out years ago. I'm terrible at it. I never go to Bible study, don't keep a prayer journal or do the morning "quiet time" thing. (In Texas we say "quite tahm.")

I only remember to pray in emergency situations. The truth is, I really don't have the time or energy for any of that checklisty stuff. Or the self-discipline, for that matter. I'm usually too busy alphabetizing my spices or searching for a good parking space to pay any sustained attention to spiritual matters.

I should probably convert to Catholicism. If I were Catholic, at least I'd have to go to confession. Maybe that would whip me into shape.

Whatever the problem was, I had to admit that none of my other friends seemed to attract this sort of attention. Well, except Liz and Maria. And Christine. Come to think of it, they were really my *only* friends. They were probably all just spending too much time with me. The thought depressed me thoroughly. I wasted a good hour obsessing about it before I remembered Maria had been targeted long before she met me. I'm embarrassed to admit how much that cheered me up.

I checked the clock, then picked up the phone and called her. "Any news?"

"None," she said. "I'm resigned to it for now. I just have a feeling it's going to be a little while longer."

"What feeling? You mean, like he's okay?"

"I think he is. Maybe that's just a mother's refusal to consider the worst. But I'm telling you, he's out there. I can feel it. I almost hear him crying."

"That sounds excruciating."

"Maybe I'm kidding myself. I don't really care. I need to believe it."

I wasn't going to argue with her. "What's the FBI saying?"

"They were hoping it was a drug snatch."

"What's that?"

"Apparently, lots of children get kidnapped and ransomed for drug money."

"Don't they know Parkland doesn't pay ransom wages?"

"They do, but they're assuming the kidnapper might not. They also thought that maybe since I'm a doctor, someone had targeted me for OxyContin or something."

"So is that what they think happened?"

"They told me today it's not likely. There's been no demand for ransom. Well, one, but it turned out to be fake. The guy had seen it on the news."

"How do they know it was bogus?"

"They checked it out. It was just some drifter."

"And they're sure? Like, positive?"

"They seem quite certain."

"And you believe them?"

"I do. They're very good, Dylan. They know what they're doing."

"What happens to those kids—the drug-snatch kids?"

"If you pay up, they bring them right back. They're usually home within twenty-four hours. Apparently it happens a lot. A lot more than you'd think, anyway."

"I never knew."

"Those cases never make the paper. Half of them never even get reported to the police. The kids are usually minorities from crackhouse neighborhoods."

"What now? Are the FBI guys still at your house?"

"They left this afternoon."

"But they're still looking for him."

"Of course. They're just not waiting by the phone. Whoever has him is not going to call—I really believe that. I'd rather have them out there looking for him than sitting in my living room, you know?"

"Are your parents still there?"

"I checked them into a hotel. I can't take care of anyone but myself right now."

"Good decision. Can I do anything?"

"Keep me company?"

It was only ten o'clock. I'd be up for hours anyway, in my state of mind.

Maria greeted me with a glass of red, and we sat in her living room listening to music and talking. An array of trucks and dinosaurs lay scattered under the kitchen table, where Nicholas liked to play. Maria was even tidier than me. Under normal circumstances, they'd all be in the bin in his room.

The wine was good. Round but not too fruity. I closed my eyes and let the flavor settle on my tongue. "How's Bob?"

"The turtle?"

I nodded.

"He seems to be taking it okay," she said. "Probably one of the advantages of being a cold-blooded creature. Escape from the curse of self-awareness. I should take him out in the yard, let him get a little exercise. Nicholas usually walks him."

I told her about the snake in my yard.

"You have the worst luck," she said.

"Everyone says that to me."

She raised her glass. "To better luck."

"For all of us."

I told her about Christine's tests and the tech's pronouncement.

"He shouldn't have said that."

"But he's right, isn't he?"

"If she blew up the balloon every time, she doesn't have asthma."

"It's maddening to not know what's wrong with her."

Maria tilted her head. "They may never figure it out. Nicholas went through something like this awhile back. We did the same routine. The whole rigmarole."

"Does he have asthma?"

"Turned out to be panic attacks."

"A five-year-old? I've never heard of that."

She nodded. "They were triggering tracheal stenosis."

"What's that?"

"It's a spontaneous closing of the trachea. Tracheitis."

"More diseases to be afraid of."

She smiled. "I don't think you need to worry too much. Odds are in your favor. You're more likely to die of the flu. I bet you don't get flu shots, do you?"

"How did you know?"

She laughed. "Um, your reflexive refusal to listen to anyone?"

"What causes it?"

"Your reflexive refusal to listen to anyone?"

I made a face at her. "Trache-whatever."

"Some people get it from a virus. Or it can be a reaction to anesthesia or intubation." She shrugged. "It's rare for anxiety to trigger it, but it happens."

I sat there a minute. The gears began to grind in my mind. "So, does Nicholas still have the panic attacks?"

"Sometimes. When he's really afraid."

"And when did they start?"

"Last fall. He changed schools in September. He'd been in a little private preschool until then—very structured. I moved him to Montessori. He got a little freaked out. He likes structure."

"So you think that was it?"

"Well, nothing else was going on. Business as usual in the Chavez house. Mom's too busy. No dad in sight. Nanny refuses to speak to him in anything other than Spanish. Bob has a fungus. Nicholas throws a fit wanting Sugar Babies for breakfast. The usual dramas."

"Tell me about the panic attacks."

"What do you want to know?"

"What were they like? What were his symptoms?"

"Rapid heart rate. Clammy skin. Respiratory distress. You know—that whole fear-escalation cycle."

"Which for Nicholas went how?"

"It started with the sweating. He'd get gray and clammy, and his heart rate would go up. He called it drums in his tummy."

"And then what?"

"Rapid breaths, increasing in frequency, decreasing in efficacy. Eventually, he'd either calm himself down or pass out. His trachea didn't start closing until several months into it. But it was like an asthma attack. Almost exactly. I put him through the same tests Christine just went through. He blew up the balloon."

"What time of day did his panic attacks happen?"

"Usually at night."

"Why?"

"Nicholas is afraid of the dark."

"I didn't know that."

"He can't go into a dark room. He can't sleep in a dark room. He won't even go into the hallway until I turn the light on for him. He's always been like that."

"What, does he have a little night-light or something in his room?"

"Superman. He has a Superman night-light. He says it keeps him safe."

"Keeps him safe? He uses those words?"

"That's what he says exactly. 'It keeps me safe.'"

I went to the kitchen, brought back the wine bottle, and filled Maria's glass. "Maria, has anyone told you what the kidnapper said to Christine?"

"I just heard that he knew Nicholas by name."

"She didn't report it initially. I think she was afraid. Scared out of her mind. But she told me that when he grabbed her, he burned his hand."

She furrowed her brow. "That doesn't make any sense."

"I know it doesn't."

"What else did she say? You're getting at something."

I hesitated. "He said he didn't want her; he only wanted Nicholas."

"And?"

I took a breath. "And…he said he was taking him to keep him safe."

"He used that phrase?"

"Yes. 'To keep him safe.' That's what she told me. Those exact words."

"It's probably just a coincidence."

"I remember your telling me that he was having nightmares."

"About that creepy white guy with the slash in his back," Maria said.

"Peter Terry."

"The one you said was hunting souls."

"Right. That's what he does," I said, my anger rushing up me like a gust of hard wind. "He's out to ruin us all." I set my glass down. "Do you still have the coloring book? That Audubon coloring book? The one where Nicholas colored the birds with the slashes in their backs?"

"I think it's in his room."

"Let's take a look."

She got the book, and we pored over each page. I hadn't seen it since last winter. I'd forgotten how graphic the images were.

For the first half of the book, the coloring was normal for a kid his age. Scribbles in the margins. Wild, happy colors everywhere. Yellow swans, bright pink sparrows. Then a sudden change. The colors grew darker, angrier. Black parakeets, blood-red lovebirds. And then finally, a dove.

Nicholas had left the dove white but had crossed out each of the wings and drawn an angry red slash in the bird's back, wing to wing.

"When did he do this one? Do you know?" I asked.

She picked up the book and flipped through the pages until she found the remains of a page that had been torn out, its edge still bound into the backbone of the book.

"This was December. He colored a picture and gave it to me for my birthday." She gestured toward the bookcase, pointing out a framed hummingbird in green and blue and purple. "He looked it up in a book to get the colors right."

The following few pages were still bright, energetic. Three pages into it, Nicholas had colored a whooping crane black.

"How often does he color?" I asked.

"Two or three times a week, probably."

"Does he always color the pages in order and do one book at a time? Or are there several books, and he just picks one randomly?"

"Nicholas is a very meticulous child." She smiled. "He's a lot like you that way."

I raised my glass. "My sympathies. Definitely in order and one book at a time, then. When's your birthday?"

"December twelfth."

"So sometime in the second or third week of December, his coloring changed. And then a week or so into that, he colors the dove. Do you remember a change in mood?"

"That was when the nightmares started."

"The ones about Peter Terry."

"Right. He'd wake up screaming."

"I guess Superman wasn't doing much good at that point."

"What are you getting at, Dylan?"

"What triggered the decline? Did something happen in mid-December?"

Maria's eyes pooled suddenly.

"It was my fault." She wiped a tear away.

"What?"

"It was a Saturday, and I was running late, racing around getting ready for work. The nanny had just come, and she was cleaning up the breakfast dishes and starting some laundry. I thought he was with her. He always follows her around in the morning because she brings him a surprise every day. Nothing big. It could be a smiley-face Band-Aid or something. But he loves it. He can't leave her alone until she gives it to him."

I watched as she struggled to retain composure. Her skin began to flush, and her upper lip trembled.

"I wasn't really tracking where he was," she said. "I just wasn't thinking about it. The nanny went to the laundry room to fold some towels. And I picked up my keys and left."

"What happened?"

"I didn't know at first. The nanny called me in a panic a few minutes later. She couldn't find him anywhere. She thought maybe I'd taken him with me without telling her."

"Where was he, Maria?"

She began to cry, tears glistening wet in the soft light. She dropped her head into her hands and began to sob, shoulders shaking, gasping air. The kind of crying you do maybe once or twice in your life.

I'm pretty good with crying. I watch people cry all the time in my line of work. I sat down next to her until she'd cried it out, then handed her a Kleenex and waited.

"The light goes off when the door closes." She wiped her cheeks with her hands. "He was only in there a few minutes." She took a rattled breath. "He couldn't find the knob. That's why he got so scared."

"What happened to him, Maria? Where was he?"

"In my closet. I'd accidentally shut him in my closet."

17

~

RAIN DRUMMED STEADILY FROM the night sky, thunder grumbling in the distance. Maria swiped a card to get through security and parked in the doctors' lot at Children's. She set the brake and was out of the car and halfway to the elevator before I'd finished admiring the covered parking space. The guard waved us through, and we walked through the double doors. I followed, almost at a trot, as Maria led us through the maze of hallways. Our wet shoes squeaked on the nonsensical painted stripes, echoing in near-empty corridors.

On the seventh floor, Maria spoke briefly with the charge nurse, then pointed me down the hall to Christine's room and said she'd be right there.

Christine was sound asleep in her bed, sprawled sideways, clutching No-Nose. Liz sat in the Lysol chair in her jammies, flipping through a magazine. She had a stack of them on the table next to her.

"It's almost midnight," she whispered. "What's going on?"

"We have a theory we want to run by you," I said. "Fasten your seat belt. It's pretty bizarre."

Liz frowned. "I can't imagine anything you could say that would surprise me at this point."

Maria came in with three cups of coffee.

"You went all the way downstairs in that amount of time?" I asked in a whisper.

She shook her head and stirred her sugar in. "Nurses' station. It's one of the big perks of being a doctor."

"Is that one of those rights and privileges they talk about on the diploma?" I asked.

"I always wondered what those were," Liz said. "Other than unfettered access to narcotics."

Maria rolled her eyes. "Yeah, makes all those long hours of medical training completely worth the trouble. That and the spectacular pay you get working at a public hospital."

"How's she been?" I hiked myself up onto the window ledge, throwing a towel over the air-conditioning vent to keep it from blowing snow up my shirt.

"She seems fine. No more attacks. She's dreaming some, squirming around. But she seems good. I think they'll let us out of here tomorrow." She looked around the room. "I will not miss this place."

Maria pulled up a chair. "I put in a page to Dr. Lindsay. He should have gotten the reports from the radiologist and pulmonologist today."

"Do you think it's asthma?" Liz asked.

"Gut feeling? No. But I want to make sure."

"What about you, Maria?" Liz asked. "Any news?"

"Nothing."

Liz shook her head. "I don't know how you're getting through this."

"I'm on fifteen-minute segments," Maria said. " 'One day at a time' was too ambitious."

"What about you?" I asked Liz. "Any word from down south?"

"I talked to Andy a little while ago. The satellite phone decided to work, finally." She took a sip of coffee and sighed. "That stupid phone cost a fortune, but it's a worthless piece of junk if the network's down. There are some problems that all the money in the world will not solve."

"How does he sound?" I blew on my coffee, enjoying the smell of it.

"Terrific. He says it's beautiful there. The kids are having a ball. They saw parrots in the trees today. He said they're wearing themselves out playing with all the little orphan children. Probably teaching them to shoplift or something." She turned to Maria. "My boys are hoodlums."

"Sweet, though," I said. "And so adorable they can get away with it."

"Yeah, they're going to be lady-killers, both of them," Liz said.

"We're foregoing a college fund for those two. We're socking away cash for a criminal-defense fund instead." We all laughed, bottling up the sound to keep from waking Christine. I watched as Maria wiped tears from her eyes. Tears of laughter, not grief or anger. I was grateful to see her eyes soften, her smile linger. The next fifteen minutes were looking pretty good.

"They keep dragging orphans up to Andy one at a time and asking if they can bring them home, like they're puppies at the SPCA," Liz said. "Like if they just find the right one…"

"Would you do that?" Maria asked. "Adopt a kid like that?"

"Maybe. I would like a little notice first. Andy's liable to just show up with a few. He's got a huge heart. He was one of those kids who always brought home lost kittens and birds with broken wings."

"Do they know about Christine?" Maria asked.

"The boys? He didn't want to scare them."

"How's Andy taking it?"

"He's worried. He wanted to turn right back around and come home."

"What did you say?"

"I said he was doing more good there than he could possibly do here. I don't need the boys yanking the pages out of Christine's chart and climbing her IV pole." She tapped me on the arm. "You know how they are. Besides, he's there for the orphans. It's an important trip. They're building a clinic. And the Angel Wing plane is flying around picking up supplies and bottled water and bringing in doctors. He needs to be there."

"Is he personally building the clinic?"

"He thinks he is. He doesn't really know what he's doing. But he loves to swing a hammer." She took a sip of coffee. "Makes him feel like a man."

"Enrique was over last week with his power drill putting some shelves up in my closet," Maria said. "So sexy."

I nodded. "I love a man with power tools. David used to prune my sycamore tree with a chain saw."

"And you broke up with him? You're an idiot," Liz said.

"He broke up with me," I corrected. "And I think my idiot status is well established."

Maria's phone rang loudly. She snatched it up before it could wake Christine, spoke briefly, then hung up and turned back to us. "That was Dr. Lindsay."

"At this hour?" Liz said. "Where can I get that kind of pull?"

"I delivered his twins. He owes me." Maria winked. "Besides, he's a night owl."

"What did he say?" I asked.

"He saw the test results. No asthma."

"What could it be then, Maria?" Liz asked. "Seizures maybe? Something neurological?"

Christine stirred and turned. No-Nose fell softly to the floor. Liz tucked him back in with Christine and pulled the blanket up over her shoulders.

We lowered our voices and told her about Nicholas's panic attacks.

"What are you saying?" Liz hugged her knees. I covered more of the register with the towel. "That Christine is having panic attacks? Is that what's behind this…what's it called?"

"Tracheal stenosis."

"Liz," I said, "I think it might be more complicated than that."

"Is this the seat-belt part?" she said.

Maria looked at me quizzically. "Seat belt?"

"I told her she'd need to buckle up for this ride." I hopped down and sat on the edge of the bed. "Think about what's happened so far. Nicholas starts having nightmares about a pale, creepy guy with a slash in his back."

"Peter Terry?" Liz said. "When was this?"

"Last fall," Maria said. "I wish I understood who he is, Dylan."

"Look, if I knew, I'd run for God."

"He's sort of a specter, I guess," Liz said. "The anti-Earl. That's the best way to explain it."

"I got him a Superman night-light," Maria said.

"Didn't he have Superman pajamas too?" I said. "I think he was wearing them the first time I came over to your house."

Maria nodded. "Those were for 'double protection' nights. I had him convinced they had superpowers."

"Why would he need double-protection pajamas?" Liz asked. "What was he afraid of?"

"Nicholas is afraid of the dark," Maria said.

"Aren't all kids afraid of the dark?" Liz asked. "My kids think their night-lights protect them from monsters. Or the boogie man."

"I thought it was bogy man," Maria said. "I hate colloquial phrases. My English…"

"It's either, really. But Andy taught them *boogie.* As in 'Boogie Fever.' He's still living in the seventies."

I laughed. "You're kidding me."

"I wish I were. He's crazy about ABBA. And you know the green shag carpet and lava lamps in our game room? That's Andy—and it's not a cool retro thing. His favorite movie is *Smokey and the Bandit.*"

"That's hysterical," I said. "I think of Andy as being so…cultured. Isn't he on the symphony board or something?"

"It's an act. Really, his childhood fantasy was to be Danny Bonaduce."

"Who's that?" Maria asked.

"*The Partridge Family,*" I said. "If it's any consolation, Liz, I wanted to be Laurie."

"Right, but Laurie was cool. That's my point. Any normal boy would want to be Keith."

"Who's Keith?" Maria asked.

"David Cassidy," I said.

Maria threw up her hands. "I'm lost."

"Evel Knievel was his second choice. Remember him?"

"I'm happy to say I have no idea who that is," I said. "If it wasn't on reruns after school *and* before my parents got home, I didn't see it. My mom didn't believe in TV."

"Well, you didn't miss much. He was always vaulting over eighteen-wheelers on his motorcycle in this horrible white Elvis suit." She took a sip of coffee. "It feels so good to laugh." She shook her head and sighed heavily. "I need to get some sleep."

"Did they give you anything?" Maria asked.

"Just Xanax. It's keeping me from crawling out of my skin."

"Dosage?" Maria asked.

She shrugged. "They're white."

"Two-point-five milligrams. Take an extra one tonight," Maria said. "A few hours' sleep would make a big difference at this point."

"Or hit yourself on the head with a hammer," I added. "Whichever you prefer."

"What were we talking about?" Liz asked. "I know it wasn't Evel Knievel."

"Nicholas believes his Superman night-light is to keep him safe," I said. "He uses those words. *To keep him safe.*'"

"The same words the kidnapper used," Maria said. "Same words exactly."

"So the man comes to the park, and Christine can tell that he's mean," I said.

"Mean, black, and with a snake," Liz said.

"Even though he was white," Maria said.

"Or maybe Hispanic," I said.

"And he obviously did not have a snake," Liz said.

"Right. So snakes represent evil in the human psyche," I said. "And power. Subverted power."

"I don't think it was a real snake," Liz said.

"And then I heard a rattlesnake in my backyard tonight," I continued.

Liz looked at me sympathetically. "How much worse can your luck get?"

"I think I'm better off not knowing."

Maria rested her elbows on her knees and clasped her hands in front of her. "Something going on that day was evil. Christine knew it right away."

"And then the man grabs Christine's arm," I said. "And he tells

Christine he's made a mistake. That he doesn't want her. He wants Nicholas."

"By name," Maria said. "He mentions Nicholas by name."

"It seems like the police would be looking for someone who knows him. Who else would know his name?"

"I asked them that," Maria said. "They said child predators are very adept at watching kids play, learning their names, and then approaching them."

"So it doesn't mean he knew the guy," I said.

"And when he grabs Christine, he burns his hand," Liz added.

Christine stirred, and Liz gestured that we should keep it down.

"Right. He burns his hand," I said. "So maybe she was getting some kind of protection."

"Maybe Earl carries a Taser," Liz said.

"I think he might," I said. "And then the guy tells Christine he's taking Nicholas to keep him safe. 'To keep him safe.' Same phrase Nicholas uses about his night-light."

Liz furrowed her brow. "But that can't mean anything. Anybody might use those words."

"Do you remember that day on the porch? When Christine said Nicholas was hot and thirsty?" I asked.

"I still feel bad about that, Maria," Liz said. "I don't know what would possess her…"

"And then that morning you were gone for so long trying to raise Andy on the radio? I don't think I told you this, Liz. But Christine woke up and asked about Nicholas. She said she thought he was in the closet. I thought she'd had a dream or something. And right after that she asked me to move the towel away from the closet door. I had it blocking the crack under the door."

"Why?" Maria asked.

"I hate eggs."

"I don't get it," Maria said.

"Not important. The point is, Christine's having these same attacks

Nicholas had. There's no sign of asthma in either child. And then all these weird little incidents."

"It's too bizarre to be coincidental," Maria said.

"Something's going on." I set my coffee down. "I think she's got a bead on him, Liz."

"Christine?"

I nodded. "I think somehow she knows what he's going through."

18

IT WAS TWO IN the morning before I walked in my door. I checked on the rabbits, stuck my head outside to listen for the snake, who was blessedly silent, then took a long bath and slipped into my softest jammies—my version of a security blanket. I spent a couple of hours flopping around in my bed, chasing my thoughts around. My brain had finally shifted, engine revving, from nagging stress to full-blown mania. The sound was deafening, inescapable. I could almost smell the rubber burning. Foul clouds of brain exhaust were flying everywhere, choking all the nice, clean, lemon-Pledge-scented air out of my bedroom.

I'd flown around this track enough times to know what I was up against. It was pointless to resist. At three that morning, I caved to the inevitable and fired up my computer, signing myself on to the Internet and checking last week's weather patterns around the country.

The Northeast was locked down in a cool front—drenched in rain for the past week, highs in the midseventies. The Gulf states and the Texas coast were muggy and windy—typical Houston armpit weather—but not unseasonably hot. The rest of Texas and the entire Southwest, particularly the desert states, were sweltering under a dome of high pressure that had parked itself between the Great Divide and the Mississippi River. Highs in the midnineties. One hundred ten in the shade in Nevada.

"Hot and thirsty" didn't narrow things down much.

I hated to consider the possibility he had been taken outside the city. But local news coverage had been breathless. Relentless. People all over the city were looking under every rock for him. If I'd just snatched a kid, I'd have lit out for Mexico by now. (Sunny, highs in the upper nineties, no rain in sight.)

I stared at the satellite image, willing the clouds to part and reveal some truth—even a tiny bit of insight—that might lead me to Nicholas. It was futile, like throwing a dart in the dark. After a while, the greens and reds and yellows began to run together on the screen and my eyes started to sting. I waved the white flag, abandoned my research, and returned to bed, managing a couple of hours of fitful sleep before my phone rang. I cracked open an eye and groaned. The sun was just peeking through my bedroom shades.

I've never had sufficient optimism or even a passable level of anticipation about the day ahead to manage a morning-person attitude. In fact, I find morning people to be obnoxious and off-putting. It's the eagerness that gets to me, I think.

Since I am not a morning person, I am famously grouchy until well into my third cup of caffeine. Even grouchier than I am the rest of the day, if you can imagine that. I know of only one person on the earth, in fact, who possesses the gall to bother me this early in the morning. He loves to call me at the crack of dawn and jar me out of bed. We both know it is the one time of day I can't possibly generate an excuse not to answer the phone.

I fumbled for the receiver. "Hi, Dad."

"Dylan, why must I stalk my own daughter? How many phone calls does it take to get a response?"

"How many is this, Dad?"

"Don't get flip with me, Dylan."

"Have you ever heard of the distancer-pursuer dynamic?"

"Dylan, don't you dare use that psychobabble on me. I'm your father. I have a right to talk to my daughter."

"People naturally distance when you overpursue."

"A father cannot overpursue his daughter." He covered the phone and said something to someone else. "It's impossible. The daughter is required to respond."

"If you wouldn't pester me so much, I'd probably call you back."

"Why are you being so difficult?"

"It's like a magic formula. You should try it."

"The magic formula is that you should treat your father with respect, Dylan. *You* should try it."

I sighed and sat up, swinging my feet over the edge of the bed.

"Abracadabra, Dad. I'm listening."

"It's about Kellee."

"Is something wrong? Has something happened to the baby?"

"Kellee is receiving the finest prenatal care in the country. Of course, nothing has happened to the baby."

"Dad, prenatal complications are not a personal insult to you."

"Dylan, your mother is having no prenatal complications whatsoever. She has the finest obstetrician in Houston. I have personally seen to it myself that—"

The whir of the ceiling fan suddenly buzzed loudly in my ears as the roots of a headache sprouted and began to crawl up the back of my neck. I rolled my shoulders and closed my eyes.

"Dad, Kellee is not my mother."

"Your stepmother."

"Kellee is not my stepmother."

"What difference does it make?"

"Kellee is your wife. That is all she is to me. My one and only mother died of cancer."

"You're splitting hairs."

"It's not splitting hairs. I'm five years older than she is, Dad. Don't call her my stepmother. It insults Mom's memory."

"You're so prickly."

"Dad, can you please tell me why you woke me up at"—I glanced again at the clock—"6:12 in the morning?"

He cleared his throat. "I need to ask a favor."

Now we were getting somewhere. "Shoot." I began mentally thumbing through my Ready-Made Excuses file.

"Kellee wants you to be in the delivery room with her."

I almost laughed out loud.

"Tell me you're joking."

"I am most certainly not joking. She asked me to personally call you myself and ask you."

"Instead of personally calling me herself and asking me?"

"Why are you so critical, Dylan? You're so critical of every single little thing. You're one of the most critical people I know."

"Thanks, Dad."

"It's a very unattractive trait. I can't stand being around critical people. They're so negative. You're such a downer, Dylan."

The man had all the self-awareness of a jackhammer.

Aspirin. I needed aspirin.

"I'm honored, Dad. I really am." My lying rhythm was coming back. I could feel it sliding into place. "But isn't that your job?"

I waited for him to answer.

"Dad?"

"She says I'll be a liability," he said at last.

I reached for my bathrobe and shoved my feet into my slippers. "And I thought the woman wasn't bright."

"I'm a surgeon!" he shouted. "How could I possibly be a liability in the operating room?"

"Dad, don't take this the wrong way—"

"Oh, here it comes."

"You'd be the worst possible person in the universe to have in the delivery room. You'd yell at Kellee if she did one single thing wrong."

"I certainly would not," he yelled.

"You'd completely take over. You'd boss the OB around. You'd want to do the epidural yourself. It would be a nightmare."

"Well, that's just rich, Dylan. Here I am calling to offer you the highest honor…"

"A Purple Heart?"

"…and you insult me."

"Oh, come on, Dad. Admit it. Patience and nurturing—not your strengths."

"Thank you for your confidence in me, Dylan. I'm touched."

"Is that why she wants me there? To mitigate the 'you' factor?"

He cleared his throat awkwardly. "She thinks you'll have a calming effect. Being a psychologist and all."

I let out a laugh. "Dad, I'm flattered. I really am. But I couldn't possibly. What would I do—carry a pager and hop a plane to Houston when she goes into labor? Besides, the baby's due in July, right?" I reached into my file and whipped out Ready-Made Excuse number 23A. "I'm out of the country for that whole month."

"It must be nice to be able to leave at the drop of the hat for a month at a time. What are they paying you over there at Southern Methodist University, Dylan? I've thought of getting one of those jobs myself, but I'm not sure I could handle the grueling hours. Don't you teach two whole classes every single semester? With the entire summer off?"

"Who's insulting whom, Dad?"

"What am I supposed to tell Kellee, Dylan? She'll be crushed."

"Kellee and I are barely on speaking terms. Why on earth would she want me in the delivery room?"

"I think she wants you to like her."

I groaned inwardly. "I'll work on that, Dad. I really will. I promise." Lie number three. "But I absolutely will not be in the delivery room when your wife delivers her baby."

"Are you sure?"

"I'm quite certain."

He sighed.

"Why don't you ask Guthrie?" I said.

"Your brother? Dylan, have you had an aneurysm? Do you need medical care? Guthrie can't keep his cats fed."

"Well, that's the whole gang, Dad. The entire roster of our dinky little family. I guess you'll have to go off the list."

"Thanks very much, Dylan. I'll keep this conversation in mind next time I need a favor from my daughter."

"Good talking to you, Dad."

The medicine cabinet squeaked as I swung the door open and

screwed the cap off a new bottle of aspirin. I should buy stock in Bayer. Over the years I've consumed vats of the stuff after conversations with my father. Three tablets at a time, washed down with a desperate gulp of water.

I spend a fair amount of time obsessing about my relationship with him. I'd spent my entire childhood waiting for my real father to arrive. You know, the standard-issue kind who mows the lawn and will come fix a flat for you if you have one. The sort of dad who screens his daughter's boyfriends to protect her from all the idiots out there.

Imagine the rude awakening when it dawned on me that my dad, to my mind at least, *is* one of the idiots out there. A man to whom I'd prefer not to give the time of day if we were stuck alone in an elevator in the middle of a terrorist attack.

I'll never forget the moment I first saw him for the man he had become. It was my sixteenth birthday—a milestone birthday, as my mother would say. Sixteen meant a driver's license, a groovy pair of jeans my mom embroidered herself with peace signs and daisies, and a cake with a car key baked inside as a surprise. Waiting in the garage was my new-to-me baby blue VW bus, complete with a working stereo and those wood-bead seat covers. My dad was supposed to bring the key that afternoon before my mom baked the cake. He never showed up. The man actually stood me up for my sweet-sixteen birthday party. Who does that? And not for an emergency heart procedure either—I could have forgiven him for that, if grudgingly. No, the sad truth is, he stood me up for a round of eighteen on the same course he still plays twice a week.

"It was my country-club audition, for crying out loud!" he'd shouted when I challenged him about it. His big chance to impress the committee.

That was the day I knew he'd sold me out. That was the day we became the disposable family.

I got up and put the kettle on, then shuffled over to the rabbit hutches. Eeyore and Melissa were both awake, so I picked them up and took them outside to relieve themselves, keeping an eye on them to guard against the lethal reptile who had taken residence under my back porch.

I turned my face to the sun and sighed, determined to enjoy the cool of the morning, if only for a few moments, before reality set in. Morning sounds are so heartening—sparrow songs and the occasional squawk of a jaybird. No rattles today.

I let the rabbits inside, fixed myself a quick breakfast, changed into shorts and a tank top, and laced up my running shoes. A three-mile run, a hot shower, and a second cup of tea later, I felt almost normal.

Around midmorning, I called my former exterminator, Randy of Randy's Right-Now Rodent Removal.

"I don't do snakes, you realize," he said.

"But you'd know what to do if you saw one, right?"

"Seeing ain't the same as exterminating, if you get my meaning. I got no experience in this area."

"Well, what do you recommend?"

He chuckled. "I'd get myself a garden hoe if I was you."

"What for?"

"Chop that sucker right in half."

I winced. "I don't think I'm up for that."

"Well, it's not my area, ma'am. Good luck to you."

Strike one. My next move was to call my favorite hardware store, Elliott's, which, of course, I should have done in the first place. Going to Elliott's is like going to the mountain. If there's an answer, they know.

"What you need is a Snake Guard Snake Trap," the man said.

"You have them, then?"

"In stock on aisle eleven. I'll set one aside for you. Name?"

"Dylan Foster."

"You might also want to consider a can of Snake-A-Way snake repellent, Miss Foster. Once you get rid of the sucker, you're going to want to create an environment that's inhospitable for creatures of this nature."

"Snake-A-Way will do the trick?"

"Every time."

"Thanks very much. I'll be by this afternoon." I hung up the phone and smiled to myself. The right hardware store can fix almost anything.

The rabbits were scratching at the back door. I got up to let them out again, but stopped in my tracks.

I cocked my head and listened, wishing like mad I was wrong. But there it was. The unmistakable buzz, loud and angry. But this time the rattle wasn't out in the yard, where a snake should be if a snake shows up uninvited. This time it was in my house, my sanctuary.

And it was coming from underneath my kitchen sink.

19

I DON'T KNOW WHAT Peter Terry's obsession is with my kitchen sink, but he has chosen it, apparently, as the front-line headquarters of his little war against me. That's where I was standing when the flies came one at a time and began to dive-bomb me. That's where the infamous rat incident occurred—the one I still have nightmares about. And now that stupid snake was parked under there, rattling away, sending a chill into my bones that could freeze-dry me solid in no time flat.

I'll spare you the details of the previous vermin episodes. Suffice it to say, both the fly and the rat incidents were traumatizing. For me and for them, though they didn't survive the experience, thank the Maker. Now here I was facing yet another plague. Peter Terry must be high-fiving himself about now. He loves this sort of thing.

Maybe the geography was a hint from the Lord. Truth be told, I treat my sink like a sacred shrine in my home. I scrub. I polish. I disinfect. I wipe it out with a soft towel every single time I use it, buffing away every last droplet to avoid leaving even the tiniest water mark. In fact, if I'm willing to be honest with myself, I must admit that I'm possibly guilty of sink worship.

The sad truth is, if I paid as much attention to my soul as I do my sink, I'd probably be a whole lot better off. My sink is pristine. My soul could use a can of Comet and some elbow grease.

Whatever Peter Terry's reason for choosing a plumbed hunk of porcelain to torment me, it was working. I stood there staring at the sink from across the room, positively exploding inside at the thought of a nasty, venomous serpent coiled up behind those cabinet doors, settled in and comfy among my cleaning products.

I couldn't decide whether to vomit or run. Probably I should have done both—in reverse order.

What I did instead was both monumentally stupid and uncharacteristically optimistic. I stalked to the pantry, grabbed a broom, and marched back to the sink.

I realize a broom might seem like an unusual weapon of choice. A shovel or, as Randy the rodent man had aptly suggested, a garden hoe would certainly have been more effective. But I have a long-held secret belief in the power of brooms. Not in the witch-transportation sense, of course. In the consecration sense. If you can sweep something, you can make it better. This is a cornerstone of my obsessive-compulsive philosophy.

Of course, you cannot sweep up a snake. Shoo it, possibly. Poke it, perhaps. But my guess is that if a rattlesnake finds himself in a fight with the business end of a broom, the moron on the other end of the stick would have a fifty–fifty chance, at best. Nevertheless, there I was, clutching my broom, staking my claim.

I flung the cabinet doors open, jumping backward into the kitchen and assuming a martial-arts stance I'd seen in all those female-warrior movies.

The buzzing stopped as soon as the doors swung open. The silence was downright creepy.

Now, anyone even passably familiar with rattlers knows that snakes are not like crickets, who become silent when threatened and wait politely for you to go away. An angry rattler is a loud rattler. The rattling, then, should have intensified when the doors flew open. Not stopped.

I watched for movement, peering into the cabinet from a nice, safe distance, broom poised and ready.

Nothing happened.

As I stared into the space under the sink, it gradually began to dawn on me that there was no room under there for a snake. I'd envisioned a monster of a serpent, its coiled form roughly the size of one of my truck tires. My vision, I realize, was perhaps a teeny bit exaggerated.

Even paring that down significantly, however, there was simply not enough space under my sink to accommodate a reptile of any kind. There were just too many cleaning products in there. The bottles and boxes were all still standing upright (labels forward, sorted by purpose and frequency of use). Not one of them had been disturbed.

My heart still pounding, I tightened my grip on the broom and moved closer, squinting to see inside the cabinet, until I was squatting between the open doors, mentally dividing the territory into grids and searching systematically for scales, a rattle, fangs—anything reptilian at all. I jabbed the broom into the cabinet and knocked over a bottle of Soft Scrub with Bleach (lemon scented, of course), which started a little bowling-pin chain reaction.

I waited. Still no movement. My confidence growing, I began pulling everything out of there, piece by piece—Brillo pads, Comet, Pine-Sol, Pledge. I poked my head inside the now-empty cabinet and looked up at the underside of the sink, then carefully inspected the piping and the corresponding holes in the wood. I'd sealed off all the openings last winter after the rat incident. There was no way anything could have gotten in and out of the cabinet without going through the cabinet doors, and those had been firmly closed. I sat back on my heels.

There was indeed no snake under the sink.

Maybe the sound had somehow been misdirected. Or had I imagined it? What if the whole thing was a big, fat bluff?

Somehow, this last thought triggered more ire than relief.

I replaced the cleaning products, first scrubbing the entire interior of the cabinet with Murphy Oil Soap and then wiping each bottle with a damp towel before I placed it carefully in the appropriate order. Then I opened the rest of the floor-level cabinets and drawers, one by one, fishing around inside each one with my broom handle, knowing even as I did it that there would be no snake there. Finally, I reached on top of the stove for my egg timer, turned the dial, then shut it inside the cabinet and listened to the tick. It was muffled and local. Definitely coming from under the sink, behind the cabinet doors. There was no way the rattling sound had somehow been projected from elsewhere.

The timer dinged like a game-show bell.

The rabbits had scuttled into the bedroom when they heard the rattle but had eventually hopped back into the kitchen. I sat down cross-legged on the floor, chin in my hand, eyebrows furrowed. Both bunnies hopped into my lap and snuggled in. They were clearly shaken and seemed to possess a misguided confidence that I could protect them.

I petted the bunnies and pondered the situation. Which was worse, I wondered—a real snake or some kind of creepo spiritual manifestation? I almost preferred the real thing. At least a flesh-and-blood snake could be trapped and removed. With the Peter Terry version, I could be up against something else entirely.

Which brought me back to the issue of Peter Terry extermination. It was time to address this problem once and for all.

Now, I realize that to most Jesus people like me, anyway, the obvious solution to such a dilemma would be to pray. At least that's the scuttlebutt. But the truth is, I'd done plenty of praying over the past two years about this very thing, and it had gotten me exactly nowhere. Was I praying incorrectly? Without the appropriate surge of faith? Maybe the high-church types were right. Maybe I should be kneeling on a hard floor under stained-glass saints instead of tossing up desperation passes while driving around in a '72 Ford pickup with muffler problems. Would it help to enlist allies? Should I be taking advantage of the thoughtfully provided little golf pencils and begin submitting items on the prayer request cards at church?

My worst fear, of course, was that God had decided that I could use the kind of spanking only a being like Peter Terry could deliver. If that were the case, I was doomed. Straightening up my life or begging for mercy wouldn't do me a bit of good.

I found my Bible and squinted at the concordance in the back. After checking every New Testament passage about demons—there are hardly any in the Old Testament, it turns out—I concluded that life reconstruction was not the answer for this particular predicament. Plenty of nice, decent people in the Bible were targeted by the dark side. They didn't do anything spectacular to deserve it, any more than the ones picked for the good stuff deserved their fate. Lucky and unlucky alike were picked because they got picked, and that was that.

I did not find this to be heartening news. I sat there for a while, staring at stubborn pages of maddeningly small print and growing more irritable by the minute, until finally I realized it was time to employ my secret weapon. The ultimate solution. It was time to go to the library.

Like all academics, I hold a deep reverence for thick, wordy books, for charts and tables and graphs and indexes. A thorough search of the literature, a posited idea, a series of incisive, illuminating questions, and a serious effort to amalgamate the information should propel me forward—or at least help me make some real progress.

If the answers are not at Elliott's or in the Bible, then they are at the library. It's a fact.

I tucked the rabbits into their hutches, securing the screen lids over the aquarium tops to protect them from the lurking serpent—in case it did happen to be the live, rabbit-eating variety. Then I got in my truck and headed out to SMU. I stopped at Elliott's on the way and talked to the man about the surefire Snake Guard Snake Trap, just to hedge my bets. I took one look at the thing and experienced a crushing wave of nausea, followed by a surge of second thoughts.

"I didn't know it was a glue trap," I said.

"Only thing for the job. They crawl right on in there and they're caught 'fore they know it."

I gulped. "I had a bad experience with a glue trap once."

"Get yourself stuck to a rattrap or something?"

"No, the rat did." I tried to scrub my brain of the image.

"That would be the point, ma'am."

"It's so inhumane."

He raised a finger. "Ah. You don't actually want to kill the snake. You want to spare the sucker so it can bother someone else someday."

"Correct."

"How's your nerve?"

"How do you mean?"

"Well, you do have an option with a glue trap. A humane option. But most people are too scared of snakes to give it a shot."

"What is it?"

"Cooking oil," he said triumphantly.

"Pardon?"

"Cooking oil. I recommend corn oil. Or canola is good. Snake crawls in the trap, right? He sticks to the glue, you find him in the morning, you close up the box, right? Then you throw the whole thing in your trunk and drive on out to the Trinity River bottom and open up the box."

"And just leave?"

"No, see, you take the bottle of cooking oil out there with you. You open the box, you douse the snake with cooking oil—oil loosens the glue. Few hours or so, and he'll be good as new."

"You're kidding."

"I never kid about varmints, ma'am."

"Okay. I'll take five."

He raised his eyebrows.

I aimed my best and friendliest "don't say anything" smile at him. "And did you say something about snake repellent?"

"Follow me." He gestured.

I trotted behind him to aisle nineteen. He stopped and picked up a plastic jar, whirled around, and handed it to me like it was a prize. "Snake-A-Way reptile repellent. One hundred percent effective and EPA approved. Keep 'em off your property for good."

"One application?"

"It's best to reapply every few months."

"And that'll do it?"

"Should do the trick, ma'am."

I pointed at the plastic container he held in his hand. It was about the size of a supersized Dr Pepper from McDonald's. "That doesn't seem like very much."

He squinted at the label. "One-point-seven pounds."

"Does it come in a bigger size?"

"It just takes a sprinkle or two, ma'am. This should hold you for a year or so."

"But it does come in larger amounts?"

"Up to twenty-eight pounds, ma'am."

"Great. I'll take one of those."

"Now, that's gonna run you a hundred nineteen dollars plus tax. Not including the price of the traps."

"Sold."

He pushed his hat back. "You got a lot of property?"

"Nope. Just a lot of fear."

He walked me to the checkout stand and scanned the items, then loaded them into my truck as the checker took my credit card. Poor as I am, I smiled as I signed the receipt. Small price to pay to protect my home from serpents into perpetuity. Who knew it would be so easy?

If only Elliott's carried glue traps for demons. I'd happily let Peter Terry squirm and moan in that stinky brown mess of glue. No corn oil for him. Gasoline, maybe. And a match.

I slid behind the wheel and resumed my pilgrimage to the promised land, hitting only a brief little snag as I tried to figure out which library to go to. Fondren Science seemed the obvious choice. All the good snake information would be there, certainly. But I ended up at Bridwell instead, all the way down campus in the theology school. If I was dealing with Peter Terry and his minions, I was going to need more than a scientific understanding of vipers.

A quick scan of the literature showed reams of material—most of it addressing the usual snake lore. Garden of Eden. Satan dressing up as a serpent and leading Eve around by the nose. God showing up and grounding His kids, then cursing the snake to a lifetime on its belly for leading them astray. Jesus's mission to stomp the snake under His heel and rescue us all.

Then there was all the mythical stuff. Once again, the dearth of comparative religion in my theology training nearly skunked me. Four years of sod-busting in seminary had taught me exactly nothing more than what I already knew—in grander proportions, of course, and to near-microscopic levels of minutia. In the end, I got out of there with a solid hermeneutical method, an encyclopedic understanding of dispensational theology, and the ability to conjugate verbs and deconstruct participles in Greek and Hebrew—all notable skills—but without even passable knowledge of anything outside one extremely narrow strip of theological territory.

When it was all said and done, I'd spent four years and a trainload of money to get indoctrinated, not educated. Lousy planning, if you ask me.

I spent several hours poring over basic texts on various world religions, simply to get my bearings. When I finally dug in, I found snakes were crawling all over every single one of them. Aside from the odd snake deity, most of the ancient religions—Greek, Roman, Egyptian, Hindu, Chinese, Muslim—held snakes in extremely low esteem. In fact, just about everyone loathed the little monsters. Unfortunately, no one seemed to have any useful hints for getting rid of them.

I was deep in the middle of the Egyptian Middle Kingdom when my phone rang and jolted me back to my library table and my stacks of books. A beam of sunshine had crawled across the table, lighting up the dust in the air and warming the pages under my fingers. I dug in my bag, avoiding the angry stare of the theology student studying next to me, and checked the caller ID. "Helene?" I whispered, shooting a fake apologetic smile at my accuser. "What's up?"

"Are you in the middle of something?" Her voice was tight. She sounded jumpy.

"Sort of. Why?"

"I just got a call from Lew Sterrett."

"The jail?"

"Yes, the jail. Of course, the jail. What other Lew Sterrett is there?"

"What did they want?"

"Parkland had them call. He'd listed me as next of kin."

"What? Who?"

"John Mulvaney. Who else do you know in Lew Sterrett?"

I felt my skin prickle, the air around me chilling, a familiar sense of dread sneaking its way up my spine.

"Why are they trying to get in touch with John Mulvaney's next of kin?"

"Because he tried to kill himself last night."

20

JOHN MULVANEY HAD FINISHED his evening meal, complete with an extra helping of tapioca pudding, then taken off his jail coveralls and tied the pants around his neck, twisting them so tightly he eventually passed out naked on the concrete floor of his jail cell. As soon as he lost consciousness, of course, his grip had loosened, leaving him with a plum-colored bruise on his neck but very much alive. Why he thought he'd die rather than pass out eludes me. But, of course, that's not the point. The point is that he wanted to check out in the first place.

I hung up the phone and put my head in my hands. In spite of myself, I felt profoundly sad for him. A drop of water plopped onto the page I'd been reading. I looked up, thinking maybe condensation was dripping from the air-conditioning vent, then back down at the page. It took me a second to realize it was a tear. My tear. I'd reached a new low. Crying (in public, no less) over John Mulvaney. What had I become?

I sat there awhile, watching the sunbeam move across the table, trying unsuccessfully to pull myself together so I could finish my research. But too much live-action information was squirming around in my head to allow me to concentrate on the canned kind.

I noted the page in the book I'd been working on, scribbled out a quick summary of my findings, shoved my notebook in my bag, and left.

John Mulvaney had tried to kill himself. Why? Was it relevant to the rest of this mess or just a sick coincidence? I couldn't knit any of it together. It just didn't fit.

I slammed the truck door, started the engine, shuddered, and said out loud, "Will somebody please tell me what's going on? None of it makes any sense." I half expected my phone to ring with the answer, but of course it doesn't work that way.

I turned on the radio to keep myself company and got nothing but static. I twisted the knob, my temper rising with each mark on the AM dial. I finally stuck my head out the window at a traffic light and discovered that my luck was indeed holding. Someone had broken off my antenna. I cursed and clicked the radio off.

As my truck squeaked and moaned, navigating the potholed streets of Harry Hines Boulevard, I took a mental inventory. I needed a new set of shocks, a tune-up, a can of WD-40, and now an antenna.

So, for that matter, did my truck.

I parked in a crummy, tight spot, smack in the hot sunshine, under a ledge populated by a half-dozen fat pigeons. They squabbled for space on the cramped ledge, then settled in and stared at me. I could just feel them eying my hood. I glared back at them for a minute, longing for my childhood BB gun. I needed to blow something away right about now. A flying rat who was preparing to poop on my truck seemed to me to be a perfect candidate.

My shoulders began to tense up as I started the hot trek across the asphalt. We'd all spent too much time at this hospital. I submitted yet another request to the Almighty to release Christine today.

Cold air laced with the foul industrial smells of floor wax and disinfectant blew out of the lobby doors as they slid open, pushing my hair back with a whoosh. I pressed the button for the elevator, then crowded in with the rest of the forlorn parents and friends and stared at the numbers until it was my turn to get off.

Liz and Christine weren't in the room when I got there. I tracked down the charge nurse, who said they'd gone for another test. Christine had developed some complications, she said. She wouldn't tell me what complications she was talking about.

"Blame the federal government," she said. "That HIPAA privacy nonsense has got us all hogtied."

I sat in the Lysol chair and made phone calls.

Molly Larken was first on my list. For some reason, I felt like she should know about John Mulvaney. I left messages at her home and on her mobile.

Maria didn't pick up either. I figured I'd have heard from her if she had any news. But I hadn't talked to her in a while and wanted to check in, at least to let her know I was thinking about her.

I tossed out a pitch to the universe and called David, though I knew there wasn't a gnat's chance he'd pick up. I left him a breezy, "Just thinking of you; hope you're well," message. Maybe if he heard my voice, he'd realize how much he missed me.

I briefly pondered whether or not to put in a call to Ybarra. I knew he wanted me to stay out of his case, but I knew equally well that I had absolutely no intention of doing any such thing. The more I considered the call, though, the more certain I was I shouldn't do it. What would I say? That Christine Zocci was somehow tuned in to Nicholas and was having asthma attacks that weren't really asthma attacks? That the spiritual radar Ybarra thought was nonsense was really quite accurate and seemed to indicate that Nicholas was longing for red Kool-Aid? That the snake represented subterfuge and stolen power? I rolled my eyes and looked around, embarrassed, even though it was just me sitting there.

It took me a few minutes to track down Martinez. He wasn't in his office and didn't pick up his cell phone when I called. He called me back a short time later, though. I was relieved to hear his voice.

"Any news?" I asked.

"A little. HP police ticketed a white Ford Fairlane for using a handicapped spot at the park that day."

"A Fairlane? They stopped making those forever ago, didn't they?"

"Yeah. Sometime in the seventies, I think. Talked to the cop who wrote the ticket. Red leather interior. Cracked. Oxidized paint on the hood. Said he thought about just towing the thing, it was such a wreck."

"You're kidding me. That's got to be the car."

"It was parked at the wrong end of the park—too far away for the guy to have been parked there when he snatched Nicholas."

"What time was the ticket?"

"Four in the afternoon."

"That's right when we got there."

"Maybe he watched for a while, picked his target, moved his car to the other end of the park, and waited."

"So they know the plate number now, right?"

"The plates don't match the make and model of the vehicle."

My heart sank. "Someone switched the plates."

"Looks like it. Plates are registered to a guy over near Harry Hines. Red Chevy truck—2004."

"Did you talk to him?"

"He's clean. He's worked at that Home Depot over on Lemmon for six years. Legal resident from Mexico. Green card, the whole bit. Family man with solid alibi for the time of the disappearance. Clean record— no priors, no known criminal associates. No history of child porn— nothing on his computer at all. He opened it right up for us. He says he reported the vehicle stolen two days before the abduction."

"You checked that out, I assume."

"Yep."

"So. Dead end."

"Right."

"But the car's right, isn't it? It's a white Ford Fairlane? What year?"

"Probably '63. Could be a '64. With stolen plates. We've got every trooper in this state looking for it."

"Let's hope the guy's got a lead foot."

"How's Christine?"

"I don't know. I just got back to the hospital. She and Liz are gone for another test. The nurse said she's had some complications."

"Maria said it's something with her trachea."

"Did she tell you the rest?"

A long pause. "Do you believe it?"

"Do you?"

"I've seen stranger things happen."

"You told me about all those summers you spent with your grand-mother in Mexico."

He chuckled. "Yaya, God rest her soul. Some creepy stuff went down at Yaya's house."

"What would she have done? To find Nicholas? Is there a spell or something?"

"She probably would have called me. She was a pragmatist."

"I talked to Joan Carmichael."

"I knew you would. What did she have to say?"

"Just that Christine probably imagined the snake. Or superimposed it somehow from something she saw."

"I think we all agree on that."

"There's this whole thing about snakes and the human psyche. It's an iconic image. I did a little research today."

"What'd you come up with?"

"People have always associated snakes with evil," I said. "That's the short version."

"So you think Christine saw the evil in this guy."

"That's my theory," I said. "I don't think Nicholas was a random choice."

"I know you don't. But that's the way it's adding up."

"How's Maria? I haven't talked to her today."

"She's holding up okay. Better than I am."

"You know, I forget how close you and Nicholas are."

"I love that kid like my own. We were going to the ball game on Sunday." His voice cracked. He collected himself, then cleared his throat. "When I catch up with the guy…"

"There's a special place in hell, Martinez."

"I intend to help the scumbag arrive, then."

"Painfully," I agreed. "Nicholas is out there," I added. "We'll find him."

"I hope we get there in time."

I winced. "How are our odds at this point?"

"Not too good, Dylan. It's been five days. A lot can happen in five days."

My phone beeped. I checked the number. "I gotta go. Call me if you hear anything."

"You're second on my list."

"Is Maria working today?"

"She's on now, I think."

"Okay. Talk to you later."

I clicked over.

"Hey, Helene."

"Are you trying to commit career suicide?"

"What are you talking about?"

"What time is it?" she asked testily.

I looked at my watch. "Four twenty-five. Why?"

"What time were you supposed to meet Harold?"

"Twelve thirty. But not until Thursday."

"Today is Thursday, Dylan."

"It's Wednesday."

"It's Thursday."

"Are you sure?"

"It's been Thursday all day long. This is a verified fact."

I felt my stomach clutch. "You're joking, right? You're kidding around."

"Why would I joke about this? Harold just called me. He's furious. Just for future reference, Dylan, when a senior colleague—a tenured professor and an endowed chair, I'd like to point out—offers his time and guidance out of sheer generosity, it is unwise to leave him sitting at a sushi bar for an hour by himself. This might seem like fairly basic information, but it is the sort of lesson you seem to have a great deal of trouble digesting." She sighed heavily. "Harold doesn't even like sushi."

I needed Mylanta. Now. "I think I'm going to be sick."

"I do hope you're not fishing for sympathy."

"Don't say fish."

"Fish, fish, fish."

"Harold doesn't get furious, does he? I've never seen him get past mildly annoyed."

"Congratulations are in order, then. You've managed to tip him over the edge."

"I don't know what to say, Helene. I thought today was Wednesday. What should I do?"

"I'd look for groveling opportunities if I were you. And in the meantime," she said, "I'd suggest you start looking for another job."

21

CAREER SUICIDE HADN'T BEEN on my agenda for the day, but with my usual efficiency, I'd managed to squeeze it in anyway. I called Harold at every number I had for him. I left contrite messages, groveling as Helene had recommended, knowing even as I did that it was a vain and inadequate effort. No amount of penitence on my part could possibly clean up a mess of this magnitude.

I sat there for several long minutes just staring at the mottled tile floor. Then I dug in my bag for my notebook, pulled out a pen, and started a list of my Recent Disastrous Failures. I put the Harold debacle first, since it was the freshest and smelliest, then worked my way backward. At the end of the list I wrote David's name, underlined it heavily, then counted the items. I couldn't take the full blame for my lousy relationship with my father but was fully prepared to accept my half. That left me with nine and a half incidents. And that was just off the top of my head.

I leaned my head back onto the Lysol chair and closed my eyes. As though the apocalyptic apprehension I'd been enjoying wasn't enough, now I'd managed to plummet myself into full-on, abject despair.

In this distressed state, there was no way I could just sit around and wait for Liz and Christine to come back. My mental health was no longer a load-bearing structure. My only hope was to keep moving, or the whole thing might collapse.

I stuffed No-Nose in my bag and lit out toward radiology, figuring that was as good a place to start as any. If they were there, I'd be able to follow the screams and find Christine and Liz in short order.

Interestingly, I made the same series of mistakes I'd made the first time, though, of course, I should have known better. Followed the indigo stripe instead of the purple one. Took the quicker elevator on the left rather than the sluggish one on the right, my chronic sense of urgency and legendary lack of forbearance winning out once again over any shred of common sense I might possess.

I was relieved to see that Patrick the gender-ambiguous guard dog was not at his post. In his place stood a fairly fluffy and pleasant-looking woman with a tight black bun, skin the color of Duncan Hines brownies, and a name tag that had a bright yellow happy face on it. I sized her up, checked the tag, and decided to go with one of the techniques a rabid stalker client of mine had used to trick women into falling for him: forced teaming.

"Hi, Bernadette," I said sweetly, as though we were old friends.

"Well, hello now." She stopped what she was doing and beamed at me. "What can I do for you?"

I pasted on a wide-eyed look of innocence. "We've got a little problem."

Her eyes widened a bit. "Do we now?"

"Yes we do. We have a little girl in there right this minute who's having a terrible time of it."

"Is that so?"

"Our little sweetie—she's my niece, actually"—lie number one—"is having a procedure today, and she's just downright terrified." I pulled No-Nose out of my bag and held him out for her to see. "You don't mind if I just nip in real quick and give her a hug and her teddy bear before she goes in, do you?"

She smiled apologetically. "Why no, honey. I'm sorry. I can't let you do that. It's not allowed. You know how that is." She winked at me as though we were just suffering this minor little indignity together, the two of us.

She'd forced-teamed me right back. Bernadette was tougher than she looked.

"Would you like me to give her a message for you?" she said with apparently genuine sympathy. Brilliant move.

"Maybe you could just check the visitors list? I think they might be expecting me. Dr. Dylan Foster?"

"Honey, we got no visitors list up here at this desk today. We're runnin' two hours behind, and those technicians are working so hard, they got no time for such things. You know how that is. I'm just as sorry as I can be."

"Could you just call back there and check? I hate to be any trouble." Lie number two.

"It won't do any good, sweetheart. Why don't you just let me take that on back to her? What's her name?"

"Christine Zocci."

She flipped through several pages on her clipboard. "No one here by that name today."

"Oh. You're sure?"

"Yes, honey. I got the whole list right here in front of me. What's she having done today, darlin'?"

"Um… Dunno."

She shrugged. "I sure don't know what to tell you."

I thanked her for her help and started to leave, then turned and walked quickly back to the desk. "Hey, do you have the lists from previous days also?"

She nodded. "It all goes in the computer."

"My brother-in-law"—lie number three—"was in here the other day. I wonder if you could just check and see if he's still in the hospital anywhere."

"I don't have that record here, but I can call down to patient information for you if you'd like."

"That'd be great."

"Name?"

"Joe Riley. I just want to see what room he's in. I think they might have moved him."

She picked up the phone. "Check-in date?"

"I'm not sure. I know he was here yesterday."

She spoke into the phone, nodded, and said, "I see," a few times, then looked up at me. "No one registered by that name, darlin'."

"So he's checked out, then."

"No, I mean we don't have a patient record for anyone named Joe Riley on that date. You sure you got the name right?"

"Could you check outpatient? Maybe he was just in for the day."

She spoke into the phone again, then shook her head and hung up. "No outpatient record either, honey."

"That's for the entire Parkland system, right? Not just…whichever part I'm standing in right now? Aren't all these buildings connected?"

"That's for the whole caboodle. Maybe you got the wrong hospital, sweetie. Why don't you try calling over to Baylor?"

"I'll do that. I guess I've got some bad luck going today. Thanks for your help."

I put No-Nose back in my bag and walked out slowly, puzzled. I was standing in the hallway, my brain spinning, when my phone rang. I checked the number and sucked in a breath. It was David.

I fluffed my hair, straightened my shoulders, and wet my lips, then waited for the fourth ring before I flipped open my phone.

"Hey, you," I said, wincing even as the words left my mouth.

He paused. " 'Hey, you'?" He let out a laugh. "Hey, you, yourself."

I made a note to shoot myself at the first opportunity. "That sounded incredibly stupid, didn't it?"

"I would say *credibly* stupid. But stupid nonetheless."

I prayed silently to the Good Lord Jesus to let me sink quietly into the floor and disappear forever.

"I can't think of one time," he was saying, "in all the time I've known you, that I've heard you say 'hey, you.' "

"I choked."

"Clearly."

"I'm nervous."

"Why? It's just me."

"I was trying to avoid the whole nickname thing."

"What nickname thing?"

"You want me to call you back and start over?"

"What nickname thing?"

"You know, that thing when you're so close to someone you never use their real name? You always say sweetie or babe or sugar pea or something instead?"

"Ah. The dreaded nickname thing."

"You only use the real name when you're mad. That's the rule."

"You know, I never noticed that."

"All my nicknames for you seemed too…"

"Intimate?"

I sighed. "Just the word I was searching for."

"We *are* intimate, Dylan. We were together a year and a half."

"See what I mean? You just said Dylan."

Another pause. "Point taken."

There was a long, awkward moment of silence.

David, bless his heart, bailed us out. "So…I got your message. Was there a reason you called me? Or were you just hoping to work out the whole nickname thing?"

"A reason. Fair question. I don't have my strategy mapped out, exactly."

"What a surprise."

"Yes, quite a shock, I'm sure. Maybe we could meet later for coffee or something."

"Give you a little time to work on your speech?"

I grinned. The man was absolutely disarming. "I need to go through a couple of drafts, then rework it. You know, do the spit and polish."

"And then there's the test-market process…"

"Exactly. I'll have to run it by my focus group."

"That would be Maria and Liz."

"Christine, mainly. She's the one with the good instincts."

He laughed. "Good call. How is she? I was going to try to get up there today, but I don't think I'm going to make it."

"She's okay. She's had some complications, though. I can't get anyone to tell me anything. All I know is they took her for more tests. I was just trying to track her down."

"Will you let me know?"

"I'd love to tell you in person."

He paused. "You're not going to freak out on me, are you?"

"You mean if we meet or if we don't meet?"

"Either. And please don't freak out because I'm asking you about freaking out. This is going pretty well so far."

"It's a fair question. I'm not taking it personally. Note how calm my tone of voice is."

I heard him chuckle. A good sign.

"I am definitely not going to freak out," I said. "Not if we meet, I promise. And if we don't—well, I guess that wouldn't be your problem, would it? So it's looking to me like a no-risk proposition for you."

"Easy for you to say."

"Oh, come on. Don't make me beg. Be a sport."

"When and where?"

"You busy tonight? I'm asking in a general sense only—not digging for information about your personal life. I'd like that to go in the official record."

"So noted."

"Well, are you? Busy tonight?"

"As it happens, I am. What about tomorrow?"

"Tomorrow will do just fine. Can I take you to supper?"

"I think that might be a little ambitious."

"A drink, then. Or coffee?"

"You don't drink coffee."

"Work with me here."

"I think we should avoid food and beverages entirely. How about we meet at SMU? Are you working tomorrow? I'll be over there anyway."

"At the school?"

"Just in the neighborhood."

For once I held my tongue, reminding myself firmly that it was none of my business what he'd be doing in the neighborhood.

"How about the Meadows?" he said.

"The Meadows? On campus? You are aware that's a museum?"

"And your point would be…"

"Last time we went to a museum, you were insufferable."

"They had a toilet on a platform in the middle of the room."

"It was modern art."

"It was a toilet."

"See? You're a redneck in disguise. I'm not taking you to a museum. Bowling maybe."

"No, really. I'm growing. We can walk around and, you know… look at art. I can improve my mind while you're busy not freaking out."

"I think there's some sort of visiting exhibit. It's supposed to be a big deal."

"Well, then, you're on."

"I'll see if I can snag us free tickets."

"Professor perk?"

"One of the few. Two o'clock?"

"You'll be late."

I feigned indignation. "I will most certainly not be late."

"Okay. You won't be late. See you at two thirty."

"Right. See you then. And David?"

"Yeah?"

"Thanks."

"See you tomorrow, Dylan."

22

I CAME DOWN HARD from my nervous high after my conversation with David and found myself standing in a bustling hallway full of strangers, feeling embarrassed and alone. *Hey, you?* Who had I become? I used to be witty. Interesting. Interest*ed.* I had sharp social skills and an innate ability to connect with people. I was a confident, assertive woman. Not a nervous, giggling simpleton who generates inane remarks in a simple exchange with an ex-boyfriend.

And I had never in my life been afraid of anything. Ever. Not until that ill-fated August day when I met Peter Terry and learned that fear-lessness is almost always based on denial.

Only the ignorant are unafraid.

The crucial error, of course, was that I had ignored my better instincts completely and given that pasty, invasive stranger the time of day in the first place. I should have cold-shouldered him the instant he showed up in the water and stood too close to me—the very second he pushed me to talk to him. I'd known in that moment that he was bad news. And I hadn't listened to myself.

Anyone who won't take no for an answer never, ever deserves a yes.

Idiot, my mind said to me.

"Exactly," I said out loud. "You are a grade-A prime idiot."

I tried Christine's room again and then Liz's cell phone. No answer at either number. On a hunch, I decided to hike the considerable dis-tance to the Parkland main patient-information desk. My feet were blis-tering under the straps of my flip-flops by the time I arrived.

Maybe it was the smell of the film-developing chemicals wafting through radiology that had triggered the impulse. Smells carry power-ful associations with time, place, and memory. Just the smell of canned green beans can knock me back to the lunchroom in my junior high, whether I want to go there or not. Whatever the cause, standing there in the waiting room on the worn, maroon carpet, trying to worm my way back there to see Christine, I had been overcome by a conviction that I needed to find Joe Riley. A man I'd met only once. A man who, at least according to the Parkland Hospital patient records, didn't exist.

The woman behind the desk tapped the keys with her long, pink fingernails and scowled at the computer.

"No Joe Riley," she said triumphantly.

"You checked Joe and Joseph, right?"

"No Joe, no Joseph. I checked four different spellings of Riley."

"Can you see if you have any record of his having checked in at all? Maybe you have a patient record from some other visit?"

"No ma'am. I'm sorry. I can't do that."

"Oh. Why not?" I felt strangely indignant, like I did when I was nine and accidentally slammed my bicycle into a wall.

"I can't go in there and look for just any old Joe Riley ever. Not without an address or a date of birth."

"Why not?"

"Patient confidentiality just doesn't allow for that sort of thing. If you had the DOB or maybe the Social, I could tell you if he *wasn't* here. But I can't tell you if he *was* here. If you get my meaning."

"I'm afraid I don't."

She pulled a Bic out of her bouffant and started on a diagram, complete with circles and arrows and underlined question marks. "See, with Joe Riley being such a common-type name, there could be a dozen or so here in our system. Like this."

She drew a bunch of squares scattered across her paper.

"If I pull up all the Joe Rileys"—frantic circling and underlining—"and you don't have an address or a DOB, I can't tell you who wasn't here, now, can I?" Four question marks in a row.

"I guess not."

"Right. So you understand the problem."

"Got it," I said, though of course I didn't. "No Joe Riley."

She slipped the pen behind her ear with a satisfied smile.

"What about John Mulvaney? Can you tell me if there's a John Mulvaney here? I think he might have been brought in last night."

I spelled the name and she tapped. "John Mulvaney. I can confirm he is here."

"Can you tell me where?"

"Unfortunately, no."

"Why not?"

"Patient confidentiality."

At this point my temper was kicking like a roped colt. I mentally straddled it and wrestled it to the ground.

"But if I step back and call you on my cell phone, you could put me through to his room, right?"

She squinted at the screen. "Unfortunately, no."

I sighed. "Why not?"

"He doesn't have a phone in his room."

"And the room number would be?"

"I'm sorry. I can't say."

I made a mental note to send my congressman a nasty-gram about these inane confidentiality rules, which were making my life unnecessarily difficult. As though I needed any help with that.

"Okay, how about this?" I said. "Isn't the locked psych unit up on eight? They haven't moved it or anything, have they?"

"I believe the eighth floor is where that unit is located," she said, flashing a secret-sharing smile my way.

"So my guess is, if I take a stroll on over to the locked psych unit, I might be able to track down a friend of mine."

"I think that might be a good place to start." She winked at me.

"Great."

I thanked her for her time and had started for the psych unit when Liz rang my cell phone.

"Where are you guys?" I said. "I've been all over the hospital."

"Christine had to get some blood drawn and meet with an infectious disease specialist."

"Why? What's wrong? Did she have another attack?"

"No, she's just dehydrated, I think. She's feverish and a little nauseous. She's got a little rash on her legs. I can't get her to eat anything."

"She was eating fine last night."

"I know. The doctor's wondering if she picked up an infection or something."

"Have you tried a strawberry milk shake? That was all she wanted the other day."

"Good idea. I'll see if I can get them to make her one."

"Are you guys back in the room now?"

"Settling in for another long night."

"Can I bring you anything?"

"Something besides Cheetos and Dr Pepper? Maybe some wine and cheese?"

"You got it."

Parkland is located in an infamously seedy area of Dallas, wedged between I-35 and Harry Hines Boulevard on the west side of town. You can't swing a dead rat in a neighborhood like this without hitting a liquor store. If you're looking for anything from beer to bourbon, you're in the right place. But the finer choices are limited, to say the least. I navigated potholed streets in search of wine in a bottle, not a box—streets populated by hookers looking for work in front of the nasty strip clubs that seem to spring up like mushrooms in this part of town. I finally wandered into a better neighborhood and found a Whole Foods, where I picked up a couple of bottles of Sauvignon blanc—New Zealand, of course—and got the guy behind the counter to recommend a couple of cheeses. I splurged on a set of Riedel wineglasses and picked up a corkscrew while I was at it.

Maria had finished her shift and was sitting in the Lysol chair when I arrived.

"I brought refreshments," I said after I'd hugged everyone. I unpacked my paper sack and set out our impromptu picnic. I'd bought pistachios too, which I divvied up into foam cups for Liz, Maria, and myself.

"You sure you don't want some pistachios?" I said to Christine. "They're the green ones, remember? Nice and salty and real super crunchy. Look." I demonstrated. "You get to break them out of the shell."

She shook her head. Her brown bangs were stuck to her damp forehead, her cheeks pink and feverish. She seemed fussy and uncomfortable, twisting around in her bed and tangling herself up in the sheets. She scratched at her legs.

"You're not hungry, huh?" I said.

She stuck her thumb in her mouth and shook her head no.

"What's her temp, Liz?" Maria asked.

"Hundred and one."

"That seems really high," I said.

"Not for a kid," Maria said. "Their temperature can shoot up pretty easily, especially when they're dehydrated." She turned to Liz. "Has she eaten anything at all today?"

"Nope." She sighed and rubbed her forehead. "They had to put her back on saline. I've been trying all day to get something in her."

"Probably just a bug," Maria said. "They drew blood?"

Liz nodded.

"How did that go?" I said.

Liz rolled her eyes. "How do you think? You were there for the x-ray, remember?"

I sat down beside Christine. "You tired of being in the hospital, sweetie?"

Christine was up on her knees and was digging around in her covers. She looked up at Liz with panic in her eyes. "Where's No-Nose?"

I got up and picked up my bag. "I took him out for a little walk," I said.

Her face twisted. The pink cheeks turned red as she burst into tears. The crying quickly devolved into shrieking. "He doesn't like the dark!" she shouted. She stood up in the bed and held out her arms. "Take him out! Take him out!"

I yanked No-Nose out of my bag and handed him over to Christine.

She grabbed him and clutched him to her chest, sobbing, as she fell back to her knees.

I sat down next to her again and tried to push her hair out of her eyes, but she jerked away. I pulled my hand away quickly, stung. "I'm sorry, sweetie. I didn't know."

I met Liz's eyes and mouthed an apology.

"He seemed pretty happy," I said to Christine. "I just assumed he liked it in there."

"He hates the dark," she whined. "It makes him scared, and he cries, and then he can't breathe."

Liz, Maria, and I looked at one another. It was as though all the air had whooshed out of the room.

Maria's chin began to quiver.

"Has No-Nose been real hot today?" I asked Christine.

She nodded.

"And thirsty?"

"Uh-huh."

"Doesn't he want anything to drink?" Maria said.

She shook her head violently. "No!"

"Why not?" Maria said gently. "I think he'd feel a lot better if he had a milk shake."

"He wants his mommy!" She began to sob again.

Liz shot a glance at Maria, who looked like she'd just been hit in the forehead with a bat. She put her head in her hands, her composure crumbling completely. Her shoulders began to heave as she cried silently.

Liz and I looked at each other and wordlessly divvied up the duties.

I grabbed a Kleenex box, sat on the arm of the Lysol chair, and hugged Maria as she cried it out.

Liz got up and sat down on the bed next to Christine. "It's okay, Punkin. Mommy's right here." She petted No-Nose. "And see? No-Nose has his mommy too. You're right here for him, okay? Settle down. It's okay. Everything's going to be ooookay."

Christine wrapped her arms around her mother and buried her head in Liz's hair.

We sat like that for several minutes until everyone had calmed down. Conversations in the hallway seemed muffled and faraway, as if someone had stuffed the doorway with cotton.

Maria eventually pushed her hair back, blew her nose, and went to the bathroom to wash her face. She came back looking exhausted but determined. She sat down on the bed opposite Liz.

"Christine, sweetie. Are you doing okay?" she asked carefully.

"Uh-huh," Christine mumbled. She lifted her head and wiped her nose on the sleeve of her pink jammies.

Maria touched Christine's forehead. "Have you been real hot all day?"

She nodded.

"And thirsty?"

"Uh-huh."

"Sweetie, do you think Nicholas might be hot and thirsty today?"

"Uh-huh."

"Punkin," I asked, "have you seen Nicholas lately? Like that time you saw him in the closet?"

She nodded.

Maria drew a quick breath. "Do you know where he is? Is he okay?"

Christine mumbled something.

"Speak up, Christine," Liz said. "Miss Maria can't hear what you're saying."

Christine lifted her head from her mother's shoulder. "It was real dark."

"Was he in a real small space, Punkin?" Liz asked.

"Uh-huh. It was all itchy."

We looked at each other. "Itchy?" I asked. "What do you mean? His skin was itchy? Or was he sitting on something that made him itchy?"

"He looked like a snickerdoodle." She wiped her cheeks and looked at me. "Miss Dylan, are you going to make Mr. David some snicker-doodles?"

"Not right now, sweetie." I said.

"But will you?"

"I promise. I'll make him some snickerdoodles. First chance I get."

"What's a snickerdoodle?" Maria asked.

"A sugar cookie," Liz said. "Except with cinnamon sugar." She turned to Christine. "You mean like when you're at the beach? On Lake Michigan? When we used to go to Grandma's house?"

Christine sighed. "I like to do sand angels."

Liz turned to Maria. "When she's at the beach, she rolls in the sand, then says she's a snickerdoodle."

"Is Nicholas sitting on some sand?" Maria asked Christine.

"He looked like a snickerdoodle, and he was all itchy."

"So what do you think?" I said. "Texas coast? Mexico?"

Maria nodded. "Lots of kidnapped kids end up in Mexico. There's a market there. Especially for fair-haired kids."

"I'll call Enrique."

I stepped into the hall and had a brief conversation with the detective.

"I'm not sure Ybarra or the FBI will find this to be credible information," he said.

"But you do, don't you?"

"Any other kid? No."

"But this isn't any other kid. This is Christine."

"I know."

"So what are you going to do?"

He cleared his throat. I could tell he was choking back a truckload of emotions. "You think she could describe anything in more detail?"

"With the right person asking the questions, yeah."

"I'll call you right back."

By the time I got back to the room, Christine was asleep, No-Nose clutched to her chest. Liz had pulled a chair up to the Lysol chair and was sitting knee to knee with Maria, talking quietly.

"What did he say?" Maria asked.

"He said he'd call me right back. Did she say anything else?"

"She said there was carpet and it was bumpy," Liz said.

"What was bumpy? The carpet?"

"What else would she have meant?" Maria asked.

I shrugged. "I'm wondering if she was talking about a bumpy ride. Dark space, small, with carpet, bumpy, maybe with sand."

"Trunk of a car," Maria said.

"Did she say what color carpet?" I asked.

"Black," Liz said.

"Where else would you find black carpet?" I said. "It's got to be the trunk of a car."

"That doesn't help us much," Maria said. "It means he's still being moved around."

"Enrique said they've got a lead on the car," I said.

My phone buzzed. Maria filled Liz in about the white Ford Fairlane while I stepped outside and took the call from Martinez.

"I'm bringing over a sketch artist," he said. "We'll be there in about half an hour."

"Christine's asleep," I said. "You might want to wait a little while."

"You think she's down for the night?"

I checked my watch. "I doubt it. It's only six. She's just tired from crying and from the fever. She hasn't eaten anything today."

"Can you wake her up in an hour or so and get some food in her? I can hold the artist off for a little while."

"I'll see what I can do."

"Just do it," he said. "I don't want to put this off until tomorrow."

23

WE SPENT THE NEXT hour listening to Christine breathe and looking through the pad of paper she'd been coloring on. Most of her drawings were unremarkable. Lots of flowers and stick-figure people. A kitty cat here and there. Lots of little purple bunnies.

She'd drawn several snakes, but that could have been because she and I had talked about snakes while she was coloring and working on her *s*'s. She'd spelled *snake* over and over on the page she'd been working on that day.

After that first, long, squiggly snake, she'd drawn the rest in two distinct configurations. The full-bodied ones were all in the same circular shape—similar to an "at" sign, with the head in the center of the coil. Each of these she drew in red. The other image was a face-only image of a diamond-shaped head, face forward, fangs bared, with a circle inside its open mouth. These images she'd done in greens and purples, leaving the circle white. The effect was highly stylized, almost primitive.

"What's the circle mean?" Maria asked.

"I have no idea," I said. "Nobody recognizes the image? It's so deliberate."

"I don't think she's ever seen a snake before. Maybe at the zoo," Liz said. "She's never drawn anything like that. It's creepy."

I picked up the book and stared at the image. "I was in the library today researching snakes as symbols in ancient religions."

"Sounds like loads of fun," Maria said wryly.

"I ran across probably a hundred images of snakes from different religions, different times in history. It reminds me of a few of those, but it's not quite the same."

"Did any of the snakes have anything in their mouths?" Maria asked.

"Not that I remember. It looks like a hieroglyph or something."

"Can you research it, Dylan?" Maria asked.

"I'm happy to poke around. But there are zillions of ancient symbols floating around out there, so I wouldn't hold my breath if I were you. There could be someone at the theology school who would know. I'll ask around." I folded the snake pages and tucked them into my bag.

Maria checked her watch. "It's a quarter of seven. Should we wake her up?"

"Let's get her another milk shake," Liz said.

"I'll go," said Maria. "I need to stretch my legs."

As she left the room, Liz stood and leaned over the bed and kissed Christine on the cheek.

Christine woke slowly with a yawn, stretching her arms, her back arching. Her fever seemed to have broken. The sweat was gone from her forehead, and her cheeks looked plump and pink. She reached down and scratched her leg lazily.

"Feeling better, Punkin?" I asked.

She nodded and stuck her thumb in her mouth.

"Ready for something to eat?" Liz asked. "How about a strawberry milk shake?"

Christine nodded again.

Maria returned with the milk shake, and Christine drank it eagerly, sucking hard on the straw and breathing through her nose, like a nursing baby. Liz's color came back at the same rate the milk shake disappeared.

Martinez showed up at seven thirty with a woman who looked like a truck-stop waitress—or maybe a professional ballroom dancer. Her hair was too black and too tall, her skin too pink with too much makeup, her lips painted an orange red. Her black spandex outfit was stretched onto her busty form like a latex glove. Martinez nodded at us. "Everyone, this is Venice."

I raised my eyebrows. "Venice?"

She smacked her gum. "I'm Italian," which she pronounced "eye-talian."

She shooed us out of her workspace and began a magical, whispered conversation with Christine, their heads almost touching as she asked one question after another, all the while moving her pencil across her sketch pad. She tsked occasionally, then switched pencils and continued drawing in quick strokes and long, fluid lines, flipping the page and starting in on a blank sheet almost without pause. Two hours later, Christine fell into an exhausted sleep, and we all crowded around the sketches.

They were remarkable. Clear, precise. Elegant in form and utterly simple. Not one extra stroke clouded the essence of the images. Yet she'd captured Nicholas as though she'd photographed him. The sweet face, the huge eyes, his small, little-boy frame. And that wild, curly hair.

Christine had described her dreams to Venice. Nicholas curled into a tight ball inside a dark space sprinkled with sand, his Cowboys jersey ripped at the numbers, sand stuck to his bare legs. Nicholas crouching in a closet, small and alone among the shirt sleeves and cowboy boots, his arms clutched tightly around his legs, his forehead resting on his knees.

The images shocked us all into numb acceptance of ugly reality. Maria couldn't look at them. A quick glance only, and she turned and walked into the hall. We saw her pacing back and forth outside the door, arms crossed, head down, as we hunched over the sketch pad, firing questions at Venice.

"Were these the only scenes she described?" Martinez asked. "Just these two?"

"She mentioned a bed and a kitchen table, but she couldn't describe either one. I couldn't get enough detail out of her to be sure of the accuracy."

"But she did suggest he wasn't spending all his time in a closet? Was there a bed in a larger room?" I asked.

"She couldn't say," she said. "These were the two images she had real clear in her head, so these are the ones I did."

Martinez sat back in his chair. "Did she describe anything else? Temperature of the room? How long it took to get there? How much time he spent in the space with the sand in it?"

"I do stills, Detective, not movies. Two dimensions only."

"What's this?" Liz asked, pointing at the closet sketch.

"She said he had a gun with him," Venice said.

"She said it was his gun?" Liz asked.

"She was real clear it was his gun, not anybody else's."

I felt my breath catch. He'd hung on to his gun.

"Good for you, Nicholas," I said under my breath.

"Did she say what the sandy space was?" Liz asked. "Was it the trunk of a car?"

"I got the feeling it might be." She pointed at a detail on the edge of the drawing. "This sounded like it might be jumper cables. She said long, thick wire with pinchers on the ends."

I picked up the other sketch. "All the clothes in this closet are men's clothes," I said. "Was she specific about that, or were you just putting in filler?"

"I don't put in filler," Venice said sharply. "She said shirts. I said shirts like your mommy wears or like your daddy wears? She said shirts like her daddy wears, but yuckier, with squares on them. And big tall boots like a cowboy wears. So I drew yucky men's plaid shirts and tall cowboy boots. Just like she said. She was real clear about that." She picked up the drawing. "See here? She said boots with two colors and one pair with metal tips. Real mean-looking, she said. So I drew mean-looking two-tone boots with metal tips."

"What about the rest of the stuff in the closet?" Martinez said. "What's this jersey hanging here?"

"She said a tank top with numbers on it. She saw a three, so I drew a three. And she said the letters *SH,* so that's what I put there. See how it's hanging between other shirts? You wouldn't be able to see the whole thing."

"Team jersey?" I asked Martinez.

"Gotta be. Looks like a basketball jersey."

"You can't see the logo, though," Liz said. "It could be from any team."

"Or just some team down at the Y. Maybe the guy plays basketball for fun," Martinez said.

"Anyone out snatching kids does not play team sports," I said flatly. They all looked at me.

"I'm not kidding. He might watch basketball on TV, but he does not play a team sport, I guarantee you. This guy is not a team player. He doesn't have the social skills. He has no friends to speak of, no peers. He's a loner."

"What are you, just profiling him? Out of general knowledge?" Martinez asked.

"Sociopaths, especially ones who abuse children, do not have age-appropriate relationships," I said.

"What makes you think Nicholas is being abused?" Martinez said. "That's an assumption."

"Kidnapping is an abuse of power. I don't know if he's sexually abusing him. I'm not saying that. I'm saying normal people with healthy relationships do not snatch kids from parks and keep them from their mothers."

"You're right about that," Martinez said.

"Plus, if the guy has friends, why haven't we heard from any of them? A guy's on a basketball team, people are going to notice something's weird with him. I don't think he'd be able to snatch a kid and keep him hidden without it affecting his behavior in some obvious way."

"People might notice something weird without putting it together with a kidnapping," Liz said.

"I think Dylan's got a point," Martinez said. "Local kidnapping with a well-publicized description of the car. Guy starts acting squirrelly, he fits the description. Someone would have called."

"And look what's in his closet," I said. "See any tennis shoes? Any sports equipment? I see ratty collared shirts and cowboy boots."

"Did you get a sketch of the suspect?" Martinez asked.

She flipped to a new page. "Might want to call the mom back in. She'll want to get a good look at him. They always do."

Martinez found Maria, who had pulled herself together once again. Her expression was steely as Venice sorted through several sketches of Nicholas's captor.

"She wasn't as sure about him. I did a few different versions." Venice found the one she wanted. "She picked this one."

You could feel our collective loathing, our rage, billow and fill the room as we all studied the drawing. The man's face was thin and sallow, with a scrubby shadow of a beard, thin lips, and small, hollow eyes. He could have been thirty or sixty. His features were weathered, worn by time, hardship, or both. His hair was thin and short, shaved close to his head.

"Did she say anything about a snake?" I asked.

"She said he had a snake on his head," Venice said. "I couldn't get nothing else out of her about that. I drew him with long hair, bald with a snake tattoo, a hat, dreads, everything I could come up with. I finally gave up and just eighty-sixed the hair. I can't account for that feature, that snake thing. I got no idea what she saw."

"So the hair?" Martinez asked.

Venice shook her head. "I can't say what kind of hair he has. I don't think it was an obvious feature, or she'd have said it. She's a pretty observant kid. I think this is a decent guess."

"This guy looks white," Martinez said. "She didn't tell you he was black?"

"She did say at first he was black, but then it came out that she meant black like mean and evil, not like black skin. Thin lips, light eyes? I think the man's got to be white. Most likely, anyway. Could be Latino."

"He looks like a druggie to me," I said. "This is not someone who eats organic and drinks bottled water."

"Dude's a smoker," Martinez said. "And a junkie."

Liz peered at the drawing. "How do you know?"

I pointed. "Look how thin his face is, how hollow his eyes are. That's heroin."

"Could be meth," Martinez said.

I gestured toward his cheeks. "And he's undernourished. Junkies don't eat."

"Look at the lines around his mouth," Martinez said. "That's the smoking, Liz. Probably since he was a kid."

"I can't believe you guys can get all that from a drawing," Liz said.

"If we had his prints, I could tell you whether it was heroin or meth," Martinez said.

"How?" I asked.

"Meth users have burn scars on their fingertips. Shows up in their prints."

I looked at Maria. She was pale, her face still, her eyes fixed on the image.

"You okay?" I asked.

She nodded.

"Collared shirt," Venice was saying. "No T-shirt underneath. Skinny neck, like you see here. Sort of sinewy. I got the impression he was average height. Hard to tell with a child witness. Everyone looks tall to them." She erased a small stray mark. "But skinny. She said his jeans were dirty and baggy. I just did the face. Nothing about the clothes was distinctive. Plus, it's been so long since she saw him."

"Shoes?" Martinez asked.

"Cowboy boots."

"Who would wear cowboy boots to abduct a child?" I said.

"What would you wear?" Liz asked. "I can't imagine fashion would be much of a decision when you got up that morning."

"He'd need to run," Martinez said. "You wouldn't wear boots if you were going to have to run."

"You'd wear sneakers or something," I said. "Something you could move in."

"She was sure about the boots?" Martinez asked Venice.

"Yep."

Martinez and I looked at each other.

"Amateur, maybe," I said.

Martinez nodded. "Could be his first time. Maybe he didn't think it through."

"Maybe it was impulsive," Maria said. "Maybe he didn't plan to do it."

"It's possible," Martinez said. "If that's the case, he's going to make a mistake sooner or later. Guy doesn't know what he's doing. He's inexperienced. Hiding a kid is no simple matter."

"Do you think Nicholas is still alive?" Maria asked suddenly.

"I do," I said. "Christine would know if he'd been hurt. I'm positive. She's having these dreams because he's out there somewhere."

Martinez gestured toward the sketch. "Is this the man you saw on the soccer field?" he asked me.

"I don't think so. That guy blended in with the soccer crowd. I doubt this guy could have pulled that off. Besides, the clothes are wrong. The guy on the field was wearing shorts and a white knit shirt."

"How about the age? Younger? Older?"

I picked up the sketch and examined it. "I can't tell how old this guy is. The man I saw was stronger looking. And sort of ageless. Not particularly healthy, come to think of it. Pale. But not like this. He didn't look nearly so…damaged."

"Do you think Christine's description was accurate?" Martinez asked Venice. "I mean of the guy. The face."

"I'd say it's pretty close," Venice said. "Seventy, eighty percent, maybe."

"So we're good to put this out there?" Martinez asked Venice.

"That's your job, Detective." She tore out the pages and handed them to him. "I've done mine."

24
~

I SAT IN MY truck in the Children's Medical Center parking lot for a good, long while that night, just staring out my windshield at the pigeon guano that was splattered all over my hood—a scatological Jackson Pollock painting. My hands were numb as I gripped the steering wheel, my mind fixed on the image of the man who had taken Nicholas. His face was everywhere I looked, the way a flashbulb leaves behind a blue silhouette when you close your eyes.

I don't know why I was surprised by the hatred I felt toward him. I think I'd expected it to feel more clinical than personal. I thought I'd see the picture and file it into the evidence folder and then get out there and start looking for him. Instead, I felt a wave of rage that confused and distracted me. I wanted to see that man suffer. I wanted to be there, personally, when something terrible happened to him. I wanted to hear his screams and watch him feel pain, and I wanted it to last a long, long time.

It scared me how much I hated him. I didn't want to think about what that might say about me.

I started my truck, the familiar rumble nagging me to schedule that tune-up. I reached for the radio and turned the knob, then remembered about the antenna. My hand fell to my lap as the cab of the truck filled with the sound of static. For some reason, I started to cry.

The parking lot was almost empty. It was late—almost eleven by now. I had plenty of privacy to sit there and blubber like a child in my '72 Ford pickup, doors locked, windows open. As though it made any sense at all to sit in this part of town with the windows open at night. As though the locks would help if the windows were down. But the warm night air was a comfort after another day of unrelenting tension and excessive air conditioning.

I dug in my bag for a Kleenex and blew my nose. The truck lurched as I released the brake, pressed my foot down on the clutch, and threw the transmission into reverse. I turned to look behind me, then felt a chill crawl up the back of my neck.

I cocked my head, listening, hoping I was wrong. But there it was. The buzz. The snake was here. Somewhere in the truck. With me.

I threw my shoulder against the door and jumped out of the truck, forgetting momentarily that I'd already put the transmission in gear. The engine belched with a jerk and rumbled to an abrupt stop. Then the truck began to roll slowly backward out of the parking space. I hopped into the cab and set the emergency brake, then jumped back out without shutting the door and stared at the truck, my chest heaving, sucking in deep breaths of hot, sulfury night air.

I was at a complete loss. What do you do when there's a snake somewhere in your pickup truck? Do you call animal control? The police? Is there someone who will come and just shoot the beast? Do we have people who do that? I looked around frantically and spotted a man in a uniform standing near the lot's exit gate, about thirty yards away.

"Excuse me!" I shouted. I began running toward him. "Can you help me? Please help me!"

He turned and bolted in my direction, moving with the agility of a running back, and met up with me under a bright fluorescent light. I checked the embroidery on his blue uniform. His name was Jeffrey, and he was a Parkland security guard.

"You ran," I said. "I can't believe you ran. Thank you so much!"

He unsnapped the walkie-talkie from his belt. "Are you in danger, ma'am?"

"Not the kind you're used to," I said, panting. "Do you have a gun or anything?"

"What's the problem, ma'am? Can we start with that?"

"There's a rattlesnake in my truck. How's that for a problem? I don't know what to do."

He blinked. "Are you sure? How do you know?"

"I heard it."

"But you didn't see it?"

"Have you ever heard a rattlesnake in person, Jeffrey? It's not really a matter of opinion."

I followed behind him as he strode toward my truck—obviously the scene of the trouble, backed as it was halfway out of the space, door standing wide open, dome light shining weakly.

We stopped a couple of yards away. I held my breath.

"I don't hear anything," he said at last.

We inched closer. No rattle. I reached over gingerly and jiggled the door, sure the noisy hinges would set the varmint off. But still no sound.

"Maybe it got out." I bent down and looked underneath the truck, then stood and scanned the lot, surveying for possible snake hiding places.

"I don't see anywhere it could have gone," he said, his eyes following mine. "Lot's empty. No trees, no grass." He looked around. "What are you doing parked way out here in Oklahoma? A woman really should park a little closer in."

I rolled my eyes. "You have no idea. Believe me, I tried. I got here…" When did I get here? I couldn't remember. "…forever ago. This was the only empty spot."

He pointed at my hood. "I see you've met our pigeons."

We both looked up at the ledge, the thought occurring to us simultaneously. There they were, feathers puffed out, sleeping with their heads tucked underneath their wings.

"I guess the pigeons didn't hear the rattler, huh?" he said, doubt creeping into his voice.

"That doesn't make any sense, does it?"

"No ma'am."

"They would have flown off, wouldn't they?"

"I would, if I were a pigeon." He pulled his flashlight off his belt and shined it up at them. "You sure you heard a snake?"

"I've had a rattler at my house the last few days," I said. "I keep hearing it, but I never do see it. Maybe it crawled under the hood of the truck when the engine was warm. Don't they do that sometimes?"

"How long did you say you've been here?"

"I don't know. Hours."

"And you believe a snake stayed in your engine all the way from— you drove here from where?"

"I live in Oak Lawn. About fifteen minutes from here."

"So a snake stays in your engine block from Oak Lawn to Children's Medical Center. That's fifteen minutes, no traffic. Then it sticks around for several hours waiting for a ride home?"

I could feel my expression tightening, the muscles of my neck starting to contract. The rage was back, rising up inside me and taking over what was left of my brain. I wasn't mad at Jeffrey, of course. He was merely pointing out the obvious. I was mad at the lousy rotten fink who had gotten me into this mess.

Peter Terry. The skunk. He loves embarrassing me.

"Sounds pretty implausible, huh?" I said.

"Afraid so."

"So what do you suggest?"

"Let's pop the hood."

We gave the truck a thorough going-over. We looked in the wheel wells and checked behind all the tires, in the bed of the truck, under the spare. We checked every cranny under the hood, Jeffrey shining his flashlight around and humoring me as I pointed at places I wanted him to illuminate. Bless his soul, he even stretched out on the hard ground and scooted himself under the truck for a look at the undercarriage.

Naturally, we found no snake.

He dusted himself off and shone the flashlight back into the bed of the truck, illuminating my newly purchased antisnake gear. "Looks like he doesn't stand a chance if you find him."

I shrugged. "I like to be prepared."

He switched off his light and wished me luck. I thanked him profusely and prayed once again to disappear into the pavement. Once again, the Almighty stamped "DENIED" on my application.

I drove home in a cloud of radio static and white-hot anger, giving in at last to the brutish day and to the long, agonizing disaster of this week.

My house was dark and lifeless when I got home. I unlocked the door, threw my stuff down, and went back out the front door to get the mail. The bulb shattered as I flipped the porch light on, startling me just about out of my skin and fraying the last of my nerves.

I stood there for a second, forcing myself to stay calm, then turned and walked back into the house, glass crunching under my feet. My house is well supplied, of course, so I opened the door to the garage and flipped the light switch. The bulb burst with a flash and a loud pop. Glass sprinkled to the concrete floor.

Standing frozen in the doorway, I counted to a hundred, concentrating on each number, determined to manage the panic—the panic that I knew was the object of the game. I absolutely refused to give Peter Terry the satisfaction.

Using a pair of pliers I found in my truck, I wriggled the shattered bulb out of the socket. Then I pulled a box of bulbs off the shelf, screwed a new one into the socket, and flipped the switch. The warm yellow glow of a 60-watt GE Bug Lite filled the garage.

I turned off the light and went back through the house to the front door, where I pulled another Bug Lite out of the box, repeated the procedure, and screwed it into the socket. It exploded in the next moment—the switch was still on—and I let fly a string of cuss words that would embarrass a sailor. (Another one of my Top Ten Terrible Traits.)

I took a deep breath and was grateful, for once, to be alone in the world. Better that than inflict my foul temper and even fouler mouth on any innocent bystanders. I sat down on the porch steps and stared up at the night sky.

I hate city lights for obscuring the stars. Someone should shut the place down after midnight, just to give city kids a fair shot at seeing the universe once in a while.

Squinting at the dim points of light, I searched for my favorite constellation, Orion the hunter. It reassures me somehow to see him up there, with his belt and his weapons all geared up for some ancient clash of grand celestial combat.

I couldn't make him out tonight. Probably too late in the year. I sighed, feeling strangely abandoned.

Peter Terry was here. I knew it as surely as I knew my own name. The bulb thing was obvious. That was his style—vandalism with a creep-out factor. But the rest of it—the snake, Christine's strange symptoms, Nicholas's disappearance—you could choke a horse with all the evil in the air.

I sat there a long time, for once appropriately reverent, my attention turned toward the heavens, where I knew the answers lay. It occurred to me to pray, so I prayed for Nicholas, for Christine, for Liz and Maria. And for myself. It took the edge off the tension, if nothing else. In the end, I felt a little less forsaken. Though at this point, I'd just about convinced myself the cavalry would never arrive.

A good half hour passed before I stood and surveyed the damage. I had to hand it to Peter Terry. He got points from me for creativity. On his last visit, he'd vandalized my water heater, which I thought was a pretty innovative way to ruin somebody's peace of mind. Days of frustration, frigid water, blue-toed showers, inadequate laundry facilities. Not to mention a sizable bill from Paulie's Pretty-Quick Plumbing Repair.

There was one more bulb in the box. I decided to make one last stand and see if I could end the day with a victory. I stood tiptoe on my front porch and reached for the socket with my pliers, thought better of it and checked to make sure the switch was off, then wriggled the base of the shattered bulb out of the socket. It took a few minutes, but I wrenched it out of there, screwed the new bulb in and flipped the light on.

The bulb blew up in a cloud of smoke and sparks, glass tinkling delicately as it landed on the porch around my feet.

"Nice touch," I said out loud, and I walked back into the house and locked the door firmly behind me.

25

ALL THE LIGHTS INSIDE the house worked. I was grateful for that much. Sometimes Jesus just gives me a little present. Maybe God had posted sentries at the doors and windows or something.

The rabbits were restless. I couldn't tell if it was because they'd been alone for so long or because they were afraid of the snake. Whatever it was, they kicked and squirmed when I picked them up. They scuttled under the bed as soon as they hit the floor, then refused to eat anything until I made them a little picnic on my bed and let them munch up there in relative safety.

While they dined on their crunchy food, I unloaded my five new snake traps and my twenty-eight-pound tub of Snake-A-Way from the bed of my truck and began placing the traps strategically around my yard. One under the front porch, one under the back porch, one beside the back gate (as though a snake would bother with a gate), one in the garage, and one under the hood of my truck—just in case.

The lid of the Snake-A-Way snake repellent had apparently been sealed with concrete. I broke two fingernails and a screwdriver before I budged the thing. I scooped out a cupful and walked the perimeter of my house and backyard, sprinkling as I went, my peace of mind blossoming as I moved. I felt better somehow, hedging my bets. I sprinkled the garage, returned the cup to the tub, hammered the cap back on, and got ready for bed. I decided to leave the glass on the porch for later. I'd dealt with enough messes today.

I slept like a stone that night, the sentries guarding, perhaps, my peace of mind as well as my doors and windows. I needed the sleep badly and woke up feeling rested for the first time in days.

After a quick breakfast, I sliced some apples for the rabbits, then walked the perimeter of my house, checking my snake traps. They were empty, as I knew they would be, though one had attracted a number of fire ants, which were now entombed in the brown, smelly glue. That left a phone call to the hospital on my morning to-do list—all was well—and I was out the door for the pool, looking forward to a long swim.

I settled quickly into a good rhythm and had finished my first mile when a group of college kids started doing cannonballs into one of the lap lanes. The lifeguard blew his whistle and kicked them out. I waved a thanks and was poised to push off the wall when I realized I recognized the face. I knew that kid.

I peeled off my swim cap and dunked my hair in the water, then hiked myself out of the pool, wrapped up in my towel, and walked to the lifeguard stand.

"Gavin," I said, craning my neck and squinting against the sun.

"Professor Foster!"

He hopped off his chair and was down the ladder in two big steps, standing in front of me, his bare chest tanned and smooth, with big Hawaiian flowers on the swim trunks skimming his knees. His hair—dyed a bright yellow blond but black at the roots—stuck out everywhere. An ankh gleamed on a leather rope around his neck.

"That was you in lane four? You have a pretty stroke."

I blushed, embarrassed that he'd been watching me. "It may be pretty, but it's slow. I'm just back in the pool the last week or so. I've been out of the water for a while." I pulled my towel tighter around me. I felt awkward standing in front of a student in my bathing suit, hair dripping. "I didn't know you were lifeguarding here."

"Hey, good sun, bikinis…" He grinned and gestured around the pool. "And hardly any little kids to yell at. Easiest summer money there is."

"You look great," I said. "How are you? I haven't seen you since… what, December before last?"

"Yeah, thanks for the C," he said, laughing. "I bombed the final. Thought I'd flunked the class."

"I get generous around the holidays. Don't tell anyone," I said. "Besides, you'd had a tough semester. I figured you could use the break."

He nodded. "Yeah, tough semester." He shifted his feet awkwardly and crossed his arms.

"Sorry. I didn't mean to embarrass you."

"No, that's okay. I just don't like to think about it. I don't have too many fond memories of the loony bin."

I smiled at him. "We call it an 'inpatient psychiatric unit.'"

"You can say inpatient whatever. I say loony bin."

"You're doing okay, though, huh?"

"Doing great."

"Are you still in touch with the DeStefanos? Did you know they're in Guatemala now?"

"I'm housesitting for them."

"You're kidding! That's great. I'm surprised they kept their house. I thought they were gone for good."

"It's just until it sells. It's a slow market, I guess. Or something. I was there all semester."

I pointed at the necklace. "I'd forgotten you wore an ankh. Was it a gift?"

"My mom gave it to me. The day before she died. For luck."

"I didn't know your mom was dead."

"She died my freshman year of high school."

"Oh. I'm sorry."

There was an awkward silence, which I decided to plug with a little fair-play self-disclosure, just to even things up. "My mom died a few years ago too. Cancer. It was awful. I'm still not over it. It's hard to watch someone deteriorate like that."

I watched him consider whether to tell me more about himself. "My mom wasn't sick. It was kind of sudden."

"Was it an accident?"

"You could say that."

I pursed my lips, unsure what to say next.

He saved me the trouble. "She overdosed." He said it bluntly, without emotion.

"Oh. I'm sorry." I was batting a thousand bringing up awkward subjects.

He shrugged. "She had a lot of problems."

"It was intentional, then?"

"I think that's why she gave me the necklace. She knew she was taking off. She said it would keep me safe."

I felt a surge of adrenaline shoot through my body. "What did she mean by that?"

"She was kind of a nut." He smiled and glanced away. "Obviously."

I shook my head. "I'm sorry, Gavin. I didn't know."

He shrugged again. "No worries. It was a long time ago."

I took a breath. "Well, it was good to see you. I'm sure I'll see you again soon. I'm determined to spend as much time as possible in the pool this summer." I slapped my thigh. "I turned thirty-five this year. Things are starting to slide south on me."

He grinned. "You don't look a day over thirty-four."

"Thanks. You're a real pal."

We said our good-byes, and I walked back to my lane, hopped into the pool, and pushed off the wall, my mind spinning.

Gavin had been a student of mine a couple of years ago. The two of us had wound up in an odd tangle with the dark side after Gavin found himself in Peter Terry's target zone. He'd almost lost his battle. I'd arranged for him to stay with the DeStefanos—to keep him safe, come to think of it. But he'd tried to hang himself in Tony's bathroom and done a little time at one of the local psychiatric hospitals.

The DeStefanos are good people, though. They'd apparently stuck with him, and today he looked whole and healthy.

I finished my swim and said good-bye again to Gavin, who promised to keep in touch, then I showered, changed, and walked across campus to Bridwell Library.

The reference librarian pulled some books from the shelves and then helped me haul a stack of them to the study area, where I settled into my favorite spot. The sun had already started moving across the table as I cracked open the first book.

I had two missions today. The snake, of course. I had to find out about the snake. I pulled Christine's papers from my bag, unfolded the pages, and smoothed them onto the table.

My second mission was to find out how the ankh fit in. Not that I was certain it did. It's just that it tended to show up when Peter Terry came around.

On his last visit, ankhs had appeared in the graffiti-like art of a murdered co-ed and in the weird mythology of her nutty psychic mother, Brigid, who had given the girl an ankh on a chain to wear around her neck for protection. I'd also discovered it stamped on the back of a necklace I'd received the day I first met Peter Terry.

And now Gavin was wearing one. An ankh his mother had given him. To keep him safe.

If I remembered correctly, Joe Riley had also worn an ankh on a thin chain underneath his hospital gown that day in the radiology lab. It hadn't seemed like a big deal at the time. But since he'd become the incredible disappearing man, it had taken on an eerie significance.

I'd spent some time studying ankhs last winter. They turned out to be an ancient symbol of protection, of life, and of immortality, and the mark of an apocryphal being named Anael—possibly an angel—whose name I'd never heard before. I'd turned up a little dirt on him, but not much. Michael, Gabriel, and Lucifer are the only celestial beings actually named in the Bible. The rest of the angel lore comes from questionable sources, at best. I'd waded through hundreds of years of speculation and pieced together some odd bits of information—just enough to make me wonder if Peter Terry could be Anael in disguise.

The protection thing confused me. Were ankhs good or bad, angelic or demonic? The whole mess was just a jumble of guesses stuck together like a big wad of gum.

As the beam of sunlight made its way across the table, I searched every reference I could find that listed ankhs and snakes in the same volume. Those wacky Egyptians, not surprisingly, were crazy about both. Many of the pharaohs—who believed, of course, that they themselves were gods—had incorporated the symbol in their names. Steve Martin's fave, Tut*ankh*amen, for instance. Interestingly, the pharaohs often wore crowns with snakes on them—to keep them safe, it turns out. Apparently a snake is an asset when it's on your side.

I struck out on finding anything resembling the snake with the circle in its mouth. I checked every reference on the table, but by the end of it my stomach was growling and I had the distinct feeling I was running around the wrong tree. I closed up the books, tucked Christine's art into my purse, and left. I needed food—and some time to practice my greetings before my big meeting with David. He'd be getting no more "Hey, yous" out of me.

I grabbed a sandwich at my favorite sub place across the street from campus. The picnic tables outside were empty, so I sat at one, ate my sandwich and chips, and drank my Dr Pepper, reveling in the heat of a Dallas summer afternoon. Why must buildings in Texas be so cold in the summertime?

While I was at it, I caught up on phone calls and checked in with Liz and Christine. Good news on that front—the fever was gone, and they were discharging her that afternoon. I left a few more groveling messages for Harold, then dug around in my bag for the card with Molly Larken's number on it. I'd forgotten until now that she'd never returned my call.

I hate it when people subject you to endless rounds of phone tag without coughing up the reason for the call. It reinforces my already-concrete resistance to calling them back. I liked Molly too much to do that to either one of us. I left her the full message—the brief but sordid tale of John Mulvaney's continuing demise—and suggested she call me back if she wanted to. I figured, she's an adult. She knows how to use those little numbers on her phone.

I spent the rest of the hour planning my strategy, writing out as many witty greetings as I could think of. It was a slim list, but anything was better than "Hey, you." At precisely ten minutes to two, I bused my table, washed my hands, glossed my lips, brushed my hair, and marched myself right over to the Meadows Museum of Art, squaring my shoulders for a meeting I was certain would determine my romantic destiny. My mission, which I had chosen to accept, was to get my boyfriend back.

It was Operation Get That Guy. I was locked and loaded.

26

As I walked across the green, shaded lawn through the center of campus, past the museum's huge, outdoor, kinetic, wavelike sculpture, up the steps past Claes Oldenburg's weeping Geometric Mouse and the crouching lumps of bronze that flanked the doors to the museum, I could feel my brain emptying itself of intelligence. One by one, all my cogent thoughts leaked out onto the St. Augustine grass, replaced by dull, cottony space bound by thick, wiry tension. By the time David walked up and hugged me—looking delicious and wearing that blasted Italian cologne—I'd forgotten my entire script. Every single word.

"Hey, you," he said, grinning wickedly.

I shot him a quick wave.

"Hi…there."

He stepped back and held up his hands in mock consternation. "'Hi there'? I thought you were going to work something up."

I moaned. "I choked again. It's so humiliating. Wait a minute." I held up a finger and fished in my bag for the notes I'd made during lunch, then unfolded the paper and cleared my throat. "Okay. Here's what I came up with. I've got, 'Hey, sweet man.' 'Hey, handsome.' 'Hey, good-looking'—obviously without the 'whatcha got cooking' part. 'Hey, former sugar pie'…"

"'Former'? How did that happen? Once a sugar pie, always a sugar pie. I thought that was the rule. I mean, absent the commission of some crime against humanity."

"Unfortunately, you forfeited your sugar-pie status when you resigned from being *my* sugar pie."

"Gyp!"

"I'd like to remind you that this was your choice, Mr. Shykovsky. You're, of course, still a sugar pie, generically speaking, but you'll not get a 'sugar pie' out of me until you reapply. Of course, that involves a committee interview, references…"

He pursed his lips, holding back a grin. "Fair enough. What else have you got?"

"That's pretty much it. Variations of *hey, hi,* and *hello.* The all-purpose, generic 'How's it going?' It's a sad list, really. Representing an embarrassing lack of creativity."

"Yet an admirable attempt to manage the nickname thing. Let's call it a victory. Did you get the tickets?"

I waved them at him. "Two tickets to the Caravaggio exhibit." I checked the museum poster beside the information desk. "It's up on the second floor, I think."

"Who's Caravaggio?" David asked.

"Some Italian. Let's walk."

We handed over our tickets and climbed the stairs toward the buttery daylight filtering in from above. We passed a sculpture of three naked women.

"Someone should put clothes on them," David said.

"The fraternities usually do. At least once a year they all end up wearing nightgowns or bras or something."

We paused to study a painting here and there, walking awkwardly side by side. It was as if neither of us knew what to say or what to do with our arms. Normally, of course, we'd have been holding hands, laughing at the naked paintings, cracking jokes, people-watching.

I pointed at the gallery across the hall. "That's the permanent collection over there. Spanish art. It's, like, a specialty. We'll do those next. Just to expand your small-town mind."

He winced. "Will it hurt?"

"Hopefully."

"I thought all the big bananas were Italian."

"They are—except the ones who are Dutch, French, English, Spanish…"

"Funny. You're very funny. If SMU is into Spanish, why are they renting space to the Italian guy?"

"Maybe he's got an uncle in the mob or something. His uncle Vito got him a showing."

David squinted at the little card beside a painting. "Says here he died in 1610."

"Okay, his nephew."

We walked slowly, still awkwardly, strolling at art-gallery speed, passing huge canvases and tiny pencil drawings, almost all of which were of religious scenes.

David stopped and stared at a painting. "Now that guy's having a tough day." He leaned in to read the card. *"The Crucifixion of St. Peter."* He stepped back. "Bible Peter, right?"

"I do believe it's Bible Peter, yes."

David whistled. "Saints have the worst gig."

I nodded. "Lots of torture and maiming."

"Who are the dudes tying him down?"

"Romans, I would assume. Probably speaking to him in British accents."

"Just like on TV."

I pointed at the image. "See how the cross is tilted? I think they crucified him upside down."

"Ouch." He nodded at another canvas. "Look at that dude."

We crossed the gallery, passing paintings of saints suffering wildly divergent variations of torment and misery, and looked at the card. *"The Beheading of John the Baptist,"* I read.

David shuddered. "At least it's quicker than crucifixion." He scanned the room. "Where are the happy paintings? Look at that." He gestured across the gallery. "Another beheading."

"What did you expect? Bunnies and puppies?"

"This is uplifting, Dylan. I'm really glad we came here."

"So much for your growth spurt."

He crossed his arms and sighed. "Who called this meeting, anyway? Does anyone have a copy of the agenda?"

I gestured toward the bench in the center of the gallery. "Let's sit."

"Is it time for the speeches?" he asked.

"It's time for mine. I didn't know you'd prepared a statement."

"I got a couple of them in the can, should the occasion present itself."

I took a breath and squared off in front of him. "The thing is, David…"

"It's almost never good news when someone starts a sentence with 'the thing is.' "

"Stop interrupting. I need to work up some speed."

"Sorry."

"The thing is, we have this chemistry."

"I can't argue with that."

"It's not just the usual romantic kind. It's this cerebral situation…"

"The repartee."

"I mean, it's like we share the same brain or something."

"That's unsettling."

"You know what I mean."

"I do."

"Don't you miss it?"

"Of course I do."

"Don't you miss me?"

He sighed and reached for my hands. I looked down at our intertwined fingers. David has great hands. They're strong and masculine but not too calloused or rough. Gentle hands. But hands that know how to run a chain saw.

"Dylan," he said. "I'd be lying if I said I didn't. I miss you every day." He cocked his head and thought about it. "Okay, at least every other day." He winked.

I concentrated on maintaining my composure. I didn't want to get all fluttery just because David Shykovsky was holding my hands for the first time in…forever. My fingers were tingling.

"I miss your hilarious phone messages that go on for days," he was saying. "I miss duct taping parts together on that awful truck you drive. I miss the way your hair falls on your shoulders, the way you always walk like you're in a hurry. I miss the way you smell—a subtle mix of expensive bath soap and Tide with Bleach."

I wagged a finger at him. "Bleach Alternative."

"Right, Bleach Alternative. Mountain Spring scent, if I remember correctly."

"Actually, I switched. I use Clean Breeze scent now."

"You wacky thing, you."

"I like to shake things up."

He looked down at his hands and rubbed mine with his thumbs. "I miss your weird, obsessive habits. The incessant scrubbing and polishing and alphabetizing. I still can't walk down the cleaning products aisle at Safeway without tearing up. I get a whiff of Pine-Sol, and I feel like someone punched me in the chest."

I allowed myself a brief surge of optimism, which, as usual, turned out to be a catastrophic error.

He met my eyes, the unspoken apology hanging in the air between us. "But I don't miss the rest of it. I really don't."

"Which part is that?"

"The part where I'm getting the short end of your life. The part where you're always running off to God knows where to put out some inferno with your squirt gun."

"Oh." I could feel my face fall. "That part." I took a breath and let it sink in. "Quite a letdown after that run of missing-me details. A girl could wait her whole life for a man to talk to her like that." I noted with alarm that my chin had begun to quiver. I was determined to maintain a small measure of self-respect before I crawled home to self-immolate.

"Don't give me too much credit. Most men are preverbal, as you know. Grunts and gestures. Not much competition."

"Stop being so funny. I'm trying to hate you here."

"I do think about those things, Dylan. I think about all the Italian food we've eaten and how mad you get when I talk during movies. How fun it is to haul you onto the dance floor after you've knocked yourself out at work and to make you forget every single minute of your day."

"I always thought it was such a fair fight, David. Do you know how rare that is?"

"I asked you out the day I met you, remember? You're the one who never seemed to understand the value."

"I do now."

"Do you really think anything's changed?" he asked. "Because from my chair, it's only gotten worse. I mean, the things you say to me sometimes…"

I began mentally scheduling my self-immolation. With a little juggling, I could work it in this afternoon.

As David listed my recent transgressions, my eye wandered to the gallery behind him. The painting on the opposite wall gradually came into focus.

"What is it with the snakes?" I said aloud, interrupting him in midlist.

"You're not listening to me."

"I am listening. It's just that—"

"What did I just say?"

"That I have a long way to go."

"And then you started talking about snakes. Out of the blue. Like I'm not even talking. Are you trying to prove my point for me?"

"But look." I stood and gestured for him to follow me, which he did reluctantly. We walked through the doorway into the next gallery, straight toward the enormous painting on the opposite wall.

David stood back and stared quizzically. "Who's the kid?"

I leaned in and checked the card. "*Madonna with Serpent.* It's Mary holding Jesus, and that other woman is…maybe her mother or something." I pointed. "Look. He's stepping on the snake. I mean, her foot is technically the one on the snake, but—"

"Right. They're letting a naked kid stomp on the head of a snake.

That should get you a child protective services file. Someone should call 911. Why am I supposed to care about this, Dylan?"

"You're missing the point. She's *helping* Him step on the snake."

"This is exactly what I'm—"

"David, listen to me."

I told him the snake stories from recent days.

"I think you're reaching," he said at the end of it.

"But Nicholas…"

He grabbed my arms. "…was kidnapped by some sicko. A human sicko. Not some weird spiritual stalker."

I shook off his grip and stepped back.

"I'm sorry, Dylan. I—"

"David, I'm not making this stuff up. I've heard that snake in my house. And in my car. Christine says she saw one on the kidnapper. And there's this whole thing about snakes and evil—"

"But what does that mean, she saw a snake? That makes no sense. She's six. She was confused."

I pulled the papers out of my bag. "This is what she's been drawing since she got sick." I handed them to him and traced the images with my fingers. "See? This coiled one, over and over. And then this one—" I switched the pages. "It's got this circle in its mouth. I went all over ancient religious literature looking for this symbol, and I can't find it anywhere, but I'm positive it's—"

"The Diamondbacks, Dylan."

I blinked. "What? What's that?"

"It's a baseball team. That's their logo."

I snatched the paper out of his hands and peered at the page. "So that thing in the middle is a—"

"A baseball. What did you think it was?"

"I thought it was some ancient hieroglyph or something."

"Academics are so weird." He looked around. "We should be at a baseball game today. It's gorgeous outside, and we're standing in a building with no windows looking at these gory four-hundred-year-old pictures."

"Is there a basketball team too?"

"The Suns."

"With the same logo?"

"Not the same logo. The same town."

I grabbed his arm, my excitement rising. "Is there someone on the basketball team whose name ends with *sh* and whose jersey number ends in three?"

"Steve Nash. Number 13. Point guard. Great floor vision."

"What's that?"

"Floor vision? It means he can see the whole floor. He gets the big picture. Never gets lost in the details. Great assists. Real team player. He always knows—"

I interrupted him. "The Diamondbacks and the Suns. Where? Where are these teams?"

"Phoenix."

"Arizona?"

"Yes. Phoenix, Arizona."

27

I WAS ON THE phone to Martinez in my next breath.

"It was a baseball cap, then," Martinez said. "She saw the logo on the cap."

"The guy I saw in the car was wearing a baseball cap."

"Remember the color?"

"I think it was black. Dark, anyway."

I heard him tapping computer keys. "Looking through the Diamondbacks' sports memorabilia Web site… There it is. Black cap with the green and purple logo. Snake with the ball in its mouth."

"What about the other one? The coiled one."

"That's the other version of the logo. The new one, I guess. It's red. Red on black."

"That's what she drew, Enrique. They're all red."

David motioned that he was going to walk around. I signaled for him to wait. But he was gone the next time I looked up.

"It doesn't mean anything, Dylan," Martinez was saying.

"How can you say that? What are the odds?"

"No. I mean, it doesn't help us."

"Why not?"

"Guy's a fan, doesn't mean he lives in Phoenix. Do you know how many fans those two teams have around the world?"

"But the sand… And she said it was hot—"

"It's summer, Dylan, for crying out loud. It's hot everywhere. You think Phoenix has a lock on sand? Pick a beach. Pick a sandbox. We can't go running an investigation based on the nightmares of a six-year-old kid."

"She gave us a good sketch, Enrique. She gave us a picture of the guy."

"I realize that. And I believe her. I do. But the possible sighting of a Phoenix Diamondbacks baseball cap by a six-year-old is not evidence. It's one little piece, and it may be the wrong piece. You don't turn an investigation on information like this."

"So what are you going to do?"

He sighed heavily and swore in Spanish. "Call Ybarra. And get every cop in the Phoenix Police Department looking for that white car."

I hung up the phone and looked around for David. He wasn't in any of the second floor galleries, so I went downstairs and walked the rest of the building. I finally found him sitting on the steps outside the museum, his face to the sun, elbows on his knees, fingers interlaced, staring out at the trees.

I sat down next to him.

"What'd he say?" he asked.

"He doesn't think it's important."

"Bet that went over like a hearse at a birthday party."

"Mortuary joke. Nice touch."

He didn't say anything.

I put my hand on his shoulder. "Talk to me."

He glanced at me out of the corner of his eye, then looked back down at his hands. I saw a tear fall to the pavement.

He shook his head, wiped both eyes, then looked up at me.

"I miss you, Dylan. I really do. But I think I miss you more when we're together than I do when we're apart."

"What's that supposed to mean?"

He clenched his jaw. "I can't do it, Dylan. I can't be last on your list."

"I'll burn my list and make a new one. David, give us another chance. Give *me* another chance."

A breeze fluttered through the live oak trees on the lawn, blowing spent leaves up onto the steps. David picked one up and twirled the stem between his fingers.

"Come on," I said. "I think we owe ourselves that much. There's too much here to throw away."

He dropped the leaf, watched it flutter all the way to the ground, then stood up. "I'll call you."

"Is that like 'don't call me, I'll call you'? Or like 'let me think about it, and I'll call you and let you know'?"

He considered. "B."

"Really? You'll think about it?"

He nodded.

"How hard are you willing to think about it? Do you mean you're sort of letting it back into the realm of distant possibility for vague, future consideration? Or are you talking about hard-core study?"

"B."

He held out his hand and helped me up. "Where are you parked?"

"Pool."

"I'm downstairs in the parking garage."

"So. See you later?"

"I'll call you."

He drew me in for a long, close hug. I breathed in his cologne, wishing I could stand there with my head on his chest and his arms around me forever. Instead, I stepped back and smiled at him.

"Thanks for meeting me," he said.

"You're welcome."

"Time well spent."

"Let's hope so."

"Bye, Dylan."

"Take care, David."

"Don't you mean, 'Take care, you'?"

I smirked at him. "Funny. You're very funny."

I sat back down on the steps of the museum, enjoying the breeze and the feeling of sun on my face, and went back over the entire conversation in my mind. I thought it had gone pretty well, considering the fact that groveling is clearly not my strength. We'd had some nice connection.

Plenty of mutual respect. A fair measure of mutual honesty. Not too brutal, but honest nonetheless. David had been reasonably receptive. More receptive than I'd anticipated, certainly.

I scored myself fairly highly, considering I was working against my natural weaknesses. I'd been reasonably polite and self-effacing without sinking into pathos. I'd limited the whining. Avoided begging altogether. I'd resisted the urge to go for it when I saw him weakening. Played it soft. Given him plenty of space. Even the dismount had been pretty clean.

I gave myself an extra half point for resisting the urge to grab him around the neck and burst into tears. All in all, a solid performance— seven-point-five on a ten-point scale, with an extra bonus point for degree of difficulty. Final score: eight-point-five. I decided to take advantage of the beautiful day and walk up the tree-lined avenue to my office. I needed to pick up mail and check messages. I was also hoping Harold might be in today. I'd already gotten a head start on my groveling. I figured I might as well complete the cycle of misery while I was warmed up.

Harold was indeed in his office. I knocked tentatively, knowing that the closed door meant he didn't want to be disturbed. I was already on his blacklist. I figured I had nothing to lose.

The door flew open. "What?" he said. Then, realizing it was me, "Oh. My dear Dr. Foster. What an"—he looked up, searching for a word—"surprise."

"Go on. Pick an adjective. *Unpleasant? Unfortunate?*"

"Unexpected," he said, stepping back and inviting me in. "That's redundant, though, isn't it? All surprises are unexpected. Nevertheless, it's always a delight to see you."

"Liar." I sat in the "student" chair across from his desk, not my usual "colleague" perch on the puffy leather couch in the seating area.

He obliged and seated himself behind his desk, picking up a pen and twirling it between his fingers like a baton.

"Where'd you learn to do that?" I asked.

"The pen? A nine-year-old taught me."

"A patient?"

"My big sister. I was seven." He shrugged. "My mom worked. I learned to smoke cigarettes that year too."

"And you still remember?"

"I never forget anything. It's a curse."

"Does that mean you can't forget my transgression?"

He winced. "Weak transition, Dylan. I expect better from you."

"I'm so sorry, Harold. I truly am. I can't believe I did that. I just...thought it was Wednesday."

I resisted the urge to blather and waited for the upbraiding I deserved. But he merely nodded, pope-like. "You're forgiven, my dear."

I waited for him to say more. He didn't.

"It's that simple?" I asked.

"Not quite. There's still the matter of your review."

"You're not going to hold this against me, are you?"

"Of course not. That would be improper. Unethical. And mean."

I exhaled, finally. "Thank you."

"But the review looms nonetheless. Are you prepared?"

"I will be."

He flipped open his calendar. "A week from today. Today is Friday, I believe." He looked up at me mischievously. "Correct?"

"Correct."

"Can you make four o'clock? Here in my office."

"You're still willing to help me?"

He looked at me over his glasses. "I believe it's called grace, isn't it? Isn't that the theological concept?"

I nodded. "Unmerited favor."

"We want you to succeed, Dylan. In spite of your many faults, you do bring a certain *joie de vivre* to an otherwise lackluster department." He looked me up and down. "The purple shoes, for instance."

I looked down at my flip-flops. Purple with daisies on them. "Thank you, Harold. I think."

"You're quite welcome." He stood and ushered me out. "I'll see you on Friday, my dear."

"Friday. Four o'clock. And Harold?"

"Yes, Dylan?"

"I owe you one."

He winked. "Indeed you do."

28

IT SEEMED AGES SINCE I'd been at the hospital—a relief I could barely allow myself to enjoy, knowing Liz had hardly seen daylight all week. As I walked through the double doors, steeling myself against the cold, I realized I'd grown accustomed to the sour smell of disinfectant—a fact I took to be a very bad sign. Hospital disinfectant doesn't exactly exude that fresh-as-a-summer-day smell I shoot for in my house. I inhaled and grimaced. You'd think with all that emphasis on cleanliness, they'd pick better cleaning products.

Christine's room was empty when I arrived. No Liz, no Christine, no flowers, no balloons, no crayons. I asked at the nurses' station where they'd moved her. A nurse informed me Christine had been released. I put in a quick call to Liz. She and Christine had just arrived at the hotel. She'd convinced Christine to stay there tonight, but Christine had insisted on coming to the house this evening for a bunny visit. We agreed on a time and hung up.

I longed to leave the hospital, but my conscience tugged at me. After a few moments of thumb wrestling with myself, I relented and made the hike to the psych unit and pushed the button beside the heavy steel door. A loud click and an orderly stuck his head out.

"I'm Dr. Foster. I'd like to speak to John Mulvaney. He came in Wednesday night."

"You his shrink?"

"Yep." How many lies was that today?

"ID?"

I handed him my driver's license. He disappeared for a minute, then swung the door open and let me in. I knew the drill. The orderly had already checked my name against the list to verify my hospital privileges. He handed my ID to the person behind the sign-in desk. I watched as she wrote down my vitals and handed the ID back to me. She pointed to a blank line on the sign-in sheet. "First initial and last name only, please."

"Mine?"

"Patient's."

I dutifully wrote "J. Mulvaney," then handed over my bag to the security guard, passed through the metal detector, and followed the orderly across squeaky floors all the way down to the end of the hall. The man was slim and dignified, with skin so black it was almost blue and an accent I couldn't identify.

"He's in isolation," the orderly said over his shoulder.

"Because he's a prisoner?"

"And the suicide watch."

"Still?"

"He tried again this morning, or he would be back in jail by now." He glanced back at me. "You used to work here, didn't you?"

"Yeah. A while ago. There's so much turnover here, I'm surprised you remember me."

"You bought me a Coke one day."

"Me?"

"I was out of quarters."

I followed behind him in silence.

"What did he do?" I said at last.

"Mulvaney? Cut his wrists."

"With what?"

"Paper clip. Found it on the floor."

"Superficial, then?"

He nodded. "Couple of deep ones. Took a few stitches."

"Is he being medicated?"

He shrugged.

"You think I could take a look at his chart?"

"Of course. I'll bring it down to you."

He took out a set of keys, opened another metal door to another hallway, and led me down the corridor, stopping midway down and showing me into a little room on the left furnished only with a table and two chairs. I raised my eyebrows with the silent question.

He shook his head. "No civilians allowed in the prisoners' rooms."

"Oh. I've never dealt with prisoners before. So I should..."

"Wait here. I'll be right back." His keys jangled as he left. Keys are the ultimate sign of power in a psych hospital.

I tapped my fingers on the desk. The fluorescents buzzed overhead, reminding me of flies and rattlesnakes and light bulbs.

A few minutes passed before I heard the jangling again. The key slid into the lock, the door swung open, and in stepped the orderly, a uniformed guard, and someone who looked a little like John Mulvaney.

The patient wore pink scrubs, his scraggly blond chest hair peeking out from the V in the shirt. The shirt wasn't quite long enough to obscure the puffy white belly that hung over the elastic waistband of the scrubs—no drawstrings allowed on suicide watch. No shoestrings, either. Instead, he wore dirty socks and his prison loafers—orange canvas Keds that were a tiny bit too big for him and flapped on the floor as he shuffled in with his hands cuffed in front of him.

His thin, brownish-blond hair was matted and sticking out in all directions. His face was gray, his beard showing several days' neglect. An ugly purple bruise circled his neck, and his wrists were bandaged underneath the cuffs. A nickel-sized blot of blood showed on the underside of his right wrist.

I stood to greet him. No hug, of course. But a measure of some familiarity and respect seemed in order.

"Hi, John. It's, um, good to see you."

He mumbled something unintelligible.

The guard looked at me. "You want him cuffed or uncuffed?"

"Take them off. Please."

He stuck his key in the lock and freed John's hands. John looked sideways with vague contempt in his eyes.

I pulled out a chair. "Here, John. Have a seat. You look like you might be tired."

John glanced at me dully and sat down. The chair squeaked under his weight. I pulled out the other chair and sat across from him.

The orderly left. The guard parked himself beside the door, just inside the room, and left the door open a few inches.

"Would it be possible for us to have some privacy?" I asked.

He pointed at a camera hanging in one corner. "No such thing."

"Do you need to stay inside the room?"

"Yes ma'am. It's for your safety."

I looked at John and then dropped my eyes, embarrassed for him. He seemed unruffled. He had obviously become accustomed to the indignities of life in jail.

The guard stepped back and assumed a stance that indicated he intended to tune us out. He gazed at the ceiling, hands crossed in front of him.

"Well," I said to John. "I'm not sure where to start. How are you?"

He looked up at me, meeting my eyes with a steady gaze—perhaps for the first time ever in the years I'd known him.

"How do you think I am?"

"Not great. That would be my guess. Not great."

He slouched in his chair, looking down at the bandages on his wrists.

There was a knock, and the orderly walked in the door with a file under one arm and a cold Coke in his hand. He popped it open for me, set the file on the table, winked, and left.

I pulled up the chart. "Do you mind?" I asked John. He shook his head no.

I pushed the Coke across the table to him. He stared at it hungrily, clearly debating whether to accept the gesture, then reached for it, tipped it back, and took a long drink.

I flipped open the chart and found a detailed intake describing his condition on admission. He'd arrived at the hospital unconscious and unclothed, the bruise already purpling on his neck. They'd revived him, pumped his stomach just in case, put him in a set of scrubs, and locked him in a room. As far as I could see, they'd run no tests to determine the extent, if any, of brain injury which might have occurred while he was depriving himself of oxygen. No medications were listed.

"Are they giving you anything, John?"

He shrugged. "Dunno."

"They haven't given you any pills to swallow?"

"Dunno."

I studied him, sizing up the grim expression, the hunched shoulders, the apathy.

"John, do you know who I am?"

"Dr. Foster."

"Do you know what day it is?"

"Dunno."

"Do you know where you are?"

"Parkland, I guess."

Two for three. I could understand the miss on the time question. There were no windows in here. I saw no clock in the room, and I figured he didn't have one in his room either. He'd arrived at the hospital unconscious. He couldn't possibly know what day it was.

"Do you remember how we know each other?"

"SMU." He mumbled something else.

"Pardon?" I leaned toward him. "I didn't hear you."

"Why are you here?"

"I heard you were having a rough time." I gestured toward his neck. "Helene called me."

"How did she know?"

"I guess you listed her as next of kin."

He nodded and looked down at his hands again.

"Do you want to talk about it?" I asked tentatively.

"About what?"

"Um...about the fact that you tried to kill yourself. Want to tell me about it?"

"Not really."

"John, you're depressed. I mean, severely depressed. I think it might help to talk."

He met my eyes again. "What difference does it make? I'll still be here."

"I know. But—"

"Do you know what happened to my mice?"

"Your mice? You mean the ones in your lab?"

He nodded.

"I think they caught them all." An easy lie. I didn't want to upset him. "They gave them back to the guy you bought them from."

"And my research?"

"I assume it's just like you left it. Boxed up somewhere. I don't think they've reassigned your office or anything. I haven't been down there."

He scratched his head and stared into space.

"Is it bad in here?" I asked tentatively. John could barely survive the rigors of normal life, he was so socially handicapped. I couldn't imagine what jail had done to him.

He nodded. A tear slid down his face.

"Do you have a good lawyer?"

He shrugged. "I don't see her much."

"Tell me her name, and I'll give her a call for you, okay?"

He looked up at me. "You will?"

"Sure. I'd be happy to. And anyone else you want me to call. Just give me a list."

He told me his lawyer's name. I dug a notebook out of my bag and wrote it down.

"Have they set a trial date?" I asked.

"Dunno."

"They don't tell you much, do they?"

"Nuh-uh."

I tapped my fingers on the table and looked around the room. I'd just about run out of niceties. What do you chat about with a person who's in jail awaiting trial and who has recently tried to kill himself? Appropriate topics eluded me.

"Listen, John. While I'm here…"

He glanced up.

"...I wanted to ask you about your blog."

"What blog?"

"The blog you have online." What other kind of blog was there?

He looked at me blankly. "I don't have a blog."

"I think the address is DoctorBehindBars. I saw it, John. You don't have to lie."

He pounded his fist on the table, startling me backward and bringing the guard another step into the room, his hand on his weapon.

"I'm not lying!" John shouted.

My eyes widened at the sudden burst of temper. I'd seen that rage once before. It was easy to forget about, obscured as it was behind his slow, lumbering demeanor.

"But, John, I saw the blog." I held my hand out to indicate I expected him to hold his temper. "It has pictures of you. Pictures of SMU. Details of your career."

"I don't know what you're talking about."

"John, you're lying."

The fist hit the table again.

"One more time, and you're back in isolation," the guard said quietly.

I looked up at the guard and shook my head. "It's okay."

"I'm not lying," John said quietly.

"I talked to Molly Larken, John."

"Who's that?"

"Molly Larken. The student you mentioned in your blog."

"I never heard of her."

My eyes narrowed.

"Red hair? Looks a lot like me?"

He met my eyes again. How many times in one conversation? Surely a record.

"I never heard of her."

"In the blog, you called her your muse."

His face twisted in anger. "Does that sound like something I would say?"

I stopped and thought about it. Bless my soul, it didn't.

"I don't have a computer," he said.

"Someone from outside the prison would have to be maintaining it."

"I don't know anyone."

"And you don't know Molly Larken?"

He looked up again. "I don't know any students."

Now, that had to be true. John had never bothered to learn his students' names. Even in his labs, when he might have had only a few students for an entire semester, he just didn't care enough about them to bother.

"What else does it say?" he mumbled.

"That you're innocent."

He glanced at the guard. "Maybe I am."

"John, I was there when—"

The fist slammed on the table again. More blood began to show on his wrist.

"That's it," the guard said. He took out the cuffs.

"Could you just give us another minute?" I asked. "I think I can handle it."

He looked at John, then back at me. He stepped back and pointed at John. "You watch it."

I took a deep breath. "Will you take some medication if I can get your doctor to prescribe it?"

"No."

"Why not?"

"What's the point?"

"John, you can't live like this. Do you see yourself? You're falling apart."

"What's the point?"

"Look, I know it seems hopeless."

"You don't know what it's like," he said quietly.

I sat back in my chair. "I don't, do I?"

He shook his head.

I stood up. "I'm going to talk to him anyway. I wish you'd consider taking something. I think it would help. You deserve to feel better than this."

"You don't know what I deserve," he said, his teeth clenched. The hatred in his voice stunned me.

His blue eyes were watery. "Don't come back."

I took a step backward, the power of his anger pushing me toward the wall.

I held up my hands. "Okay. If that's what you want, I won't come back."

"Good."

He hung his head while the guard cuffed him and led him to the door.

"Bye, John. Take care of yourself. I'll talk to the doctor for you." I held up my notebook. "And your lawyer. ASAP."

John glared at me again.

I took a step away from him.

He turned his back to me and shuffled out of the room without looking back.

29

By the time I got back to my house, Liz and Christine were parked in front, waiting for me. I greeted them with a ridiculous level of enthusiasm. I was so glad to see Christine back out in the world again.

"How ya feeling, Punkin?" I asked, leaning down to her eye level.

She shrugged unenthusiastically. "Pretty good."

"You ready to see Eeyore?"

Her face broke into a wide smile. "Did he miss me?"

"He missed you tons. Let's go see what he has to say."

I could tell something was wrong as soon as I unlocked the door. The house just felt lifeless to me.

As we stepped inside, Liz cocked her head. "What's that sound?"

"I don't hear anything."

"It's in the kitchen."

As we walked down the hall, I heard it too. A high, steady beep.

I turned around. "It's the carbon monoxide alarm. Get Christine out of the house."

Liz turned and hustled her back out to the front yard. I ran around the house throwing open doors and windows, pulled the monitor out of the socket, grabbed some batteries, and went out to the yard.

"Sometimes it goes off because the batteries are dead," I said to Liz. "If it goes off again after I change them, we'll know it's real."

"What do we do then?"

I shrugged. "Call 911?"

"But what about Eeyore and Melissa?" Christine whined.

I handed Liz the batteries and the carbon monoxide unit. "I'll go get them. I bet they can't wait to see you."

I opened the bedroom windows first, then walked over to the rabbit hutches, expecting the usual nose-twitch, ear-flap greeting. Both rabbits were lying on their sides, mouths open, ears flat. They weren't breathing.

I grabbed them up and ran to the front yard.

"Call 911," I said to Liz.

She sized up my cargo. "For the rabbits?"

"No, for the house. Tell them our rabbits died. It's a real leak."

"No!" Christine shrieked, grabbing for Eeyore. "Save them!"

She pried him out of my hands and knelt, laying him gently on the grass, then took Melissa and laid her carefully beside him.

She stood up and stared at me. "Save them," she said again.

"I don't know how," I said. "Punkin, it's too late."

"You saved me. Mommy told me."

"But you're a little girl. They're rabbits. It's not the same."

"Miss Dylan, you have to save them!" she shrieked. Tears began to puddle in her eyes.

"Punkin, I don't know how to resuscitate a rabbit. They didn't teach us that in CPR."

"Pleeeease, Miss Dylan? Pleeeease?" She was jumping up and down, tears streaming down her cheeks, nearing hysterics.

I looked helplessly at Liz, who was talking on her cell phone to the 911 operator.

"Okay." I knelt beside the bunnies and grabbed Christine's hands. "Here's what you do." I showed her how to compress their chests gently. "Not too hard. They have tiny little ribs. Like chicken bones. Just do it real soft. I'll be right back."

I took a gulp of air, held my breath, and dashed into the kitchen, yanking open a drawer and grabbing some soda straws. Back in the yard, I knelt next to the rabbits. I did Eeyore first, tipping his head back, slipping the straw into his throat, closing my hand around his mouth and nose. I leaned over and blew gently. Liz hung up the phone, grabbed the other straw, and started in on Melissa. I talked her through inserting the straw. She got the straw in and began blowing air gently into Melissa's little bunny lungs.

"On my count," I said. "Christine, stop pressing for a second." Liz and I blew into the straws. "Okay—now press down." I counted for her. "Liz, two more breaths."

We went through three cycles of compressions and breaths.

Eeyore started to kick. I looked at Liz, my eyes wide.

I gave him two more breaths, then pulled the straw out. Eeyore's ears pricked up, and he struggled to his feet.

"Is Melissa's chest rising when you breathe?" I asked Liz.

She nodded. "Her nose is getting pink."

They went through another full cycle before Melissa started to twitch. A few seconds later, she righted herself and balled up, ears back, fur puffed out, breathing heavily.

Christine began clapping wildly and hopping around the yard like a bunny.

We could hear the fire engine's siren wailing in the distance.

Liz looked at me. "Unbelievable."

"Ridiculous," I said. "I felt absolutely ridiculous. And look at them. I can't believe it worked."

"I'm glad you weren't sleeping when this happened," she said.

I swallowed. "I hadn't thought of that."

"There wouldn't have been anyone here to stick a straw down your throat."

We stared at each other, letting the thought sink in. "Do you think this could have caused Christine's first attack?" she asked.

I shrugged. "Let's ask the firemen."

The fire engine screamed to a halt in front of my house. My neighbors were pushing back curtains and stepping into their yards.

Firemen began jumping off the truck.

"Resident?" one said to me.

I looked up into a pair of liquid blue eyes.

"Me," I said, raising my hand like a schoolgirl. "I live here."

"Name?"

"Dylan Foster."

I held out my hand. He winked and shook his head, holding up his hand, which was sheathed in an enormous yellow glove.

Liz and I stayed in the yard with Christine and the bunnies as the firemen streamed into my house.

"Okay, so he's cute," Liz said, watching my face.

"*So* cute! Who knew disaster was a great way to meet men? I should have had a carbon monoxide leak years ago."

"No!" Christine said. "He's not your boyfriend, Miss Dylan. Mr. David is."

"I'm not sure Mr. David wants to be my boyfriend," I said.

"Did you make him the snickerdoodles yet?"

"Not yet, Punkin."

The cute fireman came out and pulled off his glove. "You've got a leak. We had to turn the gas off."

"Oh. What do I do now? Who fixes that?"

"I have a number you can call."

He hopped into the cab of the truck and came back with a business card. "TXU Gas comes twenty-four hours a day for emergencies."

"Is this an emergency?"

"Yes ma'am."

"Lucky me."

"Congratulations," he said.

"Thanks."

"They should be out tonight to fix it. Sometimes they get backed up." He pointed at the bunnies. "Dispatch said the rabbits died."

"She brought them back to life," Christine said. "We saved them."

He tipped his fireman hat. "Good work. How'd you do the breathing?"

"Soda straw."

He nodded. "Good thinking. You must have caught them right after they went under. They wouldn't have lasted long."

We asked him about the leak, whether it could have caused Christine's problem.

"I doubt it. If it was that bad, it should have gotten everyone in the room. Carbon monoxide is an equal-opportunity killer. It loves everybody."

"Mr. David loves Miss Dylan," Christine said in a sing-songy voice.

"Christine! Hush!" Liz said. She grabbed Christine by the hand and pulled her away.

"He's her boyfriend!" Christine shouted as her mother dragged her across the yard.

The fireman looked at me and shrugged. "Bad luck for me."

I smiled, embarrassed.

"We're sort of broken up."

"Sort of?"

"The jury's still out."

"His or yours?"

"His."

He took the card from me, fished underneath his jacket, and pulled a pen out of the pocket of his shirt.

"If he convicts, give me a call." He wrote down his name and number and handed me the card.

"Buck Bradley," I read out loud. "That sounds like a rodeo name. Or a movie star. Or an astronaut."

"Nope. Just a fireman." He tipped his hat again. "Pleased to meet you, Ms. Foster."

"Do you always hit on the women whose houses you get called to?"

Another dazzling smile. "Only the ones who know how to bring a rabbit back to life."

The firemen let Liz and Christine climb up with them so Christine could blow the siren, which sent her into spasms of delight. I sat on the curb by myself, watching the scene, twirling the card between my fingers.

I stared at it for a moment, trying to imagine myself with Buck Bradley of Dallas Fire-and-Rescue. Then I tore the card up and tucked the pieces into my pocket.

30

~

WE DECIDED THAT LIZ and Christine would smuggle the rabbits into their hotel room in Liz's duffle bag. Someone needed to keep an eye on them, and after their recent ordeal, I thought it only fair to let them enjoy their recovery in a snake-and carbon-monoxide-free environment. Plus, Liz needed a night of room service and Frette linens after almost a week of sleeping in the Lysol chair.

That left me alone at my house—just me and Peter Terry—waiting for TXU gas to come find my leak and turn the gas back on. I walked through the living room, my temper rising.

"You're losing your touch," I said out loud.

The sound of my breathing seemed to fill up the kitchen, which had fallen eerily silent. The air was still and warm. There was no knocking from the water heater—no gas, of course. The clock on the wall, which normally hums as the red hand counts off the seconds, had stopped.

The kitchen drawer protested loudly as I yanked it open and fished around for a screwdriver, which I used to pull the back off the clock.

"You've stooped to killing rabbits? Where were you in the eighties? Didn't you see *Fatal Attraction*? Come up with something original."

I popped the batteries out and pulled another AA Duracell from the pack, slipping it in and flipping the clock over to verify that the second hand had begun to move. I checked my watch and set the time: 9:37.

"I don't know what you think you're accomplishing. You're not scaring me anymore." I hung the clock back on its hook. "I'm onto you. You know that? You're nothing but a stalker. A coward."

My shoulders ached. I reached into the cabinet for aspirin and opened the fridge for a cold bottle of water.

"Hiding in the shadows, breaking light bulbs, and summoning flies and rats and snakes like a petty vandal. No one cares. Do you hear me? No one cares about any of this. Least of all me. I'll just keep swatting the flies and trapping the rats and the snakes."

The water was so cold it hurt my teeth. The aspirin caught in my throat. Another swig, tossing my head back, and a hard swallow before they yielded and slid down my throat.

"You're a fraud. A pretender. And I'm telling you, you are fighting a losing battle. Everyone seems to understand that but you."

The clock stopped again.

I stalked over, pulled it off the wall, and popped the back off.

"You keep at it. I got plenty of batteries. You should know by now I'm well supplied."

A fresh AA, and the hands started to move again. I replaced the back and hung the clock back up on the wall, straightening it carefully.

"Only a coward kidnaps children," I said to the silence. "You know that? Someone who can't handle a fair fight—that's who kidnaps kids. Losers like you who have to overpower someone small and weak in order to feel important. To feel like they have some power in the universe."

I rolled my shoulders and shut my eyes, my hair falling back on my shoulders.

"I will absolutely make it my mission in life to get him back. I will not stop until you are whining and crying and begging for mercy. Angels will come and strangle you slowly."

I looked around the room, daring him to appear. "What do you want? Ransom? What are you holding out for? Why don't you just give up now? You know we're going to get him back."

I threw the rest of the new batteries into the drawer and slammed it shut.

"We both know how this is going to come out in the end. My dad can beat up your dad."

Silence. I knew he was listening. I didn't really care to hear his response.

I finished my water and reached into the fridge for another bottle, then snapped off the light in the kitchen, glancing for the first time at the answering machine. I groaned. That blasted light was blinking again.

I considered ignoring it but caved to the guilt and punched Play, scrolling through a few messages from my father, one from my brother, and one from Helene, who wanted to congratulate me on my absolution. The last message was from Molly Larken, wanting to talk to me tonight. She didn't leave a number.

Ten o'clock is the boundary between evening and night for most people, the moment after which it becomes rude to call. My watch said 9:52. I decided to go for it. Another search through my bag—cursing that I hadn't taken the half minute required to put her number into my phone.

There were maybe a dozen slips of paper bunched up in the bottom of my purse. I pulled them all out and searched through them, looking for the card she'd given me. I got halfway through the pile before I stopped cold, staring dumbly at the card in my hand. On it were an ankh and a phone number. Nothing else. I vaguely recognized the area code.

I flipped the card over and sure enough, there was Molly's phone number in her handwriting. This was the card she'd given me.

Molly picked up on the first ring.

"Did you see the blog?" she asked.

"When? Today?"

"He posted a poem this morning. It's all about how he can't wait to get out and get back to teaching so he can be with me again. He actually used the phrase 'molding young hearts and minds.' Listen…"

I heard her tapping computer keys. "Wait, I'm scrolling down… Here it is. 'I miss molding young hearts and minds, helping them to a future in time.'"

I groaned. "That's awful."

"Let's see. What else is on here? He mentions an article from today's paper. About DNA exoneration. Claiming it will prove his innocence. 'Beyond a shadow of a doubt.' That's not the phrase, is it? It's 'beyond a reasonable doubt,' right? Is he an idiot or what?"

"He didn't write that."

"What do you mean, he didn't write it?"

"I mean, he didn't write it. He doesn't know anything about it."

"How do you know?"

"He's locked in a room on the psych unit at Parkland Hospital."

"Maybe he got a message to someone."

"There's no way in or out of there. No phone. No computer. No mail. I don't even think he can get the paper. He couldn't possibly have seen that article."

"He might have. They have newspapers in the hospital."

"I saw him today, Molly. He's barely functional. Actually, he isn't functional at all. He didn't write it."

"You saw him today?"

"I went down there. You got my message about the suicide attempt?"

"How did he do it?"

"He tried to strangle himself with his jail uniform."

"Too bad it didn't work."

"He's really a pitiful figure, Molly. He tried to kill himself again today. He sliced up his wrists with a paper clip."

"Am I supposed to feel sorry for him?"

"He doesn't know anything about the blog, Molly."

"How do you know?"

"I asked him about it."

"And you believe him? He's in jail. Why would you believe anything he says?"

"He's incapable of producing anything like that on his own behalf. I swear. He didn't know anything about it. He'd never heard of you. He didn't recognize your name at all."

"He's faking."

"You never had a class with him, right? You've never met him?"

"No, but that doesn't—"

"Even if you'd been in his class, I guarantee you he wouldn't have remembered your name. I doubt he'd even recognize you if he saw you."

"But you and I look so much alike."

"That was the only thing I could figure—that maybe he saw you and it reminded him of me and set him on one of those psycho spirals he has. But I swear, he does not know your name. He's never heard of you."

"So what does that mean? What are you telling me?"

"Whoever created the blog did it without his knowing anything about it."

"Why? Why would anyone do that?"

"I have no idea."

I heard her tapping keys again.

"Are you still online? Looking at the blog?"

"Uh-huh. I wanted to ask you about something on here."

I waited.

"Who's Gordon Pryne?"

"What does it say about him?"

"That he's a liar."

"Read it to me."

" 'Gordon Pryne is a liar when he said'—should be 'says' —'DNA is a convicts'—no apostrophe—'best friend.' His grammar is awful. 'DNA will not be his friend when he is found guilty of this crime.' "

"The blog actually names Gordon Pryne?"

"Yep."

"That's not public information."

"What do you mean?"

"I mean, only a few people even knew he was a suspect. The cops, me, and a few people who were questioned."

"So it's one of those people."

"Or someone who knows Gordon Pryne. He might have told someone."

"Where is he? Can you go talk to him?"

"He's in prison in Huntsville. Serving time for sexual assault."

"You keep good company."

"It's not like John has an avid social life. I can't imagine it's someone he knows. Maybe he has family somewhere."

I flipped over the card in my hand. "Do you remember the card you gave me with your number on it?"

"You mean…which card, exactly? Um, no. Why?"

"It has an ankh on it."

"What's an ankh?"

"It's a cross with a loop at the top."

"What else does the card say? You mean a business card, right?"

My doorbell rang. I looked outside and saw the TXU truck.

"It doesn't say anything else. Just the ankh and a phone number."

"What's the number?"

I read it to her.

"Three-one-eight. That's my old area code."

"Where? You're not from Phoenix, are you?"

"Not quite."

"Where, then?"

"Bossier City."

"Where's that?"

"Right outside Shreveport, Louisiana."

31

I BROKE THE TEN o'clock rule, of course, and dialed the number on the card after the TXU boys had settled down to work.

I knew exactly what I'd hear.

"Serenity," the voice chimed

I started to hang up. The voice continued with a Louisiana drawl you could land a plane on, it was so wide.

"Serenity is the quest of all the universe. Follow your star, no matter if it's hopeless, no matter if it's far. Please leave a message, and Psychic Brigid will call you right back."

I hung up before the beep and stared at the phone.

What in the name of homegrown tomatoes was going on? Brigid was John Mulvaney's junior-high girlfriend—probably the one female he'd ever personally touched in his entire life, not counting relatives and research rodents. She was also a wacko. A certifiable nut-job wacko.

She'd greeted me with a twelve-gauge shotgun last winter when I showed up at her house uninvited. Now here she was showing up in my life again. Definitely uninvited.

Oh, for a loaded over-and-under when you need one.

My kitchen clock was still running. I guess Peter Terry had decided to knock off for the night. The clock said 10:24. I broke the rule again and dialed Molly.

"I'm so sorry to bother you again. Especially so late."

"I'm on college time. It's early."

"Listen, do you happen to remember an encounter with a psychic in Shreveport named Brigid?"

She didn't answer me right away. I wondered if she'd hung up.

"Molly?"

"Who told you about that?"

"Nobody. I dialed the number on the business card you gave me. The one with the ankh on it."

She sighed heavily. "Okay, that was too weird. I thought you were psychic or something too. That's right—I forgot. She uses that ankh thing instead of a signature. She was a loony bird."

"So you did go see her?"

"Once. I went with a girlfriend from high school. On a lark. Well, it was a lark for me. She believes in that stuff. She wanted to find out who she was going to marry. The big-time, all-important life question for girls from small towns who end up in beauty school."

"When was this?"

"Spring break."

"That was mid-March, right?"

"Yeah. I went home for break. Why?"

"Brigid was John Mulvaney's junior-high girlfriend. Check out the picture on his blog. The one from the school dance."

I heard her tapping keys, and then she let out a long whistle.

"I'd say she's not wearing her age well, but she didn't wear youth much better, did she?"

"So you do see the resemblance?"

"Barely. How do you know she was his girlfriend?"

"I met her last January. Briefly."

"You didn't go for a reading…"

"Not exactly. I showed up on her doorstep and found myself on the business end of a shotgun. It was a short meeting."

"What were you—"

"Long story. I'll tell you over iced coffee someday."

"What do you think's going on?"

"I don't know what to think."

"She's probably the one doing the blog for him. I bet she's the one posting the content."

The game-show ding sounded in my brain. "I can't believe I didn't think of that earlier. She was nuts about him. But I don't think she's seen him since ninth grade."

"Maybe they got back in touch."

"I'm assuming you told her you go to SMU."

"I probably mentioned it. I don't remember."

"Did you fill out any paperwork? Any way she could have gotten your address?"

"I think my friend put us on a mailing list, maybe."

"Credit-card number?"

"Yep. I paid with a credit card. It was my birthday present to her."

I logged on to the blog. "Look at the copy. It's so hokey. And so badly written. Brigid's answering machine quotes that horrible song." I drummed my fingers on the keyboard and filed through the Bad Song folder in my memory. "What is it?"

"I never heard her message."

"Something about a quest and a star, no matter how hopeless…"

Molly groaned, then sang, "To dream…the impossible dream…"

I hooted with laughter. "I can't believe you even know that song. It's so old!"

"I saw it on *Gomer Pyle*. He gets to sing it at the big Marine thing. For the president."

"That show's still on? I used to watch that after school when I was in elementary school."

"Nick at Nite."

"What's that?"

"You don't get out much, do you?"

"Someone else pointed that out to me recently."

"What are you going to do?"

"I don't know. Probably have a talk with Brigid."

"You think that's wise? I mean, after the shotgun thing?"

"Probably not. But that almost never stops me."

"Want company?"

"Absolutely not. But thanks for offering."

"Don't mention it."

"Hey," I said. "What did Brigid tell you when she did your reading?"

"She said I was going to be an old maid."

"Oh. Sorry."

"Are you married?"

"No."

"Dating anyone?"

"I was." A wave of smelly shame rolled over me. "He broke up with me."

She laughed. "Hey, maybe she got us mixed up. Maybe the reading was really for you."

32

~

IT'S THREE HOURS FROM Dallas to Shreveport. A couple of hours of sleep, and I hit the road early. I was standing on Brigid's porch by ten the next morning, buzzing with a caffeine high that could launch the space shuttle right off the pad at Cape Canaveral.

A dinner bell sat on a shelf beside the front door. The sign beside it said Knock Then Ring. I complied and waited. The door swung open, and Brigid was standing there, resplendent in peacock colors—a long, tent-like muumuu made of green and purple chiffon, an indigo turban covering most of her peroxide-yellow hair. Her nicotine-stained finger-nails were sharpened into talons and painted black. She stood with her arms up, her hands resting on the inside of the doorframe as though she were accepting applause. Her eyes were half-shut, her chin lifted, her mouth painted a bright bloody red.

"How may I be of help to you, my child?" she asked regally.

I waved and flashed a quick grin.

"Hi, Brigid. Remember me?"

She shifted her eyes slightly and looked down at me without moving her head.

"You've been to see Brigid before, my child?"

"Dylan Foster, remember? I was here last January talking to you about your daughter, Drew?"

I saw her flinch.

"I came all the way from Dallas again, Brigid. Left at seven? this morning to get here. I was hoping to get a word."

Her face twisted out of the Gloria Swanson imitation and screwed itself into a hard, angry scowl. She dropped her arms and pointed a long finger at me.

"You get off my porch. This minute."

"I came to talk to you about John Mulvaney."

"Don't you mention his name to me, young lady. That name does not belong on your lying lips. You come traipsing in here and get me to show you my pictures and tell you my stories about the one true love of my life, and then you go and lie and put him in jail like a dog."

"I'm sorry, Brigid. I didn't lie to anyone about anything. I just—"

"A smart doctor like my John in prison! An innocent man! Who would think such a thing? I have half a mind—"

I held up my hands to fend off the barrage. At least she wasn't armed this time.

"I think you may be confused. John confessed to me. In detail. He told the police the same story. Did anyone tell you that? That he confessed? They found all this evidence at his—"

"That confession don't mean nothing!" she shrieked. "You trapped him with your pretty-girl ways." Her eyes narrowed to slits, her voice dropping to a low growl. "I know all about you prom-queen types."

"Now, that's not fair. I can assure you I was never a prom queen."

"You pretty girls, always making fools of the men, getting 'em to do whatever it is you want. You think he was really in love with you?" She looked me up and down. "You took advantage of him, with his soft heart and his sweet ways. You tricked him into that confession."

I took a step back. I'd clearly failed to account adequately for the nut-ball factor. I could see I'd have to reconsider my strategy.

"I saw him yesterday, Brigid. I thought maybe you'd want to know how he's doing."

The pointing hand remained poised in the air. "You saw him?"

I smiled smugly. "Yep."

"You went down to the jailhouse? Or did they let him out?"

"I went down to the hospital and saw him. Did you know he's in the hospital, Brigid? Did you know that? He's not doing well at all."

The hand dropped. Her face fell. "What's he doing in the hospital? Is he sick?"

"Yes, he is. He's quite sick, as a matter of fact. I'd be happy to tell you all about it." I gestured toward the door. "Can I come in?"

She narrowed an eye at me but stepped back and let me pass.

Brigid's house smelled of cigarette smoke and old clothes. And hair dye. I followed her down the hall, longing for a surgical mask and perhaps a nice new pair of latex gloves. We walked past a room with a beauty-shop sink in it—the kind with the U where your neck goes.

"I do hair," she said as we passed the room.

"I think you mentioned that last time."

She talked without turning to look at me, gesturing over her shoulder as she walked. "You could use a touch-up on that red job you got there. I noticed that out in that sunshine."

"I don't dye my hair."

"Don't you lie to me, honey. I can spot a dye job from a hundred yards."

There was obviously no point in arguing.

We passed another room with a purple starry sign on it that said Reading Room.

"You ever had a reading?" she asked, tossing the question out behind her.

"Um, no." I already knew I was going to be an old maid. I didn't need any peacock psychic from Shreveport, Louisiana, to tell me that.

We arrived at the kitchen, which was cluttered with tacky knick-knacks and smelled of cake. The oven was on, heating up the already fetid room. Beaters dripped pasty batter into an empty mixing bowl. Dirty, putty-colored melamine dishes were stacked up beside the sink, along with a pile of wet dishtowels.

Brigid pulled out a vinyl-covered dinette chair and gestured for me to sit. I obeyed, folding my hands in my lap, careful, of course, not to touch anything. Brigid clearly did not give two hoots about cleanliness being next to godliness.

She stalked across the room, muumuu flowing behind her, and snatched a pack of Marlboros out of a drawer. She tapped one out of the package and lit it, sucking a long drag into her lungs. She grabbed an empty Coors can, sat down opposite me, and glared.

"You start talking. Right now, young lady."

Rarely do I find myself in a situation that intimidates me. But sitting there in Brigid's filthy kitchen, surrounded by her flea-market décor and knowing there was a shotgun lurking somewhere in the house—and having been on the receiving end of that mean redneck temper of hers before—I found myself a bit cowed.

I cleared my throat. "Um, I was wondering…when was the last time you saw John?"

She blew smoke over her shoulder and tapped the ashes into the can. "I said start talking, not asking."

I considered my options and decided to play hardball. "You want to hear how he is or not?"

The finger pointed at me again.

"Don't you mess with me, Dylan Foster."

"Brigid," I said, almost touching the table, then folding my hands again in my lap. No talking with my hands today. "You have something I need. I have something you need. You want to do business or what?"

She tapped her ashes again and took another drag.

I plowed on. "Because I'll walk out that front door and drive back to Dallas in a red-hot minute. And I'm telling you right now, there's no way on God's green earth you'll get any information about John Mulvaney from anyone but me. The shape he's in, I guarantee you will not be allowed to see or talk to him. Or get any information about him whatsoever. In fact, I can make sure that's the case. Or…"

She raised her brows.

"…maybe I can arrange for you to see him. I'm sure he'd like that very much." I sat back and folded my arms. "What's it going to be?"

She considered me through narrowed eyes, smoking and tapping her ashes.

"What do I have that you want?" she said at last.

"I want to know about the blog."

"What's a blog?"

I scooted my chair back and stood to leave.

"Wait, wait!" she said. "Set yourself back down."

I sat.

A long pause. "I know what a blog is."

"I know you do. Now stop shoveling horse manure and let's get down to business. DoctorBehindBars. That's you, isn't it?"

She stared at me and smoked, then gave me one quick nod.

"Yes? Was that a yes?"

"Maybe."

"Yes or no, Brigid. Ticktock. I need to get back on the road. I've got a long, long way to go today."

"Yes. It's me. You happy? What's it to you?"

"John doesn't know anything about it, does he?"

She shook her head—a barely perceptible no.

I took a breath. "What about Molly Larken?"

"Who's that?"

I reached for my purse and started digging around for my keys.

"Stop that. What about her?"

"Why are you picking on her?"

"You two meet at a prom-queen convention or something?"

"I called her up after I found out I was being blamed for running the blog. Did you think I was just going to let that go?" I tsked. "Brigid. You know me better than that."

She dropped her cigarette into the can and reached for the pack, plucking a fresh one out and lighting it delicately with her Bic. She looked up at me without answering.

"Where did the copy come from?" I asked. "The words about Molly and me? You didn't write it, did you?"

She thought about the question, then stood up and walked into the other room. I waited at the table while she rooted around for something, shoving boxes around and cursing. I resisted the urge to go to the sink and wash up, knowing that the sink was even filthier than the table.

She came back with a school yearbook. She opened it up and shoved it across the table at me.

I squinted at the adolescent scrawl and flipped the page to find the signature. John had signed her ninth-grade yearbook, calling her his muse, his precious angel, his liaison to the rest of the world. The prose was drippy and overwritten, like something out of a book of bad Victorian poetry.

"Why use the words he wrote about you to describe someone else?"

She poked the book. "I can't write like that. I just don't have the gift. It's so beautiful."

I nodded vaguely and managed to refrain from throwing up.

"He's a genius, you know." She closed the book and held it to her chest.

I couldn't think of a polite response to that one. "Molly and I look a lot alike."

"I noticed that."

"Is that why you're picking on her? Because you're jealous of John's obsession with me?"

"He is not *obsessed*." She spat the word out. "He took a few pictures. That's all."

"He took hundreds of pictures, Brigid."

"You don't know that for a fact."

"I saw them."

She leaned back. "So you say."

I leaned my elbows gingerly on the table, drawing my face closer to hers. "Now you listen to me."

She glared at me and waited.

"You listening?"

A nod.

"John has never had true feelings for me. What he had was an obsession. A sick obsession. It's a psychological condition. A sickness. That's all it is. It has a diagnostic code and everything. It doesn't mean anything at all about me personally or about him. Or about you, for that matter." I leaned back, removing my elbows from the sticky table and making a mental note to purchase a bottle of Phisoderm on my way home. "I'm sure, in fact, that he would have quite genuine feelings for you if he knew how much you cared for him."

Her face lit up. "Did he mention me?"

I shook my head. "It wasn't that kind of visit."

She pointed at me with her cigarette. "Your move, prom queen. Let's see what you've got."

"John tried to kill himself a couple of days ago."

Her chin dropped. "He what?"

"He's on the psych unit at Parkland Hospital. They've got him on suicide watch."

The color drained rapidly from her face, leaving her white skin almost blue against her jewel-toned turban. I could see gray roots poking out from underneath the indigo fabric.

"He's very depressed," I added. "I'm sure you can imagine. I don't think he's doing very well in jail."

Brigid put her head in her hands. I watched with fascination as she pulled off her turban and ran her hands through her wiry hair, writhing with the pain she felt for a man she hadn't seen since she was in junior high school. A man who had done her more harm than she could possibly admit to herself.

She got up, snatched a paper towel off the roll, and blew her nose, then sat back down opposite me and lit another cigarette with shaky fingers, still sniveling. "Do you think he's going to be all right?"

"I don't know, Brigid." I shook my head. "I doubt it. He's not exactly cut out for prison life."

She began to cry. Big, wet, blubbery tears. Mascara ran in two black streams down her face.

I let her cry, staring at her as though she were a science project or something. She was one sad case. For the life of me, I could not imagine what she was thinking, pining away for a mess like John Mulvaney. The two of them were quite a pair.

When she settled down, I decided the best approach was the direct one.

"Brigid, look at me."

She blew her nose again and dabbed ineffectually at her ruined makeup.

"Why do you care about him so much? Why all this affection for someone you barely know? Why the loyalty? I really don't understand it." I shrugged.

"Peter Terry's the criminal. Not my John," she spat. "He and that Gordon Pryne killed my baby girl. You of all people oughta know that."

33

~

I SAT BACK IN my chair. The words hit me like a truckload of scrap concrete.

"I'd forgotten you knew Peter Terry."

Another cigarette, another flick of the Bic with shaky fingers, a long drag, a tap into the Coors can.

"I forgot you knew him too." She blew the smoke at me. "Until just now this minute."

"What do you mean Peter Terry's a criminal?"

"I mean he killed my daughter. He ruined her life and turned her into a nothin', and then she went and got herself killed by that no-good loser druggie Gordon Pryne."

"Gordon Pryne didn't do it, Brigid."

"Well, I tell you one thing, little girl. Dr. John Mulvaney had nothing to do with it. I know that for a fact." Tap, tap.

"How? How do you know that?"

"It's not in his nature. I know people. I'm a trained professional. Don't you forget that." She thumped the table with her finger for emphasis. "He's a sweet, sweet man." She teared up again and dabbed her eyes with her paper towel. "He'd a made me a great husband. I always knew it. Not like that rattrap loser I married."

I could see this was a losing battle. And one that, frankly, I did not care to fight. Let her hang on to her little fantasy about what a great couple she and John Mulvaney would have made. Maybe she could be one of those women who marries a prisoner. She'd throw herself at his feet in a second if she had half an opportunity. And he'd be a fool not to take her up on it. She was his one fan in the entire universe. The one human being standing between him and complete, invisible obscurity.

"Talk to me about Peter Terry," I said. "When did you see him last?"

"I can't get rid of that monster. Talk about a psycho. Try that one on for size, why don't you?"

"What do you mean, you can't get rid of him?"

She leaned forward, balancing on her cigarette hand, the smoke still burning between her fingertips.

"I mean," she said slowly, "he...will...not...go...away. I channeled him, and I can't get rid of him. What do you think I mean?"

"You channeled him. I'd forgotten you told me that. That was... when?"

"January 10, 1986."

"Right. The day you met your ex-husband. I can't remember his name."

She snorted out another cloud of smoke. "King Sturdivant. King of nothing. No good rattrap loser..."

"We really don't have time for that, Brigid. Stay with me here."

She quit ranting about King Sturdivant and took another drag. The air in the kitchen was becoming alarmingly blue. I looked around for a smoke detector and began to have panicky, obsessive thoughts about lung cancer and secondhand smoke.

"Why are you doing the blog?" I asked.

She paused, her lip quivering. "He deserves that from me."

"Who, John? Why would you say that? Do you owe him a favor or something?"

She got up, reached into the kitchen cabinet, pulled out a fifth of Jack Daniel's and two glasses that looked sort of clean. I checked my watch. It wasn't even noon yet. She set the glasses down and poured us both some whiskey.

I ignored mine while she threw hers back like an Irish barfly.

She looked at me with bleary, mascara-smeared eyes. "Even if my John did do somethin', it wasn't his fault. It was that Peter Terry. And I'm the one that brought him here."

"When?"

"When what? I told you, January 10—"

"No. When did Peter Terry start bothering John?"

"A while ago. I don't know. A long time."

"How do you know?"

"He told me."

"Who told you? John?"

"Peter Terry. Who do you think?" She poured herself another glass. "You want some more?"

I shook my head. "It's a little early for me."

"Suit yourself." She sipped this one, taking a small drink and setting the glass back down.

"It's that Gordon Pryne who's a criminal. Not my John."

"Peter Terry is a liar, Brigid. Surely you—"

"I know that! Don't you think I know that?"

"Then why are you listening to him?"

"He said he could fix it."

"Fix what?"

"Get John Mulvaney out of jail. Set him free."

"Brigid, Peter Terry does not set people free."

She stopped with her glass halfway to her lips, a look of shock on her face. Clearly this obvious notion had not occurred to her.

"You know that, don't you?" I said, my voice rising. Her willful ignorance was infuriating. "He imprisons people and confuses them. He does not set them free. He does not help them in any way. If he told you he'd do that for John, he's lying."

She lifted the glass to her lips. A longer drink this time.

I sighed. "Why a blog, Brigid? I mean, no offense, but you don't really seem like the blog type."

"All the prisoners have 'em now. It's the only way they can tell the world what's going on. Imagine you're locked up like an animal like that. A dog chained in a yard has more freedom than my poor John."

"But how did you think of a blog? It really doesn't seem like your style."

She waited a long minute before she answered me. "I got the idea from that Gordon Pryne. He has one." She stubbed her cigarette out on the table and dropped it in the Coors can. "Peter Terry told me all about it."

I froze in place. "Gordon Pryne has a blog?"

"That monster. Killed my baby girl. My poor, sweet baby girl."

She started to bawl again. The whiskey was getting to her. "If that murderer has one—out there saying he's all innocent and"—she made little quotation signs with her fingers—" 'clean as the driven snow'—my John should have one too."

"He used that phrase? 'Clean as the driven snow'?" I asked.

"Clean. As. The. Driven. Snow." She drew out the words, emphasizing each word with a thump of her forefinger on the table. "Am I stuttering? That's what it says."

"Are we talking about the same Gordon Pryne? The one I know can't put three words together."

"He's not as smart as my John."

"So it's the usual stuff? 'I'm innocent and the world is unfair'? He doesn't mention the murder, does he?"

"Of course he does not mention any such thing. He's not going to just tell the whole world what he done."

The timer on the stove chimed.

She looked at me smugly. "Time's up."

"This isn't a reading, Brigid. We're not doing thirty-minute segments here."

She got up, picked some potholders out of a squeaky drawer, and pulled a sheet cake out of the oven. She set it on the stove, pulled off the potholders, and sat back down.

"You want a reading? I'll do one for you. No charge."

"No thanks. I think I can see plenty of my future from here without any help from you."

She drew back and studied me. "You and my baby girl and that Molly Larken have the same aura. Anyone ever tell you that?"

"Well, no, Brigid. Since you're the only person on the face of the earth who knows the three of us, no one but you has mentioned it. What does that mean, we have the same aura?"

"It's a real nice color too. A nice, pretty orange. Means you have a creative mind underneath that bad dye job. Drew was real creative too. She was a lot like you. Stubborn as the day is long. Couldn't never take no for an answer. Rest her soul."

"Thank you. I think."

She stood to usher me out. I turned and looked back at the kitchen as I left. Smoke hung thick and gray in the air, swirling lazily in the light filtering through dirty windows.

"Y'all share an angel too," she said.

"What do you mean—like a guardian angel? I thought everyone had their own."

"They divide 'em up by aura," she said, as though she were making perfect sense.

She stepped into the reading room, rummaged loudly through a drawer, and came back out into the hallway with a small box. "You ought to take one of these. Might do you some good. Keep you safe."

I reached for it, but she snatched it back at the last second.

"Can you get me in to see my John?" she asked.

"I'll see what I can do. I'll try. I promise."

She handed me the box. Inside was a little ankh on a silver chain.

"Anael, right?" I asked. "Wasn't that his name?"

"That's his angel name. Not the one he works under."

"I don't understand."

"Angels are like pro wrestlers, honey. They all have a stage name."

I knew the answer before I asked the question: "What's Anael's stage name?"

"Joe Riley," she said as she opened the door for me. A fresh breeze blew through the open doorway. "Keep an eye out for him. He might do you some good someday."

34

IT DOESN'T TAKE A genius to know to not bank on information from a crackpot like Brigid. But at this point, I wasn't about to bet against her, either. I fastened the necklace around my neck before I started the truck to head home.

If I hadn't met Joe Riley in radiology that day, I wouldn't have believed her. But when the answers don't come, I've learned, I'm almost always asking the wrong questions. And every last one of my questions about Joe Riley had led me to a dead end.

As I thought back on it, the new questions began to emerge. How did Joe Riley know what test Christine was having? He never asked. But he described the chest x-ray in detail. And how did he know my little easy-peasy-I-have-to-sneezy thing? It's not like it's caught on in the national lexicon or anything. I made it up. About three minutes before I met him.

Why wasn't he registered for tests at Parkland Hospital? Did his records disappear? Dogged as I am, I'd have run around that tree forever, busting a lung tracking down someone who might not even exist. At least, not in the flesh.

Last but not least, how on earth could Brigid have picked that name out of the blue? It wasn't possible.

And then there was the ankh on a chain around his neck.

I fingered the ankh Brigid had given me and stared at the road, my truck rumbling toward home on the hot, black, asphalt highway, my thoughts tumbling around like lottery balls in my head. If only the numbers would settle into place. I felt certain they would eventually. But it had been a full week since Nicholas had disappeared. Seven long, excruciating days. I couldn't stand thinking what might be happening to him.

I picked up the phone and started dialing, unable to tolerate the silence in the cab. I called Maria first, then Liz, then Martinez, on down the line. No one picked up. I dialed the main number for the DPD and asked for Ybarra. He was out too. It rattled me that they were all unavailable at the same time. Something was going on.

I was just crossing the Texas state line when my phone rang at last. It was Liz.

"Where is everybody?" I asked. "I've been calling and calling."

"Christine and I are back in the emergency room. I can't speak for anyone else."

"You're kidding me."

"I wish I were."

"What's going on?"

"Christine passed out again. Out cold."

"Was it the same thing?"

"More or less. We were at the pool at the hotel. She was just sitting in her pool chair doing nothing—not swimming or anything—and down she went. I called 911, and now we're back at Children's."

"Are they admitting her? Is she okay?"

"We're waiting to hear. I think they're just going to change her asthma meds."

"Did it happen suddenly? Or was there some sort of buildup?"

"She talked all morning about having a stomachache. She said it was like something was flying around in her tummy. Then she just started getting clammy and cold, and before I knew it, she was hyperventilating and gasping for breath."

"Did her heart rate go up?"

"I didn't check, but I'd bet on it. I know mine did."

"That's a panic attack. Same progression of symptoms Nicholas has."

"I wondered," she said. "I've never seen a panic attack before."

My stomach turned, a flood of nausea washing over me.

"Something's happening to Nicholas," I said. The stripes zipping by on the asphalt seemed to speed up as my vision blurred. The cab felt cold suddenly. "Has Christine said anything about him today, Liz?"

"She dreamed last night he was back in the sandy space—the trunk, I guess. Maybe they're moving him."

"Could mean the cops are getting close." I fought to clear my head. "Maybe they're scaring the guy. Have you talked to Martinez or Maria?"

"Nope."

"I called Enrique, but he didn't pick up. What about Maria? Have you seen her? Did she come to the ER when you guys got there?"

"She's off today. We were planning to meet for lunch. I was going to call her after I called you. Where are you, anyway?"

"Driving back from Shreveport, Louisiana."

"What on earth…"

I told her about Brigid and the blog and about Anael and Joe Riley.

"So the guy who was so sweet to Christine in x-ray…" The question lingered unfinished between us. It seemed too ridiculous to say out loud.

"I guess so, yeah. I checked with Parkland. They have no record of anyone named Joe Riley in that day. Inpatient or out."

"And Christine asked if God sent him?"

"Yep. He told her she didn't need to be afraid of anything."

Liz sighed. "Let's hope he's as accurate as Earl is."

"Call me if you hear anything."

"Likewise."

I drove for a while longer, then spotted a Starbucks and pulled over to splash some water on my face, scrub my hands with my recently purchased Phisoderm, and get something to drink. Another double-shot latte might well kill me, I was so overloaded on caffeine, but I didn't think I could stay awake without it. I ordered a turkey sandwich and a sugar cookie too, just to hedge against caffeine-induced heart arrhythmia.

I people-watched as I ate, impressed by the astonishing variety of individuals parading through the place—a small-town Starbucks on I-20. I drank my coffee and wondered about their stories.

How did God keep track of it all? Was there a logarithm on a blackboard somewhere, a theorem to prove? Had Peter Terry deciphered it? Or did they all have access?

I made it back to my house by midafternoon and collapsed in the sunshine on my front porch, rocking back and forth in the swing as the lottery balls continued to bounce around in my head.

When I'd recovered from my drive, I started making phone calls again. I hated feeling disconnected from everyone. It amplified my mania to somewhere between hysteria and full-on panic.

Maria was the first one I reached.

"Did you hear Christine had another attack?" she asked.

"You talked to Liz."

"We had lunch."

"So they made it."

"We were late going, but by the time they got through Emergency, they were ready for something to eat."

"They didn't admit her to the hospital?"

"There's really not much they can do at this point."

"Liz said they were going to change her meds."

"There's no point," Maria said. "It's not asthma."

"I know it's not." I heard her sniffle. "Are you okay?"

She didn't answer. I could hear the wet, drippy sounds people make when they're crying.

"Something's happening to him, Dylan." She blew her nose.

"I know. Did Christine say anything else about him?"

"She just seemed agitated and afraid. We couldn't settle her down at lunch. She wouldn't eat anything."

"Have you talked to Enrique?"

"He's here with me."

"Put him on."

The phone changed hands, and Martinez said hello.

"Is there any news at all?" I asked. "Anything on the car?"

"We've tracked down every white Ford Fairlane of any model year registered in the DFW area. They're checking them out now."

"What about Phoenix? Are you doing the same thing there?"

"They're working on it."

"How many Fairlanes are there in Dallas?"

"Seventeen."

"Any of the owners have criminal records?"

He sighed. "Why don't you just apply for my job?"

"Well?"

"Two."

"Where?"

"One in Mesquite. One over off Harry Hines."

"Where off Harry Hines?"

A long pause. "Near the hospital."

"So the kidnapper may have known Nicholas."

Another pause. "Possibly."

"Or Maria."

"Possibly."

"Address?"

"None of your business."

"Please? I just want to know. I swear I won't go over there."

"Absolutely not."

"Is anyone over there looking for the car?"

"What do you think?"

"They're there now, aren't they?"

"What do you think?"

"Great. Maybe we're getting close. Are you going over?"

"Ybarra is on it, Dylan. We've got cops crawling all over that neighborhood. If he's there, we're going to find him. Today." He must have known what I was thinking. "You stay away from there."

"What are you talking about? I'm not going to—"

"I mean it. If we're closing in on this guy, we don't need you nosing around and tipping him off."

"Understood."

"You stay put. I'm not kidding."

"I get it, Martinez. Don't worry. I'll stay out of it."

We hung up.

I paced around on the porch for a while, then walked the yard and checked my snake traps, which of course were all empty. As the sun began to slip behind my sycamore tree, I went inside, poured myself a glass of David's favorite New Zealand Sauvignon blanc, and fired up my computer.

It took me awhile to find Gordon Pryne's blog. There was another Gordon Pryne, a landscape photographer in Maine, whose listings occupied the first five pages of Google hits. I weeded through those, then found my way to a little four-pager at JusticeForGordon.com. It didn't have quite the traffic or Web prominence that John Mulvaney's did. The home page was one of Gordon Pryne's mug shots—not a particularly inviting image. It was a young version of him, not the ragged, dried-up man I knew. But he was clearly a dangerous sort. Scrawny neck, that wild shock of hair, bad skin, angry green eyes the color of pond water. Whoever was managing his blog wasn't exactly focusing on design, marketing, or PR.

I scanned the site, which was similar to the other prisoner sites I'd seen. Proclamations of innocence, tirades against the American justice system. There were none of the background photos like John's site had—no baby pictures or hometown references. But there was a message board.

I clicked on the message board, made up an e-mail address and a screen name, and logged in as a new member. Apparently Gordon's brother was the Webmaster.

There was lots of back and forth about court dates. Some notes about Pryne's mother's impending death. She wanted to see her son out of jail before she died.

"Fat chance," I said out loud.

I scanned the message page, but there was nothing of note. A few conversations between buddies of Pryne's who were in and out of jail.

One thread about a package delivery. One thread about a bank deposit—I guess Pryne conducted some business with friends via the message board.

Back to the home page, perusing the site for the flowery language Brigid had referred to. I finally found it in one of the innocence rants: "Gordon Pryne is not the criminal you have seen in the papers. He is a family man, innocent and clean as the driven snow."

A family man? Who made up that drivel? The only child I knew of was Nicholas. And Nicholas was the product of a violent rape, the same crime for which Pryne was serving his current stretch of time.

Disgusted, I left the site and did a search for the online records of sex offenders registered in Texas. The zip codes near the hospital were pocked with them, which was no surprise. Parkland is in the barrio on the west side of town, not far from all those seedy strip joints on Harry Hines. I was willing to bet that half the men in that zip code had done jail time for something. Pryne had lived in that zip code, come to think of it. At a dump near Northwest Highway and Harry Hines called the Circle Inn.

I printed out the map, yanking it out of the printer and staring at the little yellow stars pinpointing the spots. They all centered around the intersection of Northwest Highway and Harry Hines. Not far from the house where the Fairlane plates had been stolen.

I felt my heart jump. Martinez had said they were over there right now looking for the Fairlane. We were close. I knew it as surely as I knew my own name.

I looked around the room. "You're going down, you know that?" I said to the ether. "We're going to snatch that little boy right back out of your filthy white hands and take him home to his mother where he belongs."

The clock buzzed to a stop.

35

I SAT THERE TAPPING the tabletop for a solid hour trying to figure out what to do next. What I wanted to do was get in my truck and drive over to Harry Hines and join the hunt. But Martinez was right. I couldn't go over there. Armed men were combing the neighborhood looking for a kidnapper. Any interference could turn out to be disastrous. But I couldn't just sit on my hands, either. I finally grabbed my keys and headed that direction.

I stopped down the street from the first address I'd printed out, looking up and down the road to get my bearings. I backed my truck into an alley and checked out the neighborhood. Mostly postwar-era houses with siding in various states of disrepair and sparse, unkempt lawns. Almost every block, though, had some holdout who tended rosebushes, watered the lawn, or placed a pot of flowers on the porch. You had to admire the determination.

There weren't many people out at this time of the evening. Yellow light shone through windows up and down the street. Blue TV screens flickered in living rooms. The neighborhood looked completely normal. You'd never know all those cops were there. Wherever they were, they were discreet.

I don't know what I was hoping to see. Some guy walking down the street wearing a sandwich board that said, "Shoot me, I'm the kidnapper"? After a few minutes, I started up the truck and threw the transmission into gear. I pulled into the street and began passing liquor stores, gas stations, convenience stores.

I began stopping at each one, hitting all the businesses on the south side of the street. At every stop, I went inside and spent a couple of minutes talking to whoever was behind the counter, asking them about the white Fairlane. They'd all seen the news reports. The ones who spoke English took my card and said they'd call if they saw or heard anything.

I was just about to give up my quest when I spotted one business I knew a little about—a strip club called Caligula. Gordon Pryne had been a customer there, which meant it was a hangout for users and dealers. Exactly the place where the guy in the sketch would hang out.

I pulled into the club parking lot and sat there for a while, watching men park their cars and walk in. After a few minutes, I threw my weight against the squawking truck door, squared my shoulders, and went inside.

Caligula is on Northwest Highway—a major thoroughfare situated between the wealthier parts of Dallas and DFW airport. It's one of those places you drive by regularly, averting your eyes, and then forget about as soon as you've made it around the bend. Among strip joints—already a foul business, to my mind—Caligula had a reputation for being one of the seediest. The Metro section of the paper referenced it occasionally as a crime scene. I knew it had been shut down for a number of years—the door boarded, the sign dark—until a year or so ago.

At any rate, suffice it to say, I'd never been to a strip joint, never considered what it might be like to go into one. And never imagined myself stepping into this one, of all places. But here I was, yanking the door open and stalking up to the bouncer like I knew what I was doing.

I stopped short. The man's biceps were the size of melons. His black T-shirt and jeans were stretched taut over a superhero body—enormous shoulders, muscular bulges, tiny waist, and chiseled quads. Beside him stood a live Barbie doll—Strip Club Barbie. Same measurements as Malibu Barbie but a tinier, sluttier outfit. I'd never seen that particular shade of blond hair, but it was somewhere between egg-yolk yellow and cream-cheese white. Tattoos fanned out from her bellybutton to her G-string.

Strip Club Barbie looked me over. "Twenty-dollar cover."

I felt my face flush. "I'm not a really a customer." I looked around, as though someone might catch me here and send me to the principal's office. "I just wanted to ask the manager a couple of questions."

"Twenty-dollar cover," she said again.

I reached in my bag, found a ten and nine ones. "All I have is nineteen."

Her face didn't move.

I leaned in. "Listen. Do I look like your regular customers?"

A barely perceptible smile. "You'd be surprised."

"I doubt it. But I'm not here for the show. I swear. I'd just like to ask the manager some questions."

"Reporter or cop?"

"Psychologist."

The man with the melon biceps raised his eyebrows. "You a shrink?"

"Yep."

"I got a problem with my wife," he said.

"What is it?"

"I can't get her to leave me." He threw back his head and laughed.

"I can probably help you with that."

He cocked his head toward the door, waving me in. "Straight through, all the way to the back on the left. Name's Hardy."

He refused my nineteen bucks, so I stuffed it back in my bag, pulled open the door, and stepped inside.

It took a moment for my eyes to adjust to the dark. I found myself in a small entryway dominated by an enormous fish tank. A thick velvet curtain walled off the little room from the rest of the club. I'd have to pull back that curtain—touch it personally with my hands—if I wanted to get back there. I grabbed one of the free newspapers from the stand by the fish tank and used it like a glove, shoving the curtain aside and stepping into what my grandmother would have labeled dramatically, a "den of iniquity."

The music was loud and thunky, the room's air stale and humid, the lighting nonexistent except for the spots aimed at three long runways jutting out into the room between tables with weak candles on them. A few women were gyrating on the runways.

In spite of myself, I stopped and stared.

I should add here that it is an essential truth in the universe that all women obsessively compare themselves to one another. Why we engage in such futility is one of life's great mysteries. But as any married man knows, this should be accepted as fact without argument.

It's inevitable. It's a reflex. Just make peace with it now.

So as I stood there, mouth open, staring at the room in front of me, I gave the dancers the once-over, looking for the usual suspects: sag, cellulite, poor muscle tone, jiggles. I'm happy to report that all the dancers checked out as completely average in every department. Except, of course, in the areas that were surgically enhanced. But that's another conversation.

Feeling better about my thighs than I had in months, I sauntered back to the office, past a succession of seemingly regular-looking men. None of them were drooling or making inappropriate sounds or gestures or anything like that. In fact, several tables held groups of men who weren't watching the dancers at all. Stacks of paper covered one four-top, its occupants punching numbers into calculators just like they were sitting around a conference table at the office.

I shook my head—not exactly the scene I'd expected—and found the office door. A sign on the door read "Private—Do NOT Enter!"

I knocked.

No response.

I knocked again.

Still no response.

The third knock was the charm. I heard someone push a desk chair back and stalk to the door. It flew open, and I was staring at a lovely woman in a tailored business suit. She was about my age.

"Um, hi. I'm looking for…the manager? Mr. Hardy?"

"I'm Eileen Hardy. What can I do for you?"

I failed to keep the raw consternation out of my voice. "You're the manager?"

She shifted her weight to one foot and crossed her arms. "Can I help you with something?"

"Could I come in?" I glanced back at the dance floor. "It's a little loud out here."

"You a cop?"

"No. Just an interested party."

"Interested in what?"

"Nicholas Chavez."

I couldn't tell if the name registered, but with the last week's news coverage, unless she'd been in a coma the past week, it should have rung a loud, clanging bell. Eileen Hardy stepped back. I walked in and looked around the room. I could have been standing in any office—drab furniture, industrial fluorescents, putty-colored file cabinets. A whiteboard on the wall had a list of girls' names, along with their shifts. I scanned the list: Bambii, Freedom, Sugar. There were fifteen of them.

She led me to a seat, then settled herself in opposite me, crossing her legs and waiting for me to begin. Her gaze was steady. If I didn't know what she did for a living, I'd have thought she was a lawyer or something. I probably would have invited her for coffee.

"I didn't expect you to be a woman," I said at last.

"Surprise, surprise."

"Are you the owner? Or what?"

"I'm the manager and part owner."

"Do you mind if I ask how you got into this line of work? I mean, I'd think places like this would be managed by men."

"Now why would you think that?" she said, clearly enjoying my discomfort. She got up, walked over to a credenza, and poured us both some Pellegrino. She handed me a glass and sat down again.

"Well, uh, I guess I assumed since it's a club for men… I mean…"

"Ninety percent of the employees are women," she said. "Don't you think they could benefit from female management?"

I let out a breath. "I hadn't thought about that. Good point."

She pointed toward a stack of paint swatches and floor plans piled on her desk. "If you know this place, I'm sure you know the old Caligula. We bought it last fall. We're gutting the place next month—completely redoing everything. We've hired a new chef, and we're holding auditions for new dancers. Our goal is to elevate the whole place to a new level."

I tried to look enthusiastic. "Wow. Great. Good for you."

"I know Caligula has always had a bad reputation—"

"Terrible."

"But we're changing that." I could see her considering what to say next. "I knew the dancer who was killed this winter. And I know her killer met her here." She said it like she was confessing.

"She was a nice kid."

"She was."

"It was terrible, what happened to her."

"We're looking to attract a different crowd now. Nothing like that should ever happen here. These girls should be safe."

I didn't say anything. If she was looking for absolution, she'd come to the wrong place.

"Our target market is men ages twenty-five to sixty-five with incomes of forty-five thousand or more."

I sighed. I hadn't come to discuss her business plans. "Do you remember a customer named Gordon Pryne?"

"Very well." She sipped her Pellegrino. "No longer our target market."

"He's back in Huntsville, so I don't think you'll need to worry about it."

"Did you want to talk to me about Gordon Pryne?"

"Not exactly. I'm actually wondering if any of your customers drives a white Ford Fairlane."

She gestured toward the walls. "We're a business with no windows. I come early. I leave late. I eat at my desk. You looking for anyone in particular?"

I pulled out my sex offender list and read her the names.

"I don't recognize any of them."

"It was worth a shot," I said. "I thought maybe there was some connection."

"To what?"

"Nicholas Chavez's kidnapping. I'm sure you've heard about that. The kidnapper drove a white Ford Fairlane, we think, and may have lived in this neighborhood." I took a sip from my glass. My stomach hurt. "I think this was a wild goose chase. I'm sorry I wasted your time."

She stood and offered her hand. "You didn't introduce yourself, by the way."

"I'm sorry." I extended my hand. "I guess I'm a little overwhelmed. This is not exactly familiar territory for me. I'm Dylan Foster."

"You're not a cop. A reporter?"

"Just a friend of the family." I handed her a business card. "Will you call me if you hear anything about that white car? Or anything about Nicholas?"

"Of course." She walked me to the door. "Did you talk to Wayne yet?"

"Who's Wayne?"

She pointed. "The bartender. He knows more about the clientele than I do. If there's anything to find out, he's your man."

"Thanks."

I kept my head down as I walked to the bar. I didn't want any more images from this place in my head.

I sat down on the edge of a bar stool and worked on maintaining as unfriendly a demeanor as I could muster to discourage anyone from even thinking of hitting on me. Since I'm naturally hostile, this was the one part of my evening that was a snap. I was careful not to touch the bar—I didn't want to contemplate where the customers' hands had been. As I waited for the bartender to come my way, I glanced up at the bar. My rotten luck was holding. The bar was mirrored to make sure patrons seated there could have a full, unobstructed view of the dancers behind them. I grimaced and looked away.

The bartender made his way over. "What can I get you, little lady?"

"Nothing. I just wanted to ask you a couple of questions. Do you have a minute?"

He gestured toward the packed bar.

"Do I look like I have a minute?"

"Please? It will only take a second. Eileen Hardy suggested I talk to you."

He leaned on his elbows and looked at me. "What do you want to know?"

"Do you know if any of your customers drives a white Ford Fairlane? Probably a '63 or '64?"

He jerked his head at the wall behind him. "See any windows? I'm behind the bar pulling drinks. Why don't you talk to Rocky?"

"Who's Rocky?"

He nodded toward the door. "Bouncer. He keeps an eye on the lot. He might know about a car like that. You don't see many of 'em."

"Thanks. I'll check with him on the way out. I don't suppose you've overheard anyone talking about Nicholas Chavez?"

"The kidnapped kid? That's what you're after? You a cop?"

"No."

"Private detective?"

"Just a friend."

"I haven't heard a thing. I guarantee you if I had, I'd a called it in first thing. That's sick, taking a kid like that. They ought to string that guy up by his—"

"Any of your regulars stop showing up suddenly?" I asked. "The kidnapping happened last Saturday."

He looked up toward the ceiling, thinking. "Not that I can think of, off the top of my head. With a little time, I could give you a better answer, probably."

"Any of your customers Phoenix fans?"

"Suns or Diamondbacks?"

"Both."

"Lots of 'em, probably."

"If I have someone bring you a sketch of the suspect, will you look at it and see if you know the guy?"

"Sure. What's he look like?"

"He has a Phoenix Suns jersey, number thirteen."

The bartender nodded enthusiastically. "Steve Nash. Point guard. Leads the NBA in assists."

"I know. Great floor vision."

"What else you got?"

"He's kind of scrawny. Probably a meth addict. Narrow, sharp features. Sallow complexion. White guy, or maybe Hispanic. And he wears cowboy boots. We think he wears long-sleeved collared shirts. Lots of plaid. All old and worn out. And he wears an Arizona Diamondbacks cap. A black one, we think. The one with the snake head on it."

"Sounds like Googie."

My heart stopped. "Googie who? Do you have a last name? Address? Anything?"

"Never heard a last name. He comes in here every now and again. Dealers don't sit still. He never stays long."

"You don't have a credit card slip, do you? Anything?"

"Dealers always pay cash. Besides, I haven't seen that much of him since...oh...January? Used to come in here with his running buddy."

"Do you know why they stopped coming?"

"I think his buddy got sent up to Huntsville. Doing time for rape."

I could feel my hands go cold. "What's his buddy's name?"

He cocked his head again, thinking. "Jeff? George? No...Gordon. I think it was Gordon something."

"Was it Gordon Pryne?"

He slapped the bar and pointed at me. "That's it. Gordon Pryne."

36

I CALLED MARTINEZ AND Ybarra, but neither of them picked up. I left messages for both, then sat in my truck and stared at the steering wheel, trying to figure out what to do. Men walked in and out of Caligula, passing my truck without noticing me. The glow from the streetlight was greenish gray. It made everyone look dead.

I couldn't imagine how Gordon Pryne could be connected. As far as I knew, he'd never even seen Nicholas. He had shown up at Maria's out of the blue, stoned out of his mind, one time that I knew of, and tried to give Nicholas a teddy bear. I don't think he ever got into the house, though. That was last January.

My phone rang. I dug in my bag and checked the ID. It was Maria. I almost answered it. I wanted so badly to tell her my news. But I didn't know where it would lead. And I didn't want to frighten her. Gordon Pryne was a soulless, violent man. His attack on her had been cruel, brutal. Just the sound of his name could drain the color from her face. If Nicholas was in the hands of one of Pryne's buddies, there was no telling what had happened to him by now. I rubbed my eyes. My head was beginning to pound.

I started the truck and pulled into the street. I had only one lead. I intended to follow it as far as it took me, and then I'd go home and wait for Martinez to call. I couldn't stop now. Not when I was so close.

I drove a couple of blocks west to find the Circle Inn, the crummy pay-by-the-week motel where Gordon Pryne had lived. I parked my truck alongside the few ratty cars that were parked in the lot. Curtains in most of the windows were askew or had been replaced with towels or sheets. One window had been covered over completely with aluminum foil. Lights were on in four of the rooms.

I stepped out into a parking lot littered with cigarette butts and walked quickly toward the office. I reached into my bag for a Kleenex and used it to pick up a hypodermic I found on the ground. I could just see some little kid picking that thing up and getting some terrible disease. I held it at arm's length, walked over to the Dumpster, dropped in both the Kleenex and the hypodermic, and wiped my hands on my jeans.

The office was locked, so I knocked like the sign said. A minute later, an elderly man poked his head out. His white, feathery hair flew out in every direction, and I could see the collar of a terrycloth robe around his turkey neck.

"What?" he shouted.

"I'm looking for someone named Googie."

"What?" he shouted again.

I noticed a hearing aid. I leaned in and enunciated my words, raising the volume of my voice a few notches.

"I'm looking for someone named Googie."

He squinted at me. "Boobie? I don't know any Boobie!"

"No, Googie." I drew a *G* in the air. "G-o-o-g-i-e. With a *G*."

"If you're a cop, where's your badge?" he shouted, jabbing his bony finger at me.

I held up my hands. "I'm not a cop."

"I don't know any Googie."

"Are you sure? Because he used to run with a guy who lived here. Do you remember a man named Gordon Pryne?"

He slammed the door. I heard him throw the lock.

I knocked again. I could hear him shuffling around in there, but he never came back to the door. I sighed and looked around. What was I thinking? Standing in the middle of a high-crime neighborhood, at a drug motel, knocking on doors. At night. Alone. Of all the idiot moves I'd made recently, this one had to be the dumbest. Or at least in the top ten. I started mentally cataloging my idiot moves as I walked over to the row of rooms and knocked on the first door where a light was on.

I could hear a TV through the thin walls.

The door flew open, revealing filthy carpet littered with Solo cups, beer cans, and cigarette butts. Clothes were strewn around the floor. The bed was unmade. A man wearing a wife-beater tank top and boxer shorts gestured toward the television set.

"I'm in a meeting."

"I just need a minute," I said. "I'm—"

"I don't want no Girl Scout cookies."

"I'm not selling anything." I held up three fingers. "Scout's honor."

He squinted at me. "You're looking for smack, you come to the wrong place. Charlie don't live here no more."

"I don't want any smack. I'm looking for someone named Googie."

"Don't know him."

"Are you sure? Because I know a friend of his who used to live here."

"Lots of people used to live here, lady." The man turned casually and slammed the door in my face.

I moved on to the next lighted window. No answer.

Gripping my bag, I looked around the parking lot, which was uninhabited except for an emaciated gray cat licking its paws beside the Dumpster. I clutched my keys between my fingers anyway, following the ridiculous advice all girls get about being out alone at night—have your keys ready in case you need to jab someone's eyes out to defend yourself. As though that would stop an attacker with a half ounce of determination.

Cars zoomed by on Northwest Highway. The warm night air was still and humid as I climbed the stairs. I could feel myself starting to sweat, my hands getting clammy. I tossed out a prayer—maybe Joe Riley was on duty and God could send him on over. I wondered if you lost your angel-protection privileges if you indulged in moronic behavior.

Another lit window, another knock. No answer.

A light came on next door. A man flung open the door, grunted, and brushed past me, then stomped down the stairs and off into the night. A woman wearing a pink satin bathrobe and full makeup stepped out of the room with a pack of cigarettes. She looked me up and down.

"You lost, honey?"

"I'm just—"

" 'Cause this is Fat Daddy's territory, and he'll cut you if he knows you're working it."

"No, I'm not… It's not like that. I'm just looking for someone."

She lit her cigarette, pulled a long drag into her lungs, and leaned against the doorjamb. She closed her eyes.

"Long night?" I asked.

"Just gettin' started, honey." She blew a thin stream of smoke into the air, opened her eyes, and turned to me. "Who you looking for?"

"Someone named Googie."

I watched her face. Nothing registered.

"Who's looking for him?"

"Do you know him?"

"You don't hear too good, do you?"

"My name is Dylan Foster."

"You a cop?"

"No. A friend of the family."

She laughed. "He got a rich uncle or something? Who are you, lady? If you're not a cop."

"I'm looking for Nicholas Chavez."

"The kid? The one that got kidnapped?"

I nodded.

"You a private detective?"

"I told you. Just a friend of the family." I held my hand out. "And you are?"

"I saw that kid's mom on TV. Rich doctor, right? What's the reward?"

"She works at Parkland. She doesn't have any money."

She studied me. "You look like you might have some money."

"I've got nineteen bucks on me. You want it? If you'll tell me what you know about Googie, you can have every dime."

She pointed her toes and admired her pedicure. "Mama needs a new pair of shoes."

"All I have is nineteen dollars." I pulled my wallet out of my bag and showed her. "Look. A ten and nine ones. I might have some change in my truck."

She took another drag and pointed at the street. "ATM's right over there, honey."

I followed her point with my eyes. There was indeed an ATM across the street, at Nuevo Laredo Bank, which was situated between another strip joint and a bar called Spanky's.

"You want me to walk over there and withdraw money at night, in this neighborhood, by myself? Do I look like an idiot to you?"

"You want to know about Googie or not?"

"I've got a call in to the cops. I'm sure they'd be glad to ask you themselves. Maybe you could call Fat Daddy and let him know he's about to go out of business."

She leaned her head back against the door, eyes closed, and sighed, clearly bored with my threats. "Two hundred dollars."

"I'm calling 911."

"I'll be gone by the time they get here, sweetie." She jerked her head toward the motel room. "I pack real light."

I stared across the street at the ATM, then looked back at her.

"We're talking about a little kid," I said. "A little kid's life is at stake."

"Ought to be worth a couple of singles, then, huh?"

I sighed and dug in my purse for my ATM card, then stomped down the stairs and across the parking lot to my truck. I threw the door open and felt around under the seat for my flashlight. My hand closed around it, and I pulled it out, wielding it like a club. It's one of those long metal ones that could double as a baseball bat. Holding my weapon in my hand, I stalked across the street and pushed my ATM card into the slot. It took me a minute to remember my PIN. My fingers were shaking as I punched the numbers in.

The machine spit the money out, and I jammed it quickly into my pocket, gripping the flashlight again and heading back across the street.

Upstairs at room eleven, I handed the woman the cash, which she counted.

"This is only two hundred," she said.

"You said two hundred!" I shouted.

"The price is two nineteen."

"You're really something, you know that?" I dug in my purse for my wallet. "Unbelievable." I was just about to start a rant when she snatched the money out of my hand.

"Googie lives with his mother," she said.

I froze. "Where?"

"Over off Inwood. Behind that Home Depot."

"What's the address?"

"Don't know."

"Do you know what kind of car Googie drives?"

"Googie doesn't have a car."

"What about his mom?"

"Never saw a car."

"What's her name?"

"Juanita Garcia."

"There have to be a hundred Juanita Garcias in this town."

She sucked on her cigarette. "Nice lady. She made me tamales one time."

"You've been to her house?"

She nodded.

"Tell me where it is. I want to know exactly."

"I don't remember the street."

"For two hundred nineteen dollars, you'd better remember the street," I said, my hand tightening on my flashlight.

"She owns a day care."

"What's it called?"

"Little something."

"Little what?"

She looked up, trying to remember. "I'm blank."

"Picture the sign. What color is it?"

"White, maybe. With balloons."

"What color are the balloons?"

"Red, yellow, and blue."

"And the sign says 'Little'...what?"

She shrugged. "I don't remember."

"What color is the house? Do you remember? Anything noteworthy about the yard? There's play equipment, right? Is it a chain-link fence or a wood one?"

She snapped her fingers. "Little Blue School House."

"Is the house blue?"

"Turquoise."

"And it's off Inwood behind the Home Depot?"

"A few blocks in," she said. "You can't miss it."

37

IT TOOK ME ABOUT twenty minutes to find the house. I was dialing Martinez frantically the whole time, but I got sent straight to voice mail every time. It was late. Maybe he'd turned his phone off. I left him a rambling message about Googie and his mother and the Little Blue School House. I failed to mention, of course, that I was going over there right this very second. No need to get myself into any more trouble than I was already in. Especially if this whole thing turned out to be another one of my harebrained debacles.

The Little Blue School House was on a scrubby little lot in a crumbling residential neighborhood near Love Field. The turquoise paint was peeling, but the yard was neat. It was one of the "exception" houses—one of the few in the neighborhood whose owner seemed to be trying to maintain the property. A chain-link fence revealed a playground in the backyard. A wooden fort with swings and a slide dominated the yard space. Beside the fort sat a small sandbox and a seesaw with duck-shaped seats. I parked down the street and watched the house. It looked to me like no one was home—or maybe everyone was asleep. I couldn't see any lights on.

A streetlight in front of the house illuminated the front yard, which was brown but tidy. There were no cars parked in the driveway.

I got out of my truck and walked quickly toward the house, staying in the shadows of trees, then sneaked up to the garage and peeked inside, fully expecting to find the white Ford Fairlane. The garage, though, had been converted for the day care. Inside were three cribs, an array of play equipment, and a small fleet of tricycles and strollers.

I crouched down in the dark and made my way around the perimeter of the house. Under each window I stopped, listened, then poked my head up and peeked in the window. All the curtains on the front of the house were closed tight. I scaled the chain-link, careful not to rip my already-ripped jeans, and let myself down into the backyard, repeating the window procedure on the backside of the house. The only window that wasn't curtained was the kitchen, which looked out onto the backyard. The kitchen was plain but seemed clean. Baby bottles were drying on a rack by the sink. Beside the dinette set sat a child-sized table with little-kid chairs.

I crept from the house to the alley, still hoping for a glimpse of the white Fairlane. But the alley was empty. I began walking down the alley, looking for a carport, maybe. As I got to the next yard, I heard a low growl. I stopped in my tracks and shifted my eyes to the gate. Behind the chain-link fence, a mixed-breed pound dog bared its teeth at me. I held up my hands reflexively, then slowly moved my right hand down and reached into my purse. I fished around and found what I was looking for. I slipped my emergency supply of Nature Valley granola bars out of my bag, ripped open a wrapper, and held a piece out gingerly to the dog. He sniffed at it, wagged his tail happily, then began barking maniacally.

I dropped the granola bar, bolted down the alley to the corner, hopped into my truck, and lit out for home.

Another spectacularly bad idea. Still, I was batting five hundred today. My visit with Brigid had been fruitful. My bold trek to Caligula had yielded a name, Googie. But then I'd started smacking fly balls right at the center fielder.

It was late now, and I'd about had it for the day. I'd been up forever—I'd been in Shreveport only this morning. That seemed days ago now.

My house was dark and depressing when I got home, as usual. The answering machine light was blinking, as usual.

The first call was from my dad, barking orders to call him back. Another call from my dad, angrier this time. And then a call—horror of horrors—from Kellee. I rolled my eyes. They were laying it on thick. Delete, delete, delete.

The next call was from David. He was ready to talk. Could we meet tomorrow sometime? I felt tears pool in the corners of my eyes, the rush of emotion catching me by surprise. I'd forgotten to obsess about him in all the fuss. Now I fell headlong into a tar pit of loneliness and fear. I saved the message and moved on.

The last call was from Liz. They were heading back to Chicago in the morning and wanted to know if they could bring Melissa back by tonight. I checked my cell phone—she'd left the same message there two hours ago. I must have missed the call while I was spiraling into a fit of neurotic, misguided behavior. I pushed Return and dialed her.

"You're up late," she said when she picked up the phone.

"So are you. I was hoping I wouldn't wake you."

"I've given up sleep entirely. It's bad for you, I've decided."

"How do you figure?"

"Every time I go to sleep, something terrible happens. So I'm just going to stay up."

"For the rest of your life?"

"Possibly."

"Great plan, Liz. Let me know how that works out."

"Where have you been?"

I told her about Caligula and the Circle Inn and the Little Blue School House.

"No Ford Fairlane, huh?"

"Nope. I wish Martinez would call me back."

"He's in Phoenix. Or probably still in the air. That must be why he isn't picking up."

"What's going on? Did they get a lead?"

"They found a white Fairlane whose owner has a criminal record and who disappeared last week. Last time anyone saw him, he was headed east. The wife reported him missing and says she thinks he's in Mexico now. Martinez flew out with another detective to talk to her."

"What day was he driving east?"

"I don't think it's him, Dylan."

"Why do you say that?"

"Christine said it wasn't him and that Nicholas wants his mommy."

I let the air out of my lungs. "I'm exhausted. Can we make the bunny exchange in the morning?"

"Sure."

"What time does your flight leave?"

"Whenever we want."

"Oh. I forgot. George."

"Don't start," Liz said. "What time do you want us to come by?"

"Not too early. Maybe tenish? I'm going to try to sleep in."

"What if we all go to brunch before Christine and I head out?" A tired sigh. "I can't get her excited about going back. She keeps crying that she needs to find Nicholas first."

"We all need to find Nicholas first."

"Get a good night's sleep, Dylan."

"You too. See you in the morning."

It stormed again that night, thunderclaps almost knocking me out of bed half a dozen times before I nodded off. I slept hard, though, until 3:30 a.m., when I heard the rattlesnake again. I didn't know whether I'd heard it in my dreams or in reality, so I did a cursory check of the house, shot up a quick prayer, had a brief, hypothetical conversation with Joe Riley, then opened my bedroom windows and smelled the rain.

The snake wasn't real. I was convinced of that. What I wasn't sure of was how much of the rest of it was. Was I chasing phantoms? The white car. The sallow-faced man in the sketch. Googie and his mother and the Little Blue School House. And Gordon Pryne.

I crawled back into bed, my head full of disturbing images. I tossed in bed for the next few hours, worrying them all until I'd beaten them half to death and worn myself out completely. I must have fallen into an exhausted sleep, because when I woke with a start, the sun was up. I looked at the clock: 7:33 a.m.

I wrapped my robe around myself and padded into the kitchen, feeling surprisingly rested after such a short sleep. Maybe it was the rain. Or maybe I was entering some sort of manic episode. I peered out the kitchen window. The rain had stopped for now, but the skies looked heavy and wet. I put the teakettle on and woke my computer up. I found myself staring at Gordon Pryne's mug shot again. I was still logged in to his blog. I put my chin in my hands and studied the picture. He had the animal energy of a wild dog—wiry, aggressive, vicious, predatory. His eyes were empty of everything but rage. Why would anyone want this man released—even his mother? He was so obviously a threat to society. I clicked on the message board, scrolling down through the messages.

Gordon's brother's screen name was Piper. I knew a kid once whose nickname was Piper. He was a pot dealer. Pryne's mother's name wasn't mentioned, and since she hadn't logged in, she didn't have a screen name. In the messages, everyone referred to her as MA. Capital *M*, capital *A*.

I started in on the messages.

"MA keeps asking about Gordie. Meeting with ATTY on Mon."

"Good luck man. Spring him."

All the exchanges were like that—brief and cryptic. Many of them mentioned MA or the "ATTY"—presumably, Gordon's lawyer. MA's cancer was bad, Piper said. "Eating her insides out."

A few of the messages mentioned a pending court date at the Dallas County courthouse. I couldn't figure out why he'd be in court. Maybe it was related to the offenses he'd committed last winter while he was on the run.

I paged through the rest of the messages halfheartedly, then picked up the phone and called the courthouse. It took a few transfers, but I found out Gordon Pryne's case was due for a hearing in the Dallas County court on Tuesday. I wondered if prisoners got bused in from Huntsville to appear at their court dates. Maybe Gordon Pryne was at Lew Sterrett.

His attorney of record was someone named G. Perry Eschenbrenner. I got his number from the state bar Web site and called it, expecting to leave a voice-mail message. To my surprise, a live voice answered.

"I'd like to speak to Mr. Eschenbrenner, please."

"Who's calling?"

"Dr. Dylan Foster." It helps to whip out the credentials when attempting to intimidate the hourly help.

"Ms. Eschenbrenner is unavailable," the woman said. "May I take a message?"

"Oh. She's a woman. Sorry. Perry?"

"Gail Perry Eschenbrenner," the woman said. "May I take a message?"

"I'm calling about Gordon Pryne. Do you happen to know if he's been transferred up here for the hearing?"

"This is an answering service. We don't have access to that kind of information. I can have Ms. Eschenbrenner call you if you'd like to leave a number."

"When would that be?"

"Monday's a holiday. Tuesday she's in court all day. I'd say Wednesday. Would you like to leave a message?"

I hesitated, my mind stumbling over *holiday*. What holiday? Then the fog cleared. I'd forgotten Monday was Memorial Day.

"Is there any way you could page her or something?"

"I'm sorry, Dr. Foster. Would you like to leave a message?"

I sighed and left my number. "Just tell her it's about Gordon Pryne."

"I'll give her the message," she said curtly, and she hung up.

I saw a flash of lightning outside the window and heard an immediate crack of thunder. The lights in my house flickered, then buzzed out. My computer screen went black as the sky opened up again, dumping buckets of gray rain onto the already soggy ground.

I fixed my tea and returned to the kitchen table, sipping and staring into space, the gloom of the day descending on me. It occurred to me to pray, but the swamp of hopelessness I was wallowing in made that an impossibility. Begging seemed possible, so I tried that for a while, eventually shuffling into my bedroom and cracking my Bible open in another attempt to find the scene where God shows someone the angels. I finally found it in Second Kings—not a book I spend a lot of time in. God shows Elisha the angels surrounding the battleground in chariots of fire.

"Where are my chariots?" I shouted.

A flash of light, and the sky cracked again. My lights flickered back on. The computer buzzed to life.

"Wow," I said, amazed. "Thanks."

My energy renewed, literally, I sat back down and logged in, searching Google for MA Pryne, Piper Pryne, Gordon Pryne, Googie. I found a few newspaper articles about Gordon Pryne—the most recent was a year old. There was nothing in it of note. Nothing at all on the other searches.

Back to the blog. I checked every screen name on the message page, hoping for a break. Anything. But they were all nonsense to me. Nothing rang a bell.

I was studying the list of threads again when my phone rang. It was Martinez.

"Are you insane, Dylan? Is that the problem here? Should I take you down to Parkland for involuntary commitment?"

"What are you talking about?"

"What are you doing poking around at Caligula?"

"I got a name, Martinez. Did you notice that? Have you started looking for Googie yet? Because I found his mother's house. She owns a day care over by Love Field."

"What? Slow down."

I told him about the events of the night before.

"You paid a hooker two hundred dollars and you believe what she told you? Go back to your day job, Dylan. You're not cut out to be a detective."

"You think she'd lie to me?"

"You're kidding, right? Tell me you're kidding. How could anyone in your line of work be so naive?"

"It's a gift," I said defiantly. "From the Lord."

"Well, keep it stowed. It's not helpful."

"So you're not going to send anybody over there?"

"Of course I'm going to send someone over there. I have to. We're going to have to waste man-hours on this now."

"It's not a waste. It's a lead."

"We're already looking for Googie. But he's probably long gone by now."

"What makes you say that?"

"Dylan, listen very carefully. When a reasonably well-off white woman starts walking around a neighborhood like that one asking questions about someone, the person in question usually assumes that is not good news."

"But you guys do it. Detectives go down to places like that all the time and ask people questions."

"We take them down to the station, Dylan. So they won't be seen talking to cops. That way," he said in a sing-songy voice you'd reserve for a five-year-old, "they don't get their throats cut, and our suspect doesn't get tipped off by someone who overhears the conversation."

"Oh. I didn't think of that."

"Do you get that these people are not on our side? Do you understand you can't trust anything they say? Are you grasping this basic fact of law enforcement?"

"I don't know what to say, Martinez."

"Then keep your mouth shut, for once. For crying out loud, Dylan."

"Where are you?" I asked, more to change the subject than anything.

"Getting on the plane in Phoenix."

"You're coming back? Already? Did you find the guy?"

"He was at his girlfriend's in Juárez. Passed out after a bender. We've got half a dozen witnesses who put him with her all week. The car never left the driveway."

"Well, I guess I'll see you when you get back, then. Have a safe trip."

We hung up, and I sat there making phone calls for a while. I checked in with Maria, who seemed to be on her last leg. I returned my dad's calls, knowing he'd be on the golf course, and there was no way he would pick up the phone. I did not call Kellee, of course. I had not taken complete leave of my senses. My last call was to David.

"Hey, you," he said.

"Very funny." I stood and began pacing as I talked. "I hear the jury's in."

"You got my message."

"Hence the return phone call."

"Are we feeling a little oppositional today?"

"You have no idea." I stopped and braced myself against the breakfast bar, my heart suddenly racing. "So. What's the good word?"

"The word is, I'd like to meet and talk."

"When?"

"Tomorrow? I'm free in the evening if you are."

"Wow. A nighttime meeting. I must be out of the basement."

"Not yet, sugar pea."

"Ooh. A nickname. Working my way up."

"I'd better get off the phone before you make up my mind for me."

"What time tomorrow?"

"Eight o'clock?"

"Great. See you at eight thirty."

"Right."

I got off the phone determined to think positive, happy thoughts. David had called. He wanted to talk. Surely he wouldn't banter with me like that if he'd decided to cut me loose. To celebrate my anticipated good fortune, I got up from the table and made myself a peanut butter and honey sandwich, savoring it with a second cup of tea. It was the first encouragement I'd had in a while, and I intended to enjoy it.

I went back to my computer and stared again at the list of threads on Gordon Pryne's blog, the words blurring together. I was reaching for the phone to dial G. Perry Eschenbrenner's service again when my hand froze in midair, my eyes locked on a message from Piper posted a week ago today.

"Gordie says to pick up the package ASAP."

I scrolled down, looking for the response. There wasn't one. I combed backward through the messages again until I found what I was looking for.

There it was, in black and white.

"Gordie says the package isn't safe."

38

~

I MADE MORE FRANTIC phone calls to Ybarra, who was clearly deter-mined to ignore me, and to Martinez, who was on an airplane with no access to his cell phone. I couldn't think what else to do, so I threw on some clothes, got in my truck, and pointed it toward Lew Sterrett.

I'd been there once before—to visit Gordon Pryne, as a matter of fact. But I'd been escorted by a detective that time, so I'd been whisked through security without any problems. This time, I'd brought along some props. I would have to con my way in. With a little luck, some help from the Almighty, and the assistance of my recently polished lying skills, I just might cross the Rubicon and gain an audience with the devil.

I knew the drill. I handed my bag to the guard, walked through the metal detectors, and allowed myself to be wanded by a young guard who looked as though he had orders to shoot on sight. I did as I was told, for once, and passed through step one without incident. Step two is to show your ID to the guard at the desk, who then checks your name against the prisoner's allowed-visitors list.

"Name of prisoner?" the guard said.

"Gordon Pryne."

The woman thumbed through a list, going back and forth between pages. My heart stopped. If his name wasn't on the list, he was still in Huntsville and hadn't been transferred up for his hearing.

Her pen stopped on a name and put a little red check by it. My heartbeat resumed.

She squinted at the page. "Says here he's got a hearing on Tuesday."

"That's right. First thing." I handed the woman my ID and pulled a file out of my bag.

She studied the picture, matched it to my face, wrote down my name, and began thumbing through the visitors list.

"I may not be on there," I said, trying to sound helpful.

She looked up. "You can't go in unless you're on the list."

"I know. I'm with his attorney's office."

"Which one?"

Once again, my weak preparation skills were inhibiting my already meager prospects for success. I cast about for the name but drew a complete, black-hole blank.

She kept her pen poised over the page, bored and impatient. "Eschenbrenner or Vittato?"

A little gift from Joe Riley. I breathed a quick sigh of relief.

"Eschenbrenner. I just need ten minutes. I promise."

She held her hand out for the file, which I had stuffed with some random mail I'd had on my desk at home. I pulled it back and held it to my chest.

"I'm sorry. It's privileged."

She looked at me over her glasses, her eyes landing on the hole in my jeans. "You don't look like you work for a law firm."

"I'm technically off today. Everyone else is out of town for the holiday. You know how it is."

She didn't seem sympathetic.

"Look, I just need to take care of this and get back to Ms. Eschenbrenner. Ten minutes." I smiled, pasting on a look of apologetic sincerity. "I promise."

She gave me a disapproving look, wrote my name down on the allowed list, and waved me through. I completed the rest of the security-check obstacle course—another flash of my ID, a verbal review of the procedures for prisoner visitation, and another guard, who wrote my name down again.

"Name of prisoner?"

"Gordon Pryne." I repeated my explanation, smiled innocently, and was eventually led to a seat. I waited almost half an hour before someone came and got me and escorted me into the visitors' area—a grimy room with a thick wall of glass down the middle, divided by little booths with phones on both sides of the glass. Prisoners were hunched on one side, huddled over the phone, talking to attorneys or relatives through the phone lines. One woman had brought her children with her. The littlest girl—she looked to be about three and was wearing a pink ballerina tutu—had pressed herself up against the glass and was trying to kiss her father, who was crying on the inmate side of the window.

I sat where I was told to sit and waited by the phone. The Formica was filthy. I couldn't even contemplate what was on that phone. I kept my hands in my lap and lambasted myself mentally for arriving without a bottle of hand sanitizer gel and a fresh pack of Handi Wipes.

A few minutes later, Gordon Pryne sauntered in, wearing his prison whites and a pair of bright orange Keds loafers.

When I'd seen him last, he'd been shackled at the hands and feet and was three days into detox from a wicked meth addiction. He'd also just been arrested for murder and had a recent run-in with Peter Terry. Not surprisingly, he had looked like death on toast. Old, dry, cracked toast. With an extra helping of sour mayonnaise.

Today, though, he was clear eyed and rested. The rage was still there, but five months without drugs had brought some color back to his face and straightened his back. He didn't look broken anymore. He looked arrogant and mean.

He picked up the phone and sneered at me. "Lookee who's here," he said in a flat redneck drawl.

"Mr. Pryne. Do you remember me?"

"He said you'd come."

I furrowed my brow. "Who said I'd come?"

He glared at me with those muddy green eyes. "You take me for a fool?"

"Pardon?"

"You think you can walk in here and lie to me like I don't know who you are?" He leaned toward the window and whispered. "I know who you are."

I leaned back from the window reflexively. "I'm not sure what you mean about knowing who I am, Mr. Pryne. I'm just here to ask you a few questions."

I shot a nervous glance at the security camera in the corner. I was living on borrowed time. The second they figured out I wasn't who I said I was, I'd be kicked out on my rear end into the bright May sunshine without the answers I'd come for.

"We've only got a few minutes," I said. "Do you mind, Mr. Pryne, if I ask you a few questions?"

"Mr. Pryne? Ain't we formal, now?" He sat back and crossed his arms tightly across his chest. "I got some questions for you too." He spat out a foul epithet, one he'd used repeatedly the last time I saw him.

"You won't get any answers out of me using language like that, Mr. Pryne," I said firmly.

He shot the word at me again.

I took the phone away from my ear and was preparing to slam it onto its hook when I heard his voice, tinny and distant through the phone line: "I got what you want."

I eased the receiver slowly back to my ear, Martinez's advice ringing in my ears. *These people are not on our side. You can't trust anything they say.*

"Give it to me, then," I said. "If you've got what I want."

"I'll give you what you want." He looked me up and down hungrily. "But you gotta pay."

I thought of my two-hundred-nineteen-dollar investment, which had yet to fully pay off. I hoped Pryne didn't have anything more graphic in mind.

"What's the price?" I asked warily.

"You give me what I want," he said through gritted teeth. "What I asked you for last time."

"What do you want, Mr. Pryne?"

"I told you to get 'em to stop."

"Get who to stop what?"

He growled at me. "You know what I mean, you lyin'—"

I flinched. There was that word again. I wasn't about to leave, though, until I found out what he knew.

"They got their eyes on me," he was saying, his voice raspy now. "In my head." He jerked his head around wildly as though he was chasing a fly, then calmed himself and looked again at me. "You said you'd get rid of 'em."

"I don't know about any eyes in your head."

He glared at me, still twitching. "You know 'em. You know who they are."

"I don't. I swear, I don't."

"You're a liar," he said quietly, his jaw tight.

"I'm sorry you feel that way, Mr. Pryne."

He leaned in. "He told me you'd lie."

I pushed back from the glass again.

Pryne was still talking, almost to himself. "I said, 'No sir, she wouldn't lie. Not a citizen like her with her fancy life. She wouldn't do nothing like that. Not when I got what she wants.'" He shook his head, his eyes locking on mine, a look of disappointed condescension on his face. "But he was right. You're a liar. A lyin' piece of trash. Just like he said."

I felt my skin prickle. My hands felt like I'd plunged them into a bucket of ice water. "Who said I would lie?"

"Who do you think?" He sat back and narrowed his eyes at me, daring me to say it.

"Tell me. Who are you talking about?"

He waited a moment, then said quietly, "Peter Terry." He said it like he was spitting out a broken tooth, wiping his mouth after the words came out. "That's who I'm talking about."

I blinked. Peter Terry knew Gordon Pryne. I was certain of that. But I hadn't known until this moment that Gordon Pryne knew Peter Terry. Not by name, anyway.

"How do you know Peter Terry?" I asked, the cold creeping from my hands into my arms.

"How does Peter Terry know me?"

"I don't know," I said. "Honestly. I don't."

"Make him stop." Pryne's eyes darted around the room again.

"What's he doing?"

"Watching me!" he shouted. Then more quietly, looking around suspiciously, "He's always watching me."

The cold had taken over my whole body. I shivered, feeling suddenly faint and tired. "Is he watching you now?"

He leaned into the window again and sneered, showing me his brown teeth. "What do you think?"

He began to laugh. Insane, cackling laughter, bursting out of him and hitting the glass like gunfire. I looked around nervously. The last thing I wanted was to draw attention to myself. But everyone was just going about their business. Even the guards seemed uninterested.

I needed to pull myself together. I shook my head and warmed up one hand on my jeans. The other, still holding the phone, stayed cold as a stone.

"Mr. Pryne…"

The laughter slowed.

"Mr. Pryne…"

He sing-songed, "Mr. Pryne, Mr. Pryne."

Only a chuckle now.

"Mr. Pryne. Can you hear me?"

I glared at him silently.

He put the phone to his ear again. "What?"

"Listen to me."

The manic laughter drained from his expression, leaving the raw hate and the impenetrable mistrust from years of a hard, bottom-scraping life.

I was the one who leaned in this time. "Are you listening?"

His eyes locked on mine.

I stared right back at him. "If I knew how to get rid of Peter Terry, I would tell you. I swear I would. He won't leave me alone either."

"We got something in common, then," he said, a look of angry lust on his face. He ran his eyes over me again.

I shifted uncomfortably. "You're right. We do."

"You got something for me, then? Since we got so much in common?"

I considered my answer for a long minute before I spoke. "Do you know Joe Riley?" I said finally.

His look was blank.

"You don't, do you?"

He shook his head, a quick no.

"I think he might be able to help you get rid of the…eyes in your head."

"He a priest or something?"

I shook my head. "Just put him on your visitors list."

"Ain't got no room, what with all my friends and relatives," he said sarcastically.

"I don't know if he will help you. But if you listen to him, he might." I swallowed. The feeling was coming back to my hands. "I would if I were you."

The argument was already raging in my head. What are the rules pertaining to angel management? Is it even possible to loan out your angel? Surely even losers like Gordon Pryne have angels of their own. Maybe his was an apprentice or something. It was a theory, given the lousy job he was doing.

What was I thinking, offering up help to a scumbag like Gordon Pryne? But who more than he needed the help? Wasn't that the point, after all—to offer the help to the ones who need it the most?

Pryne was looking at me like I was the one who was nuts.

"That's all I have to give you." I set my jaw firmly for the fight I knew was coming. "Your turn."

He pushed back his chair and stood to leave.

"Who's Googie?" I shouted into the phone.

He stopped, clearly shocked that I'd learned his accomplice's name. He turned and stood, the phone still in his hand. I motioned for him to raise it to his ear, which he did reluctantly.

"Don't know no Googie."

"You don't need to lie about it, Mr. Pryne. I know you know him. I just don't know where he is. Tell me where to find him."

"How should I know?" He shrugged. "He ain't in here."

"You're the liar," I said, my anger beginning to burn. "You want to keep the package safe? You tell me where to find Googie."

His expression tightened.

"The package isn't safe," I said. "Not in the hands of someone like Googie. The package belongs with his mother. She's the one who can keep him safe."

He sat down, a look of dumb amazement on his face. I watched him struggle, his face twisting as if he were receiving a punch. He put his head in his free hand and ran his fingers through that shock of wild, curly hair, so like Nicholas's. A few minutes passed in silence. His expression and body began twisting as if he were in terrible pain. I watched the battle rage in his mind as Gordon Pryne fought with what was left of his conscience.

"He wants the package," he said at last.

"Who does?"

"Who do you think?"

My mind raced. "Peter Terry? Peter Terry wants Nicholas?"

He darted a look behind him at the guard, who was standing a dozen feet away.

"Don't know no Nicholas, lady. I'm talking about a package. That's all. Just a package."

"Peter Terry wants the package?"

He nodded a quick, almost imperceptible yes.

"Did you have Googie pick him up to keep him safe?"

A long wait—an eternity—before he gave me another quick nod. I could barely breathe.

"Why?"

He mumbled something.

"I didn't hear you. Talk into the phone. Why did you have Googie pick up the package?"

He ducked his head and hunched over the phone. "Wouldn't want him to have the eyes in his head."

"A sudden burst of fatherly concern?" I couldn't hold back the sarcasm.

He looked up at me with the first sincerity I'd ever seen on his face. "They shouldn't go after the kids."

My jaw dropped. I was stunned by this sudden burst of decency.

"His momma take good care of him?" he asked, his eyes cast downward.

"Yes, she does," I said. "Where is he, Gordon? Tell me where he is. If you care about him at all, you have to tell me."

"Don't know."

I felt the blood rush back into my extremities. My face was hot. "You lying pig," I said, my temper finally beginning to boil. "You tell me where he is right this minute."

He looked at me calmly. "If they told me, I'd know, now, wouldn't I?"

I froze. "What are you saying?"

He leaned in, almost touching the glass, and said quietly, "If I know where the package is, I'm not the only one who knows. You see what I'm sayin'?"

"No. I don't see what you're saying."

"If I know where the package is, the eyes can find out where the package is." He licked dry lips, his eyes flicking from side to side. "And the package ain't safe no more."

We stared each other down for several long seconds. Finally I said, "How can I find the package, then? Tell me how to find Googie."

He leaned back, stretched his legs out, and crossed his ankles. "Don't look for Googie."

"What, then? What should I do?"

"Look for May Ran," he whispered into the phone, his eyes weary, defeated. "You find May Ran, you find the package."

And then he stood, hung up the phone, turned his back to me, and walked away.

39

~

YBARRA AND TWO OTHER detectives were knocking at the door of the
Little Blue School House day care an hour after Martinez's flight landed
from Phoenix. A brief interview with Juanita Garcia confirmed that her
son's nickname was indeed Googie, that he did live with her, but that
she hadn't seen him in several days. Not since he brought his girlfriend's
little boy over to play for a few hours before he left town.

"Is this the boy?" Ybarra had asked, hands shaking with rage as he
showed a picture to Googie's mother.

She'd nodded and looked up at the cop, seemingly ignorant of what
her son had done. "He's not in some kind of trouble, is he? Is he hurt?
You haven't hurt my Googie, have you?"

They'd cuffed her, stuck her in the squad car, and called the day-
care kids' parents to pick up their kids, who had all been parked at day
care on a holiday weekend by blue-collar parents who couldn't afford to
take the day off. Someone had lined them up in plastic kiddie chairs in
the backyard with Popsicles melting on their hands. A couple of cops
were talking to them gently, one by one, while others combed the day
care. The Physical Evidence Section of CAPERS showed up in a white
van and unpacked their gear.

The closet in Googie's room was exactly as Christine had described.
Venice's drawing had been almost surgically correct. Boots, collared
shirts—all worn, many of them plaid. The Phoenix Suns jersey was
hanging right there. Nash. Number thirteen.

Martinez was there when they bagged and tagged the Nash jersey.

"Great floor vision," the PES investigator had commented as he
took a picture with gloved hands and folded the shirt into a brown
paper bag.

As he left the house, Martinez called me and told me the whole story.

"Does he own a 1963 Ford Fairlane?" I asked.

"Ms. Garcia developed a sudden inability to understand English when we asked her that question," Martinez said. "We eventually got her to admit that her precious Googie borrows it from a friend sometimes."

"She give you a name?"

"Batiste. Carlos Batiste."

"Is it the guy you were looking for?" I asked. "The one with the criminal record?"

"Nope. Just another unemployed loser living at his mother's house."

I gave him my news about Gordon Pryne.

He whistled. "If you hadn't come out of there with this, I'd be hauling you to the woodshed right now. What were you—"

I cut him off. "Save the spanking for later. Who or what is May Ran?"

"How should I know?" Martinez snapped.

Over the next hours, the cops took the day care apart, confiscated everything in Googie's closet, and emptied the sandbox into bags, hauling it all down to DPD headquarters for a thorough going-over by PES.

The Fairlane was soon located a few blocks away—parked inside a garage and covered with a tarp, and still sporting the stolen plates. Its owner was promptly arrested, and the car was towed to the pound. PES investigators ripped the black carpet from the trunk and began examining it.

I was with Maria when Martinez and Ybarra came to tell her what they'd found.

Martinez sat beside her at her kitchen table as Ybarra methodically laid out the evidence.

"We found hairs consistent with Nicholas's in the sand we took from the sandbox."

Maria looked at me, tears already forming in her brown eyes. "The snickerdoodles. At least he got to play outside. That's a good sign, don't you think?"

I nodded, reached across the table, and gripped her hand.

"Hairs consistent with Nicholas's were found in the carpet we lifted from the closet, as well as from the carpet we took from the trunk of the Fairlane. We also recovered sand consistent with the sand from the day care's sandbox in the trunk of the Fairlane." Ybarra paused and took a breath, glancing first at Martinez, who reached for Maria's other hand. "Along with a trace of blood we've typed to match Nicholas's."

Maria gasped and crumbled. Martinez hugged her while she sobbed. I got up to fetch Kleenexes and a glass of ice water, all the while vowing to kill Googie and Gordon Pryne with my bare hands if I ever got the opportunity.

When I returned to the table, Maria wiped her face with both hands, accepted a tissue, refused the water, and squared her shoulders. Ybarra looked at Martinez, who nodded for him to continue.

"It'll be a few days before we have DNA on any of this, but the evidence strongly suggests we're on the right track."

Maria nodded numbly.

"I wouldn't worry too much about the blood," Martinez said gently. "Don't think the worst. Not yet."

"How much blood was there?" I asked.

"Trace amounts. Almost nothing. Could have been from a skinned knee," Ybarra said. He put his pen down onto the neatly printed notes he'd been reading from. "Nothing suggesting anything like a mortal wound."

"Had the carpet been cleaned?" Maria asked.

"No. The carpet was full of sand and hairs. It hadn't even been vacuumed."

Martinez spoke up. "It helps when you're dealing with morons."

Ybarra nodded. "They left us all the evidence we needed. They might as well have written us a letter."

"Or drawn a map," Maria said grimly. "That would be helpful at this point, wouldn't it?"

"What about Gordon Pryne?" I asked. "Have you gotten anything out of him?"

"His lawyer won't let us near him," Martinez said. "Your 'employer'"—he shot a look at me—"is already claiming any information he gave you is inadmissible."

"*Is* it inadmissible?" I asked.

"That's a question for the DA," Ybarra said.

"I don't care if it's admissible or not," Maria said. "I just want my son back." She took a sip of water and turned to me. "Dylan, do you think he'd talk to you again?"

I thought about it but shook my head. "I don't think so, Maria. I think he's told me everything he knows. He'd made a point to not know the particulars. So Peter Terry couldn't get the information out of him."

"Who's Peter Terry?" Ybarra asked.

The three of us looked at one another.

"Gordon Pryne's inner demon," I said at last. "Think of him as an imaginary friend's evil twin."

Ybarra checked his notes. "The name Joe Riley ring a bell?"

"Why?" I asked.

"Pryne added him to his visitors list today. He doesn't work for either of the lawyers—"

"He put him on the list?" I said.

"Why? Who is he?" Martinez asked.

I shook my head, not believing it myself. "Long story. It's not important."

"You sure?" Ybarra asked. "Can I get an address? I'd like to know why—"

"I don't have one. I wouldn't have any idea how to get in touch with Joe Riley. Any luck on May Ran?" I asked, anxious to change the subject.

"Nada," Martinez said. "And we're still looking for Googie. Nobody we've talked to will admit to knowing where he is."

"What about the girlfriend?" I asked. "His mom said he had a girlfriend."

"We can't find anyone who knows who she is," Ybarra said. "And Ms. Garcia has lawyered up and developed a severe case of amnesia."

"Nothing in his room to suggest who the girlfriend might be?" Maria asked.

"Nothing we've found so far." Martinez looked at his watch. "They're probably still over there."

Ybarra and Martinez left. I spent some time with Maria, the two of us spinning optimistic scenarios like puffy clouds of cotton candy at a carnival. Maybe Googie and his girlfriend were holed up somewhere and Nicholas was playing in a hotel pool, thinking he was on vacation. Nicholas might be playing on a swing set in the summer sunshine. Or making sand castles. Maybe he finally got to have Sugar Babies for breakfast.

I left them as the sun was going behind the clouds and checked my messages for the first time, realizing with a shock that I'd forgotten to meet Liz and Christine for the bunny exchange. I dialed Liz. My apology came tumbling out at the first sound of her voice.

"Don't worry about it," she said. "I figured something was up when I couldn't raise you. I couldn't get Christine on the plane today anyway."

"She didn't have another attack, did she?"

"No. She just doesn't want to leave until Nicholas comes home."

"But that could take—"

"I know," she said. "But she said he needs her. I believe her, Dylan."

"So do I."

I filled Liz in on the day's events, and we agreed to meet at my house. I hung up and perused the list of calls I'd received. Four more calls from my father, one of which was from his home number—which meant it was probably from Kellee. And one message from a number I didn't recognize. I pushed Return and waited.

"Gail Eschenbrenner," the voice said.

I gulped and briefly considered hanging up. I assumed she was calling to castigate me for interfering with her client.

"Ms. Eschenbrenner, this is Dylan Foster. Returning your call."

Her tone was professional and neutral. "Thanks for calling me back. You got my message, then?"

"Um, no, actually. I just saw the number on my caller ID."

"I wonder if we could meet?"

"Um…sure," I said, already thumbing through my excuse file and preparing my cancellation story. I was consumed with regret that I'd ever called her in the first place. What could she possibly have to say to me but to tell me to go straight to red-hot hell? If I were her, I'd string me up by my thumbs and beat me silly.

"When did you have in mind?" I tried to keep my voice nonchalant.

"Are you free this evening?"

"I'm on my way to meet some people." I checked the clock, hoping she wouldn't be available later. "It would have to be late. Nineish."

"That would work for me," she said. "I just have to leave by ten to pick up my son."

I checked the clock. "Let me button my friends down, and I can come meet you after I check in with them."

"That would be great."

We agreed to meet at her office, which was near downtown, not too far from my house.

Liz and Christine were parked in my driveway when I arrived. I pulled in behind them. We were ridiculously glad to see one another.

Together we carried the bunnies into the house and gave them a snack. Christine was unusually quiet. I took her into the kitchen, poured her a glass of milk, and set a plate of Oreos in front of her. She dipped the first one three times and took a bite while Liz and I caught up on the day's events.

"Christine's had a bit of a tough day," Liz said. "Haven't you, sweetie?"

"When are we going to find Nicholas?" Christine asked.

"Soon," I said. "Real, real soon."

"She's been thinking about him a lot, and I think she dreamed about him again last night, but she couldn't tell where he was. Right, Punkin?"

"Uh-huh."

"Do you think he's okay?" I asked. "Is he safe?"

She nodded. "He misses his mommy lots."

"I'm sure he does," I said. "She misses him lots too."

"Want to hear the news Andy gave me today?" Liz asked.

"Good news or bad news?"

"Good news, I think. Once I get used to the idea."

Christine spoke up. "I'm having a baby sister."

I raised my eyebrows at Liz.

"It's true," she said. "Andy and the boys can't part with one of the little orphan girls. He called to see if it was okay if we adopted her. They can't bring her home with them now, but he can start the paperwork."

"And you said yes? Just like that? Without even meeting her?"

"I know, it's crazy. I just have a feeling it's the right thing. Something good in the middle of all this mess."

"Wow. That is unbelievably massive news. Congratulations."

"Poor kid has no idea what she's getting herself into, right, Punkin? It's tough being a sister in this family. Rough duty."

"She can have my toys," Christine said. "I don't need them anymore."

"You're giving her all your toys?" I said, feigning incredulity. "That's pretty generous, Punkin. You sure you don't want to keep one or two of them?"

"I'm six," she said proudly.

"All grown up, now, aren't you?" Liz said, stroking Christine's hair.

"Uh-huh." Christine started in on another cookie.

"So tell me about this little girl. How old is she?"

"She's four. Her mother just died. I'm not sure when. I don't think she has any other relatives."

"And how did they pick her? Out of all those kids they wanted to bring home?"

"She picked them, actually. Andy said she wouldn't stop following the boys around. She kept making them necklaces out of string and telling them they were from her mommy."

"Necklaces?" I asked. "She made them necklaces?"

"Andy said her mother made jewelry or something. She's probably still missing her mom."

I could feel my mother standing in my kitchen at that moment. I swear I could. I could have reached out and touched her, she was so real to me. And at that moment, one of the lottery balls in my head fell into place. An old one that had been bouncing around for a good long while.

I got up and went to the buffet and came back with a pouch and a ring box.

"Did I ever show you this?" I asked Liz, pulling a necklace from the pouch.

She took it and examined it—a beautiful rough stone rimmed in silver and hung on a black leather cord.

"I've seen you wear it," she said. "It's beautiful."

"It was an anonymous gift. It came wrapped in a box the day I met Peter Terry at Barton Springs. I'd always assumed it was from him."

"He has good taste," Liz said, touching the stone.

I studied the workmanship. "David got me another one for my birthday last year. Different, but from the same designer. Her name is Rosa Guevera. See the mark on the back?" I turned the necklace over and showed her the tiny ankh stamped on the back, next to the initials R.G. I pointed at the ankh. "This is a symbol for protection."

She squinted at the mark and rubbed her finger over it.

I pushed the ring box across the table to Liz. She put the necklace down and opened the box. Inside was a delicate diamond wedding ring.

"That same day," I said, "I got my mother's wedding ring back. The necklace and the ring were wrapped exactly the same way. Plain white box. White paper, white ribbon. No card. I never knew who gave them to me or why. Or what they meant, for that matter."

I took the ring out of the box and held it up so it sparkled in the light. "Now I think they both might have been from my mother."

"I thought your mother died years ago."

"She did."

Liz looked at me knowingly and handed me the ring box. "Maybe she knows Joe Riley. Maybe he's the one with the good taste."

"I wouldn't be surprised."

I slipped the ring on my right-hand ring finger. It fit perfectly.

"Rosa Guevera is part of a women's co-op in Guatemala," I said. "My mother gave her some money to start her jewelry business." I watched Liz's face as the information registered.

Her eyes widened. "A Guatemalan woman made this necklace? You don't think this little girl…"

"…is her kid?" I shrugged. "What are the odds? But—"

"I'm going to have a new sister." Christine had finished her cookies and climbed down from the table. "Sister, sister, sister," she chanted, then stopped and looked up at me. "Miss Dylan, do you have a sister?"

"No, sweetie. All I have is one brother, but he lives far away."

"I thought your dad's wife was pregnant," Liz said. "Isn't she going to have a girl?"

I looked over at her, startled. "She is."

"Well, then, I guess you have a sister," Liz said.

"You just haven't met her yet," Christine said gleefully.

"You know what, Punkin? You're right. I guess I hadn't looked at it that way."

"What's her name?"

"Kellee Shawn," I said.

"I want to be her friend," Christine said.

I fought back unexpected tears.

I wound the leather cord of the necklace, tucked it back into the velvet pouch, and handed the pouch to Liz.

"Keep this for your new little girl. She can wear it someday when she's older. To mark the day her luck changed."

"Don't you want it?" Liz asked.

"I have the one from David," I said. "I think that's the one to hang on to at this point." I held out my hand and admired the ring. "Besides," I added, reaching over to hug Christine, "I'm thirty-five, right, Punkin? All grown up. I don't think I need it anymore."

40

AT A FEW MINUTES before nine, I pulled into the parking lot at the building where G. Perry Eschenbrenner officed and hauled myself out of my truck for what seemed like the thousandth time that day. The day had outlasted my stamina by a good hour at least. I was losing steam fast. My legs were wooden and heavy, my eyes itchy and red, and my attitude quickly becoming as rotten and sour as an old tomato. I wanted to be home in a bubble bath, not walking the plank to be chewed up by Gordon Pryne's defense attorney.

I pressed the button at the door. A loud buzz and the door clicked open. I walked into the building, the door swinging silently shut behind me. The building was an old one—not quite vintage, but one step away from shabby. It was warm inside. They must have adjusted the air conditioning after office hours ended on Friday.

I checked the directory by the elevators, got in, and pushed the button for the sixth floor. As the elevator rose, my stomach tightened. I began mentally preparing my defense. The elevator doors swished open, and I stepped out onto navy blue industrial carpet and walked down smudgy halls to an unimpressive wooden door with a sign that read, "Eschenbrenner, Coving & Ford, Attorneys at Law."

The door to the office suite was locked, so I knocked and waited a moment. A stocky, middle-aged woman in sweatpants and an oversized T-shirt opened the door and extended her hand. She wore no makeup, and her gray hair was pulled back in a simple ponytail. She looked like she'd had a day at least as long as mine.

"Dylan Foster?" she said.

"Guilty." I decided to take a shot a humor. "Not literally, though.

Actually, I'm quite an innocent person. In spite of what you may have heard."

My joke landed with a splat. She gave me the sort of look you might give a disobedient pet and motioned for me to follow her, which I did almost at a trot. The woman was faster than she looked. We went all the way down the hall to the corner office. I followed her inside, and she offered me a seat in a stiff wing chair. She sat down beside me in the other one and crossed her thick legs. A pair of scuffed Birkenstocks revealed unpainted toenails.

"First of all," she said sternly, "it was completely improper what you did today. Impersonating an employee of mine to gain unauthorized access to my client."

I felt a surge of defiance. "I realize that."

She looked at me calmly, waiting for me to say something.

"If you're looking for an apology, you're going to have a long wait," I said.

"I expected better from a fellow professional. Imagine if I contacted one of your clients that way."

"My client list isn't a matter of public record," I snapped. "And to my knowledge, my clients haven't kidnapped any children lately." I could feel my face burning. "But if they have, Ms. Eschenbrenner—"

"It's a mouthful. Call me Gail."

"Thank you. If they have, Gail, I expect you would employ any means at your disposal to find the child in question."

"I'm a criminal-defense attorney, Dr. Foster—"

"Dylan."

"Dylan. Of course. I'm sure you'll understand that my job is to defend my client, not investigate a crime my client couldn't possibly have committed." She stood. "I'm afraid I failed to offer you any hospitality. Would you like coffee? Water? A soda, perhaps?"

"What I'd really like is to know why you wanted to see me," I said. "I've got guests at my house, and it's been an extremely long day."

She walked to a credenza and picked up an envelope. "I take it personally when the rights of my clients are violated."

I sighed impatiently. "Honestly, Gail, I couldn't care less if you take it personally. I'm not an attorney, and I'm not a cop. I'm not bound by the same rules you are." I scooted up to the edge of my chair. "Nicholas Chavez is one of my favorite people in the entire world. And as I'm sure you understand, his mother is anxious to have him back where he belongs. As far as I'm concerned, that trumps your client's rights every time. And if you had a shred of common decency, you'd agree."

Her mouth tightened. "Given what I do for a living, I'm sure you understand that I can't share your point of view."

I was working up a good head of steam here. I needed to be careful to not blow my stack and make things even worse for myself than they already were. "I didn't violate anyone's rights. Your client voluntarily talked to me. He wasn't coerced. He knew exactly who I was and why I was there."

"He doesn't know where the child is."

"I'm aware of that. Is that what you wanted to tell me?"

She handed me a plain brown envelope—the big kind with the metal fastener on the back. "I've been asked to give you this."

"By whom?"

"I'm not at liberty to say."

"You're keeping a lot of secrets on behalf of a very sick man," I said.

"You do the same every day," she said. "You of all people should understand."

"Do you want me to open it now?"

"I'd rather you didn't," she said.

"What's in it?"

"You'll find out soon enough." She sat back down.

I studied the envelope. It felt empty. Someone had penned my name on the front in black marker.

"I've been asked to convey to you that the material in the envelope is for your eyes only. You are requested to keep the information to yourself."

"Or what?"

"It's a request, Dr. Foster, not a threat." She stood and extended her hand. "Thank you for coming."

I shot her my best look of disdain. "I'm being dismissed?"

She walked to the desk, picked up one of the framed photos propped amid the stacks of papers and files, and handed it to me.

It was a picture of a beaming young man, his face covered with ice cream, sitting on a swing on a bright, sunny day. He looked to be about twenty.

"As I said, I have to go pick up my son at ten."

I could tell she was waiting for me to notice something. I looked more closely at the photo. "Your son has Down's?"

"All three of them do, Dr. Foster." She took the picture back and held it up proudly. "Alex is in seventh grade in a public school. Ben lives at a home for the developmentally disabled in Terrell. And this is Steve, who works at the movie theater. He's a ticket taker. It took him six months to learn to count change, but he did it, and he's got a job"—her voice cracked—"and I'm so proud of him."

She composed herself and set the photo carefully on the desk. "There might be more to people than meets the eye, Dr. Foster. You might want to keep that in mind before you make your judgments."

Once again I prayed to the Lord Jesus to open up a hole in the ground for me to hide in. And once again He declined, preferring instead to leave me there to face yet another of my Top Ten Terrible Traits.

I trotted behind her again as she escorted me out. She stopped at the door and extended her hand. "Thank you for coming."

I shook her hand. "I'm sorry I was so harsh earlier. It's just that… we're all so anxious to find him. Any little scrap of information—"

She put up a hand to stop me. "I understand completely. Please give Dr. Chavez my best. I hope she finds her son very soon."

After I'd recovered from my near-crippling shame attack at my abominable behavior toward G. Perry Eschenbrenner, attorney at law and apparently quite a decent human being, I sat on the bench seat of my truck, engine running and dome light on, and ripped open the envelope. Inside was one sheet of paper.

It was an arrest record. From 1973. A shoplifting offense adjudicated in juvenile court in Montgomery County. The offender was sixteen years old, and his name was Gordon Weldon Pryne.

I squinted at the blurred copy. It was the old kind with purple letters, common before Xerox machines were cheap and plentiful. The words were smudged, the county seal wrinkled from a coffee-cup stain.

Gordon Pryne had been arrested for stealing a transistor radio from TG&Y. His height and weight were listed, and his prints ran along the bottom of the page. There was no photo—that probably would have been on a separate page. I wondered if it was his first arrest.

The report noted that his mother had brought him down to the station and made him turn himself in. She couldn't possibly have known at the time that her son would doom himself to a lifetime of drugs and crime. It made me feel better somehow, that she'd tried to do the right thing. That someone sometime had once tried to help Gordon Pryne.

I couldn't imagine why he'd wanted me to have the arrest report. I pored over it again and again but came up dead empty every time. There was nothing on it that had anything to do with Nicholas.

I slipped it into my bag and started back to my house. I got halfway there before I pulled over and yanked the paper out of my bag.

There it was, on the bottom of the page in smudged lavender ink. An address. And a name.

41

In 1973, Mary A. Pryne had lived on Cooper Lane in a little town called—you could measure the irony in tons—Cut and Shoot, Texas. A quick call to my cell phone's handy information service indicated there was no such town. The first dead end. I drove home in a rush, running perhaps a light or two but feeling sure the Good Lord would excuse me for such a worthy cause. I pulled into my driveway in record time.

I parked the truck under the sycamore tree and shot to the front door, flipping on lights (which stayed on, thank you very much) as I made my way through my house and plopped down at my computer once again.

A little research revealed that at some point, Cut and Shoot had been absorbed into Conroe, Texas. There was no current listing for a Mary A. Pryne on a Cooper Lane in Conroe. Four more phone calls to the surrounding municipalities yielded a big fat nothing. I did a people search online and quickly discovered there were exactly zero Mary A. Prynes out there. Not a development I'd anticipated.

I fumbled about for a while until, in a stroke of genius—or perhaps in a generous gift of inspiration from the Lord Jesus Himself—I began calling hospitals and nursing homes in the Dallas area. Twelve phone calls, and I got a hit. A Mary A. Pryne was registered at a place called Golden Acres in Mesquite—a shabby suburb on the far eastern edge of the city.

"But she's not in residence right now," the receptionist said when I called.

"What does that mean? Did she leave on a pass or something?"

"I'm afraid Ms. Pryne has been transferred to hospice."

I felt a shot of electricity run up my spine. The blog had said Gordon's mother was dying of cancer.

"Do you know which hospice? I'm a friend of the family, and I want to be sure and get by there and say good-bye. You know, while there's still time."

"Hold a second, sugar."

I tapped the table nervously while I waited for her return, praying mightily that just this once God would overlook those ridiculous HIPAA regulations and tell me what I needed to know.

The nurse clicked back on. "Got a pen, honey?"

She gave me the address, which I wrote down in a near-illegible scrawl. I ripped the paper off the pad, checked the map on my computer, and stuffed the address in my bag, grabbing my keys and slamming the door behind me.

The hospice was also in Mesquite, all the way on the other side of LBJ Freeway. This would normally seem like a laborious and unpleasant drive to a city girl like me who had the good fortune to live about thirty seconds from her place of employment. But tonight the miles flew as I drove, my mind racing around wildly like a helicopter missing a rotor. What was I doing? Should I have called the cops? Was I screwing things up by going alone? Why did Gordon Pryne lead me to his mother, and why had he insisted I keep her location to myself? Was he setting me up? Was Gordon's mom a gangster or something? Maybe she packed a .45 underneath her bathrobe.

By the time I squinted at the address on my crumpled paper and matched it to the house in front of me, I was haggard and weary from the mental activity alone.

I parked my truck and stared out my window. I'd expected some sort of hospitalish building with double doors and fluorescent lights. Instead, I found myself parked in front of a rundown house in a rundown neighborhood. Apparently Mrs. Pryne was getting home hospice care instead. I hadn't counted on this arrangement at all.

The house was dark, of course. It was late. But as I crept around the perimeter, I saw a light on in the rear of the house. I made my way back to the front door and knocked quietly.

To my surprise, the porch light snapped on, and the door swung open. The woman standing there wore green scrubs with bunnies on her shirt. I took this as an encouraging sign.

"I'm here to see Mary Pryne," I said.

"She's sleeping right now," the nurse said. "You want to come back tomorrow morning? She does a lot better in the morning."

"Do you mind if I just come in and sit with her for a minute?" I asked. "I know it's late, but I came a long way."

To my delight, she simply opened the screen door and stepped back.

The living room I stepped into was plain but neat. A gold chenille throw covered a worn sofa flanked by a couple of recliners. The entire arrangement pointed at a massive TV. There was nothing on the coffee table. A round mirror was the only decoration on the wall above the couch. A picture of Jesus hung on the wall by the door.

We walked on worn shag carpet through the living room and into a lit kitchen, where another nurse sat waiting to finish a card game. My escort showed me to a room behind the kitchen. I knocked gingerly, then stepped into a dimly lit bedroom dominated by a single hospital bed. Beside it sat a single wooden chair.

The nurse closed the door, leaving me alone with the shriveled figure in the bed—a small raisin of a woman in a nylon gown, socks on her tiny feet, her hair pulled back by a soft headband with flowers on it.

I sat on the chair and stared at her. Even in her decrepit state, I could see the resemblance. The shape of her face. The thin brows, the sharp chin. And the wild, curly hair. Hers was gray, of course, and was limp and matted, but I'd have recognized that head of hair anywhere. As I looked at her and watched her breathe, it dawned on me that I was sitting with Nicholas's grandmother. I felt tears spring to my eyes and my throat tighten. This tiny woman would keep Nicholas safe if she had a breath left in her body. I was as sure of that as I was of anything I'd ever known in my life.

The nurse came in and offered me Kool-Aid, which I declined. I sat with Mrs. Pryne for almost an hour before she stirred. I scooted my chair to her bedside as she opened her eyes.

"Who's there?" she asked, her voice weak and mewly like a kitten's. Her eyes were open, but it was clear she couldn't see me. Gordon's mother was blind.

"I'm a friend of Gordon's, Mrs. Pryne."

"Gordie? My Gordie? Will you tell me where he is? I can't get anybody to tell me where he went off to. He was in the army…"

She held out her hand for me. I took it. Her fingers were thin and cold in my hand.

"I'm not sure, exactly, Mrs. Pryne. What did they tell you?"

"They tell me this and that. They think I don't know anything, like I've gone and lost my senses or something."

She squeezed my hand, the life coming back into her.

"You haven't, though, have you?" I said.

"I most certainly have not. What's your name, honey?"

"Dylan Foster."

"How do you know my Gordie?"

I hesitated. "It's a long story, Mrs. Pryne."

"He's in trouble again, isn't he? My Gordie was always in trouble. I haven't seen him in so long." She sighed wearily. "I've prayed and prayed for him."

"You have, haven't you?" I said, tears stinging my eyes again.

"Didn't make a lick of difference. My poor Gordie. God love him."

I thought I saw a twinkle in her sightless eyes as she motioned for me to lean in. "I think the Good Lord just might've given me a lemon."

I held back a smile, forgetting momentarily that she was blind.

"Do you know his little boy too?" she asked.

I froze. "I think I might have met him once. What's his name?"

"He's the spittin' image. He's got my Gordie's pretty eyes. And his curly hair." She reached up and patted her head. "Gordie got that from me." She sighed again, more deeply this time. She was tiring. "Gordie's eyes are so green in the light. He got that from his father, God rest his soul. They tell me the boy's eyes are blue, though. Can't see 'em myself, of course. I'd give my left foot to see those eyes. But Piper told me. He's not a bad son."

"Piper. That's Gordon's brother. Is that his given name?"

"After my father. And I could feel the curls in his hair when he came to see me. Such a sweet little boy. Piper doesn't have the curls. Gordie got 'em all."

"Nicholas, right?"

"Nothing like his daddy, thank the Lord." She said it like *loward*. "Such a sweet child."

"When did you see him last?" I asked.

"Gordie? I think it was in nineteen—"

"No, Nicholas."

"What time is it now?"

I tried to keep my voice calm, natural. "You mean you saw him tonight?"

"Well, sure, honey."

"He came by to say hi?"

"He came in here and kissed me good night. Such a sweet little—"

"Where is he now?" I interrupted. "Do you know?"

"He's in Gordie's room with Jeremy. 'Course, this is Piper's house now, and it don't look the same…"

I scooted my chair back and stood. "Mrs. Pryne, I need to run to the restroom a minute. Can I get you anything?"

"I'd love some water, honey. Or maybe some ice chips. Those nurses love to give me ice chips. Like it's the Lord's cure for every little thing."

I stuck my head into the kitchen and beckoned the nurse. "Mrs. Pryne would love some ice chips. Could you just point me to the restroom?"

"Second door on the right, honey."

I walked into the darkened hallway, my heart pounding all the way through my clothes. Behind one of these closed doors, Nicholas Chavez was sleeping, safe and sound in his grandmother's care. And behind another one was at least one person who knew he had no business being there.

I waited, heart pounding, for my eyes to adjust to the dark. Then I realized, of course, which door was Nicholas's. The one with the light coming from underneath. I walked over and opened it, and there he was, curled up on the bottom bunk of a set of twin bunk beds. Another little boy slept soundly in the top bunk.

I crouched down beside Nicholas, out of sight of the top bunk, and tried to figure out what to do. Like a fool, I had left my bag—and my cell phone—in Mrs. Pryne's bedroom, so I had no way to call the cops. And I was standing in a lit room—dimly lit, but lit nonetheless—with two sleeping children in a house full of people who didn't want me there.

I thought briefly about going back for my phone. But I wasn't about to let Nicholas out of my sight, so I crept over and touched him gently on the shoulder.

"Nicholas," I whispered, "it's Miss Dylan. Wake up, doodlebug."

Nicholas stirred but didn't open his eyes. I had a second to look at him and see what sort of shape he was in. He looked good, actually. His face was clean, and he was wearing a pair of Superman jammies that fit him—a good sign of at least decent care. He seemed thin to me, though. Christine was right. He hadn't been eating.

I touched him again on the shoulder. This time he opened his eyes. I held a finger to my lips, cautioning him to be quiet.

His huge blues eyes looked up at me, and it was clear he didn't realize who I was for a second. Then he lunged for me and grabbed me around the neck, latching on and pulling me down toward him.

"Where's my—," he said in full voice.

I shushed him again and pried him away from me. I whispered into his ear. "We have to be real, real quiet, Nicholas. We don't want to wake anyone up. Okay?"

He nodded and whispered loudly, "Where's my mommy?"

I put my mouth next to his ear again. "We're going to go find her right now, but not another word, okay? We have to be real quiet. Like little mice, okay?"

He nodded solemnly. I stood up with him wrapped around me, his head resting on my shoulder, and thought I might pass out from the alternating waves of ecstasy and abject panic which were crashing in on me. I didn't know which feeling was more likely to knock me over, but it was a close contest.

We tiptoed from the bedroom and into the hallway. I closed the door quietly behind me just as another door opened at the other end of the hall. I put my hand over Nicholas's mouth and ducked quickly into the bathroom next door, pulling the shower curtain back carefully and stepping into the tub. I crouched down in the dark, still clutching Nicholas, who had realized by now what was happening and was beginning to hyperventilate. I pulled away from him again and held my finger to my lips, then pressed my lips to his ear. "You need to calm down now, Nicholas. Breathe real slow and quiet, and calm down. You're safe. I'll take care of you."

I felt his breaths deepen and his neck relax, his head dropping limp on my shoulder.

The light clicked on. We both held our breath as someone shuffled into the bathroom, used the toilet, flushed, and then left.

"He didn't wash his hands," Nicholas whispered to me when the room was quiet.

I couldn't help but smile in the darkness. "You're right, sweetie, he didn't."

"My mommy said to always wash my hands."

"You're exactly right. That's a very bad habit not to wash your hands."

"Did you come to get me?"

"Yes, I did, doodlebug."

"Will you squeeze me?" he said.

I began to cry as I squeezed him tightly in bursts and he coughed out my name in a whisper. Then I saw a look of dismay cross his face.

"I need my gun," he whispered frantically.

"No, you don't, sweetie. You're safe now. We need to get out of here quick, quick, quick."

He started to cry. "Mr. Enrique gave it to me."

"Sweetie, I am absolutely positive he will get you a new one. Let's get out of here. Now, be quiet like a little mouse. Just like we said, okay?"

I stood and stepped out of the tub, Nicholas still draped over my shoulder, and peeked into the dark hallway. The doors were all closed again. I'd just about made it back to Mrs. Pryne's room to get my bag when Nicholas leaped from my arms and ran back to the bedroom where he'd been sleeping. I followed and watched, unable to breathe as he fished under his pillow and pulled out his toy gun. He'd hung on to it all this time. He wasn't about to let it go now.

He raced back to me and hopped into my arms. We slipped through the hallway door and into the brightly lit kitchen.

The hospice workers were in the kitchen, still playing cards at the breakfast table.

"Could you do me a favor?" I whispered.

They looked up at me, apparently unconcerned that I had one of the household's children in my grip.

"Sure, hon."

"Call 911, give them the address of this house, and let them know the boy they're looking for, Nicholas Chavez, is here."

The woman's eyes widened.

"Just do it. Please."

I heard another door open in the hallway. I put my finger to my lips and whispered, "Not a word."

The nurse nodded, and I slipped back into Mrs. Prynes room, Nicholas still wrapped around me. I was reaching for my bag when I heard a man in the kitchen. I left the bag where it was and slipped into the closet, stepping back into the clothes, letting them come together in front of me. I was afraid to reach into the room to close the door, so I tried to make my shoes blend in with the others and scooted behind a long wool coat.

"Did Nicholas come in here and get a glass of water?" I heard the man ask the nurses. I held my breath.

"No, Mr. Pryne. I haven't seen him. I think he's still in bed."

"He's not there. He's hiding somewhere."

The door to Mrs. Pryne's room flew open, and a man I took to be Piper Pryne stalked into the room. Nicholas clung close to me. I could feel him clutching his gun tighter behind my neck.

"Did Nicholas come in here, Ma?" the man said.

The tiny form in the bed stirred and said weakly, "Nicholas? Who's that, honey? Have you seen my parasol? I want to go out for a walk."

"Whose bag is that? Is that the nurse's?" I watched through the crack as he pointed at my bag.

"We're taking the Greyhound to New Orleans in the morning. Don't you just love New Orleans? Where's my parasol? I just saw it yesterday..."

The man swore at her, slammed the door, and left.

I waited a minute, listening as he opened doors and called Nicholas's name, waking the rest of the household. My only hope was that the nurse could call 911 without getting caught. I crept across the room and reached for my bag. I'd just picked it up when Mary Pryne's hand shot out and gripped my wrist.

She pulled me down to her and whispered in my ear.

"Keep him safe, honey."

"I will, ma'am. Thank you. How did you..."

"They don't give an old lady never mind, but I know what's what." She patted my hand, then reached up for Nicholas, who climbed down and gave her a hug. She kissed him and touched his face and whispered something into his ear.

He nodded. "Yes ma'am." He walked back over to me and held my hand, still clutching his gun.

"They're coming for me tonight," she told me calmly. "You take care of my grandson for me, and I'll see you on the other side."

"I'll take care of him, Mrs. Pryne. I promise."

"I know you will." She nodded. "And, honey?"

"Yes ma'am."

"Call me Mary Anne."

We slipped out the back door with the words ringing in my ears.
She said it just like her son did.

May Ran.

42

I DIDN'T THINK MARIA had any tears left, but she cried buckets when she saw Nicholas, who was still clutching his toy gun and wearing his Superman pajamas when we pulled up at her house, accompanied by four patrol cars. Martinez met us there, and we all stood there in Maria's yard, watching and bawling, hugging one another and thanking God above and congratulating ourselves and everyone else—just like at the Oscars.

Nicholas had stories to tell. Googie, whose name Nicholas had never learned, had snatched him, stuffed him into the trunk of the Fairlane, and driven off with him as Nicholas wailed and banged on the trunk lid from the inside. They'd driven for a long while—Nicholas didn't know how far or for how long—then stopped in an alley, where Googie popped the trunk and handed the child a vanilla cone. He'd told Nicholas they were going to see his grandma and that his mother couldn't keep him anymore. Then he'd closed the trunk on him again, driven him to Piper Pryne's house, and dropped him off.

Every morning after that, Googie would pick him up, sometimes putting him in the trunk, and drive around for most of the day, dropping him off at Piper's house after the sun went down. This was the routine until the white Fairlane popped up on the news. After that, Nicholas spent most of the daytime in Googie's closet at his mother's house, which, it turned out, was not air conditioned. After the day-care kids left, he was allowed to play in the yard under Juanita Garcia's watchful eye.

They'd told him it was to keep him safe.

Under relentless questioning, Piper Pryne admitted he knew the boy had been kidnapped. He claimed to believe he was hiding the boy for his own good. His brother had been emphatic that the boy was in grave danger and that only an extended stay with Mary Anne Pryne could protect him. Piper had assumed Nicholas to be the vig for a dope deal gone bad.

"It was just temporary," he said, "till everything got worked out. We never even knew he had a kid. I tell you, one look at him and bam, I know he's my brother's kid. Gordie don't know where Ma lives. She ain't listed or anything. He ain't seen her since he was, like, nineteen. Before Nam. So there was no way they could find him, see?"

They threw him in a holding cell and filed charges against him, along with all the other adults involved except Googie. The cops were still searching for him.

The morning of his return, Nicholas finally got to have Sugar Babies for breakfast. Liz, Christine, and I showed up that afternoon with the bunnies. "To finish my birthday," Christine said.

I'd spent the morning in the kitchen and produced another non-crunchy strawberry cake. Christine brought Nicholas the pink Barbie tiara, which had lain in the dust after his abduction and which she'd saved for him, "For when you came back."

As we sat in the backyard that Memorial Day afternoon, the breeze soft and the sun gentle after all the hard rain, Christine said suddenly, "My grandma and your grandma have the same name."

"What, Punkin?" Liz asked.

"My grandma and Nicholas's grandma have the same name. Mary Anne."

"I hadn't noticed that, sweetie," Liz said gently. "But I don't think Mary Anne is really Nicholas's grandma. Not the way yours was."

"She was nice to me," Nicholas said, strawberry cake smeared on his face.

"She was?" Maria asked, tearing up again. She handed him a napkin. "Wipe your face, sweetie. What nice things did she do?"

"Mary Anne said I could have my Superman jammies."

"She did?" I asked. "How did she know?"

"She prayed to Jesus to keep me safe, but I told her my Superman jammies were for double protection, and she told Mr. Piper he had to go to Wal-Mart and get me some right now. But they're scratchy because he didn't wash 'em."

Maria hugged him. "They worked great anyway, didn't they?"

"And I got cookies and Kool-Aid. The red kind. And I got to have bedtime stories in her bed."

"Did she make up the stories herself?" I asked.

He stuffed another huge bite into his mouth and said through the cake, "She had Dr. Seuss."

"The books?" I asked. "She read to you from books?"

"Uh-huh." He drained his milk. "*Green Eggs and Ham* and the cat one and the Horton one."

Liz looked at me quizzically. "Why, Dylan?"

I poured Nicholas some more milk. "She's blind."

"Was she, Nicholas?" Maria asked. "Could she see the books?"

He shrugged. "I got to pick books from the shelf in Jeremy's room, and then I could climb up, and she would read them to me until she got sleepy and it was time to talk to Jesus again."

"Maybe she had them memorized," Liz suggested. "I bet I could quote every single one of them by memory. Dr. Seuss is the only book-length poetry I've ever memorized in my entire life."

"Elegant, yet simple," Maria agreed.

"Sophisticated and surprisingly complex," Liz added with a grin.

I raised my milk glass. "With a tart hint of grapefruit and a soft finish of green apple."

We had a laugh—the first in forever that wasn't weighed down by the terrible unknown.

When Martinez arrived for the party, Nicholas leaped from his seat and raced into the detective's arms. You could have thumped Martinez once on the forehead and knocked him right out, he was so lightheaded with joy. We all were. We were floating in the air like those people in *Mary Poppins*.

He settled in with us, and the kids left the table to play with the rabbits. Nicholas ran back every minute or two to touch his mother and then ran back to his games.

"Any luck on Googie?" I asked.

"We'll find him." Martinez took a bite of Maria's cake. "Pretty soon they're all going to figure out it's every man for himself, and someone's gonna offer him up. Ybarra's working on 'em. He's our best interrogator. It's like a gift with him."

"Want some cake?" Liz asked.

He washed the bite down with some of Maria's milk. "No thanks."

"What's going on with Gordon Pryne?" I asked.

"Not a peep out of him. The man has a good lawyer." He picked up the fork again and took another bite of Maria's cake. "You met her, Dylan. What did you think of her?"

"Tough lady. She's got three kids with Down's. And I think she's a single mom."

"Makes me hate her a little less," Maria said.

"I tried to hate her," I said. "I mean, I really strained at it, you know? And this is not something that's usually difficult for me. But she was actually pretty decent. She believes in what she's doing. And sick as he is, Gordon Pryne is getting good representation from her, which is his right, I guess."

Liz shook her head in disgust. "He's one of those people...you don't even know what to think about him. I can't believe there are people out there who are that soulless."

"His mom obviously tried to save him," I said. "I guess there must be some subterranean streak of decency in him. And in some sick way, I think he does care about Nicholas."

"Dylan, you can't be serious," Maria said.

"The man is tortured by Peter Terry. Absolutely tortured. I think he was trying to spare Nicholas that. I believe him."

"That arrest record, the one from 1973?" Martinez said. "He went in the army after that—they were taking anybody because of Vietnam. He did a tour in Nam and left with a dishonorable discharge for stealing supplies. After that, he disappeared into the streets."

My fork stopped halfway to my mouth. "He was AWOL that whole time? From his own family?"

"Yep. Started writing letters from prison a few months ago, sending them to his brother through his lawyer. He didn't even know his own brother's address or whether he was still alive. I guess the lawyer tracked him down. Then Piper started the blog and started trying to get him released before their mother died." He took a swig of Maria's milk. "She passed last night, by the way."

I batted my eyes to fight back the sting of tears.

"Did the lawyer know about this? That Nicholas was kidnapped?" Liz asked.

"She's got a pretty good reputation," Martinez said. "I'd bet money she didn't know anything about it. Not at first, anyway."

"I think she would have found a way to let someone know sooner," I said.

"Even with privilege?" Maria asked.

Martinez took another bite and pointed at me with his fork. "It's like you guys. You have exceptions to confidentiality, don't you?"

I nodded. "Even if we didn't, I would violate the rule and save the kid. I think she would have found a way."

"Pryne's not going to make it to court tomorrow, by the way," Martinez said. "His lawyer's going to ask for a postponement."

"I hope he roasts in hell," Maria said.

I was silent as she and Liz toasted with their milk glasses.

"Eschenbrenner saw the tape," Martinez was saying, "of Dylan here doing her dirty work in the visitors' room."

"Who gave them the tape?" I asked suspiciously.

He smiled sweetly at me. "I did."

"Oh, technical foul!" I said. "You ratted me out?"

"Who do you think gave her your number?" He laughed and drained Maria's milk glass. "She thought you were working for us." I poured him another glass and got Maria another slice of cake.

"Did you ever find out anything about the other guy?" I asked him. "The tall one in the park?"

Martinez waved my question away. "I think you—hey, kids, slow down."

He snagged Nicholas with one arm as he came careening around the corner, Christine in tow. Both children giggled, then came over and climbed into their mothers' laps. Christine reached over and dug her finger into her mom's icing.

Martinez looked at me. "You must've made that guy up, Dylan. No one else in the entire park saw him."

"Saw who?" Christine asked.

"Nobody, sweetie," Liz said.

Christine furrowed her brow. "You mean Earl?"

"Earl what?" Liz said.

"No one else in the park saw Earl?"

"Earl wasn't at the park, Punkin," I said.

She nodded vigorously. "Yes, he was."

We all looked at one another.

"Earl was in the park?" Liz asked. "How do you know?"

"I saw him."

"Where was he?" I asked.

"Cutting the trees," she said matter-of-factly.

"Nobody was cutting down trees, honey," Liz said. "I think you might be letting your imagination run away with you."

"Maybe she means the gardener," I said. "The one cutting the shrubs."

"What gardener?" Liz asked.

Maria chimed in. "I don't remember any gardener."

"He was clipping shrubs with clippers and raking up the leaves," I said. "I can't believe you didn't notice him. I haven't seen anyone use a rake since Jimmy Carter was president."

"There was no gardener," Liz said.

Martinez went to the car and came back with a notebook opened to a diagram of the park. "Where was he?"

I pointed at the map. "Clipping the shrubs on the far end of the park—here. About twenty yards away from the tennis courts. East of the swings. You guys don't remember that? He was the only black person in the whole park. Pretty hard to miss."

"They can't see him," Christine whispered to me.

I leaned down and whispered back. "Maybe they just didn't notice him."

She was emphatic. "No! They can't see him. It's just us."

Martinez was thumbing through pages. "No one else mentioned a gardener. And no one admitted to seeing the tall guy at the soccer game."

"He's mean," Christine said.

"The tall man? You saw him, Christine?" I asked.

She nodded. "Super-duper-duper mean."

I looked around the table. "None of you saw this guy? You're kidding me. We can't be the only ones."

We all stared as the possibility settled in.

Maria's eyes were wide. "You think the tall guy…"

"…knows Peter Terry?" Liz finished the sentence.

Martinez whistled.

I shook my head, not believing it. "If he does, it looks like Googie got there just in the nick of time."

～

That evening at eight sharp, David Shykovsky pulled up in front of my house, walked to my front porch, and knocked politely. I answered, equally politely (so as not to seem eager), and we stood awkwardly in the entryway.

He wasn't wearing the Italian cologne.

"It's a college-acceptance-letter moment," I said.

"Come again?"

"You know, the envelope test. If the envelope's thin, you got rejected. If it's fat, you got in."

"So what's the parallel?"

"If you ask me if I want to sit down, it's a rejection letter. If you ask me where I want to go to supper, I'm in."

"Wrong again, sugar pea."

"Aha! A nickname." I smiled knowingly. "Early admission."

"Wrong, wrong, wrong."

"You're blowing my theory."

"I realize that."

"So. What's your plan?"

"My plan is that I'd like to know what that incredible smell is." I sniffed the air. "What smell?"

"Cinnamon."

I grinned wickedly. "I baked."

"You did not."

"I did."

"You never bake."

"I do."

"You don't."

"I didn't before."

"But you do now?"

"I do."

"Why now?"

I winked at him. "Bribery."

His face lit up. "What's the currency?"

"Snickerdoodles."

He threw back his head and laughed. "Tell me you didn't call my mother."

"I didn't call your mother."

"No, seriously. When did you talk to her?"

"I didn't. I swear. Why?"

"Snickerdoodles are like heroin for me. I'm going to end up free-basing them in an alleyway someday, my life gone to ruins."

"Morally and financially bankrupt?"

"Inevitably. I'm obsessed."

"You never told me that."

"You never asked."

I sighed deeply, sinking for a moment under the weight of my regrets. "I didn't, did I?"

"No, you didn't."

"I'm on a self-improvement plan."

"Is this the same as your Thigh Recovery Program?"

"Exactly the same, yes. Which worked, by the way."

"I did notice that."

"I'm going to take a systematic approach to my personality problems."

"And your plan is?"

"I'm going to knock out my list of Top Ten Terrible Traits, one by one."

"Sounds a little ambitious," he said skeptically.

"I should be done by the time I'm, oh, eighty-five or so. About fifteen minutes after I die."

"And in addition to that ambitious goal, apparently you intend to bake."

"Not often. But occasionally. Now and again."

"Now and again? You were really moving up in the rankings there for a minute."

"It's tough love, David. I mean, I don't want to be an enabler. You've got an addiction. You need help."

"I can't believe you baked snickerdoodles. Of all the possible cookie choices out there. Are these alleged snickerdoodles for me, or is there, like, a bake sale at church?"

"They're for you," I said indignantly. "I made them personally, in my own oven. From scratch. With a recipe and everything."

He took my hands. "Who told you I like snickerdoodles?"

"I'm not at liberty to say."

"Oh, come on."

"Let's just say the information came from a reliable source."

We stared at each other for an awkward moment.

"So," he said at last.

"So?"

The two of us stood there for an eternity, looking at each other, the terrible unspoken question hanging in the air between us. Finally, he opened his arms, and I stepped into them. I took a deep breath, inhaling the smell of him, and had my answer.

Tide with Bleach Alternative. Clean Breeze scent.

I was in.

ACKNOWLEDGMENTS

An enterprise as unwieldy as a novel necessarily involves legions of supporters, most of whom I hope to thank here. I will inevitably forget someone, and for that, I blame myself and the mercury...

I'm indebted again to the good people of the Dallas Police Department Crimes Against Persons Division (CAPERS), Homicide Section, for their time and generosity. These are exceptional people, and I feel both privileged to know them and grateful that our city is in such capable hands.

Sergeants Larry Lewis and Eugene Reyes were kind enough once again to allow me access to their squads. Detectives Phil Harding, Robert Quirk, and Eddie Ibarra—fine professionals and even finer gentlemen—let me follow them around, answered hundreds of pesky questions and bought me lots of club soda at the dugout. I'm also grateful to Officer Chantell West of the Highland Park Police Department for letting me button-hole her and grill her for information. Any authenticity in the police-related elements of this story is due to the help of these wonderful individuals. Deliberate inaccuracies are mine, for the sake of the story.

Lieutenant Commander Doug Halter (U.S. Naval Reserve) provided details about airplanes, flight patterns and travel times. Pam Lindsay, MD, lent her medical expertise to the details of this story. Again—the authenticity is theirs, the mistakes mine.

I'm indebted to my agent, Lee Hough of Alive Communications, whose regard for my work and faithful advocacy on my behalf humbles me and spurs me forward. Lisa Taylor, my publicist—who has become my champion and my friend—is relentless in her quest to help my books find their way into the public eye. The good folks at Waterbrook-Multnomah, in particular Tiffany Lauer, Joel Kneedler, and Ken Peterson, stepped in at just the right moment to support this book. For that

I am deeply grateful. Mark Ford, who designed the cover, also deserves a mention, genius that he is. And Anne Buchannan, who edited this novel, has an eye for detail that I can only envy. Her time line alone had me slack-jawed. Thanks also to Julee Schwarzburg and Amy Partain for herding this book through the process. Good shepherds, both.

Dennis Ippolito (perhaps the most patient human in the universe) once again read and reread the manuscript as it evolved over time, offering his usual incisive suggestions. His endless forbearance and insight (and his enormous vocabulary—*fungible,* indeed) have been invaluable. Trish Murphy, a fellow writer and my sister in the fight, continues to supply encouragement, kinship, and plenty of fried chicken on the awful journey of the creative life. Our writing trips remain the lifeblood of my projects. I'd be lost without the synergy her winsome presence in my life provides.

The indefatigable members of the Waah Waah Sisterhood have listened to me whine for years now and yet remain steadfast, loyal friends. The staff at LifeWorks keeps the ship running while I'm absent or preoccupied with book-related tasks. Particular thanks to Harry Cates and Abbie Chesney for their efforts toward this end.

Thanks to Elizabeth Emerson and Christine Carberry for countless editing and proofing insights. Again their capacity for detail stuns me. (E-beth, will you organize my closet for me, please?)

And much thanks to my readers, who always seem to shoot me an encouraging e-mail just in the nick of time.

It should never be perfunctory, a writer's thanks to the people who have helped a novel along its way. To those individuals mentioned here, much gratitude and Godspeed.

Here's an excerpt from the first
Dylan Foster novel from Melanie Wells,

When the Day of Evil Comes.

Available now.

SOMEONE SAID TO ME that day, "It's hotter than the eyes of hell out here." I can't remember who. Looking back, I wonder if it meant something, that phrase. Something more than a weather report. But as it was, I let the remark pass without giving it a thought. It was hot. Hotter than the eyes of hell. That was true enough.

If I'd known enough to be afraid, I would have been. But I was a thousand years younger then, it seems, and I didn't know what was out there. To me, it seemed like an ordinary day.

I was making a rare appearance at a faculty event. I hate faculty events. Generally, truth be told, I hate any sort of event. Anything that involves pretending, in a preordained way, to like a bunch of people with whom I have something perfunctory in common. Faculty events fall into this category.

This particular faculty event was a picnic at Barton Springs in Austin. The picnic was the final fling of a faculty retreat—my definition of hell on earth, speaking of hell. They'd all spent the weekend at a retreat center in the hill country of Texas, getting to know each other. Or bonding, as we say in the industry.

Imagine the scene. A dozen puffed-up psychologists (I include myself only in the latter part of this description, for I do admit I'm a psychologist), wallowing in all the clichés. Bonding exercises. Trust falls. Processing groups. Sharing. I could imagine few things more horrific.

I'd begged off the retreat, citing a speaking engagement in San

Antonio. A speaking engagement, might I add, that had been carefully calendared a year before, timed precisely to oppose the dreaded faculty retreat.

So I'd spent the weekend in the hill country too. But my gig involved talking to entering master's-degree students about surviving graduate school. A topic on which I considered myself an expert, since I'd done more time in graduate school than 99 percent of the population of this grand country of ours. Hard time, in fact. I'd won my release a few years before by earning my PhD and promising myself I'd never breach the last frontier—the suck-you-in quagmire known as "postgraduate education."

Over the weekend, I'd let those entering students in on my secret—higher education is all about perseverance. It has nothing to do with smarts or creativity or anything else.

It's about cultivating the willingness and stamina for hoop-jumping.

Jump through the hoops, I'd said. Do it well. Do it relentlessly. And in a few years, you can join the elite of the American education system, secure in the knowledge that you too can endure with the best of them.

After sharing this little tidbit, I'd decided to take my own advice and jump through a hoop myself. The aforementioned faculty picnic at Barton Springs.

Barton Springs is a natural spring-fed pool in the heart of Austin, which is in the heart of Texas. And since it was the heart of summer, the water would be sixty-eight degrees of heaven on a hundred-degree day.

I like picnics, generally. And anything that involves water is a good thing in my eyes. I'd started swimming competitively once I figured out that swimming is like graduate school. Perseverance is the thing. And I'm pretty good at that.

So I drove to the picnic that day with a fairly good attitude, for me, considering this was a herd event for professional hoop-jumpers.

I parked my truck in the shade, saying a quick prayer of thanks for the shady spot. I don't know why I do things like that, pray over a parking spot, as though the Lord Himself is concerned about which parking space I get. Surely He has more important things on His mind. But I said the prayer anyway, parked my truck, grabbed my swim bag, and set out to find my colleagues.

They were bunched up in a good spot: near a group of picnic tables, under a live oak tree, and next to one of my favorite things in life. A rope swing. What could be more fun, I ask you? Rope swings are childhood for grownups.

I said my hellos and settled in at one of the tables next to my department head, Helene Levine. I liked the name. It had a swingy, rhymie sort of rhythm to it. One of the matriarchs, as she liked to describe herself, referring to her Jewish heritage.

Helene is indeed matriarchal. She's an imposing woman, with a big battle-axe bosom and a manner that is simultaneously threatening and nurturing. I don't know how she pulls that off, but I love her. And she loves me. For some reason, as different as we are, we hit it off from the beginning. I signed up as daughter to her nurturing side.

This day, she was in threatening mode, at least with everyone else. Foul-tempered in the heat, I guess. And probably sick of babysitting her faculty charges. In any case, she brightened when she saw me, handed me a plate of fried chicken and potato salad, and poured me a cold soda. I settled in to eat.

The food was good. Few things in the world sing to my heart like picnic food. Especially good fried chicken, and I knew Helene had fried this chicken herself. I ate a breast and a wing, two helpings of potato salad, and a huge fudge brownie, all washed down with the national drink of Texas, Dr Pepper. A meal of champions.

Then the rope swing beckoned.

Since most PhD'd folks spend lots and lots of time bent over books or lecturing halls full of students, they don't get outside much. Hence, they tend to be white and lumpy. They are also not very much fun.

I am not terribly lumpy by nature and try to grasp at any fun that is to be had, being determined as I am not to sacrifice my life on the altar of academe. So while everyone else stayed safely dressed and sheltered on the shore, I availed myself of the dressing room, changed into my bikini, and jumped in the pool.

For a while, I was self-conscious, with all those psychologists watching me frolic by myself. Surely there was something Freudian in my behavior that would get me duly diagnosed and labeled. I kept at it, though, and eventually they lost interest in me and returned to their conversations.

After some diligent practice with the rope swing, I discovered that if I timed it just right, letting go at the very zenith of the arc as I swung out over the spring, I could hit a deep well in the pool, falling into cool, dark water that seemed to take me somewhere safe and almost otherworldly. I did that over and over, sloughing off my stress from the weekend (I had been working, after all) and leaving it on the cold smooth slabs of limestone at the bottom of the pool.

After several minutes of this, I climbed onto the shore, ready for another go, and discovered that someone was competing for my toy. A man stood there, holding the swing tentatively. I found everything about him unsettling.

His skin was chalk-white and he was hairless as a cue ball. He looked like a cancer victim. Not a survivor, which conjures up sinewy visions of strength and triumph, but a victim. Someone weak and bony and sickly, just this side of death. Next to me, with my against-dermatologist's-advice summer tan, he looked like death itself.

I'm not shy, so I walked up next to him. "You want a turn?"

"What do you do?" His voice was strong and deep, incongruous against his appearance.

I wasn't sure if he was asking what I did for a living or what you do with a rope swing. Since I don't like to tell people what I do for a living, I opted for the rope swing question. "You just grab on and swing out," I said. "And then let go as far out as you can. I'll show you."

I took the rope from him and walked backward to the rock I'd been jumping off of, then made a run for it, landing again in my favorite spot.

When I came up for air, he was in the water right next to me. I suddenly felt uncomfortable.

I fell back on a lame old line. "Come here often?"

"Never," he said. "I'm not from Austin."

"Where are you from?"

"I live in Houston now."

Which made sense, since that's where the big cancer center is. Maybe he was just there for treatment or something. I felt sorry for him, but something about him wasn't sitting right with me. I have pretty good instincts about people. I decided to listen to myself and end the encounter.

"The cold water's starting to get to me," I said. "I think I'm going to get out. Nice meeting you."

"We didn't actually meet. I'm Peter Terry."

I gave him a little nod and said, "nice meeting you" again. "I'm Dylan," I said, and immediately regretted it.

"Nice meeting you."

Okay. Done meeting this guy. I swam for the shore and climbed out onto the bank, making a point to look back at him and wave after I got on solid ground.

I felt my stomach clench as he turned to swim away. His back had a big gash in it, red and unspeakably violent against all that pasty white skin.

I strained to see it clearly. The wound was jagged and severe, brutal enough to be fatal, it looked like to me, in my quick view of it. It ran horizontally, between his shoulders, blade to blade. It was red and ugly, shredded, pulpy flesh pulled back from a scarlet strip of bleeding muscle.

My mind started casting about for a better explanation, needing to make some sense of what I was seeing. Surely it wasn't a real gash. No one with a wound like that would be walking around.

I finally decided it could be a tattoo. In fact, it must be a tattoo. That was the only logical conclusion. Which just confirmed my impression that something was off with this guy. Anyone with a tattoo like that had some issues, in my professional opinion. Good riddance.

I toweled off and walked back to my group, glad to be with the lumpy whities. Suddenly they looked pretty good to me. I sat down next to Helene and reached into my swim bag.

I found a surprise. A box, ribboned and wrapped.

I held it up. "Hey, what's this?"

Helene looked over. "I have no idea. I got one too. I thought it was from you."

The others started looking into purses and bags. Eventually, each person came up with a box, all identically wrapped. We opened them together, accusing one another of being the thoughtful culprit behind such a fun surprise. No one copped to it, though.

Each box contained something different, but they were all personal gifts. Expensive personal gifts. No one at that picnic could afford such extravagance on faculty salaries. Even those of us who were in private practice wouldn't have spent that kind of money. We didn't like each other that much.

Someone must have a secret, I assumed. Someone who was equally wealthy and codependent. And slightly manipulative.

I didn't really care. I like presents.

My gift was a black leather cord necklace with one big, rough black stone trimmed in silver. It was beautiful and very funky. Perfect for me, since I'm sort of a hippie and like strange jewelry. Whoever picked it out knew me pretty well.

We accused each other for a while longer, until it became obvious that no one was going to confess. Finally, we packed up our stuff and called it a weekend, the faculty retreat officially over. I suspected every-one would show up Monday morning wearing or using their gifts. John would mark his appointments in his new leather Day-Timer. Helene would be using her fountain pen. And you bet I'd be wearing that nifty necklace.

I said my good-byes and walked to my old, worn-out pickup truck—a '72 Ford I'd purchased for seven hundred dollars—yanking the door open and promising myself once again I was going to buy a can of WD-40. That door was stubborn as a donkey and twice as loud.

I threw my bag in and started to scoot onto the seat when something caught my eye.

It was another package, wrapped just like the necklace had been. Identically.

I picked it up, examining this one more closely. The paper was expensive. Not the kind of wrapping paper you get at the drugstore. The kind you buy from specialty stores that sell handmade journals and twenty-dollar soap. The ribbon was fresh, unwrinkled satin. Off-white paper, off-white ribbon. Lovely and tasteful.

Warily I pulled one end of the ribbon and eased the paper away from the box. The box was generic, as the others had been. Thick pressed white cardboard, expensively made. But no store logo on it. Nothing that would identify where it came from.

I tilted open the lid, took a peek, and dropped the box. Inside was an engagement ring. It was platinum, an antique setting, with a beautiful 1.2-carat diamond set among a few dainty smaller stones.

The reason I knew the weight of the diamond is that I knew the ring. Intimately. It was my mother's ring. And it was supposed to be on her finger, six feet under at the cemetery outside her hometown.

I'd decided to bury her with it instead of keeping it for myself. I'd seen it on her finger before they closed the lid. That was two years ago last March.

I fished my new necklace out of my purse, opening that box carefully, suspiciously. The necklace was still there, funky and chunky. I took it out of the box and closed my fingers around it in a fist.

I got out of the truck, slammed that noisy door, and marched back to the water's edge. I stood on my launching rock and wound up, throwing that necklace as far as I could into the spring. It was a good, long throw, reminiscent of years of childhood lessons from my brother. The necklace hit with barely a plop and sank to the bottom.

I sat down on the rock for a minute. Queasy and green with emotion.

I waited there until my head stopped spinning, then walked out to the parking lot and got in my truck. It started with its usual rumble, reminding me that I needed a new muffler too. But it got me home, which is where I wanted to be.

I pulled up in my driveway in Dallas four hours later, relieved at the impending comfort of my house and looking forward to a warm, soapy bath. I unloaded my gear, tucking the box with the ring in it carefully into my swim bag, and hauled all my stuff to the front door.

And there, hanging on my front doorknob, was that necklace, still dripping with the cold water of Barton Springs.

HER CAREFULLY ORDERED WORLD IS UNRAVELING, ONE THREAD AT A TIME...

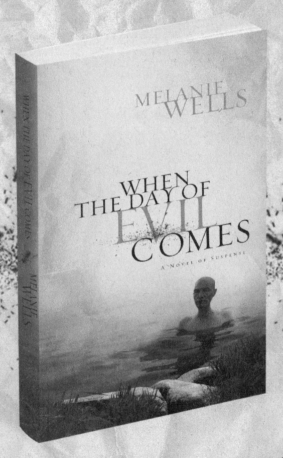

MELANIE WELLS

WHEN THE DAY OF EVIL COMES

A NOVEL OF SUSPENSE

Dylan Foster is about to get a crash course in spiritual warfare —and a glimpse of her own small but significant role in a vast eternal conflict. But when the dust settles, will anything be left of her life as she knows it?